MW01514964

1967
San Francisco

Also by DH Parsons

from Bliss-Parsons Publishing
>The Muse: Coming of Age in 1968
>Eat Yoga!

from All Things that Matter Press
>The Diary of Mary Bliss Parsons
>>Volume 1: The Strong Witch Society
>>Volume 2: The Lost Revelation
>>Volume 3: Beyond Infinite Healing

All available on Amazon

San Francisco

1967

My Romance with the Summer of Love

D H Parsons

HAIGHT

600—
ASHBURY

BLISS-PARSONS
BP
PUBLISHING

1967 San Francisco
My Romance with the Summer of Love

Copyright 2018 by DH Parsons

Illustrations by DH Parsons

**Editing, layout, and design by Susan Bingaman,
Bliss-Parsons Publishing, Columbia, MO**

All rights reserved

No part of this book may be reproduced or transmitted in any form or by any means without the written permission of the author and publisher.

Disclaimer

This story is an impressionistic account of people and events in the life of the author as recorded by him in 1967. The names of the participants, and certain specifics of some of the events have been altered for the preservation of anonymity and the exercise of artistic license. The work is based on journal entries and, as such, accurately depicts the experiences and thoughts of the author of that time.

ISBN: 978-1-948553-01-8
Library of Congress Control Number: 2018952585

To Annie

Introduction

I don't remember driving to the airport or getting on the plane, but I do remember the takeoff out of LA and the flight to San Francisco. It was a bumpy flight, and only my second commercial airline experience—the first, just the week before, was even worse—so I wasn't a happy flier. My friend, Manny, was the one who insisted we take a whole week and make it an adventure, and he had to work hard to convince me.

"Go to San Francisco? Why on Earth would we want to do that?" I asked him on that summer day in 1967. I'd just returned a few days earlier from a whirlwind trip to that fabled city with another high school friend, Bart. There had been a few good times, but it had been a tiring ordeal.

"Because that's where it's all happening!" Manny informed me, as if I had no idea what was going on up there.

"What do you think is happening in San Francisco, Manny?" I asked. "I just got back from there. It's a fun city—kinda crowded, but nothing out of the ordinary."

"You and Bart weren't there long enough, and you got there during a lull in the action. There's tons of stuff going on now—the whole hippie thing! Crazy music, interesting people, new philosophies, and girls that never wear bras flopping around all over town day and night!" Manny was more excited than I'd ever seen him.

"All of that huh?" I wasn't as thrilled by his reasons to, once again, travel four hundred miles north while seated inside a heavy metal tube thirty thousand feet in the air, praying the whole way that the plane wouldn't lose a wing. That braless thing though …

"Come on, DH, Frisco's where it's happening *right now*. There's never been anything like what's going on up there. Not just the hippies and the boobs, but an entirely new way of lookin' at life. There's a place up there called City Lights Bookstore that's a major hangout for a bunch of hard-core dudes that make the existentialists look like amateurs!" We had been studying existentialism in college the previous semester.

"Oh? And who might they be?" I knew full well who they were. Bart and I had been to the City Lights Bookstore when we were there, and the place was almost empty.

"The Beats! Kerouac's buddies—Gregory Corso, Allen Ginsberg, Gary Snyder, Bill Burroughs, Neal Cassady, Lawrence Ferlinghetti …"

"I'm quite familiar with those guys, Manny, but the actual Beat movement ended in 1960, give or take a year or five."

"Just the popular movement. Some of the old Beats are still around and they live in San Francisco. Most of those guys are still alive and kickin'. Who do you think inspired this Hippie stuff?"

"Milton Berle?" I was well aware that the Beats were still an influence in the American literary and music scenes, especially in San Francisco. I had a girlfriend whose memory I've never been able to shake from my head. Her name is Abby. Her pedigree is 100% Beat, and she exudes Beat from every pore. She taught me a lot of stuff, even in total silence. She lives up there now, somewhere.

"Come on, DH, it would be a blast!"

"I don't know Manny. I can dig the Beat stuff but I'm not as enamored by this whole hippie thing as you are. I don't have a lot of money saved up, and I'm not sure my parents would be too supportive either. This will be my second trip there in two weeks."

"Yeah yeah, and the excuses go on and on and on. Your parents are pretty cool, DH, and besides they're on a camping trip all next week. They won't even know you're gone. It won't cost much—we'll only be there for a week, and we can probably find some hippies to stay with if it gets too tight."

"Great. Stay with some hippies. I'm not even sure I've figured out what a real hippie is, Manny."

"They're just people! They eat food, play music …"

"Take drugs, get drunk …"

"That's just what the newspaper people say. You can't believe anything they write. Come on, I think it's worth the risk."

"I never did like that word, risk," I told him. "Okay, I'll go, but you have to promise never to tell anyone about this. I'm not sure I want to be associated in any way with the hippie thing. I'm trying to be an artist, not a hippie."

"You have my word. I'll never tell a soul."

Three Days Later

Three days later Manny and I were, indeed, sitting in a big metal tube thirty thousand feet up in the air and headed for San Francisco, about to become a part of a scene unlike any other—a magical moment that would rock the world for ages to come—living out a role at the very center of a cultural revolution that would become a historical moment in time: 1967, The Summer of Love.

I had $200 in my pocket.

I also realize now, fifty years later almost to the day, that because of my own lack of enthusiasm—unlike Manny—for the hippie movement at the time, I interacted with San Francisco not as an excited young hippie wannabe on a pilgrimage to the West Coast Mecca, but as an observer or a reporter. I kept careful notes in my journal the whole time I was there, recording objective, on-the-scene impressions of the people I met and the experiences I had.

I'm sure that for all of the hundreds of thousands of people who were there either as tourists or as residents of San Francisco during the Summer of Love, there are as many different tales to tell—some better, and some worse—but the variations should not invalidate each other. The stories told by those who lived through the warm, chaotic summer days of 1967 should not be censored or criticized, but read together like chapters in a book to gain a clearer picture of a brief, colorful episode in American history that affected society and politics for decades—if not for generations—one way or the other.

The pages that follow relate my own personal experience with the Romance of the Summer of Love as recorded in my journal. I cherish every memory that I now share with you.

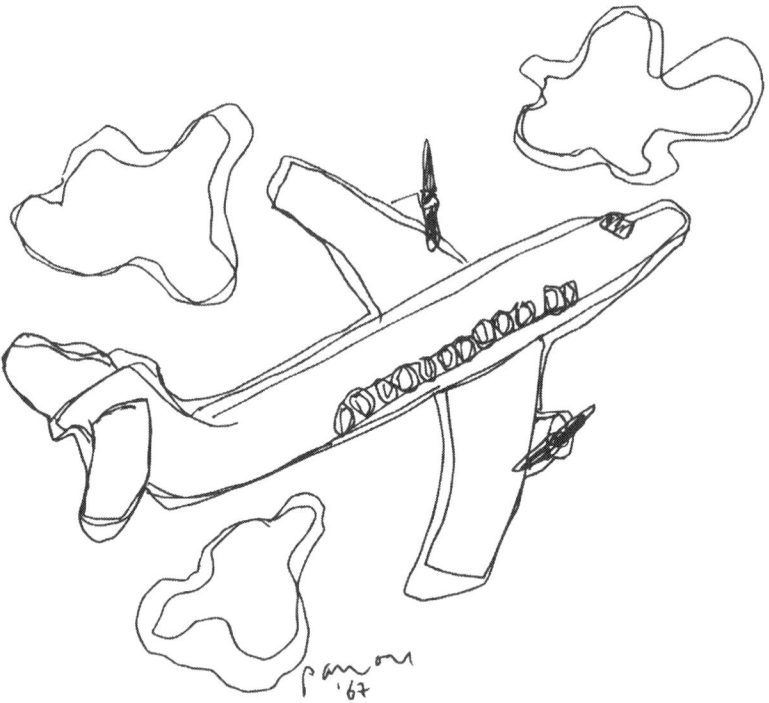

Day One

The plane ride wasn't too bad. I held my breath most of the way, but there was very little turbulence and the landing was smooth. Manny and I travel light with just the bare necessities packed into one backpack each: two changes of clothing, a razor, a toothbrush and whatever other little items could be stuffed inside. We didn't know where we'd be staying or what we'd be doing, so these would be easy to carry in case we had to carry our stuff around with us.

The airport is several miles south of the main part of the city, and the roads in between are definitely not pedestrian-friendly, so we caught a bus just outside the terminal to take us into town. We had no idea what we were doing. This was Manny's first trip to a big city other than LA and, even though I had just been to San Francisco with Bart the week before, memories of that whirlwind trip were just a blur. We had picked up a map at the airport but it didn't show where hotels and motels were located, so we figured we'd head into the heart of San Francisco and just walk around looking until the right one jumped out at us.

At the Commodore International Hotel

We walked around for a while after we got off the bus and were standing on the sidewalk trying to get our bearings. I looked up and realized where we were.

"Hey, Manny. This is where Bart and I stayed last week."

"I hope they changed the sheets since then," he replied drolly.

I am now seated at a little desk by my bed in the Commodore Hotel on Sutter Street, San Francisco, recording the day's adventures in my journal. I have just finished writing a letter to my parents, which I will drop in the mail when we go out again in a little bit.

Letter home from the Commodore Hotel

Here I am, obviously. The plane ride was all right, but unfortunately we sat in the middle and couldn't see the ground because of the wing. Our hotel costs $14 a night, or $7 apiece; it's about as cheap as possible. You wouldn't believe the prices!

We arrived at 9:05 am; took a bus to the Hilton ($1.10). Walked a mile (uphill) to the Commodore, opened the door, got our room, took the elevator upstairs (4th floor), opened the door to our room, walked in, changed clothes, went out the door, went downstairs, locked up our money, and walked 4,000,000 miles to Haight-Ashbury (where we saw 20 hippies and about 40,000,000 tourists). After a while we got bored and took a bus back to the hotel (15¢). Then we walked another twenty million miles to Fisherman's Wharf, ate some crab and walked forty million miles back (we took the long way, over Nob Hill, it's great) Now we are here. We have ordered a chicken dinner, which will be delivered soon. Then we will go to Fillmore Auditorium and see a groovy rock band. Adios, Din. P.S. I'll send you a postcard.

☮

Our legs are aching from all the walking up and down hills we did today, but that won't stop us from heading out again soon for the Fillmore Auditorium. We aren't sure where it is, even though I was there just last week — my sense of direction is so bad that I can't find my way out of a paper bag.

We can't come to San Francisco without catching at least one concert. That's what this hippie stuff seems to be all about — the music, the bands, the performers — and the Fillmore Auditorium gets them all. I think Buffalo Springfield is gonna be playing tonight, but I'm not sure — that's just what some kid down in the lobby told us earlier. He also said that The Doors and Jefferson Airplane are supposed to be there soon, maybe even tonight, so I have no idea what we're gonna get. I just hope we can find the place on foot. We really can't afford to take buses everywhere we go. Taxis would be great because the taxi drivers know the city so well. But that's out of the question — we'd be broke after just a couple of trips.

The biggest disappointment of the day so far has been Haight-Ashbury. There were thousands of tourists with cameras and tote bags all over the place — a lot of them were my parent's age! I thought this hippie thing was a kids' deal. Manny and I counted only twenty possible hippies on the entire block we were on, but they could've been tourists who were dressed for the part and wanting to blend in with the real things. But if that's the case, where are the real things?

One rather thin girl with stringy dishwater hair and large nipples poking through her shirt looked like she might be the real deal, so Manny struck up a conversation with her. She was standing by a street lamp in front of a music store. Her bright yellow t-shirt had a guitar printed on the front, so I'm guessing she might have worked in the store.

"Is this where it's happening?" I couldn't believe Manny actually said that.

"What?" she replied with a dreamy slur.

"We came up from the south to catch some entertainment," he explained. "Are we in the right place?"

"You mean, like, music and stuff?" she asked.

"Yeah, that. That and whatever."

"You gotta go to Fillmore or to the park for the best music. The park's free, Fillmore's not."

"What's Fillmore?" I asked her. Manny rolled his eyes at my dumb question. We'd been talking about the Fillmore Auditorium earlier, but when the girl just said "Fillmore", it confused me.

"You really aren't from around here are you? Fillmore Auditorium. That's where the biggie's play. Reed, the Dead, the Holding Company, Zeppelin, Cream, CCR, Zappa, Pink Floyd. You gotta pay to get in though. Or if you go to the park you can usually catch somebody playin' somethin' for free. Sometimes one of the biggies drops by and strums some tunes."

"You mean Golden Gate Park?" I asked her.

"That's the one." The tone of her voice and her expression let me know I'd asked another stupid question.

"We thought there'd be more going on here at Haight-Ashbury, but it's kinda dead," Manny said.

"It'll get livelier later. Everybody's sleepin' it off. I'm just up and around 'cause I got a job in there." She pointed to the music store. "I'm one of the unlucky ones. I gotta work for a living."

"That's unlucky?" I asked. "Aren't you lucky you have a job? I bet jobs are hard to come by around here. Lots of competition."

"Ha! The lucky ones don't have to work. Lots of 'em have money when they come here to play at being a hippie. Others do the street thing."

"What's the 'street thing'?" Manny asked.

"Hookin'. Laying on your back for five minutes and making twenty bucks, or bending over in an alley for ten."

"You mean …" At a loss for words, Manny clears his throat.

"That's exactly what she means, Manny."

"I tried that for a while, but it's undependable. Gets cold here in the winter too." She shivered with the memory.

"Well, it seems to me that a job is better than doing that," I said.

"Yeah, but I gotta keep regular hours with a job. I'm not much for that."

She looked at me thoughtfully. "Say, you wouldn't wanna spend a little time with me in that alley over there would you?" She smiled bigger than she should have.

"Uh … no …" Now I'm stuttering. "I'm afraid Manny and I are in a hurry to get somewhere."

"Afraid you'll catch somethin'? I ain't got nothin'." Her voice was teasing, but her eyes showed scorn.

"No," I said quickly. "It's just that we have an appointment we need to keep and we're already late."

"Right." I could tell she didn't believe me.

I grabbed Manny's arm and pulled him back toward the hotel

saying goodbye to the girl as we went. She told me her name was Angel and that I could find her there at the music store any time if I ever wanted her. Apparently she slept in a room in the back of the store.

"You're crazy! We could have had some fun with her," Manny said as we walked away.

"You mean you believed her when she said she didn't have any diseases?"

"Well, she didn't look sick!"

"Manny, what am I gonna do with you? She was emaciated, dirty, and way too eager to go into that alley. What does that tell you?"

"I don't know. But please tell me we didn't fly all the way up here just to walk up and down hills."

"I'm sure we're gonna have a lot of fun now that we're here. But we wanna be careful not to screw it up."

Manny's disappointment was quickly forgotten as his excitement for the adventure returned. "She had hair under her arms. Did you see that?"

"Yes, I saw that."

"She's gotta be the real thing—a real hippie. That's the way the girls are I hear. They never shave their pits."

So our first experience with a real hippie in Haight-Ashbury was kind of a bust and nothing much to write home about, making my letter to my parents a bit short. I certainly wasn't going to tell them about getting invited into an alley for a few minutes by a hippie girl. But, like Manny, I do hope we have some sort of fun while we're up here, and that we don't just spend our time walking around looking for stuff to do—we do enough of that at home. We get in a car on a Friday night and Manny says, "Now what? What do you want to do?" And I say, "I don't know, lets just drive around and see if we can find something." And we end up driving around finding nothing.

Fisherman's Wharf was nice — atmospheric and with lots of good food. We sampled bunches of seafood while we were there, including a whole crab that we split between us. Not a lot of hippies there, though. It's more of a conventional adult tourist area with grownup things to do and see.

We took the scenic route back to the hotel from the Wharf, through the Russian Hill neighborhood, and up into Nob Hill. The quiet streets were lined with beautiful mansions, fancy hotels, parks, etc. — very nice. Part of me wishes that I had the money to live there, but I'm not sure that I'd ever like being in San Francisco full time. The place is kind of hectic. There's some sort of action goin' on just about everywhere you look. And the people! We've only been here a little while and we've already seen an assortment of eccentric characters dressed in some pretty weird outfits. I'm not talking about hippies; I'm talking about regular residents. To be honest, I'm not sure that some of them aren't quite right upstairs. It's gonna be an interesting week.

We were well up into the Nob Hill area when Manny decided he couldn't walk any more; the new shoes he had bought for this trip had worn a painful blister on his heel. We didn't know how much further it was to the hotel, or where the nearest trolley or bus stop was. We could've hoofed it, but it would've been a long painful walk for Manny. While we were deciding what to do we spotted a passing taxi, so we flagged it down to take us the rest of the way back.

We were both concerned about the extravagance of the taxi ride, so our conversation in the back seat turned to our dwindling cash. We had started with about $300 between us for the whole week, but there was the bus from the airport, the hotel — not as cheap as we had planned — and now this taxi. And food — food is more expensive here than we had thought. Even if we buy our food at a market, how are we gonna cook it? Do hotels have stoves we can use? Our room doesn't have a stove. A whole week? Geez.

Having overheard our conversation, the taxi driver offered a suggestion. "If you get hard up, you can always do what all the other kids in town are doin'. Go beg some beans from the Diggers." His speech was punctuated with a fine spray of brown tobacco spittle.

Even though I'd have to witness the spittle spray again, I had to ask him, "What or who are the Diggers?"

"Is that another band?" Manny asked.

"Naw." The driver rolled down the window and spat out a big wad of brown goo. "It's a group of actors and misfits that hand out free food in the park."

"Are there a lot of people here that need free food?" I asked.

"Since the hippie crap started up we gots tons o' no-accounts comin' in here from all over. They don't bring no money wit 'em neither."

"So the Digger guys feed them."

"The city council don't want outta state hippies dyin' here in The City. Gotta feed 'em ta keep 'em alive. Can't get rid of 'em neither. They's comin' in droves and they ain't leavin'. I guess the city'd rather have the Diggers fatten 'em up a bit. That'll be three bucks—for the ride. The advice is free."

In my concern over the state of our finances I had not noticed that we had arrived at the hotel. We thanked the driver and paid him the three dollars. Although it was less than I had expected, it was still three dollars that we no longer have. And it's still just the first day of our visit.

We called the front desk when we got back to our room and asked if they had a nurse who could look at Manny's heel—that new shoe had really done a number on it. They didn't have a nurse, but they did send up a girl wearing a cute little outfit that made her look like anything but a nurse. She pulled a bottle of mercurochrome and a pack of wide bandages out of a brown bag she was carrying and went to work. She seemed to know what she was doing. She got a wet towel from the bathroom, washed off Manny's foot, swabbed it with antiseptic, and then put on a bandage.

"That feels better," Manny said. "I just hope I can keep the bandage on with all the walking we have to do."

"I'll wrap some tape all the way around your foot and leave the extra stuff with you in case you need to put on a new one," she said, smiling sweetly.

"That's very nice of you," I told her. "Are you a maid here?"

"Ha, no. I don't work here. I was in the lobby visiting my friend, Tricia. She's the reception clerk downstairs. She asked me if I'd run this stuff up here 'cause she can't leave the phones right now. I've been coming in here for years—know the place like the back of my hand—so I help out when I can."

"Well, you seem to know what you're doing."

"Our hotels get a lot of people with the same problem. Tourists come here and think they're gonna do a walking tour of The City, but this isn't the best city in America to walk in if you're not used to it. It looks small on the map, but the streets have lots of miles and lots of hills. It tires a person out pretty quick, and if you don't have proper footwear then you're gonna have sore heels just like young Manny here."

"Hopefully my shoes will break in soon and I won't have to worry about it."

"He's pretty tough. He can make it," I said.

"You're probably right," she said. "So, what are you guys gonna do tonight? It's a big town."

"We're gonna try to find Fillmore Auditorium and catch a concert," I told her.

"Great! The Fillmore's the place for concerts, that's for sure."

"You know where it is?"

"Sure. It's over on South Van Ness, I think. I'm not too good with street names, but I've been there a few times and I can get there in my sleep."

"Can you draw us a map?" Manny asks.

"I can do better than that. I can take you there!"

"Really?" Manny and I spoke in unison.

"Sure, I'd love to. My sister can pick us up. She has a car and would love to come with us."

"I didn't think anybody in San Francisco had their own car," I said.

"A lot of people don't, but Sissy does. She's going to school at UCLA and she needed a car down there, so when she comes up here to see me she drives instead of flying in a plane. She hates to fly."

"That makes two of us."

"Three," she said. "I'm terrified of flying. That's why Sissy has to drive up here to see me. I don't have a car and I won't fly."

"Well, it seems like we have our evening planned. Hey, we don't even know your name."

"Angela, but everybody calls me Angie."

"What a coincidence," Manny said. "We just met a girl over on Haight Street named Angel."

I nodded in confirmation. "The only two people we've actually met here are both named for heavenly beings."

"Well, it seems like the Angels are looking after you two. That can't be bad," she said with a wink.

The Concert at the Fillmore

Angie and her sister, Sissy, came by the hotel and picked us up about an hour before the concert was to begin. That was a good thing because I don't think Manny's heel could have taken any more serious walking. The two sisters look very much alike; they aren't identical twins but you can sure tell they are related.

Angie's hair is reddish blonde, maybe more blonde than red, a little longer than shoulder length. She was wearing it in a ponytail poked through the hole in the back of a baseball cap. She's cute and much younger than I thought she was when she came to our room earlier. My first impression was that she was about twenty-five years old, but she's only nineteen. She has an all-American face with a few freckles on and around her soft little nose; blue eyes, full lips — a lot like a young Doris Day. In spite of living in San Francisco, her passion in life has little to do with music or hippies, but with baseball, of all things. In fact, she's on a team with a 5-0 record in the citywide league this season. She plays first base and, according to Sissy, Angie is the team's most reliable home run hitter. How cool is that? I'm not into sports much these days, but I used to be when I was younger. My brother, Jim, and I used to watch baseball games all the time. Hardly a day went by in the summer that we didn't have the radio tuned in to a game. We kinda lost our taste for it when pro baseball started looking too much like any other big business. I might be able to develop an interest in a city team like Angie's, though. They don't have contracts, don't get paid, they all get along and have great fun. And at least one of them, Angie, is cute as a button.

The concert was loud and wild—the noise and activity set my teeth on edge. We thought The Doors would be playing but the headliner was Cream, the same group Bart and I saw last week. Apparently they were so popular that they were held over. We got there early and found space to sit on the floor in front of the stage where we could watch the band play up close and loud. The band members came down and chatted with us a little before the concert and during intermission, which was kinda neat. Manny was in seventh heaven when Ginger Baker, the drummer, had a conversation with him for a good fifteen minutes about drumming techniques—I never knew there was such a thing as a drumming technique. It was a kick watching Manny's face throughout the exchange. He was clearly in awe of the drummer whose frizzy red hair looked like it was on fire during his wild performance. It must have been the lighting combined with Baker's sweat that caused his hair to glisten brightly as he whipped his head around as he played. The girls in the audience went crazy over it.

The band members talked and behaved as if they were high on pot or some other drug, or tipsy with booze—or maybe both. Angie told me later that it's hard to tell if a hippie or a rocker is really high or not, because they seem to feel that they have to act like it even when they aren't. It's all part of the show.

We watched Eric Clapton prance around the stage as he tried to get all the guitar and microphone cords unscrambled before the concert. He was fully aware of the girls amongst the early arrivals in the auditorium. They swooned dramatically at his every move, even when the band wasn't playing. Every now and then he turned and flashed a smile into the audience, driving the girls totally bananas. It was quite a show, both onstage and off.

"Are you telling me that even on the streets, the real hippies out there all like to fake being high or drunk?" I asked Angie during a break in the action.

"Even on the streets—although there are a lot of real dopers out there. It's just hard to tell the difference if you aren't used to them. The rule of thumb though, is that if they're really quiet and just sitting in a corner somewhere, those are the ones that are doped up. If they're loud and obnoxious and full of themselves, those are the ones that are drunk. If they're sober, well, they're back home in Kansas."

We all laughed at that.

"So these Cream guys may be just acting drunk?" I asked.

"Hard to say. Rock bands are in a class by themselves. They can be totally sober and still act silly and obnoxious."

Manny rose to their defense. "They're entertainers!"

"It's what they do," Angie agreed.

"I guess the wilder they act the more famous they'll get," I said. "I think these guys are on the road to being pretty famous already, so it wouldn't hurt if they started drinking more to speed up the process."

"It's hard to tell if a band will make it big," Manny said. "There are some really bad bands out there that are gaining fame quickly, but the market's getting saturated."

"I think The Doors are gonna be pretty big," Angie said. "Morrison's pretty good looking, and good looks sell more records than talent these days. The girls will eat him up."

"If he doesn't get too crazy with drugs or whiskey. That can ruin a career pretty quick," Manny said.

"I can't help but wonder where some of these guys will be twenty years from now — if they stay alive long enough to get there," I said.

"Hard to tell," Angie said. "I know for a fact that some of them aren't gonna get there because of their bad habits. Janis Joplin's heading in a bad direction. So's Hendrix. Maybe Morrison. It's hard to tell."

"Such is life," I said. "We wish them well. Anyway, this Fillmore place is pretty popular. It'll probably last a while."

The band is taking one last break before the concert ends. The music has indeed been loud and wild, and I'm getting a little concerned about possible damage to my ears — they are ringing in between the songs. In fact, it's never quiet; even when there's a lull in the music the crowd is in a constant state of movement and uproar. I think it's the cheering of the crowd that bothers me the most. In all fairness though, all concert music is loud. I've been to ballets that have almost taken the top of my head off because the orchestra was so loud. But at a ballet or a Mozart concert, the audience isn't in a constant state of motion like it is here. The classical audiences are well-behaved and except for the occasional person getting up to go to the bathroom, quite motionless. Good behavior is just expected at classical performances. But not here — there are no rules here. When the musicians in the band stop playing, that's the cue for the audience to push the silly button.

I'm not much on giving a play-by-play analysis of a rock concert; I'll let Manny do that. He's been giving us the titles to the songs as Cream plays them, but the only Cream song I think I've ever heard is "Sunshine Of Your Love;" I recognized that when they played it earlier. I'm not so familiar with the other songs. They're doing something called "Sleepy Time Time" right now. Of course, the crowd doesn't care what the song is; they go crazy every time Clapton does anything on stage, or every time Ginger Baker flails his arms wildly as he pounds out the aggressive beats.

Not everybody gets a chair here at the Fillmore. A lot of kids are sitting on the floor in front of the stage; luckily or unluckily, that's where we are. I'm not sure how sanitary this floor is. I imagine a lot of sweat and spit have been tossed all over it during the time this place has been open and holding these events. I'm trying not to touch the floor with my hand. Oddly enough the kids up here on the floor around us are the most well behaved. Even at the end of songs when the audience goes crazy with applause most of them remain seated, but that's probably for fear of losing their place. It's kind of cool being able to sit right in front of the stage like this—you'd pay big time to do that at a ballet.

Any way, this has been an experience. I'm glad I came tonight just so I'll have something of a shared interest to talk with Manny about over the next few years, like "Remember that time we went to that Cream concert up in San Francisco?" Or something like that.

What luck! A gaggle of young girls a few feet back from where we are sitting on the floor got up and offered us their chairs. They said they were here for the Airplane and the Airplane wasn't on the bill. It looks like we'll be able to finish the concert in comfort.

Back at the Hotel

We were all pretty tired after the concert so we headed straight back to the hotel. We invited Angie and Sissy up to our room for a while to kind of unwind and talk about the evening. Along the way, Sissy, being twenty-two, pulled into a liquor store and bought some wine. She came out with two gallons.

"I bought a gallon of white chablis, because girls like white wine. And guys like something more robust, so I got a gallon of burgundy for you two. You are old enough to drink, right?" she queried.

"Well, actually …" I began.

"You're kidding—you look old enough. Damn. I could get in trouble buying you this stuff."

"Oh don't worry about it, Sis," Angie said. "Who's gonna know? We're gonna be in a hotel room. If we don't get rowdy, all will be well."

"We won't get rowdy, I promise. Manny and I don't really drink that much, and when we do we usually just talk all night."

And that's pretty much what happened after we got back to our room—we just drank and talked. The girls came in and plopped down on the floor. There was no radio so we didn't have to worry about the music being too loud. Manny was a little unsettled by that because he's one of those people that has to have music goin' at all times.

"We should have brought a radio," he said. "We just came from an incredible concert, and now we're met with total silence."

"That's probably a good thing, Manny," I said. "Since you and I are drinking illegally it's best we don't have any unnecessary noise to raise the suspicions of anyone passing by out in the hall."

"Or in the rooms next door," Angie added.

"So, Manny, you're a music lover?" Sissy asked.

"Manny's part of a band at home," I told her.

"Really?"

"It's not much," Manny said. "Just one of the billions of garage bands popping up all around the country—a lead guitar, a bass player, a singer, and drums. I'm the drums part."

"Glad you didn't bring your drums," said Angie, laughing.

Sissy got up to get four of those plastic cups you find in hotel rooms. She unwrapped them and filled them almost to the brim with wine—two red and two white. She handed a red to Manny and to me, a white to Angie, and kept a white for herself. She raised her cup and made a toast.

"To the four of us!"

She downed her wine in one take, refilled her cup, and sat back down on the floor.

"Sissy likes her wine," Angie whispered to me.

"I guess so," I replied.

"So what kind of music does your band play, Manny?" Sissy asked.

"Right now we're sorta into Buffalo Springfield—that kinda thing. We're not too interested in the heavy-duty hard-core stuff. More mellowish."

"Do you write any of your own songs?" Angie asked.

"Some, but not many," Manny said. "We're just tryin' to get our feet wet. I doubt anything will ever come of it."

"You never know, Manny," I tell him. "I make most of your practices, and you sound good to me."

"We need more discipline," he said.

"What do you mean?" Sissy asked.

"I wouldn't mind becoming famous, but the other guys are too undisciplined to make anything out of themselves. Too much ego. They just like goofing around and wasting time."

"Do you play an instrument, DH?" Angie asked.

"I play guitar a little, but it's not really my thing," I answer. "Acoustic, not electric. Just a few folk songs and the like. I'm not very good at it."

"So, if you aren't in a band what do you do, DH? Do you have a job?" Sissy asked.

"I teach yoga part time, if that counts for anything." I smiled self-consciously.

"Yoga!" Angie looked impressed. "I've always wanted to try that."

"It's good for you," Manny said. "DH is a good teacher. I've done a few of his classes. He's pretty popular because he doesn't hurt people with those crazy pretzel postures they teach in some classes."

"I do the old-fashioned style of yoga. It's pretty simple stuff, but it works."

"Is that your only job?" she asked.

"I also have a real job shoveling oranges out of freight cars—at least for the summer. Although I might not have it any more since I chose to come up here instead of report for work this morning. I haven't really made my mind up about what I'm going to do, career wise."

"You mean you don't know what you want to be when you grow up," Angie said.

"Kinda. Right now I'm playing with lots of different ideas."

"Like what?"

"He wants to be a rocket scientist." Manny butted in.

"Right," I said, rolling my eyes at Manny.

"Really?" Sissy looked impressed.

"I'm taking some astronomy courses and Manny thinks that's funny for some reason. I'm interested in the cosmos, but I also toy around with philosophy and art. I'm just not sure yet. I figure I've got some time to kick it around."

"Wow! Astronomy, philosophy, art—what a cultured man you're becoming. I think that's great," she said as she poured more wine for us all.

"What kind of art do you do?" Angie asked.

"Mainly I paint, but I also fiddle around with pottery, sculpture, even art history."

"Is he a good painter, Manny?" Sissy asked.

"I don't know. I guess. I'm not much of a judge of that, but he's got some cool looking paintings. I think I like those."

"Thanks, Manny. What a glowing endorsement. I'm flattered."

"What do you paint?" Angie asked.

"Lot's of things. People, landscapes, seascapes …"

"I've always wanted to have a portrait of me in my baseball uniform," Angie said. "Holding my glove in one hand and a ball in the other."

"You and that glove." Sissy rolled her eyes at her sister. "She carries it with her everywhere she goes," she explained to Manny and me.

"Not everywhere," Manny said, grinning. "She doesn't have it tonight."

"What do you think is in that brown bag right next to her on the couch?" Sissy said.

"You're kidding!" I said. "You've been carrying that bag all night. I wondered what you had in it."

Angie gave us a smug grin, reached into the bag by her side, and pulled out a light brown, well-used Rawlings deep well pocket baseball glove.

"You've gotta be kidding. You actually lug that thing around everywhere you go?"

"It beats a wallet," she said.

"But you can't carry things in a baseball glove," Manny said.

"Wanta bet?" Angie smiled, slid her hand into the glove, and pulled out some keys. "My house keys. I've got a couple of other things in there too, but they're girlie things — personal."

"Well, I'll be." I was flabbergasted.

"I'll drink to that," said Sissy. Then she downed a big swallow of her wine. Manny took a gulp of his in agreement.

"Angie, if I had any way I could pull it off I'd paint that portrait for you while I'm here. But my paints and brushes are all down south."

"Maybe you could at least draw it for me — maybe just a pencil drawing? I'd cherish that forever." Angie reached over and took my hand.

"He does some pretty cool drawings," Manny said. "He drew one of me and my drums once. I still have it hanging on the garage wall."

"Thanks, Manny." And this time I mean it. It's not exactly the Louvre, but it's the thought that counts.

"And what about you, Sissy?" I turn to face her. "Manny's a musician, Angie's a ball player, I'm almost a painter. What do you do? You're goin' to UCLA right?"

"Yes, I am. I'm a French major."

"Really? What do you do with a French major? What kind of job?"

"Basically there are two options for French majors. One is to teach French to other students — so they can grow up to teach more French to more students, who will become more French teachers — and the other is to be an interpreter for a company or a government office. I have a friend working in the State Department who's already pulling strings for me."

"Wow, I'm impressed. You must be pretty fluent."

"She certainly is," Angie said proudly. "She talks it like she was born in Paris."

"Even when I'm tipsy," she said, raising her cup and taking another large swig of chablis.

We all raised our cups and toasted Sissy.

"To Sissy," I said. "The smartest one among us. May we all get tipsy tonight so we can forget the cares of the world and move forward into fun things on the morrow."

"Here, here," agree Manny and Angie.

"I don't know about being the smartest among us," Sissy said. "But I know about the cares of the world, and I'm all about forgetting them."

"I know all about being tipsy," said Angie. "I'm getting that way rapidly, but I don't care. This is fun being with you guys. What a treat! I never expected the evening to turn out like this. I was gonna just watch some TV and head off to bed."

"And all because Manny bought some new shoes last week for this trip," I said.

"That's right," Angie said. "If Manny hadn't done all that walking and gotten those blisters, you never would have called the office for a bandage, and I never would have met you."

"And we never would have found the Fillmore," I added. "We would have wandered around the city with Manny moaning and groaning and ended up at a coffee shop drowning our sorrows in bad coffee all night."

"Just like we always do back home," Manny added.

Sissy looked at her empty cup and said, "I think I'm getting drunk."

"Great," Angie said. "You can't drive like that, and I never learned how to drive a stick shift, so we can't drive home tonight."

"I can sleep out in the hall," Sissy said.

"Why don't you just stay here?" I offered. "You two can have the beds and Manny and I can sleep on the floor in here."

Angie protested. "Oh we couldn't do that!"

"Why not, little sister? I bought the wine. The beds can be pay-backs from these free loaders." Sissy grinned at Manny and me.

"Look at the couch." I pointed over to Manny. He had been lying on the couch most of the evening, but now his eyes are closed and his chest is rising and falling slowly.

"Is he asleep?" Angie whispered.

"He's like that," I said. "He can drop off any time, any place. I guess all that drummer talk with Ginger Baker wore him out."

"I'm tired too," Sissy said as she lay back on the floor. "Who needs a bed? This floor's just fine." She closed her eyes.

"Well, I guess we can all just sleep here on the floor," I said. "But there's no need for you to rough it, Angie. You might as well go into the bedroom and sleep in a real bed."

"I'm not much for sleeping on hard hotel floors. You said there are two beds in there. Why don't you take one and I'll take the other. No use having a good bed go to waste."

"Are you sure that's a good idea, sleeping in the same room with a guy?" I asked.

"Are you afraid I'll attack you in the middle of the night?" she teased.

"I should be so lucky," I muttered under my breath.

"What?"

"Nothing. Uhhh … okay. You take one and I'll take the other. I hope I don't snore."

"Don't worry about that. I'm a jock; I probably snore louder than you do. But I think I'm gonna take a shower first, if you don't mind. You can go ahead and turn off the light. I can find my way in the dark."

Day Two

I could tell you that I got into bed last night, and that Angie went into the bathroom, took a shower, came out naked and dripping wet, and crawled into bed with me. I could also tell you that we made love all night long and woke up with smiles on our faces. But I won't, 'cause we didn't. Sorry.

I crawled into my bed alone and exhausted by the walking, the concert, the wine, and the talking. I fell asleep hard and fast and didn't hear Angie when she came out of the bathroom and got into the bed on the other side of the room.

The Adventure Begins

I woke up a few minutes ago, took a quick shower, and dressed in fresh but wrinkled clothes—I guess I'll have to practice my folding and packing skills if I'm going to do much of this traveling stuff. Right now I'm sitting on my bed writing these words while sneaking glances at Angie's sweet head peeking out from under the covers. The rest of her is completely hidden by the light blue hotel blanket. Darn.

Did I say that Angie is really pretty? I think I mentioned her innocent face; kinda like Doris Day with freckles. Does Doris Day have freckles? I think she does. She definitely looks like a tomboy. In my head, I see her standing alert at first base, the bill of her cap pulled down in front to keep the sun out of her eyes and her ponytail streaming out the little hole in the back, chewing gum for concentration, ready and eager for whatever comes her way. I wonder if Manny and I can catch one of her games or a practice session before we have to fly back home.

She's starting to move around a bit; I think she's close to waking up. She looks so peaceful there with her eyes closed, her left arm tucked up and under her head, a little bit of drool making a wet spot on the pillow. I can hear her breathing softly. Her eyes are fluttering like they're about to open.

"You're already awake and dressed?" she asks dreamily.

"For about half an hour I guess." I can't help smiling at her.

"Oh geez … my hair must be a mess." She tries to comb the tangles out of her hair with her fingers.

"No. Actually you look very pretty laying there like that. You remind me of a painting I saw once."

"I'm going to have to watch out for you aren't I, Mr. Romantic." She smiles at me as she sits up in the bed, carefully holding the sheet and blanket up around her breasts, which I am assuming are bare.

I smile back. "I'm harmless."

She looks at me with raised eyebrows.

"Sort of. I'm sort of harmless."

"That's better." We both smile.

It's an awkward moment. I'm really not sure what to do and I don't think she is either. I've never been in this kind of situation before with a girl I hardly know. I don't want to say or do anything that will shut her down or turn off this new friendship because I really like being with her. Her company beats the heck out of hanging around with Manny. Not that Manny isn't a good friend—he is—but he is trying to grow a mustache. And what am I doing sitting here writing while there's a naked girl under the sheet not ten feet away from me? Control yourself, buddy.

It's warm in here and Angie's let the blanket fall down, so now there's only a thin sheet between her and me, and one of her nipples is looking at me from the other side of the sheet. Good grief … I wonder if she shaves her armpits …

"I'm hungry." Angie's voice breaks me out of my musing, thank heaven.

"Uhh … me too." I hope she didn't notice my distraction. "I'm hungry too. What would you like to do? Should we all go out to eat somewhere, or pick something up from the market?"

"I love going out to eat, but I'm not too hot on normal breakfast places with bacon and eggs and stuff," she replies.

I try to think quickly. "I have no idea where the good places are around here. If we were in LA I could take you to a really nice Middle Eastern place that serves a great breakfast."

Picking up the thread, Angie says, "I know of a little Chinese place that opens early. They must have something. We could try it out."

"I love Chinese," I tell her. "Should we wake up Manny and Sissy and head on out?"

"They had a lot of wine last night. Maybe we ought to just let them sleep it off for a while. Sissy gets cranky if you wake her up too early. We can leave them a note," she says.

"Okay, sounds good to me."

"Great!" she says, and I am blinded by another knockout smile from the freckled-faced baseball player.

Not wasting any time, Angie gets out of bed and walks quickly into the bathroom to get ready—giving me a full view of her naked backside as she wiggles through the bathroom door. I've re-evaluated my earlier opinion; I think I'm really gonna like San Francisco this time around.

Breakfast At The Chinese Restaurant With No Name

I'd love to be able to record the name of the restaurant that we're sitting in now, but I don't have a clue as to what it is. The garish pink and green neon sign outside is written in Chinese letters, or characters, or whatever they're called, and there's no English translation on the wall or the window. We've been here for a few minutes and haven't seen a waiter or waitress yet.

The ambiance isn't too great, either. It's just one large room with a dozen small tables, a counter with a cash register near the door, and that's about it. No paintings, no cheap Chinese travel posters—nothing. The walls are painted light green and the tables are red Formica, no tablecloths or even paper place mats. At least the chairs match the table. It's kind of like being in a cave; when we talk our voices echo off the walls.

Angie is glancing around, looking more concerned as the minutes go by.

"How long do you think we ought to sit here?" she asks.

"I guess we can go any time. It doesn't look like anybody's around. You look scared. Are you scared?"

"Not really scared, maybe a little cautious though. I don't want to be kidnapped and shipped off to Shanghai." I think she's only half kidding.

"Do they really do that in this day and age?" I ask.

"San Francisco used to be notorious for that. I don't think it happens too much today though. At least, I hope not."

"Maybe we oughta leave." I prepare to get up.

Just as I move my chair back so I can stand up, a short, rotund Chinese girl comes through the door in the back and approaches our table.

"Hello?" My greeting is as much a question as it is a statement. "We thought we'd stop in and see if you're serving breakfast."

Again, I would love to tell you what the girl told us, but it is quickly becoming apparent that she doesn't speak or understand a word of English. Angie starts making signs and motions with her hands in an effort to make the girl understand that we'd like some food.

"I don't think she speaks American Sign Language, Angie."

"Surely she should be able to figure out that we're here for food. This is a restaurant—why else would we be here?"

The girl smiles broadly and motions for us to remain seated, then she turns and walks back through the door. Now what?

"Maybe she's going back to get some big Chinese men to come out here and tie us up and maybe gag us so we don't make any noise as they carry us out the back and stuff us into a seedy-looking van," Angie says seriously. I think she's read too many Agatha Christie novels.

"You think?" I'm getting a little nervous, but what if she's right? We wait in silence for a few more minutes.

The Chinese girl returns with a couple of plates and some chopsticks. She sets the plates down in front of us, then pulls some cloth napkins out of her pocket and arranges them on top of the plates. Now she's making motions that seem to mean that she understands that we want food. She motions for us to wait, and exits through the door.

Angie leans across the table and whispers, "Do you think they'll drug the food?"

I whisper back, "They might drug yours 'cause you're cute enough to steal, but I doubt they'll drug mine. I'm just an ugly, out 'o work guy."

Angie leans back in her seat and says in a normal voice, "Thanks a lot. That makes me feel better."

The girl is back again. This time she has a large teapot and two cups, which she sets in the middle of the table. She motions for us to help ourselves. Now she's making all kinds of gestures with her hand, pointing first to the cup and then to the sky, and then drawing something in the air with her hand. She seems to be getting frustrated with the failure to communicate.

Wait. What's she doing now? She's taken her left breast in her hand and is leaning over one of the cups on the table. Now it looks like she's squeezing it into the cup.

"Aww … geez … what the heck is that?"

She looks up at us, beaming with pleasure at her flash of inspiration.

"I think she's asking us if we want milk in our tea," Angie says, laughing with appreciation and understanding.

"No thank you," I say, placing my hand over my cup.

I'm really beginning to wonder about this place. What kind of rating do the health code people give it? The girl is cute even though she's a bit plump. She's dressed in a short tan skirt and a blue shirt. The skirt is old and worn, and the shirt is unbuttoned halfway down so that her boobs can be seen fighting with each other every time she moves.

A movement at the back of the room turns out to be an older man coming through the door. He's carrying a monster-sized tray holding three or four large plates of steaming food. He sets the tray down on the table next to ours, and spoons out helpings the size of Texas from each of the dishes onto our plates. The food is very pretty—full of colorful, mostly unidentifiable bits gleaming in shiny, fragrant sauces—and it looks clean. Angie and I look at each other, each daring the other to take the first bite.

"What the heck," I say, "shall we take a chance?"

"It looks good enough," she says. She leans over her plate and inhales the vapors wafting from her food. "And it smells really good."

"I think if they were gonna drug us they would have put it into the tea and not the food," I say, going back to the Agatha Christie scenario. "I mean, why go to all the trouble of making such a fantastic meal for a couple of kidnap victims?"

Picking up the challenge, Angie takes the first bite—brave girl. I watch for a few moments before raising a bite of food to my mouth.

"Angie! Angie! What's wrong?" Her eyes have rolled back, her head is lolling to one side, and she is slumping over in her chair.

She laughs and sits up. "Just kidding. It's delicious. I don't know what it is but it's really good."

While Angie attacks her food with gusto, I am a bit more cautious. "We may not want to know what it is. It could be sheep brains or something really bizarre."

"But it tastes like chicken," she says around another mouthful.

"Everything tastes like chicken until you find out what it really is, and then it's too late."

"But if it doesn't make you sick and it tastes good, then what's the harm?"

"You really are a tomboy, aren't you? You see everything as an adventure or a challenge."

She pauses her eating and raises her eyes to meet mine. As she does, her gaze softens. "Would you rather I be something else?"

"No, I pretty much like what I've seen so far."

"Well then," she says brightly, "let's eat this delicious food, and make some plans for the day.

30 Minutes Later

Finished eating. It really was pretty good stuff; sort of bland, but in a good way — the kind of food that sticks with you for several hours. I don't know why people say that when you eat Chinese food, you'll be hungry again 30 minutes later. Not this stuff. It really filled me up.

Angie sets down her chopsticks with a satisfied sigh. After studying me in silence for a minute or two, she says, "Can I ask you a question?"

"Sure."

"What in the world are you writing about? I watched you scribble in that little notebook of yours all last evening , and now here you are today doing the same thing. You know it's rude not to pay attention to a girl when you're on a date."

"I'm sorry. Do you want me to stop?" Wait a minute — what did she just say? "Is this really a date?"

"I want to know what it's all about before I tell you to stop. And yes, of course this is a date."

"This is my journal," I explain while I let what she just said sink in. "I started keeping it last year. I've decided it would be really neat if I recorded important events in my life, then someday in the distant future I can go back and try to make sense out of it all. I might even write a book."

"Wow, you are a visionary aren't you?" I'm not sure if she's teasing me. "And you think this little restaurant experience is so important that you need to record it? I don't see anything around here that's earth shattering enough to make note of."

"Oh, but it's very important to me because you're here with me. If I were alone I'd be writing about something boring, like the latest book I'm reading or the state of the world in Eastern Europe or Southeast Asia."

Angie smiles at me. "You think I'm important enough for you to ignore great literature and current events?"

"I do." I smile back.

She gets up, walks around to my side of the table, and kisses me deeply. We are interrupted by applause. Looking up, we see the man and the girl standing at the back of the room. They are grinning broadly and speaking rapidly in Chinese. Although we can't understand any of it, we get the meaning. Our simple breakfast visit to their establishment has been like a soap opera for them. They've been caught up in a sweet and innocent romantic moment between two young people they don't even know, and it's made their day.

"Angie ..."

"Yes?"

"I'm really glad we came in here this morning."

"Me too." She runs her hand through my hair.

"I'd leave those two a really big tip if I didn't have to pinch pennies in order to make it through the next week. They're pretty cute, and they've been really nice to us."

"That's okay. Breakfast is on me and I'll even leave them the tip," she says brightly.

I study her face. "You know, I really have no idea who you are, or what you do. Last night you didn't mention anything about your personal life except that you play baseball. What are your interests? What about your family? Do you have a job? How can you afford to buy my breakfast?"

"Well, I have a lot of interests. I can't really go into all of them right now. Maybe that's something we should do later—the four of us," she says, returning to her chair. "Some of my interests are the same as yours. I love art and good music. I hate most contemporary music. Even that concert last night was just a bit silly to me. Sorry."

"Don't apologize. I don't understand what the big deal is with that kind of music, either. I just go because Manny seems to get off on it."

"I prefer classical, and not the usual stuff you hear all the time—except for maybe Beethoven; he's a bit over played, but I do like him. Mozart's kind of nice. He's over-popular too, but he can be fun to listen to when you're in the right mood."

"Beethoven's good, but I really like some of the Russian composers, especially Tchaikovsky," I tell her.

"Oh, I love Tchaikovsky! Francesca da Rimini is my favorite. It's so romantic."

"That's my favorite too." And it really is. "Do you like jazz?"

"Of course I do. I live in The City. You can't live here and not like jazz."

"I was introduced to jazz last year by a girl I knew." I pause briefly reflecting on the memory. "She was a Beatnik and she knew a lot of neat stuff. She turned me onto lots of jazz musicians but I really like June Christy and Doris Day. I guess they're kinda easy jazz though, not really the heavy stuff."

"We've got them all up here, jazz is big in this town, so are the Beats. You need to make it over to City Lights Books while you're here if you want to check out the Beat scene."

"It's in my plan," I assure her.

"What else do I like?" Her eyes go soft, like she's looking out into the distance. "Let's see, I like simple things like sitting in the park under a tree while watching the clouds go by. And yes, I have a job. I work and I enjoy my work."

"And?" I probe for more. "What's your job? You didn't tell us last night."

"I'm a stripper at the go-go club downtown on Market Street. Lots of pay and big tips."

I am dumbstruck.

"Gottcha! I'm just kidding, but you should see the look on your face."

"Whew!" I close my gapping mouth and wipe my forehead in an exaggerated gesture of relief.

"You're so much fun to tease. You'll fall for anything."

"You may be right."

I look into her eyes and hold my gaze there. She picks up the thread of her life story without looking away. "I'm not sure what to tell you about my serious loves in life. I grew up on baseball. Oddly enough, I hate most of the other sports. I can't stand basketball, it's too fast for me—sweaty men running back and forth and back and forth again on that little court, totally random, aggressive movement, very little strategy. Not like baseball. You have to be able to think to play good baseball."

"I always liked baseball, too. Go Dodgers! Never cared much for football, though. Never even watched a hockey game. Always hated basketball for the same reasons you do," I said.

"Baseball is a civilized sport." Angie's serious expression makes her look seriously cute. "It's a game of strategy and very often grace. You don't have to be in perfect shape to play it either. Look at Babe Ruth and his potbelly. Of course he didn't have to run very fast, since he hit nothing but home runs, for crying out loud."

"What did you say?"

"I said Babe Ruth hit home runs."

"No, you said 'for crying out loud.'"

"I guess I did. I say that a lot."

"So do I, but I've never heard anybody else say it."

"I got it from Pops. That's what I called my dad. He said it all the time."

"I got it from my dad, too. How neat is that? Does your Pops love baseball as well?"

"He loved all sports—past tense, he's in Heaven now—but baseball was his favorite. He taught me everything I know."

"Oh … I'm sorry …"

"It's okay. It's been a couple of years now. He died of heart failure. Too much stress in his life."

"I hope your Pops would have approved of you being here with me. I mean, this looks like a pretty seedy place to take his little girl. We didn't get kidnapped, but you never know." I look around, doing my best Charlie Chan imitation.

"Pops would've loved you. You've got a good head on your shoulders. He liked people who think a lot. He was an odd mix—he loved sports and manly things, but he wasn't what you'd call an airheaded jock. He kept up on the news, followed world events, and he read a lot. I never saw him without a book."

"What did he like to read?"

"Just about everything, but mainly the classics. I think the last book he was reading was some sort of old English thing, Chaucer I think."

"Wow, he did like to think. I struggled through Canterbury Tales last semester in English Lit at RCC."

"RCC?"

"Riverside City College. I love the place and the teachers are great, but it's hard work."

"What are you taking?"

"Mainly the required stuff. I just finished my first year, and I'll have an AA degree in one more. Then I'll probably go on for a BA somewhere."

"I gather from the conversation we had last night that you haven't really declared a major yet."

"Heavens no. Not sure what I'm gonna study. I'm leaning toward art, but I've had fun in a couple of my English classes taught by a professor named Bill Hunter."

"What's so special about him?"

"I really haven't quite figured that out yet. He's just different. He's an odd duck. He's married, but he spends a lot of time alone on his sailboat out of Oceanside. His mind seems to work a mile a minute. You never know what's gonna come out of his mouth, but when it does it always makes you think. You know what I'm talking about?"

"I think so." She nods thoughtfully.

"So, what about you? Why aren't you at work?"

"Boy, that came from out of nowhere." She narrows her eyes at me. "Are you trying to get rid of me?" she asks with mock suspicion.

"Of course not. I just don't want you to get in trouble hanging around with me if you need to be at work."

"I can't get in trouble. I don't have to work today," she gloats.

"So, can you really afford to buy me breakfast?"

"I can manage it," she assures me. "I don't have a lot of expenses so I can handle picking up the check now and then. Don't sweat it."

"You really are something, Angie. You do live up to the 'Angel' in your name."

Her cheeks turn an attractive shade of pink. "I like making people happy."

"I should have planned better for this trip—saved more money to bring along. It was a last minute thing; Manny's idea really, and I wasn't too keen on it."

"Well, if Manny hadn't had the idea, I never would have met you, and we wouldn't have had this fine dining experience together."

We both laugh as we look around. This place—the decor (or lack of it), the absence of any other customers, the old guy and the young girl who must be his daughter watching us from their seats over by the cash register—makes me feel like we're in some sort of stage play. It's all just a little bit bizarre.

"Yes, I am something, aren't I," Angie says. "And so are you, DH. And so is this little Chinese restaurant. This has been one of the most enjoyable dining experiences I've ever had."

"Really?"

"Really. This is fun. Different, but fun. I'm having a great time."

"Well, the day is young." I say brightly. "I have a whole week to spend here so maybe we can have lots of fun together."

She reaches across the table and puts her hand on mine. "I hope so," she says warmly.

"But I'm afraid our hotel days are over. Manny and I can't afford to spend any more money on a hotel. We'll be broke in a couple of days if we do, and then we won't have any money for anything else."

"But if you give up the hotel room, where will sleep?"

"I have no idea. We'll just have to play it by ear. I want to explore the city—do some things I'd never get to do back home."

"You mean have a real adventure and not just be a tourist."

"That's exactly what I mean."

"Don't worry about me. I'll stay out of your way if you'd like. I might slow the adventure down."

"Are you kidding? I'd love to have you with me on my adventure."

"I may not be able to be with you every day, but I can pop in now and then. I'll give you my number so you can call me anytime."

"I'd like that."

"I've already written it down for you." She reaches into her brown bag and pulls out a piece of paper with her phone number on it. "Here, put this somewhere safe."

"Did you get that out of your magic baseball glove?"

"I did. That's where I keep my most valuable possessions."

I take the piece of paper and put it in my wallet behind the picture of a painting by D. G. Rossetti that I always carry. Angie walks up to the counter where the Chinese father and daughter are now standing behind the cash register. I can't see exactly what is going on but Angie is reaching into her brown paper bag again. She pulls out her baseball glove, and probes around inside it. I can't tell how much cash she gave them, but the Chinese folks look happy. The young girl is pointing to the glove and laughing loudly. Laughter echoes off the walls as her father and Angie join in.

Back At The Hotel

Back in our room Angie and I find Sissy and Manny sitting on the couch. They are sipping wine and chitchatting about the experience we all had at the Fillmore the night before. They seem to be really hitting it off, even though Sissy's direction in life is quite different from Manny's. Manny is a laid back kinda guy with very few thoughts for the future, and his entire world is pretty much centered on music and popular musicians. He's told me many times that he'd love to be a celebrity drummer for a major rock band, but the competition is fierce. He's quite realistic about the small chance he has of fame any time soon, so he does the next best thing — he practices constantly, and he talks about it when he's not practicing.

"We're back!" I announce as Angie and I entered the room.

"'Bout time," Sissy says.

I look at my watch as she takes a sip from the plastic cup in her hand.

"You gotta be kidding. You guys are drinking wine already? It's only ten o'clock!"

"Welcome to my world," Angie says with resignation. "Sissy does love her wine."

"Only on my days off, Angie. I hardly drink at all when I'm down south. You gotta have a clear head for university."

Manny gives me a sheepish look when I confront him. "You hardly ever drink, Manny. What's the deal?"

"I don't know. I think it's just the atmosphere here. It's different than back home. There's something in the air that screams out, 'Let your hair down!' So I'm following a primal hippie call of nature I guess. Besides, it's kind of fun being tipsy all the time."

"You're gonna fit right in down on Haight Street," Angie says.

"I hope so. When are we gonna head over that way. It was a bust yesterday when we got here — not a hippie in sight. Here we are, Day Two, and not much in the way of the hippie thing we came up to see."

"Actually, Angie and I were talking about that on our way back here. She says there's some sort of street carnival planned for the whole day, so today should be a good day to go there."

"All the stores are gonna have tables and booths out front selling their stuff," Angie explains. "It should bring out a pretty large crowd."

"Sounds good to me," Manny says. "I'm anxious to meet some people and maybe even do some socializing while we're up here."

"What are we, chopped liver?" Sissy says with feigned indignation.

"That's not what I mean, Sissy. You guys are great. You're fun to be with, but you're regular people. I'm talking about meeting some hippies, some street people, some crazy musicians. I wanta know what all this fuss is about up here."

"So I guess you'll be too busy for me to take you to a baseball game, then," Angie says.

"Wait a minute!" I break in. "I'd love to go to a game with you. Are you talking about one of your league games or something else?"

"A league game. It would be my team, but I could sit the game out so I could be with you guys in the bleachers. That would be kinda fun for a change, yelling and cussing at my own team."

"When could we do that?" I ask.

"We have another game in a couple of days. If I can tear you away from the hippies we can do it then."

"Great!" I tell her. "But if you think you're gonna sit out the game you're crazy. I wanta see you play!"

"You gotta play, Ang," Sissy says. "It's an important game and your team would be ticked off if you sat it out. You're the best hitter they got."

"Oh, alright," Angie concedes, "I'll play."

I would love to see an amateur ball game, especially if Angie's playing. I want to see what she can do out there on first base. But it would also be nice to have her there in the bleachers next to me. It would feel good to have her warm legs touching mine.

Sissy turns to face Angie. "Say, where have you guys been anyway?"

"We went to that little Chinese place down around the corner, and had some breakfast."

"You mean the one without a name?"

"That's the one."

"That place scares me," Sissy says. "I was in there once and sat there for ten minutes. Nobody ever came out to wait on me. And it's really dark in there."

I smile at her recollection. "Yep, we had the same experience. Somebody finally did come out, and after we talked in sign language for a while, they brought us some very good food."

"Especially the tea with milk." Angie grins teasingly at me.

Manny looks at her quizzically.

"The waitress brought out some tea and offered to squeeze her tit milk into DH's cup," Angie explains, still grinning.

"That isn't exactly what happened," I say, still a little uncomfortable with the image.

Sissy is put off by the mental picture. "Eeewwww," she says. "That's gross!"

Manny just nods his head and says quietly, "Interesting."

I try to correct things before they get too silly. "She was actually trying to communicate with us. She was wanting to know if we'd like milk for our tea."

"Was she preggers?" Sissy asked.

"No, she wasn't preggers," Angie answered. "She couldn't speak English so I guess she thought the next best thing was to act it all out."

"Did she actually pull her tit out?" Manny asks.

"No, she did not, Mr. Manny. It was all just sign language," Angie said.

This conversation is getting way out of hand.

"I hate to interrupt this lofty discussion, but Manny and I will only be here for another five days. We need to get this show on the road."

"I'll drive," Sissy says.

High Noon In The Haight-Ashbury District

We are sitting on a bench under a tree a few feet from the corner of Haight and Ashbury streets. There are lots more people here today than yesterday, and I'm learning to tell the real hippies from the tourist hippies. The tourists are dressed in clothing that looks newly-bought from J. C. Penny's, and they are festooned with an overabundance of beads and flashy hippie-style jewelry. The girls are spotless; with their sparkling clean hair and carefully applied makeup they look like they stepped out of a commercial for Breck Shampoo or Yardley cosmetics. The guys all have clean hair that is either cut short or styled longer.

In contrast, the real hippies — guys and girls alike — are wearing clothes that are well used at best. There are lots of faded and ragged jeans, shirts of all kinds, including no shirt at all. Some of the clothing appears to be handmade or hand decorated with once-colorful patches and inserts, and many of the girls are wearing flowing scarf-like constructions as dresses, skirts, blouses, and even pants that look like something from the Arabian Nights. There is very little jewelry except for the occasional peace symbol medallion or button, or something like that, but their hair — usually long, tangled and unwashed — is often adorned with flowers, feathers, and ribbons. While the girls wear little or no conventional makeup, there is an abundance of face and body decoration on both sexes, either by means of makeup and body paint or actual tattoos. Their footwear matches the rest of their wardrobe; that is, it could be anything — sandals, sneakers, moccasins, boots, or nothing at all. The common theme, again, is well worn and less than clean, including bare feet.

Don't get me wrong here; none of what I just wrote is meant to be a put-down of the hippies. Frankly, there's something to be admired in the apparent honesty of their style. They seem to be attempting to express their own true essence while trying to merge with nature by going against established customs and behaving without constraint in all ways possible. At least I hope that's what it's about and that it's not just because they are too lazy to bathe, or wear clean clothes, or get a job. Unfortunately, I can see this all becoming a fad or a fashion statement as binding as the conventional standards they claim to reject.

I have to confess that I find myself attracted to some of the dirtiest, and greasiest girls among them. They're definitely more attractive than the fake hippie girls with all their new jewelry and stinky makeup. I'd rather smell the natural scent of a girl any day, than the cloud of perfumed sweetness that follows so many of the tourists. There's something to be said for female body odor in the right circumstances.

The Circus Parade

Well now, there's a group that stands out even in this crowd—a small flock of Catholic nuns. There are six of them, all smiling, wide-eyed, and chatting among themselves. One of them, a bit older than the others, seems to be in charge. She is acting like a tour guide, pointing out various things of interest as they make their way along the sidewalk. They have stopped in front of the music store where the girl we met yesterday, Angel, works. They are looking at the display of guitars in the window. There is a break in the crowd and I can see that the smallest and youngest nun in the group is doing a rather good imitation of Eric Clapton playing an imaginary guitar—body movement, facial expression, and all. Uh-oh, tourist guide nun has just noticed, and she's not happy. She's taken the little nun by the arm and is pulling her away. The rest of the nuns follow, and they are moving through the crowd again like a flock of chicks following a mother hen.

As the nuns disappear down the street, another act takes the center ring. Two clowns—real, not figurative—on unicycles make their way along Haight Street. Their forward progress is slow as their actual route takes a path of curves, circles, and reversals that seems to function more to draw attention to the pair rather than to avoid collisions. One of them is juggling what appear to be oranges as he competently negotiates his way through the milling crowd. The other one is making an exaggerated show of effort to stay mounted on his wheel and avoid falling over into the throngs of people. Their performance has a surreal quality that accentuates the circus-like atmosphere that has settled on the Haight-Ashbury neighborhood. It's easy to get caught up in the carnival scene of the moment, but I think the real hippies have something more serious in mind.

When we first took our front-row seats here on the bench, a young girl approached us and asked for spare change. She looked like she hadn't slept in days so I gave her a quarter. She thanked me and as she was about to melt back into the sea of moving bodies, she turned and looked at us—her eyes had a clarity and directness I had not noticed before. She said, "Life's a circus, man." She smiled enigmatically, turned away, and disappeared into the crowd. I'm not sure if she was sharing knowledge she had picked up on the street, or if she was saying that the four of us are the performers in her life. Perhaps she was making a comment as one observer to the other members of the audience.

As a group, the four of us are not readily identifiable as hippies, wannabes, or tourists. I suppose I look the most like a tourist. My hair is reasonably short—not quite shoulder length—and well groomed, and there is nothing distinctive about my clothing; it's clean and not new, but not visibly old either. Angie and Sissy could pass as a member of any group they care to mingle with. They are both dressed in jeans; Sissy is wearing a short-sleeved white shirt, and Angie has on a yellow tank top with no bra. Neither is wearing makeup or jewelry, and their over-all appearance is fresh-faced and wholesome. Their look and their clothing is clean enough to fit in with the tourists, but well worn enough to blend in with the hippies. Angie really is lovely. It's difficult not to just sit here and stare at her and let the rest of the world go by; she's like a classical symphony in the middle of a rock concert.

Manny fits in with the crowd on the street the best of all of us. Ever since he's been in his band, he's been working hard to look the part. He had let his shaggy black hair grow long, but this morning he found some scissors and cut it much shorter. He said something about the humidity up here by the bay making his hair frizz up and look bad, but I think the real reason is that he doesn't want to look like a hippie—or worse, a wannabe—while he's here. He'll never be mistaken for a tourist though, as the rest of his carefully crafted look consists of ancient sneakers, not-quite-threadbare Levis, a well worn—but clean—white tee shirt, and a faded black sport coat. He would look good on the stage of the Fillmore.

The day has gotten quite warm and I'm starting to sweat. This little tree by the bench we are sitting on isn't giving us much shade, and there is hardly any breeze. The crowd on the sidewalk is getting thicker, as is the traffic on the street. The morning fog has been replaced by a smog of car and truck exhaust, cigarette smoke, perfume, incense, body odor, and a hint of what I think is marijuana. I've only smelled pot a few times in my life, but it is distinctive.

I'm surprised at the number of kids I see smoking cigarettes. Just about every one of them, male and female, has a cigarette in their mouth or their hand, and there seems to be almost a competition to see who can blow the most elaborate smoke rings. For the last few years there's been an increasing number of advertisements about how bad smoking is. The idea seems to be catching on, at least around where I live. Most of the people I know are either trying to quit, or are just not smoking in the first place. I guess these hippies don't watch TV or read magazines or newspapers — or their cigarette packs.

The odors of sweat and smoke — tobacco and otherwise — is increasing as the crowd grows. The people are flowing into the neighborhood in waves; the next one coming before the previous one recedes, like the tide coming in at the beach. The flood of hippies — there are almost no tourists and wannabes among them now — has filled the sidewalks and spilled over into the street. No more cars or trucks can get through, and the ones that are already here can't move. Where did all these people come from? Do they live in the buildings here in the neighborhood? Haight and Ashbury Streets are lined with little mom-and-pop businesses — except for The Unique Men's Shop here on the corner — and each of the businesses has a couple of upper stories that look like they might be apartments. Could all of these hippies be living in those, a half dozen or more in each apartment? How the heck do they get up there to the apartments? I don't see any outside doors except for the main store entrances. They must have to go through the business entrances below and take a stairway inside. Or maybe there's an alley and an outside stairway in the back. I'd like to go check it out but if I, or the four of us, got up now we'd be sucked into the tide of people and swept away to who knows where. It's almost like one of those cattle stampedes you see in John Wayne movies, only in slow motion. More like a mudflow. Or lava. Lava … geez, it's getting hot. And the odor is becoming more of a stink. Which word is stronger, stink or stench? Use that one.

"Hey guys, whattaya think?" I shout over the noise of the crowd.

"I think it really stinks here," Angie yells. A couple of hippies standing in front of us turn and give her a dirty look. "We need to move somewhere where it isn't so crowded."

Sissy wrinkles her nose. "It smells like piss," she shouts.

I turn to Angie so she can hear me. "Where can we go?" She's the only one of us who really knows the town.

"We can head off to Golden Gate Park," she yells. "It's gonna be crowded there too, but we should be able to find a fairly quiet spot. It looks like everybody in The City decided to come down here today, and they're still coming. If we're gonna go, we'd better go now or we'll be trampled on the way out. When we get up off this bench we'll have to force against the flow to get to where we want to go." She waves her hand in the direction the crowd is coming from. "Thataway!"

The flow of the crowd has slowed. People continue to arrive, but instead of moving forward, they are just milling around, filling in every available space; the people behind me are so close I can feel their butts pressed up against my back. Our little bench is in danger of being submerged in the oozing mass of smelly, overheated bodies. There are two girls standing directly in front of me at this moment. Their vacant eyes and vague smiles could be because they are a little stoned — or maybe they are just happy to be here and not working some waitress or clerk job for the day. They seem oblivious to our presence here on the bench. They are standing so close that their crotches are just inches from my face. There is a strong smell of old urine.

Angie wrinkles her nose. "Eww! Can you smell that?"

One of the girls moves in a little closer, moving her feet apart as she does. A dark stain appears at her crotch and spreads down her leg. A small puddle forms on the pavement directly in front of us. That does it for me.

Speaking loud enough to be heard over the noise, I say, "Let's get out of here."

The girl finally acknowledges our presence. She looks down at us with a smug expression as if challenging us to react.

Angie's face flushes with outrage. She starts to get up, pulling her arm back and making a fist.

Sissy quickly stands grabbing Angie by the arm. "Come on, Sis, it ain't worth it," she shouts as she starts pulling her in the direction we need to go.

"They'd never find her body under all these people," Angie yells, directing her statement at the girl. The girl makes a sour face and sticks out her tongue.

Manny steps between the two girls, grabs Angie's other arm, and tries to clear a way for us, pulling Angie along as he goes. "If you deck her they might all come and pee on us," he yells.

1:30 PM in Golden Gate Park

The four of us linked our arms together and pushed our way through the crowd. We managed to navigate our way through the sea of hot, steamy, smelly bodies and into Golden Gate Park in about thirty minutes.

The events we witnessed while sitting on the bench were disappointing and disturbing, but I don't blame the hippies or pass judgment on them. Something bigger is at play in this town, for better or worse. Something here is out of sync—not quite right—something that the "hippie on the street" is maybe not even aware of. This whole thing is supposed to be about peace and love, but right now it just seems like a big, disjointed, unorganized free for all. I hope I can at least start to sort it out before I have to go home.

The root cause of the smelly crotches and crevices of the hippies is that most of them have no place to stay, have no money, own few clothes, and don't have a way to wash the clothes they have. It's hard enough to find a restroom, let alone a shower. Sprinklers are watering the lawn just down the hill from where we are now sitting, and people are running and jumping through the spray. The system has either been turned on for the benefit of the kids, or the kids are just taking advantage of a scheduled irrigation of the lawn for some fun and refreshment.

I wonder if, in a couple of days, I might not have a little more in common with the hippies. We're good for one more night at the Commodore, but I have no idea where we'll sleep for the next five days. That means that I, too, may be looking for a shower and a restroom. I won't pass judgment on the folks wandering around Haight-Ashbury too quickly. I might get lucky and find a spot to sleep in one of the apartments above the mom and pop stores—I have no idea. One thing I do know though, I'll never try to pee on anybody.

I look up from my writing. "Well, Manny, whattaya think? That was quite an experience back there."

"I'm not sure what I expected, but that wasn't it," he says. "Those guys were like a bunch of zombies just wandering around aimlessly."

"What's the point? What are they really here for?" Sissy asks.

"Peace and love, they say," Angie replies.

"But there's gotta be more to life than just wandering around with a flower in your hair," Sissy says. "I think if this world's ever gonna adopt real peace and love as a way of life, a whole lot of changing has to be done. All of those guys out there on the street aren't really helping if they don't do anything constructive to back up their words. Part of the change has to be them."

"They're doing something," Manny argues. "They're bringing the problem to the surface where everybody can see it."

"But what's the problem," Sissy asks, "Viet Nam and corporate

America? That's all I've heard."

"That's part of it."

"Looks to me like if they wanted to change things, they'd join the army and help fight so the war would end quicker. The ones that aren't able to fight could at least get a job here and help build the economy," Sissy says.

"I think it's a lot more complicated than that," I say. "I'm not convinced this is really about the war or the corporations. I think a lot of it could just be a bunch of kids out for a lark. And who's paying for all this? Somebody has to be picking up the tab for all the disruption they're causing here — food, housing, medical expenses, trash pickup. Did you notice all the trash on the sidewalk back there?"

"This is a laid back city, DH," Angie says. "Our politicians don't seem to care about all that stuff."

"That's probably because they don't have to. The people pay for it all, one way or another," I say.

"And the people keep voting in the same politicians time after time," Angie says resignedly.

I shake my head. "Doesn't make sense to me."

"What does make sense in this world?" Sissy asks.

"That over there." Manny, always one to have his priorities straight, was pointing to a scene of activity across the park. "That makes sense," he says grinning.

There is a pile of clothing on the grass and three girls are running around and jumping in and out of the sprinklers — completely naked. Everything they have is flopping and bouncing up and down as a crowd gathers around them, some of them joining them in the sprinklers, with or without clothing. Here come the cameras; looks like the press to me. I doubt those pictures will be on the front page of any newspaper, but the photographers are snapping away like crazy. The girls have grabbed one of the reporters and they are dragging him into the sprinklers. He's not putting up much of a fight. His camera is getting soaked but he's laughing and grinning.

He's grabbed one of the girls by the butt. She turns around and slaps him — so much for free love.

"There you have it," Sissy observes. "Peace and love, and maybe a little war — she slapped that guy hard."

"They're just having a little fun," Manny says.

The activity at the other side of the park catches my attention. "Here come the cops." Five police officers have joined the party. They stop just outside the range of the sprinklers and watch the naked girls frolic in the water, obviously enjoying the show.

"At least the girls are getting a free shower," Sissy says sardonically.

I inhale deeply for the first time since we left The Haight. "The air is fresher around here than it was back there," I observe.

"I imagine the four of us are gonna start smelling pretty soon," Angie says. "I'm sweating like crazy." And she was. I had been trying not to notice the increasing dampness of her tank top.

"Me too," Sissy says. "Manny, how do you stand it in that sport coat you're wearing?"

"He wears that old thing everywhere," I explain. "He thinks it makes him look cool."

"I'm fine," Manny says, trying hard to look cool.

"Do we have any plans for today or are we just gonna watch naked girls bouncing on the lawn?" Sissy asks.

"I'm good with that," Manny answers enthusiastically.

"What would you like to do, Sissy?" I ask, ignoring Manny.

"I don't know, but it's kinda boring just sitting around like this without any wine to liven it up."

"I'm getting kinda hungry," Angie says.

"We could find a restaurant and get something to eat," I suggest.

"But I'll be the only one drinking 'cause you guys are all under-age," Sissy says, "and in the daylight you look underage too, so we can't fake it."

"How about we go back to the hotel and send out for pizza? We can stop and get some wine along the way," Angie suggests.

"That's not a bad idea," I say. "We can just visit for a while and plan what we want to do for the evening."

"That sounds kind of boring to me," Manny grumbles.

"I don't think so," I say. "I don't know about the rest of you but I'd kinda like to learn more about everybody. I know just about everything there is to know about Manny, but I know very little about you two girls — just what you told us last night. We didn't really go into detail about anything though. We're only gonna be here for seven days, and we're in our second day already. All I know about you two is that Sissy goes to UCLA and speaks French, and that Angie plays baseball."

"Angie and I don't know anything about you guys either," Sissy says. "For all we know, you could have escaped from a mental institution in Arkansas and you've both been lying to us all along."

"Not too far from the truth," Manny says.

"Well, you did come from Southern California," Sissy says, "the land of fruits and nuts."

"I always thought that was San Francisco," I say.

4 PM Back at the Hotel

We're back in the Hotel and the pizza has been ordered. Sissy stopped and got a couple of gallons of wine on the way, so we've already started drinking. Manny finally took off his sport coat. His shirt underneath was soaked with sweat, so he's taking a shower and changing into fresh clothes. We took a vote on that.

Sissy is down in the lobby waiting for the pizza, and Angie and I are sitting on the couch just chitchatting. We're saving the discussion about who we are and what we do till we're all back together as a group.

Sissy ordered the pizza from what she claims is the best pizza place in town. They all taste pretty much the same to me. Just how much can you do with tomato sauce, cheese and veggies on a piece of bread — unless, of course, you add anchovies, which I love. That's always been the secret to my being able to eat all the pizza I want at parties. No one else on planet Earth likes anchovies, so I always order pizza with anchovies. Nobody will eat them but me.

"So … what's goin' on in that mind of yours, DH?" Angie asks.

"I'm thinking about pizza."

"And here I thought you'd be thinking about me."

"I'm reserving that for when I get to know you better. After you reveal your life story to us when we're eating, maybe then I'll start thinking more about you. You might be a lunatic, too."

"I'm actually quite boring. You can ask Sissy."

"I doubt that."

"I suppose I could add a few exaggerations to my life just to make you think I'm something more than I really am," she says.

"You don't need to do that," I tell her. "I'm not interested in a girl just because she's done a bunch of wild things in her life. A baseball player sounds just fine to me."

"I've played some pretty wild games in my life, and I got hit in the head once with a fast ball. I could be nuts."

"Hmm … that might be fun too."

"Actually, I was fully nuts long before that. But it did hurt. It knocked me out cold. I had to be carried out on a stretcher. Went to the hospital to have stitches and everything. See, here's my scar."

Angie brings her head over closer to me, pulls her hair up on the left side and there it is, a scar several inches long showing through her hair.

"Wow! That's quite a scar. Did you have a concussion?

"The doc said I had a mild one. I was lucky. The ball kinda glanced off my head, but it was fast and hard enough that it tore my skin away as it glanced."

I bent down a little and kissed her scar.

"I think it makes you look even cuter. But you really blew it."

"How?"

"You could have shown me that scar and made up all kinds of stories about how you got it. You could have spun a Sherlock

Holmes tale around your life, and I would have eaten it up. I'm pretty gullible."

"I wouldn't do that to you; I like you too much. Although it might have been fun to tell you I was abducted by aliens and came back with the scar."

"Yep, I would've believed that."

"Do you actually believe in aliens?" she asks.

"Yes, I do. I'm not sure why, but something inside me has always made me think that things aren't entirely as they seem on this chaotic little planet."

"Really? I believe in aliens too. Always have. You're right, it's kinda like an inner thing. Something on the inside trying to speak to my mind, trying to correct my thoughts sometimes. I'm not saying I hear voices, but I get these thoughts periodically that don't make sense in relation to what we're all being taught here on this planet."

"Maybe you're psychic. Psychics hear voices all the time."

"My mother's psychic. She seems to know things long before anybody else."

"My mother's psychic too. In fact, I think it runs in the family. I have a couple of aunts that are well known for their strange abilities."

"So, maybe you're psychic too!" Angie's eyes sparkle playfully as she smiles at me.

"I knew you were gonna say that," I respond.

"Very funny. But being psychic isn't the same as all the alien stuff. Have you ever seen a UFO?"

"Yes, I have — more than one." I love talking about these kinds of things. "When my family first moved to California from Oklahoma, we lived in a neighborhood called La Sierra. The house was on five acres of land with lots of big old pepper trees, and my granddad helped me build a tree house in one of them. I spent a lot of time sitting in that old tree, day and night. I spotted several UFOs while sitting in that tree. I remember one especially; it was shiny and metallic, and it sped across the sky at an incredible speed. There was a jet plane flying over at the same time, and the UFO passed it like it was standing still."

"Wow!" Angie says looking eager to hear more—kinda like a kid listening to ghost stories around a campfire—so I continue.

"Once when I was in high school, I was with some friends at the Rubidoux High School football field just before a game. A UFO rose up on the horizon, flew along the crest of the hills behind the school, and then sped away. Lots of people saw that one. It even made the papers."

"What did all the people do?"

"They just stood there gasping and saying silly things like, 'Look at that!' 'What is that?' It was obvious what it was—one of those cigar-shaped UFOs you hear about all the time. Definitely not anything manufactured on this world."

We both sit quietly for a few minutes, pondering the possibilities.

"The only time I might have seen one was out in our back yard one night while my family was having a picnic on the grass," Angie begins. "It was about 9 PM and it hadn't been dark for very long. When I looked up in the sky, I saw something moving rapidly from right to left. I could tell it wasn't a plane because it was much faster—like the one you saw from your pepper tree. It flew in a perfectly straight line for a ways, and then all of a sudden it shot up into the sky at an incredible speed and just disappeared into nothing. It was a UFO in the true meaning of the phrase, but whether or not it was from another planet, who knows?"

"I don't know what UFOs really are," I say, "but something inside me refuses to believe that they're actually from other planets. We're pretty certain that there are no other intelligent life forms in this solar system, and the nearest other star system is 4.3 light years away. How can a clunky metal ship travel that distance and survive the trip? We're talking trillions of miles and probably hundreds, or even thousands of years to get here. I suppose the ship might make it, but no human-type being would be alive when it got here. I'm thinking there must be some sort of inter-dimensional travel involved, rather than physical distance in space."

"You seem to have thought about this stuff a lot, DH."

"I love astronomy, and I have a questioning mind."

"I think you're right," she continues. "I've often wondered how space ships can go from one solar system to the next, considering the time it takes to travel such vast distances. It just doesn't seem possible, no matter how you figure it."

"You're right, Angie. In order for beings to travel from one planet to another they'd have to do it in a completely different way—some form of inter-dimensional travel, like I said or, who knows, perhaps by the power of thought alone. They could be so much more advanced than we are that all they'd have to do is think their way here. Just sit down and imagine they're moving from point A to point B in space, and shazam! Here they are."

"That's different," Angie says.

"I'm sure that thought isn't original to me. Most likely some astrophysicist has already thought of it, and he's working on a way to make it happen even as we speak."

"Wouldn't that be neat!" she says. "We could just think, 'Take me to Mars,' and in a split second we'd be there."

"That might not be a very good idea," I say. "We'd freeze the second we arrive. I think Mars is really cold, and the atmosphere there isn't like ours. I don't think we could breathe."

"Well, maybe one day scientists will fly to Mars and bring with them the materials to build a city so people can go visit. Imagine a vacation on Mars. You could look out your condo window and see Earth up in the sky."

Our conversation is interrupted by Sissy. "Pizza's here!" she announces as she enters the room.

Manny, freshly showered and dressed, enters from the bathroom. "Well, I feel better now. Remind me not to wear that coat the next time we go out in the middle of the day."

"You may have to get that coat cleaned before you can wear it again," I tell him.

"I did sweat it up pretty good, didn't I."

Sissy has set three large pizza boxes on the coffee table. "I didn't know what we were gonna be doing exactly, so I thought I'd be prepared. We might be too beat to go out again. This way we'll have enough wine and pizza to last all evening," she says.

"And," Manny adds, "if we have any left over, it'll be good for breakfast in the morning."

"Well," I say, "I don't care if we stay in or go out.

"Me neither," Manny says.

"We can play it by ear," Angie says. "Didn't we say we would talk about each others lives, history and all that? That might take some time."

"How long can it take? I'm only 19." I turn to look at Angie. "And I've already told you a lot anyway."

"We're all young," Sissy says. "I'm the oldest, but everyone here has had an interesting life, or at least we all have interesting dreams and visions for the future. We should share some of that."

I second her proposal. "Sounds good to me. Everybody fill your cups, grab some pizza, and we'll get started. Just don't spill anything on the carpet — I don't wanta have to pay for it in the morning when Manny and I check out."

"Check out?" Manny asks around a mouthful of pizza.

"I don't think we have much choice. We can't afford to stay here any longer."

"Well, I'm not ready to go home yet, and anyway, our return plane tickets aren't good for another five days."

"We're not going home yet, but we will have to rough it for the next five days. It'll be an adventure!"

"But where will you sleep at night?" Angie sounds concerned about the new development.

"I have no idea, but I bet we can figure something out."

"You can always sleep in Golden Gate Park," Sissy says. "A lot of the hippies sleep there. Of course, you won't get too much rest because depending on what kind of mood they're in, the cops might come along a shoo you out."

"What do you mean by mood?" I ask her.

"I don't know firsthand, but from what I read in the paper just a minute ago while I was waiting on the pizza downstairs, the cops have a dilemma on their hands. There are so many hippies and tourists in town that most of the hotels are filled up. A lot of people have no place to stay. Some of the wannabes didn't bring hotel money with them, so they don't have a lot of choice. They sleep in the park on the benches or on the lawns, and the cops aren't sure what to do with them."

"Why don't they just let 'em sleep?" Manny asks.

"Because there are city regulations that don't permit that," Sissy explains. "The problem is that there are so many people that the cops don't know what to do with them if they force them to leave the park. They can't put them up anywhere, and they can't let them just roam the streets all night. So about the only thing they can do is let them sleep in the parks and keep an eye on them."

"But what about the mood problem you mentioned?" I ask.

"There are some cops that do everything strictly by the book. If one of those guys is on the night shift, he just might wake you up and warn you to leave the park. But I think there aren't too many of those left any more. The problem has gotten so big that even the police have thrown away the book. As long as the hippies don't cause any trouble, they just let them sleep, but they do come along and wake them in the morning to get them moving so they aren't too visible to the non-hippie tourists who are here for reasons other than studying a hippie convention."

We laugh at the image conjured by her last statement. It is a lot like a big convention, except this one was not planned. When, for instance, the Southern Baptists decide to get together, they plan where they're going to stay, what speakers they'll invite, what they're going to eat, and all that. What is happening here instead is that people just started flocking into The City from everywhere, and more keep arriving every day. Judging from what we saw this morning on Haight Street, it looks like it's almost out of control.

It's hard to tell where it's all going, or how it's going to turn out, but if it doesn't slow down soon, it's going to shut down The City. How can businesses operate if throngs of hippies are jamming the sidewalks, blocking entrances to stores and oozing off into the streets and blocking traffic? I realize that this phenomenon is being written up as "romantic"—all back to nature, peace and love, if it feels good, do it kind of stuff—but the romance fades if you have to wade through what we encountered earlier today every morning on your way to work. I'm trying to keep an open mind about the whole thing. I want to believe it's all for the good.

I'm sitting on the floor with my back against the couch and my legs stretched out in front of me. Angie is sitting on the floor next to me, and Sissy is seated on a chair facing us. Manny is sitting cross-legged on the floor next to Sissy's chair. The coffee table occupies the center of the space, and the pizza boxes are on the table within easy reach of all of us.

Sissy pats Manny gently on the head like a little puppy and tells him, "Why don't you go first, Manny. Tell us all about yourself. Give me your cup."

Manny obediently holds up his cup. Sissy fills it to the brim with wine, then fills her own. "Anybody else?" she asks, holding the jug aloft.

"No thanks, I'm good," Angie and I respond simultaneously.

"What do you guys want to know?" Manny asks. "I told you a lot last night. I'm just me. I'm pretty simple."

"Tell us about your home, your family," Angie prompts.

"I live in Riverside, with my Mom, Hester, and my sister, Shanie. My mom's single …"

"And she's gorgeous," I add.

"So everyone tells me," Manny says, his look telling me to say no more. "She is pretty though," he continues, "but she doesn't do a lot of dating. She likes men but she says they all disappoint her."

"I hear that," Sissy says quietly.

"This isn't going to become a women's support group thing, is it?" I ask.

"I won't let that happen," Angie grins. "I like men," she affirms, then she winks at me. "A lot," she adds.

"Just adding my two cents," Sissy says. "Some men are okay, but others are stinkers."

"Like women can't be stinkers, too?" Well, someone has to defend half the population. "Go on, Manny," I say.

"My sister, Shanie, and I are pretty close. She's been having some health issues lately and I'm kind of worried about her."

"I'm sorry," Angie says. "What's the matter with her?"

"Not really sure—she just passes out every now and then. We've had to rush her to the hospital more than once in the past few months."

"Wow," Sissy says softly as she hugs Manny's head against her thigh. "I'm so sorry. That must be frightening for her."

"Yeah, it is," Manny says. "It's tough on all of us. We think it's something to do with her brain. We're worried that we're gonna lose her one day soon. The docs have already told us that's a real possibility."

A shadow seems to settle on the four of us as we process what Manny has just told us. Breaking the silence and lifting the mood, I say, "Tell us more about your mom and your band, Manny. His band's really good." The last remark is directed to the sisters.

"My mom's had a lot of different jobs since my dad left us. She's worked in a clothing store down at the Mall, she was a receptionist at the police station for a while, she even worked as a mailman once—or mailwoman ..."

"There's absolutely nothing male about Manny's mom," I say. "She's all woman."

"DH is in love with my mom ..." Manny teases.

I leap to my own defense with, "I wouldn't say that."

"... just because he saw her half naked a few times."

"What?" Angie turns quickly to face me, and Sissy is grinning broadly.

"I'm not in love with your mom, Manny," I say more for Angie's and Sissy's benefit than for his.

Laughing, Sissy says, "You saw her naked? That must have got the little boy juices moving." She is enjoying this way too much.

"She wasn't totally naked," I protest.

"Mom was lying on the couch asleep in the living room. DH came to the door and rang the bell, but he didn't know it didn't work so it didn't wake her up. Since he was there to meet me for a gig we were goin' to, he just walked on in."

Angie raises her eyebrows. "He just walked on in?"

"He does it all the time," Manny explains. "It's okay. My family's his family, his family's my family—all that *mi casa es tu casa* stuff. I walk into his house all the time too."

"And your mom was lying on the couch naked," Sissy says still relishing the image.

"She wasn't naked. She had a skirt on but she had taken off her shirt and bra to get comfortable. She was tired from work, and fell asleep on the couch before she got any further," Manny clarifies.

Angie is not finding this as humorous as her sister does. "Why don't you tell us what happened, DH," she says.

"It wasn't any big deal! I walked in the front door. It was a little dark in there because she had the curtains closed, so I didn't see her at first. I walked over by the couch and was about to yell for Manny, when I saw her lying there."

"And …" Sissy is on the edge of her chair, her wine forgotten for the moment.

"And … she didn't have a shirt on and her breasts were just kind of lying there hanging over to one side. They're pretty big."

"And you wanted to grab them, didn't you!" Sissy says gleefully. She's having much more fun with this than the rest of us.

"I wouldn't have ever grabbed them!" I object.

"But you wanted to," Manny accuses playfully, "and Mom

probably would have liked it." To the girls he explains, "She likes DH."

"Oh my …" Angie buries her face in her hands. "Pour me some more wine, Sissy. I think I'm gonna need it."

"Uh-oh …" Sissy shakes her head. "Do we have one of those older woman younger man things going on down there in River City? Sounds like Peyton Place to me." Sissy is not letting this go.

"It wasn't that bad! I am an artist, you know. I couldn't help but look. And I decided the best thing to do was to back out of there as quickly and quietly as I could. So I started to back up …"

"And?" Sissy and Angie prompt in unison.

"And Mom woke up," Manny said. "And she had no idea DH was standing right there so she sat up …"

"Her large boobs flopping down into her lap," Sissy interjects. I scowl at her.

"I didn't know what to do." I tell them. "There she sat, rubbing her eyes and then stretching her arms up … and …"

"For crying out loud, get to the point!" Angie wants to get this story over with as much as I do.

"And without even looking up to see me, she says, 'Hi DH. How ya been?' She must have known I was there all along. And she made no effort to cover up."

"And that's when I walked in," Manny says.

"Then what happened?" Sissy asks.

"I pulled the comforter from the back of the couch and laid it in Mom's lap. I said, 'You might want to put this over you.'"

"But she didn't," I continue. "She just sat there smiling at me, and asked me what Manny and I had planned for the day."

"That would be my mother." Manny shakes his head and looks down at his lap. "She has this thing for men—even the younger ones. She hates them and loves them at the same time. She won't date any of them, but she flirts for all she's worth."

I'm beginning to feel a little less defensive and add, "The whole situation really shook me up. I had no idea what to do or what to say."

"He honestly didn't," Manny said. "DH didn't do anything wrong. That's just the way Mom is."

"What would have happened had you not come into the room, Manny?"

"Use your imagination, Angie," he says.

"DH would have had a really good afternoon," Sissy says, smiling suggestively.

"Well," Angie says, "we certainly learned something about Manny's Mom, but not much about Manny. The point of this little exercise is to learn about each other."

"But everyone's a part of their own family. We're all kind of who we are because of the relationships within our family," I say.

"Very insightful of you, Dr. DH," Sissy says, nodding her head at me in a bow of playful acknowledgment.

I just want to talk about something other than Manny's mom. "Come on Manny, tell them about your band," I urge.

"I already told you about it. I'm the drummer. We have a lead singer, a lead guitar player and a bass player. We practice in my garage several times a week and we play anywhere we can find a gig."

"Who's your singer?" Angie asks.

"Her name's Pet, at least that's what she likes to be called. She has a great voice."

"Is she attractive?" Sissy asks. "If you ever want to make it in the music business your lead singer has to be attractive."

"I think she's cute. What do you think, DH?"

"She's cute, blonde, kinda looks like George Harrison's girlfriend."

"Patty Boyd?" Sissy asks.

"Yeah, she looks a little like her," Manny agrees.

"Patty Boyd is kind of pretty, but a little rough around the edges," Angie says.

"So's Pet," I say.

"Does she have big boobs too, DH?" Sissy asks, waggling her eyebrows like Groucho Marx.

"As a matter of fact she does. But I thought we were leaving the boobs thing behind now."

Angie gives her sister an irritated look and says sharply, "Yeah, I'm tired of boobs talk." Turning her attention to Manny, she asks, "Where has your band played, Manny?"

"Just local stuff. A couple of high school gigs. Once at RCC, the local college."

"And it's rock music like Cream?" Angie asks with genuine interest.

"Well, not exactly like Cream—I don't think we're that good yet—but a similar style."

"I actually played in Manny's band once," I boast.

"You're kidding! You told me you didn't play any instruments."

"I don't really. And I didn't play one the night I was in his band."

Sissy's brow wrinkles as she tries to figure it out. "I don't get it. Did you just hum along?"

"Nope. The band has one of those tabletop keyboard thingies. It was broken but they took it to a high school dance anyway and set it up on the stage just so they'd look like a classy band. Somebody got the brilliant idea to have me stand there on stage behind the keyboard and act like I was playing it, just to see if anybody would notice that nothing was coming out of it."

Manny, who's grin has been getting broader as I get closer to the punch line, slaps his knee as he lets out a laugh. "It was a hoot! DH was a champ. He was moving over those keys like a pro, bobbin' around behind the keyboard like he was Jerry Lee Lewis, and not a sound was coming out of the machine. Nobody had a clue. Our music was so loud nobody could really tell if the keyboard was playing or not. Every time we took a break, people came up and told DH what a fantastic keyboard player he was, and at the end of the concert they went wild over him."

"I always wanted to know what it felt like to be in a rock band. It was fun and the crowd loved me."

"That's one of the funniest stories I've ever heard," Sissy says after she wipes her eyes and catches her breath.

"It does make you wonder though," Angie says seriously.

"Wonder what?" Manny asks.

"I wonder about all these wild, loud bands today," she continues. "Are they really playing or are some of them pulling off a big scam? I mean, how would the audience really know? They could have a loud recording going and not even be playing their instruments. That Cream concert last night … geez. It just about broke my eardrums. Who'd really know who was playing what, or if one or more of them weren't even playing at all?"

I've wondered that myself. "You've got a point, Angie," I say.

"I think we can rest assured that the entire Cream band is legit," Manny says.

"I think Manny's right on that point," I say. "They did some little solo bits along the way that pretty much prove they all know how to play their instruments."

"Ginger Baker sure wasn't faking it," Angie says. "I don't think you can fake the drums like that."

"If he was faking, he's one heck of a good actor," Manny said.

"Well now," I say, putting on my moderator hat, "I'm tired of Manny's life. I think we should move on to Sissy. I'd like to know more about you, Big Sister."

"Let me fill my cup first, I may talk for hours. Maybe I should fill two cups so I don't have to stop talking to do that. Oh wait, I already have two full cups, don't I, DH?" Sissy puts her hands under her breasts and squeezes them, pushing them upward, and shaking them back and forth vigorously. "Remind you of Manny's mom? Or maybe you'd like some milk in your tea."

Angie rolls her eyes. "Geez, Sis, I can't take you anywhere."

"Oh alright!" She drops her breasts and fills two of the plastic cups—with wine, that is. "Where do you want me to start?"

"How about your family? Manny told us about his," I suggest.

Sissy doesn't look too enthused about that subject, and neither does Angie. "We spend a lot of time with our Mother."

I recall my earlier conversation with Angie. "Angie told me your Dad died. I'm sorry you lost him. He was pretty young wasn't he?"

"Yes, he was." Angie looks down so I can't see her face.

"So … it was just stress?"

"Yeah … that was it … stress." The sisters look at each other in silence, sharing the memories and the grief. It is clear that neither one wants to talk about their dad. Sissy speaks first "But we still have our Mother," she says, making an effort to speak brightly. "She's a wonderful lady and we love her very much."

Angie smiles and nods in agreement. "Yes, we do love her very much. She's a champ in our book. A hard worker, a strong religious woman, and she's devoted most of her life to getting Sissy and me to where we are today."

"She sure has." Sissy's gaze has turned inward and she is speaking softly—almost to herself—as she recalls the efforts of her mother. "Especially me. I was the rebel of the two daughters." Then she is herself again. "Little Ang over there was always the sweet little tomboy. Never did anything wrong. Never got into trouble. I was the wild child. If it weren't for Mom I'd probably be out there sleeping on the streets with the hippies. I was heading to nowhere at breakneck speed. Then Dad died. That slowed me down a bit. I needed to be stronger for Mother, just to help her get through everything. That's when I decided to get serious about my own future. I was already taking French here at the community college, but I knew I needed a better education if I wanted to establish a career, so I transferred down to UCLA and the rest is history."

"So, you're keeping your nose clean down there without adult supervision."

"I'm still a bit of a wild child, but I don't do anything illegal." Sissy grins then swallows more wine from the first cup. I'm pretty serious about my French degree and maybe getting that embassy job. That's some pretty big bucks, not to mention an exciting career."

"Tell us more about your mom," Manny says. "Who is this Titan of a woman who raised these two gorgeous daughters?"

Angie smiles at him. "Aww, thanks Manny." Turning to me she says, "You have the nicest friend, DH."

"I know I do." I look steady into her eyes. Angie tries to look away but she can't.

"Hey you two," Sissy shouts and waves her hands. "I'm talking here."

"Sorry, Sis." Angie smiles sheepishly.

Sissy continues, "Our mother is sort of retired. We have a little family business here in The City that she used to be more involved in, but Angie's been running more and more of it since Dad died. She takes care of most of it now, and Mother pretty much does what she wants to. She has a couple of degrees in business and mathematics, so she could do any number of things if she wanted to, but she puts in a lot of time leading a ladies group at church."

"What kind of business does your family run?" I ask.

"Just a little sporting goods store." Sissy and Angie share a knowing look.

"That figures. Your Dad loved sports; Angie loves baseball."

"Yep, sports are a pretty big deal to our family. Even Mom still listens to baseball games when they come on the radio. It's in the genes I guess." Sissy prepares to take another swallow from her first wine cup and finds it empty. She puts that one down, picks up the second cup, and drinks deeply. I have no idea how she can hold so much and still function.

"Just out of curiosity what church does your family attend, Sissy?"

"We're Baptists. Have been since way back in our family history."

"But Sissy and I don't really attend much any more," Angie adds. "Mother's kinda the last holdout in the family."

After a loud belch and another mouthful of wine, Sissy continues, "We're not sinners or anything like that. We just don't have time to get involved in church any more. You can't just go to a Baptist church—you have to do stuff. They want you to join every group, be at every meeting."

"Well, maybe we are just a little bit sinners," Angie concedes. "But Sissy's right. It's hard to run a business, go to school, keep up with community stuff, and be involved in church the way the church wants you to be involved."

"My grandparents are Baptists. I was sort of raised in a Baptist church. Grandad built one from the ground up practically single handed," I tell them.

"You mean he was a Baptist Pastor?" Sissy asks.

"No, he was a deacon, but I meant it literally. He was a carpenter. He literally built the church. From concrete foundation all the way up to the wooden rafters and the roof itself," I explain proudly.

"Wow," Angie responds. "Carpentry's quite a talent. And that must have been a heck of a job creating an entire church building without any help."

"It wasn't a huge church. Just a small country church outside the Riverside city limits, down the street from where I live in Mira Loma. But it was a lot of hard work. I think when he got up to the rafters and roofing though, he had to have a couple of men help him get the lumber up there. But other than that, he drove every nail."

"I am impressed." She looks it, too.

Since we're sharing our family stories, I continue. "He loves sports too. There isn't a Friday goes by that Grandad doesn't watch boxing on the TV. I don't give a hoot about boxing but I watch it with him as much as I can. I'm like you ladies though, I'm pretty busy trying to get through college to become an astronomer … or maybe a painter. I'm still thinking about that. Or I should say I'm being haunted by that idea, because it just sorta came out of nowhere and I can't get rid of it."

"I think you ought to be a painter, DH." Angie says seriously.

"Why's that?"

"So that one day you can illustrate that diary you're writing in all the time." She's teasing me, but I can see that she means it as well.

"Yeah," Sissy says, "what's the deal with that? Are you copying every word we say?"

"Not every word, but lots of them. I seem to have been gifted with the talent of speedwriting. I can take dictation faster than a stenographer. Of course nobody can read my writing except me."

"Ain't that the truth," Manny says.

"How would you paint me, if you could paint me, Mr. Artist?" Angie asks.

"Naked. With big tits." Leave it to Sissy to bring up boobs again.

"Very funny," I tell her.

"But both of you do have big tits." Manny says with a Groucho Marx leer. "You two are pretty close to being twins in every respect."

"I'd jump right into painting your face before I tackled the rest," I explain to Angie, gazing into her eyes.

"But you'd have to study it first wouldn't you?" she asks, returning my gaze.

"I already have your face memorized."

"Gawd …" Sissy rolls her eyes up into her forehead. "Why don't you two get a room?"

"This is a room, Sissy," Manny observes.

Angie and I ignore them both.

"And what would my face look like on your canvas?" she asks.

"I usually paint portraits in an expressionistic style, but with you I'd try to make the face as realistic as possible. I'd try to capture the general shape of your face first, and that would be tough, because it kinda looks round at first — like a little girl's face — but when you really look at it, you can see it has more definition, more angles. It's really more like the face of a Nordic girl or a German girl who's used to doing physical things outdoors. I think it just looks round because you're always smiling."

"Wow, you really do take this art stuff seriously." Sissy is looking at me as if seeing me for the first time.

"I'd try to outline those big German eyes of yours with the perfectly clear blue-grey irises, the gentle, delicate eyelashes, the reddish blond — sienna, really — eyebrows …"

Angie seems almost mesmerized by my words, then she speaks. "I was expecting you to just tell me, 'I'll start with the nose, then do the mouth, and catch the eyes before I work my way over to the ears …'"

"He doesn't do simple when it comes to his painting," Manny says. "He analyzes everything first. But when he actually paints—get out of the way. He's crazy. Paint flies everywhere."

"Speaking of ears," I continue, "you have the prettiest ears. Such a perfect shape, so feminine … delicate … like you'd find on a faerie skipping about from leaf to leaf. Your ears are in exact alignment with your nose. The top of your ears are perfectly level with the top of your nose, the bottom of your ears are level with the bottom of your nose. Your nose is not angular and aggressive like noses usually found on athletes. Yours is softer, rounder, as if Aphrodite herself placed it on your youthful face …" I'm really on a roll now.

Sissy shakes herself as if she's coming out of a trance. "I need some more wine." She fills both of her wine cups, and half empties the first one in one swallow. "Is this guy for real, Manny?"

"He's perfectly in character, Sissy. I assure you." Manny says, holding out his cup. "You can top me off, too, Sissy."

"Angie, if you don't quit messing around I'm gonna steal DH away from you and run away to parts unknown." Sissy raises her cup in a salute to Angie.

"Better not try," Angie replies. I think she means it.

My wellspring of poetic inspiration gives me one last burst before it runs dry. "Your sparkling hair, blonde with a touch of sienna, flows as a gentle stream back into that fluffy ponytail that wiggles every time you laugh. And I'm not sure I could even paint your smile, Angie. Soft, light pink lips, the upturned corners, glistening white teeth—I don't think any artist in all of history has ever painted a mouth like yours and done it justice. Who am I to pretend or to profess that I can be the first?"

"My oh my," Sissy says. "I think I'm gonna swoon."

"You're just jealous," Angie tells her.

"You bet I am."

"I think I'm gonna barf," Manny says. "Are we about done with this life story crap?"

"I guess we could be." The mood of the moment has changed

and it is time to move on to something new. "What do you have in mind?"

"I don't know. It just seems that we've come all this way to see San Francisco, and here we sit in a hotel room just talking about us."

"He's got a point, DH," Angie says. "Sissy and I have seen all of it many times. We have it memorized, but you guys haven't even begun to see The City."

"Just no more concerts," Sissy says firmly.

"I'm not even into that," Manny says. "But we do need to do something. What's there to do around here at night? It's still light outside but it won't be for long."

"Why don't we go down to the wharf and hang out a bit?" Sissy says.

"You mean Fisherman's Wharf?" Manny asks. "DH and I were there yesterday."

"But we didn't really explore the area. We just ate some crab and left. That's when Manny's heel started hurting."

"That's a great idea," Angie says. "The Wharf's really pretty at night, and there are some places around there where we can just sit and stare up at the stars."

"Sounds good to me," I say. "Since we've already eaten all this pizza we won't need to buy any dinner."

"I hope Sissy can drive us," Manny says. "I'm not into walking that distance again."

"Sure I'll drive," Sissy agrees. "The Wharf's just a few blocks away. We can drive up Jones Street and be there in a few minutes. We'll have to pay to park if we can't find a place to stick my little buggy."

"I'll pay for parking if need be," Angie offers.

"Okay, let's do it."

8:30 PM on Fisherman's Wharf

There aren't nearly as many people here as I thought there would be, and we were able to find a place to park not too far away in spite of all the tourists in town. Of course, a lot of the tourists fly in and then use public transportation, so they don't have to park. San Francisco has lots of buses and trolleys, but it's confusing trying to figure out which one goes where. It was a stroke of good luck when Manny and I met Angie and Sissy. What one of them doesn't know about The City, the other one does. I have no doubt that without them we would have gotten hopelessly lost.

We spent some time walking around just looking in shop windows, reading the menus posted outside the restaurants, and listening to the music drifting out of the bars. Now we are sitting at the end of one of the piers that extend like fingers into the bay — pier 41, I think — watching the sun go down. The city is behind us on the other side of The Embarcadero — the road that runs between the city and the wharfs and piers. Very few hippies venture down to this part of the city, as the attractions down here seem designed to appeal to people who have more conventional tastes and some cash to spend on an evening in a restaurant or a bar. Those places can cost some big bucks in this neighborhood, and hippies don't have big bucks. Some of them don't have any — like Manny and me. Those places also have dress codes.

The only structures along the water are the piers where the fishing and ferryboats tie up and the wharf where the wholesale fish markets have their offices and warehouses. There is little activity here at this time in the evening, and the bustle and lights of the commercial area are far off behind us on the other side of The Embarcadero. There are only a few dim lights along the pier, so we should have a good view of the stars over the bay when it gets darker. The rhythmic sound of the water lapping against the pilings under the pier combines with the sharp odors of salt water, seaweed, tar, and fish to conjure up images — almost memories — of voyages to places distant in both space and time.

"I think it's dark enough now," Sissy says. She looks around discreetly before she pulls the jug of burgundy out of her backpack. "If a cop sees us drinking out here on the pier we'll all catch hell for it, especially since you guys are all just children. But I don't see anyone around."

Manny reaches into his coat pocket and pulls out four plastic hotel cups. "We should have brought a couple of fishing poles so we could look like ordinary fishermen. They wouldn't bother ordinary people catching fish," he says.

"Actually they would," Angie says. "This is a no-fishing area. Besides, I don't think there are many fish in this part of the bay."

"It would be cool though, just to sit here holding fishing rods — sort of complete the picture."

"Speaking of pictures, Manny, did you bring a camera?" I ask. "I brought mine but I don't think I brought enough film. If we had yours, we could take more pictures."

"I don't own a camera, so I didn't bring one."

Sissy looks at Manny, both amused and amazed by his complex simplicity.

"I wouldn't take any pictures here tonight, at least not with a flash. That would attract attention to us and I don't think we want that," Angie points out.

"You're right," I agree, "we certainly don't."

"Okay … here we sit." Manny says. "Just like we sat back at the hotel. Now what? We just gonna talk like we were talking back there?"

"We can gaze at the sky and watch the stars come out," Angie says. "That's enough for me."

"Whoopee," Manny mutters under his breath as he lays back on the pier, his knees up and his fingers laced together behind his head.

"I'm with Angie," Sissy says. "As long as I have some wine to drink and a nice view to look at, I don't really need anything else. I'm not big on concerts and parties. I like quiet evenings."

"I'm that way too," I say. "I don't even listen to the radio much any more. The music is mostly one group trying to be louder or more shocking or play longer than the others, with maybe one or two exceptions, and the announcers get on my nerves. They talk fast and loud, and they interrupt themselves every five minutes trying to sell you something you don't need and aren't interested in.

"I wonder if stars make sounds," Angie says. "I wonder if anyone's ever sent a microphone out into space and captured the sound a star makes while it's sitting out there being a star."

"Wow, Sis, I don't think I've ever heard anyone ask that before." Sissy pauses to consider the idea. "That's an interesting question."

"It is interesting," I say. "What brought that on?"

"I don't know," Angie says. "I was just thinking about all this hippie happening stuff, and it got me wondering about what all these invading hippies are doing here and why they are doing it. They've come all this way to San Francisco, and they've brought with them their own thoughts and ways, and I guess they're trying to merge what they believe with the thoughts and ways of the hippies that have been here for a while — the ones that seem to have started it all."

Manny looks baffled. "So … what does that have to do with stars making sounds?" he prompts.

"It's just how my feeble little mind works. I got to thinking that if stars make sounds, then do they all make the same sound or does each star make it's own individual sound? And if that were the case, then what would happen if the sound of one star merged with the sound of another star hundreds of light years away? What kind of sound would that then become? What kind of music would the two sounds make when merged together?"

"That's a really deep thought, Angie," I say.

Manny's forehead wrinkles in perplexity. "But what does that have to do with hippies?" he asks. "Unless you're talking about George Harrison and Paul McCartney. I guess you could call them stars. I heard a rumor that they're around here somewhere this week. That'd be cool if we ran into them along the way."

Angie continues earnestly. "It's just an analogy," she says. "The hippies that grew up here in The City — the ones who really started all this movement stuff — have their own little thoughts and sounds that they're trying to change the world with. What happens when all of the different thoughts and sounds of the invading hippies start to slowly mingle with and dilute the thoughts and sounds of the resident hippies? What'll be the result?"

"I don't know, Ang," Sissy says.

"I don't either," Angie says. "That's my point. Will all of the thoughts and sounds mingle and mix and actually blend together nicely to create a new series of thoughts and sounds, or will they clash? Will the invading thoughts clash with the resident thoughts and create a brand new, but disrupting sort of sound that doesn't do what anyone intended, but maybe instead it does the opposite? The invading hippies, in effect, don't really know what's goin' on up here. They had no part in and have no knowledge of the circumstances that brought the community together in the first place. They're just coming here for the circus. Technically they're fake hippies—wannabe hippies. Their thoughts and actions are not motivated by the same concerns as those of the residents who started the movement. What happens when the competing thoughts collide? At the very least won't the whole process be watered down? Will the real reasons for the movement be lost? What happens in a year's time when the tourists get bored and go home, and all that's left is a bunch of vagrant resident hippies? Where will the philosophy of their movement be then? Will it even still exist? Or will it just be a memory?

"Are you implying that the tourist hippies and wannabes are actually ruining everything?" I ask. "Rather than strengthening and adding support to the movement, they're actually weakening it and destroying it from within?"

She gazes off into the distance as she ponders her reply. "Sort of. But I don't know if I'm right or not. All I know is that when a person has a really good idea and another person comes along and adds their slant to it, that doesn't always make the original idea better. Sometimes it makes it worse. Sometimes it destroys it altogether. Things get watered down or even made into something entirely different."

Sissy nods her head in understanding. "That's what happens in some churches," she says. "I remember hearing about three small Baptist churches somewhere back in the Midwest that decided to merge together to form one large church. They were all kinda petering out on their own—losing members or just not growing. They decided that if they all got together and pooled their ideas and resources they'd be stronger. So they formed one bigger church, but within a year the bigger church disbanded. Kaput."

"Why?" Manny asks. "That doesn't make sense."

"Because each one of the three little churches had it's own pastor and it's own board of directors. When they merged together and tried to share ideas for growing and strengthening the congregation, the pastors and boards could never agree on anything. They each still wanted to do it their way—the same way that caused them to fail in the first place. So instead of succeeding as a bigger, stronger church, they failed completely. It's all about ego, really."

"Ego screws everything up," Angie agrees. "There's a part of me that would really love to join with this hippie movement thing. But I have a feeling it isn't all that it appears to be on the surface. I need more information."

"Now you're talkin' like DH," Manny says. "What exactly do you mean?"

"I'm not sure, but I'm smart enough to be wary of wolves in sheep's clothing. I think there are a lot of young, reckless, good-hearted people up here, residents and tourists alike, who genuinely desire to bring peace, love, simplicity and whatever to this world, but are they really being led to the slaughter? Are their innocent and naive little minds being manipulated into thinking in ways that'll benefit somebody that no one ever sees? When you watch a puppet show you never really see the puppet master, just the puppets. You never really know what's in the mind of the puppet master. All you ever know is the script the puppets mouth while on the stage of whatever play they are in. I'm just being honest here. I think it's really dangerous to join any movement without learning everything there is to know about it. Okay, so corporate America is run by evil men at the top that you never see and can't control. Who's to say this hippie uprising isn't the same—controlled by evil men somewhere, men you never see?"

"Geez …" Sissy looks just a little bit frightened. "What in the world is coming out of your pretty little mind tonight, Sister Dear?"

"That's a depressing thought," Manny says.

"I get it." Angie's words have crystallized my thoughts. "I understand what she's saying. I've thought the same thing at times. This movement didn't just happen spontaneously. It looks chaotic on the surface, but someone who knows what they're doing had to organize it. I think Angie is questioning the true motives of those who are organizing the movement."

"You're right," Sissy says. "There have been some disturbing things happening—marches turning into mini-riots, cussing out the police. I saw a couple of fistfights in Golden Gate Park just last week—what's the deal with that? That ain't flower power."

Manny has been processing this conversation in increasingly glum silence. "I don't know …" he says. "I think you guys are over analyzing this. Couldn't it be that it's really just a simple thing? Simple kids and simple hippies and simple rock bands wake up one day and decide, 'Let's go to San Francisco and have some fun!' And so they do. And here they are. And here we are. And I'll bet they're having more fun than we are talking about all this maudlin crap. I'm gonna take a walk down the wharf."

"What about your heels?" I ask as he stands up.

"I'm not goin' very far. I just wanna see what all those lights are over there across the street, and my heels seems to be getting better. I think the wine's healing them."

"Wine heals everything," Sissy proclaims as she refills her cup.

With that, Manny turns his back to us and strolls off toward the lights of The Embarcadero.

"I hope I didn't offend him in some way," Angie says as she watches him walk away.

"Nah, that's just Manny being Manny. He's kind of an introvert. He likes being alone and he's also almost single-mindedly focused on music. It's his life, and he takes it all seriously. I think he's a little disappointed with what he's seen of the music scene up here. He was expecting more of an outpouring of talent and heart. The Cream concert was a bit too wild even for Manny — too much show biz. There was some talent, but it was overpowered by noise and showy gyrations. He wanted to hear the instruments and get some ideas for his own band. During the concert he told me he wished the crowd would shut up. I've never heard him say that before."

"I hope he wasn't upset because I was talking about star music," Angie says. "I didn't mean to trespass into his area of expertise. I really don't know what I'm talking about half the time anyway."

"I assure you, Manny heard every word you said, and right now he's pondering the entire conversation. I think you actually made a lotta sense to Manny and he's gonna be mulling it over for quite some time."

Sissy has been quietly sipping her wine and gazing into the sky over the bay. Now she's tugging on Angie's sleeve and pointing into the darkness. "Did you two notice that those crazy little stars you were talking about are starting to pop into view right up there?"

"You're right." Angie turns her attention skyward. Her delight at the sight makes her look like a little girl.

I look up, too. "They are beautiful. I've always loved the night sky — ever since I was a kid."

"You really ought to become an astronomer," Angie says.

"I doubt that I ever will," I say, slowly shaking my head.

"Why not?" Sissy asks.

"I don't know. I just don't have that feeling that I will."

Sissy rolls her eyes. "Here we go with the psychic stuff again."

"Maybe, but I'm still young and I've got a lot of interests. I just don't know which path I'm gonna take when I come to the next crossroads in my life."

We sip our wine in silence while we ponder the stars and

the possibilities.

Sissy speaks first. "That's what the stars make me think of."

"What, crossroads?" Angie asks.

"The future. When I look out into deep space it always makes me think of the future, kinda like what DH just said. Which road will I take? How many crossroads are there gonna be between now and the time I finally become what I'm supposed to become?"

"Who's getting deep now, Sis?" Angie teases.

Sissy looks at Angie and grins. "Yeah, I got it in me, Ang." She gets serious again. "Maybe this whole visit here with you guys is doing something to me on the inside. When I came up here I thought Angie and I'd just get together, watch a couple of baseball games, spend some time with Mom. I never figured on the boys from below becoming part of the mix." She turns to me and winks.

"From below?" I ask.

"Yeah, some of us up here refer to Southern California as 'below' and Northern California as 'above.'"

"Tell him the truth, Sissy," Angie says.

"Okay. Not really below and above—it's hell and heaven. We're the heaven part and you're the hell part."

"Because it's a lot hotter down there?" I ask, knowing that isn't the real reason.

"It's a San Francisco snooty thing," Sissy says. "We up here think of ourselves as being higher and mightier than you folks down there. But after having lived in LA for a while, I think we have it backwards. I've been down there for long enough now to see the difference. People are crazy everywhere, but they're really bananas up here. People here in The City do things that nobody thinks anything about, but if they did those same things down in LA they'd be arrested. It's just a very different scene."

"I think that's why the hippie thing happened up here and not down there," Angie says. "It was allowed to happen up here. Even encouraged. It would have been treated more seriously down in LA I suppose."

"The cops down there are more hard-core for one thing," Sissy says. "They don't put up with stuff like they do up here. They actually arrest people. The cops often look the other way at some things here in The City."

"Really? That's not a good thing."

"I don't think it is either," Angie says. "And I don't know why they do it. I mean, the law is the law right? Or is there another law that's hidden in the shadows of The City that we don't know about?"

"You mean politics?" I ask.

"Oh yeah," Angie says. "Politics up here is like a jungle and you need a machete to cut through it. That really used to aggravate Dad when he was with us. He hated the political structure of San Francisco. No matter what the people wanted, even if it was in the majority, The City politicians always got their way—usually the direct opposite of what a lot of the people wanted."

"It hasn't changed any either," Sissy says. "In fact I think it's worse."

We fall silent again, each of us lost in their private thoughts. "Twinkle, twinkle little star …" I recite softly as I follow my own musings.

Sissy swallows the last of her wine, refills her cup, and raises it to salute the now totally dark sky. "Back to the stars."

"You brought 'em up," I say.

"I guess I did. And we should stick with the stars because politics is really depressing."

Angie leans back on her elbows to take in more of the sky above us. "I wonder if there are people on other planets sitting on a pier somewhere looking out into their night sky, wondering about what we're doing here on the other side of the galaxy?"

"I have no idea," Sissy says. "But I just drained the last of that wine jug. Don't worry; it was half empty when I brought it. I would have brought the full one, but that would have been heavy to carry."

"What are you really saying?" I ask.

"I'm saying I'm gonna walk down the wharf and find a place to buy another bottle. Maybe I'll bump into Manny along the way and we can cheer each other up. You two gonna be okay unsupervised for a while?

"I think we can manage quite nicely without you, Big Sister."

"I'll bet you can, naughty Little Sister." Sissy looks at me with a twinkle in her eye. "Don't worry, I won't tell Mom."

"Better not!"

Sissy takes off in the general direction of our last sighting of Manny before he disappeared from view. I think Sissy has taken a liking to him. They just might be made for each other. It's either like peas in a pod or that opposites attract — I'm not sure which.

"So, Angie, would your mother not like you hanging around with a crazy guy from down below?"

"You mean, would she think you're a devil?"

"Something like that."

"No, I honestly think she'd like you. My mother has a good sense of judgment when it comes to people. She'd be able to figure you out pretty quick."

"And what would she figure me to be?"

"I think she'd say you're a very nice young man with a good head on your shoulders."

"But would she trust me with her daughter?"

"Good heavens no! What Mother would?" Angie laughs.

"That was a stupid question," I say, shaking my head ruefully.

Angie looks at me for a moment and says, "Why don't we just quit talking for a while and ponder the stars?"

"I think that's a great idea."

She leans toward me and scoots her hips up next to mine. "Lay down close to me. As close as you can get."

Day Three

Well, we did it. Manny and I cast our fate to the wind and checked out of the Commodore Hotel this morning. We are now sitting on a bench in Golden Gate Park wondering where we're going to sleep for the next few nights. Like many others here in San Francisco, we are homeless.

Last night was great—the conversation, the pizza, the stargazing on the pier, and the long night with Angie back at the hotel. Sissy and Angie decided that since it was the last night we'd be in the hotel they would spend it there with us rather than go back to their own home. We sorted ourselves out the same as we had the night before—Manny and Sissy in the living room, Angie and I on the beds in the bedroom. I don't know what Manny and Sissy did in the living room all night, but they seemed to be having a good time. Angie and I spent most of the night sitting on her bed and talking.

Angie is the easiest person to converse with that I've ever known. Of course, most of my time recently has been spent with Manny and the guys in his band. Manny is fun to talk with, and the lead singer, Pet, is certainly nice to be around—for all kinds of reasons—but the bass player and the lead guitar player are, quite frankly, a little hard to get along with. All they want to talk about is the big name rock groups and the latest hit songs. It's no wonder that success is slow in coming to the band—they spend too much time envying the celebrity of the famous and not working on the quality of their own music. Manny has often said that he'd like to just break it up and start all over with new players. But then I remind him that he might get three more just like them. He just sighs and says, "You're right, DH. Maybe I'll just run away with Pet. Move to Florida, live in a shack on the beach and catch fish all day."

Running away with Pet would be every man's dream. She's an odd chick, but there is more to her than meets the eye. She has a good mind and she can hold a conversation. She's odd because she has odd interests. She's a little infatuated with the hippie movement, trying to mimic Grace Slick in her fashions and in her style of singing. But she also likes to cook, and she told me once she'd like to inherit the family pig farm. Yep, pig farm. Her parents raise pigs out near Hemet.

"There's a lot of money in pigs," she once told me. "And they really aren't that much work. They're messy, and muddier than any other job on earth, but they're also pretty smart. Do you know that a pig's digestive system is almost identical to that of a human's?"

No, I didn't know that until she told me. She loves pigs. They always smile. Did you ever notice that? Look at them sideways and you'll see that they always have a grin on their faces. She told me that, too. And no, I didn't know that either.

Pet even carries photos of her parents' pigs in her purse, and now and then she pulls them out and shows them off. One day she thought Manny and the band guys would be over at my place, so she drove over with some wine. I invited her in. We were beginning to wonder where the others were when Manny phoned to say that he and the guys wouldn't be coming. So what does Pet do? She pours us each a glass of Red Mountain, sits down on the bed, and starts talking about pigs.

I think I learned more about pigs that morning than anybody else in America. Pet doesn't hold her wine well, and the longer she was there the drunker she got. At some point in the conversation she reached into her purse and pulled out some photos. Smiling proudly, she handed them to me and said, "Look at these. Remember how I told you if you look at a pig sideways they always have a smile on their face?"

"Yes, I do remember that, Pet."

"See there! Was I lying?" She grinned.

"No, you weren't lying. They really do have smiles," I said, and they really do.

"You know what else?" She was looking at those pictures of her pigs like a mother looks at pictures of her children.

"What?"

"Look at those pictures carefully. Look at that pig's butt. Do you know that a pig's butt looks just like a human's?" Then she stood up, turned around and bent over. She lifted up her skirt in the back and pulled down her skimpy green panties, baring her own butt to me in all it's lily-white glory.

"See? I mean, forget about that little tail, just look at the ass. A pig's ass is bigger, but they look alike don't they?"

Pet is a lot of fun to be around—the stories I could tell. I'd miss her if she and Manny broke up the band and left for parts unknown.

10 AM in Golden Gate Park

"So, what are we gonna do today?" Manny is nudging me to bring me back to real time. "It ain't the same without the girls hanging with us."

"No, it ain't."

The girls phoned their mom this morning when we all got up and she asked that they come visit her for a while. She said she needed some help at the sporting goods store, and she'd appreciate it if they'd go down and put in a couple of hours. From what I understand, Angie has part ownership of the store and does most of the management—when she's not goofing off with me that is. Anyway, that's where Angie and Sissy are spending today and maybe even tomorrow. It looks like Manny and I are gonna be on our own for a while. But that's okay; it'll give us an opportunity to expand our adventure in the city. My original idea was not to come all this way just to sit around, talk, and eat pizza all day. I want to see things I've never seen before, do things I could never do at home—nothing dangerous, I'm not that brave, but things that are different from what I'm used to. Well, maybe take a few risks along the way.

"Sometime today I wouldn't mind heading into the downtown area just to roam around and check out some of the older stores,"

I tell him.

"That might be fun. As long as there aren't a million bazillion hippies cluttering up the sidewalks and peein' on our shoes."

"They may not be interested in that part of town," I say. "I think they mostly hang around the Haight-Ashbury District, or some of the parks where they can spread out, play music …"

"… do nothing and contribute nothing to society." Manny sounds disillusioned, almost bitter.

"There's that," I say. "Whatever happened to the Manny who was on fire to come up here and join with this great hippie crusade? You couldn't wait to get here and chat with all the local garage bands, run into famous rock stars, listen to loud music …"

"I don't know. I think dreams are always better when you're asleep. When you meet them wide awake they aren't always so sweet."

"Gosh, Manny, that's pretty deep."

"You know what I mean. When I came up here I thought I was gonna find a well-ordered, meaningful movement that was created for the purpose of logically changing society for the better. A movement filled with nice clean young people who couldn't wait to find reasons for their future, and make decisions to go to work in jobs that would contribute to the well-being of all civilization. Instead, here we are. We haven't found any of that; just a bunch of lazy kids who aren't working, don't bathe, smoke dope all day, and clog up the entire city so that the people who do have jobs and responsibilities can't get to work on time."

"I hope you're not getting all depressed on me."

"I'm not depressed. Just disappointed. All that these guys are gonna do is get their little party in the history books as some sort of freak show."

"I'm not so sure it is all just a freak show, Manny, and I've got an idea."

"What?"

"Why don't we spend the day goin' in search of the real movement?"

"What do you mean?"

"We can walk around town tomorrow, but today, let's go back over to Haight Street and explore a bit. Maybe we can find that Angel chick and ask her where some of the real movers and shakers of the movement are staying. Maybe we can talk to some of them, and find out where they hope this is all gonna end up."

"That's not a bad idea."

"I have a good one now and then."

"I wonder where Angel lives?" Manny is sounding more like himself now. "Maybe she could invite us over to her house and introduce us to some hard core people, instead of those street performers we saw the other day."

"She might just do that. Didn't she say something about her living in a room in the back of the music store she works at?"

"Oh yeah! She also said something about being a hooker," Manny says with a Groucho Marx waggle of his eyebrows.

"Don't get any ideas, Manny. That ain't what we're looking for."

"Well, it seems like its part of what we're looking for. What about all that free love stuff we heard about before we came up here?"

"I don't think Angel's free. She said she only bent over in the alley when she needed money to eat."

"Now that's an image I can enjoy for a while."

"Besides, what about Sissy?" I ask. "Aren't you two getting pretty tight?"

"I don't know. She's a lot older than me, DH. She is kinda hot though."

"She's only three years older. That's not much. She's single, smart, very responsible, and you're right about her being hot. She looks a lot like Angie."

"Yeah." Manny looks at me and grins. "Speaking of Angie, what did you two get up to in the bedroom last night? If you didn't do something with that chick I'm gonna find a psychiatrist somewhere and make you an appointment."

"The point I was trying to make, Manny, is that you don't need a hooker." He does have a one-track mind. "That isn't what we oughta be looking for. No kidding, this could be fun—an experiment! We search for the truth behind the hippie movement. You might even run into some of your rock star idols along the way."

"Okay, let's do it. But right now I'm really hungry. What are we gonna do for food today?"

"You see those guys over there under the trees by the sidewalk?"

"You mean the Diggers? You really want to eat their stuff? Is it safe? Who knows what's in it."

"The cabdriver that brought us to the hotel told us they serve beans fresh every day. They can't be spoiled or anything."

"But look at those huge iron pots they're stirring over there. Are they sanitary?"

"I say we wander over and check it out. It can't hurt to look."

"And smell—I can smell rotten food from twenty paces," Manny says.

"Okay, I'll let your nose be the final judge."

Lunch on the Lawn with the Diggers

The Digger beans passed the Manny nose test, so we decided to take a chance. What the heck, it's gonna be a while before we're able to find other food. Beans have protein; they can last for hours and will keep us going for the rest of the day.

We each took a paper plate from a stack on the table next to the large bean pots and got into line. The line went pretty fast, and before we knew it, we were sitting here where we are shoveling beans into our mouths and I'm catching up on my journal. Guess what? The beans are great! Today the Diggers are offering a choice of refried beans or baked beans. Manny and I both chose the baked beans because we saw the cooks put chunks of beef in them and not in the refried beans. They smelled good so we decided to take a chance and let the guy behind the pot load up our plates.

We found a comfortable place to sit under the trees near to where the Diggers are ladling out large servings to the people standing in a long, crooked line. Not all of the people here are young; some appear to be in their fifties, and some may even be older. One guy with a long grey beard and stringy grey hair falling out from under a straw hat looks like he could be in his late sixties, or maybe even seventies. I heard someone call him Sweet John. Lots of these resident hippies have nicknames, or "street names" as one girl called them — the names they use now while they're living this life they live. Back home these same people have ordinary names like Doris, Kerry, Bill, Mike, Emma, Abby.

Manny and I have been joined by two of the Diggers, Big Bob and Digger Auntie, who decided to sit with us and share "mealtime" together. I hope this isn't one of those cult things where you get lured into the food pantry only to get preached to while you eat so they can get you to join their cult. I suppose these guys could be some of those Hare Krishna folks in disguise, but that's not what we've heard about the Diggers. We've been told that they're local people who just want to help out the cause. Not only do they hand out food, they also operate a few houses or buildings in town where some of the more destitute of the hippies can flop. Two of the servers here in the park are wearing Hell's Angels jackets. One Angel has a long bowie knife strapped to his right leg. He also has a tattoo of a laughing Buddha on his right forearm, which I think might be an oxymoron of sorts, or at least contradictory.

Manny, who has been busy savoring his beans, takes one last bite and says, "I can't believe how good these are. I thought my mother made the best baked beans in the world, but these are even better."

Digger Auntie smiles broadly at Manny's obvious pleasure in his food. Using her spoon to point, she says, "You see that guy with the Hell's Angels jacket serving beans over there on the right?"

"The one with the dark glasses and the great big knife?" Manny asks, a little bit in awe.

"That's him," she replies. "He ain't really a Hell's Angel. That other guy over there by that portable stove — now he's a real Hell's Angel, an' so's his woman right there next to him. But Bean Man ain't. He's in disguise. He's really a chef at one of the biggest hotels here in The City. Makes a ton o' money but comes down here once or twice a week and shovels beans. His hotel pays for all these beans."

"You're kidding," Manny says.

"I don't kid, Sonny."

Digger Auntie looks to be about forty or older, but she had told us earlier that she was thirty-five. She's kind of attractive in a rough sort of way. She reminds me of some of the rancher women I've seen in Western movies — skin like shoe leather, dark tan, almost to the point of becoming wrinkled but not quite. She's about five foot eight, with long brown hair hanging down in the back, a little dirty and oily of course. She's not skinny, in fact if anything she's a bit muscular — well built and sturdy like maybe she really does work on a ranch somewhere. She isn't wearing any of the regular hippie attire. She has on the shortest pair of cut off Levi's I've ever seen. They're wedged up deep between her legs and her butt cheeks hang out the bottom in the back. She is also wearing a man's white V-neck t-shirt with the sleeves cut off, leaving gaping holes for her large and pendulous breasts to fall through every time she moves, regardless of how she moves. I don't want to be too graphic in this journal, but she doesn't seem to have many inhibitions. At this moment her left breast, including the nipple, is hanging out of a sleeve hole. Digger Auntie clears her throat and scratches the nipple as if it itches, but leaves it right where it is. No shame. No indication of anything out of the ordinary. In spite of the first impression, she's not an ugly woman. There is something lovely about her in a primitive, older woman sorta way, and I can see that Manny's gaze is riveted on what I just described.

"Where are you from, Digger Auntie?" I ask.

"I live just a few miles over that away," she says, pointing east, "near a little place called Walnut Creek. I've got about 60 acres and a few head o' cattle."

"You own a ranch?" Can I call 'em or what?

"You bet yer ass I do. Belonged to my grandpa, then my daddy, and now me. And now yer thinkin', 'What's this woman doin' dressed like that, pullin' beans out of a Digger pot? She owns a ranch! She's gotta have money, and she's dressed like one o' them hippies out there.' Am I right?"

"I don't know what DH is thinking, but you hit the target with me," Manny says, grinning.

"Ha! I like you little fella. Yer blunt. That means yer honest. Well the answer is I'm jus' doin' my part to take care o' all these people comin' up here. I don't want 'em to starve, and if I help out a bit it might move it along faster."

"Move what along faster?" I ask.

"We can get 'em the hell outta here quicker. They're messin' up everything they touch."

"Well, I wasn't expecting that. But I understand what you're saying. This has to be a real pain in the neck for the people who live around here."

"It's been goin' on for months," she tells us. "It ain't that I don't like kids or hippies, but it ticks me off they got no respect for the locals and the land owners. They trashed some property not too far outta town the other day. It looks like the county dump now, and it's gonna take 'em weeks to clean it all up. In the mean time, all the rotten food's drawin' flies and maggots. I don't like that goin' on just five miles from my ranch. I don't wanna lose any of my cattle 'cause of that nasty garbage."

Manny and I set out to interview people about this movement, and it looks like we aren't going to have too much trouble finding people who'll share their feelings. Digger Auntie is certainly not afraid to tell it like it is.

"How did you get your street name, Digger Auntie?"

"My nephew, Steve, gave it to me. When I told my family I was gonna come down here and help out, Steve said, 'I guess we'll have to start calling you our Digger Auntie now.' My real name's Glinda, but I thought if I came down here calling myself Glinda, all these hippies'd be callin' me the Good Witch of San Francisco. Didn't want that. I need to keep a low profile so's they don't come an' start campin' on my land. They move in and take over people's land just like they owned it themselves. None of 'em's got work, and none of 'em are worth a hoot, but they act like this all belongs to them, even though we who do own the land worked for generations to get what we have today. But these guys don't wanna work. They wanna steal what we own, then they trash it when they come an' squat on it. Nice bunch. The hope of the future."

"Aren't there laws against that?" Manny asks.

"There are, but they don't enforce 'em. What are the cops gonna do? There's an army of these characters, and even the cops don't wanna come out to where these guys are camped."

"They look pretty harmless to me," I say.

"I'm not talking about violence. I'm talking about crap. We've got thousands of people out in the woods around here pissin' and crappin' all over the place. If you were a cop would you like to slip and slide through all o' that? It's stinks and it's unsanitary. Ain't that what caused the plague way back when—tossin' crap out into the streets?"

"Have you met any of these people you do like?"

"Sure I have. I like most of 'em. They're as nice as peaches. But that ain't the problem."

Big Bob is sitting next to Digger Auntie and is looking everywhere except at her while she speaks. He seems uncomfortable at what she's saying, and I can tell that he doesn't agree with her on everything.

Big Bob is one of those ageless characters. He is big, no doubt about that, not fat, but lots of muscle. I'm pretty sure he isn't a Hare Krishna clone. In fact, he looks like he might be a real hippie. He has the straggly brown beard, the long hair, the faded clothes, and the dirty hands—all the badges of honor that seem to go along with being one of the inner circle. Kind of a rough looking dude who'd be just as comfortable in one of those Hell's Angels jackets as he is in that beat up old jacket he's wearing.

"You just have to have patience, Auntie. They'll all be gone when winter comes around," Big Bob says. "And just look at what this is doing for The City — you can't beat the press coverage," he finishes sarcastically.

"Are you a local, Big Bob?" I ask. "Do you actually live here in The City?"

"Born and raised here. Right now I'm livin' over on Haight. Got an apartment with some other folks."

"So, what's your story?"

"Whatta you mean?"

"Do you have a job?" Manny asks.

"Not at the moment. I used to manage a motel on the edge of town, but it closed about five years ago and I couldn't find work. I met some girls in the market and we got to talkin' 'bout how things are changing here in San Francisco — the direction things are going, and how that's so different from what it used to be. I'd just been kicked out of my apartment because the money ran out and when the girls heard that, they said I could sleep over at their place for a few days. I've been there ever since." He smiled.

"And you haven't found a job in all that time?"

"I never needed to. Both of the girls work, and there are three other people living with us. Two of them work. I stay home, keep the place clean, do the cooking. I love to cook. That's how I got this gig with the Diggers. They don't pay anything but it's something to do."

"So, there are six people living in your apartment. It must be a big place." Manny says.

"Not really — two bedrooms, a bath, a kitchen and a living room. The living room's where we gather most of the time. At night three of us sleep in the living room on the couches and the floor, the two girls I mentioned share one of the bedrooms. They're a couple, you know what I mean?"

"You mean they're a *couple* couple?" Manny asks.

"Yep, they share a bed," Big Bob confirms. "And all that comes with it."

"What about the other bedroom?" I ask.

"That's where Mandy sleeps. Mandy owns the apartment so she gets her own room. We don't care 'cause she lets all of us live there for free. Beggars can't be choosers." He smiles. Bob smiles a lot.

"I guess not," I agree. "What's Mandy's story?"

Before Bob can answer, Manny butts in. "Let me guess. Mandy's an older woman—retired. Her husband left her years ago and she's mad at the world, so she's hooked up with the hippie thing in order to express all her latent feminist ideas."

"What?" Bob and I both respond to Manny's outburst.

"Please don't make me repeat all that," Manny says.

Big Bob laughs. "You got it all wrong man," he says. "Mandy's the daughter of the people who own the building. She's about 25, I think. Her parents have an appliance store on the ground floor. They live in a nice house at the edge of town and they gave Mandy the apartment. Mandy isn't really a hippie, either. She's just having fun with all this. I think she goes to Stanford—working on an MA in geology or something like that."

"Well, Manny, looks like you aced that one," I tease.

"Win a few, lose a few," he says. "This whole hippie thing just doesn't make sense to me. Nothing fits together. Nothing about it is logical."

"I kind of agree with you on that," I say.

"You guys are right," Big Bob says. "It doesn't make any sense—none of it. But I think that's what draws everybody into it, especially the young people.

Digger Auntie adds, "Young people don't have any sense."

"You may be right about that, Auntie," Big Bob continues, "but this world isn't making a lot of sense right now either. The kids kinda see it as a flip of a coin thing—heads we go the way of the world, tails we drop out and seek something better. It's a fork in the road for them, but both roads seem to be leading to chaos and questions. I'm not really a kid—I'm 35—but even at 35 I can't make sense out of any of this."

"So what do the others at your place do during the day?" I ask.

"What kind of jobs do they have?"

"Mandy takes care of the appliance store downstairs when her parents are busy with other things. Bev and Reann, the couple, work at the McDonald's down the street. Frankie works at an automotive store about a block from here. The store sells parts he salvages from the wrecked cars they keep out on the back lot. And Jesse … well … little Jesse is kinda the house mascot. She doesn't work. Quite frankly, she couldn't hold a job right now. She's a hard-core stoner. You name it, she takes it, drops it, smokes it, or swigs it. She's pretty much comatose all the time. She's really a sweet little thing, cute as a button, and a ringer for that blonde actress in the TV show Lost In Space—what's her name, Marta something—only she looks really young if you look at her just right, like twelve or thirteen, even though she's supposed to be nineteen."

"Marta Kristin." Leave it to Manny to know something like that. "So you and this Jesse are the only two out of six that aren't employed," he says.

"Yep, and it isn't that I'm lazy, because I'm not. I'd get a job somewhere if I could. But you try getting work out there this summer with all these out of town hippies flooding the market."

"You mean they come here and get jobs?" I ask. "I thought they were just tourists."

"A lot of them are, but just as many are here to spend some goof off time. Some of them wanna stay and live here, which means they have to do something in order to eat. So they take up all the local entry-level jobs. Bev tells me they come into McDonald's in droves every day asking if they can sweep the floor for a few bucks. And that's another thing; you're gonna see a lot of panhandlers while you're here—bunches of 'em holding out hats or bean cans or whatever trying to get people to drop coins in. I think there used to be a law against that, but not any more. The cops walk by and just ignore 'em. But what are they going to do? Just look around; there are tens of thousands of people in the streets around here—maybe even over a hundred thousand. I'd say about half or more are homeless and jobless."

"Wow." What else can I say?

"I knew there was a buttload of hippies on Haight yesterday when we were sittin' on that bench, but a hundred thousand?" Manny asked.

"Probably more," Big Bob says. "If you could see an aerial view of that area on a festival day, or a be-in day, you'd see what I mean. It's like an ocean. Constantly moving. You can't see the ground between the people, they're packed in so tight."

Digger Auntie clears her throat—that usually means she's about to say something. "You can't get nowhere when they're like that. If there's an emergency, or an accident—well then, good luck. Yer just gonna lie there an' die, 'cause ain't nobody gonna come help ya. They can't get through all the meat."

"Isn't there anything positive about this hippie movement?" I ask. "According to the newspapers down south, all is well up here—everything is peace and love, daisies and unicorns. People are handing out flowers, everybody's kissing everybody else, and it all smells like roses. Can either of you give me some positive comments?"

Digger Auntie laughs. "Well it don't smell like roses, that's for sure, but I guess there's some good in all this. There's a lotta young folk out there that don't have no dream in life. They don't like what's goin' on in the world. This hippie thing gives 'em somethin' to think about—a dream to hold on to."

Big Bob continues to smile as Digger Auntie speaks, but I can tell that he does not entirely agree with her. "That's baloney, Auntie. At least part of it," he says. "While what you say may be true, it's no excuse. I got my first job when I was twelve, and I've been able to find work ever since—until all these people flooded into The City. I had all kinds of dreams, and even though I lost my job, live in a hippie house, and I'm 35, I haven't given up on those dreams. And I pull my weight around the house, cooking and cleaning and stuff for our little 'family', and my time down here on the food line counts for something, too. I think a lot of the kids are just damned lazy and they see this hippie movement as a way to keep from working. An excuse. But look at them. Most of them are young and healthy. The guys are well-built — some of them are pretty muscular — and the girls don't seem to have any handicaps either. I mean, look at Jesse back at the apartment. She's 19, in perfect health — at least for now — not seriously stupid, and really good looking. She could do just about anything. She could get hired just about anywhere. But all she does is lay around the house getting stoned and waiting to be fed. She's so helpless she even pisses her pants sometimes because she's too lazy to go to the john."

"Why do you keep her in the house?" Manny asks.

"Because if we didn't she'd die. She'd either die on the street from an overdose, or she'd be picked up by somebody, screwed, strangled, and left in an alley for the rats to feast on."

"He's right there, guys," Digger Auntie says sadly. "You ask me if there's anything positive up here — well, Big Bob and Mandy are two of the positive things. They got big hearts."

I reach over and shake Big Bob's hand. "Big Bob, it's my pleasure to know you. You've had a tough time of it, but you still haven't lost hope. And I'm bettin' there's more like you out there in that ocean. I just don't believe the picture is as dark as we think."

"Digger Auntie, you aren't too bad either," Manny says. "You say you hate the hippies being here, but you still come down and feed them. I don't think that's all about trying to get rid of them." He smiles at her knowingly.

"Well … I can't let 'em starve," she says modestly. Is she blushing? "Take a look at some o' these kids. Skinny. Grey skinned. Half of 'em look sick to me. What the hell are they doin' here? They ain't accomplishin' anything. It's all just a party inside their heads. Where are their parents? What are their parents like? They need to be home bein' loved on by their families."

Big Bob stands up and wipes the palms of his hands on his pants. "Well, they think they're doing something. Anyway, I gotta get back to work. That line's getting longer." He turns to go back to the bean pot.

"Hey Big Bob," I call out after him, "Manny and I don't have any place to sleep tonight. Do you know any cheap places we can stay around here?"

"Sure. Hang around for another hour and you can follow me back to my place. I'm sure Mandy will let you flop there for the night."

"Well, that was easy," Manny says.

"We've always got room for more," Big Bob says.

"That's really nice of you," I tell him, relieved by the thought of sleeping indoors at least one more night.

"I'm a pretty nice guy," he responds. Giving us one last flash of his warm smile, he heads over to the serving tables, picks up a large ladle, and resumes his job of feeding the motley crowd of flower children.

"Big Bob's a sweet guy," Digger Auntie says. "I've know him a few weeks now, and I ain't never heard a bad word come outta his mouth. He loves everybody. He's got reason to be a bit pissed at the world, but he ain't. Nothin' seems to bother him."

She's right. "The world needs more people like him. And you, too, Digger Auntie."

"Aww shucks." I think she's blushing again.

After Big Bob and Digger Auntie went back to work the food tables, and Manny and I took a short nap under a nearby tree. Now we're just killing time until Big Bob is done with his bean-serving gig. Actually, killing time is not the best description of what we've been doing for the last few hours. The Diggers' soup kitchen attracts large numbers of hungry people, and our spot here by the tree puts us close to the action but out of the way and unnoticed. This is the first time we've really been able to sit quietly and observe the hippies in a more relaxed atmosphere — to study them in their natural habitat, so to speak, kinda like Jane Goodall studying chimpanzees in the jungle — no offense to Jane Goodall.

Hundreds of people passed by us this afternoon while we ate, chatted, and studied the crowd. I'm beginning to see the truth of what Angel said on our first day here — it is a circus. The parade of eccentrics included a straggly old man sporting a long white beard and carrying a tiny blue toy poodle in one hand and a guitar in the other.

A family of five apparently local residents — a mom and dad and three small daughters wearing conventional non-hippie style clothes — passed by. The girls all carried a brown paper bag from which they pulled fistfuls of red rose petals, tossing them into the air. Each family member was accompanied by a brightly colored helium balloon bobbing along overhead, tethered by a string tied around a wrist.

Since no circus is complete without acrobats, we were treated to one of those too — a pretty blonde girl wearing a short yellow go-go dress came skipping by a few minutes ago. Since she punctuated her progress with cartwheels every few steps, it became obvious that the tiny dress was all she was wearing. A huge hairy dog — Manny said it was an Irish wolfhound — trotted happily along side her, licking her hand between cartwheels.

Right now there seems to be some activity under the next clump of trees. I see four men and a woman, all dressed in typical hippie fashion — long hair, jeans, and assorted shirts on the guys, and the girl is wearing a long tie-dyed skirt and a tank top. Her long matted hair looks like it hasn't been washed or brushed in some time. They're pulling out some musical instruments, and I can see a trombone, a drum, a couple of trumpets, and a saxophone. They look like a brass band, but not like any I've ever seen. Brass bands are guys in uniforms with shiny buttons and funny caps; this one just doesn't look right. A crowd is starting to gather around them though, like they know who they are. For all I know, they may be famous — I'm afraid I don't keep up on these things.

"What the heck …" Manny says, nudging me with one hand to

get my attention while pointing with his other in the direction of the growing commotion off to our right.

I look to see what he is pointing at. It's a giant fish about two hundred feet away and coming closer. A big white and blue fish.

"What the heck?" I say.

"That's what I said," Manny says.

"It's supposed to be a dolphin, I think." Big Bob has joined us and is watching the procession. He must be done serving beans. "Dolphins are big up here right now for some reason. Some of the kids think they're more intelligent than humans." He smiles wryly. "I can't argue with that. A lot of hippies think dolphins are aliens from another planet."

"Whatever," Manny says, shaking his head, "but somebody put a lot of work into that thing."

"It looks like it's made out of cardboard," I observe as the dolphin approaches us.

It's closer now, and I can see that it's constructed mainly of papier-mâché. It's about twenty feet long, a bit rough in spots, but neatly done overall. It's resting on a large cart with tiny wheels that keep getting stuck in the mud. Two large-breasted girls with blue painted faces and wearing blue and purple bikinis are tugging at a long rope attached to the cart to pull it forward, while a fat sweaty guy pushes it from behind. It would be much easier with a bigger cart, or at least bigger wheels. Ooh—the guy in the back just fell on his face. His feet must have slipped on the grass. He's up again—covered with mud, but back to pushing the big fish. I can't tell if his expression is one of pain or humiliation.

We watch as they move out of our line of sight. Manny takes a deep breath and lets it out slowly. "I guess I've seen everything now," he says. "Those girls do know how to put on a show, don't they?"

"The blonde just took off her bra and threw it at the bean tables," Big Bob says.

Manny lets out another long sigh. "I love San Francisco," he says.

"It's a circus," Big Bob mutters softly. "A bloody circus."

I nod my head in agreement. "I've heard that before."

5 PM in Mandy's Apartment on Haight Street

We followed Big Bob back to Mandy's apartment above her parent's appliance store in The Haight. I am sitting in the living room on one of the two worn but comfortable couches, trying to acclimate my lungs to the various odors permeating the room.

The stairs outside in the alley are broken so the only entrance to the apartment is through the store. Mandy's parents greeted us with big smiles when we came through the front door, but they looked a little disappointed when they saw Big Bob come in behind us — I think they were hoping that we were customers. They were very nice to us anyway.

"Nice to meet you," Mandy's father said when Bob introduced us. "I'm Andy and this is my wife Sandy."

I had noticed the sign out front proclaiming, "Gandy's Appliances," So my next question was the obvious one, "And your last name is Gandy?"

"Yes it is." Andy smiled.

Manny grinned and said, "And your daughter's name is Mandy?"

"Yes," said Andy, still smiling.

"So, you're Andy, Sandy and Mandy Gandy," I said, trying to keep a straight face.

"Isn't that something," Big Bob said, laughing. "Andy, Sandy, and Mandy Gandy!"

"You're like a puppet show or something," Manny said.

"I've already told them they ought to be in their own TV show," Big Bob said.

After the introductions and a little small talk, Big Bob took us upstairs. He gave us a brief tour of the apartment and then went out to buy some wine, leaving Manny and me here to get used to it all.

The only entrance to the apartment is through the kitchen. The stairway from the appliance store is about twenty steps leading to a landing at the top. There is a door on each side of the landing, one opens into the kitchen, and the other onto a little deck overlooking the alley behind the store. There's supposed to be a stairway from the deck down to the alley, but Big Bob said that it broke off years ago. If there's a fire here, I guess it's just too bad for anybody inside.

The living room where we are sitting is not very big, but it's big enough to hold two couches, a large well-worn green-and-white-striped stuffed chair, and a coffee table in front of one of the couches. There is a bright cerulean-blue shag carpet on the floor, a stereo set flanked by an unruly stack of albums under one of the two windows that overlook the street outside, and a fireplace in the wall opposite one of the couches.

What I noticed when I first walked in, though, was the smell. Geez, I hope I get used to it. It doesn't smell like urine like the hippie crowds, but it does smell like the accumulated odors of too many people living in too little space for too long—cigarettes, marijuana, cooking, less than well-washed bodies—all sucked into the furniture and the walls. With six people living here, it's no wonder.

The kitchen isn't too bad; the visible surfaces seem to be free of deep-seated grime, but there is about a three-day accumulation of dirty dishes on the counter and maybe two-days worth in the sink waiting to be washed. Big Bob told us that this is Jesse's week to wash dishes, but as she's been "a bit under the weather," the dishes sit until someone else gets the time or inclination to wash them. The stove is in pretty good shape but only three of the four burners work. The refrigerator works fine but the inside light went out about six months ago.

The bathroom is kinda pretty. It has green and pink art deco tiles on the walls and a shower with a glass door. Big Bob told us they take turns showering, and the couple, Bev and Reann, always shower together so that saves time and water. Only one toilet for six people though—that's gotta be tough sometimes. While the bathroom itself—toilet, sink, tub and shower, etc.—is clean, there is an abundance of clothing strewn about the place. Lots of panties, soiled Levis, and dirty socks, but no bras. I'm beginning to think there isn't one girl in The City who wears a bra. According to Big Bob, when the pile of clothes gets too deep they get washed in the bathtub, which is used only for laundry and never for bathing. Big Bob does most of the washing since he has the time and Jesse is seldom awake.

The small bedroom used by Bev and Reann is actually tidy. The bed is made up neatly and there aren't too many items of clothing lying around. A little white poodle on top of the bed surprised us when we opened the door. It started yapping for all it was worth until Big Bob calmed it down. "This is Fifi," he said. "She's only noisy when strangers come into the apartment. She's not so bad when she gets used to you. Just give her a few bites off your plate when we eat dinner tonight and she'll be your friend for life."

And that was the tour. The other bedroom belongs to Mandy, so Big Bob didn't take us in there. "That's her private world," he said. "This is her casa so we all respect her privacy. You're gonna like Mandy. She's a real sweetheart."

What about Jesse? Bev, Reann, and Frankie are all at work, so what's Jesse doing with her time? Well, she's lying on the other couch, sound asleep—I think she's sound asleep. Big Bob tells us to get used to it because that's how she is most of the time.

Jesse has given no sign that she even knows we're here. She didn't move when we walked in, she didn't wake up when we toured the apartment, and when Fifi started yapping, she didn't bat an eye. As I sit here writing, she's lying on her back with her head tilted toward us. There is a dark spot where she has drooled on the worn red velvet pillow under her head, and there is a small stream of snot making its way from her nose and across her lip. In spite of the drool and the snot, her face is actually rather pretty. Given her drug use, I'm surprised she doesn't look lean and haggard like most of the kids up here that use drugs. Her body seems sturdy enough and looks good—not like she works out or anything, but healthy. She's wearing dirty Levis, of course, and a pink tank top that's not doing a very good job of holding her breasts in. Her bright pink nipples are both tumbling out from the top. Her hair is almost a platinum blonde—natural, not bleached. It could be very pretty, but even from where I am sitting across the room I can tell it's filthy. Big Bob told me that she hardly ever bathes. When I asked him where she sleeps at night, he told me, "Wherever she falls." It looks like the couch might be where she's falling tonight.

The wide mantle over the fireplace is decorated with an assortment of photographs of different people. I asked Big Bob earlier who they are. "All the people we left behind," he answered somewhat wistfully. "Not necessarily family, just people we knew and loved. Some of us don't have a loving family back home. The mantle is kinda like a shrine for all of us. Every day you'll see one or more of us standing here just looking at the photos."

I guess it's their way of acknowledging that they are separated from their families and may never see them again in this life. It's a sentimental way of pretending that at least they'll be reunited with their loved ones at some time, perhaps in another place.

Big Bob just came back carrying a large box with several bottles of wine into the kitchen. He's asking me and Manny to come in and help ourselves. We'll meet the rest of the group later when they get off work and return home to what Big Bob and the others have named "Hippie Haven."

8 PM in Hippie Haven

Everyone but Mandy has made it home from work. Bev and Reann came in first, enriching the atmosphere of the apartment with the odors of hot grease, burgers, and fries clinging to their work uniforms. They were surprised to see Manny and me sitting on their couch. Big Bob was in the kitchen putting something together for dinner when they arrived. I got up and introduced Manny and myself, and told them about meeting Big Bob in the park. They were fine with everything, and when Big Bob came out into the living room we all had a nice chat. They both work at the same McDonald's where Bev is the manager, and Reann works at the cash register. They both have degrees from Stanford—Bev's is in business and Reann's is in physical therapy. I can't imagine what they are doing here in Hippie Haven and working at a McDonald's. They are attractive, intelligent, and well qualified. What makes them want to live like this?

They are an interesting pair. Bev, twenty-eight, is a bit rounder than the typical hippie girl—a little like Mama Cass, but not so much. She has a pretty face and a nice smile that shows a gold tooth on the left side of her mouth. Her hair is a natural red, curly and quite clean, again unlike most of the hippie girls. I guess that's because she holds down a job in food service. Her speaking voice is rich and mellow, but she chats mostly about her day at work, which is a bit boring. I can tell by the looks on their faces that the others have heard it all before.

Reann, also twenty-eight, is tall and attractive in an exotic way. Her face is long and lean with a rather regal Roman nose, large dark eyes, and a generous mouth that is truly lovely when she smiles. She resembles a Jewish friend of mine in Riverside, and I was surprised when she mentioned in conversation that her father is a rabbi in Oakland. Her most striking feature is her posture—ramrod straight like a ballet dancer's, even when she's sitting. I commented on that, and she told me it's because she's been doing yoga for years. It shows. Every movement she makes is effortless and graceful.

The last of Mandy's permanent house guests is Frankie. He is a young guy—about nineteen—and works at an auto parts store down the street. Out of all the residents here, he looks the most like the stereotypical hippie. His black hair is long and dirty and his lean face is covered with pimples. He is tall and thin, with long arms and hands tipped with fingernails rimmed with oil from pulling used parts out of derelict cars all day. He is wearing the regular uniform of worn Levis and faded shirt—today it's a tattered blue and white plaid with a peace symbol button on the pocket. Thick layers of oil and grease hide the original color of his boots, which have seen better days. The sole of the left one has come unglued so that it flops up and down with every step. His clothing reeks of cigarette smoke.

Manny and I are seated on one couch, and Bev is in the large chair by one of the front windows. There is music coming from the stereo under the other window and Frankie is seated on the floor next to it, sorting through the stack of albums and pulling out the ones by the Beatles. I guess he's a big fan. Bev is a Beatles fan, too. She said she owns every Beatles album, including the earliest ones that were produced in England. I don't know how she got hold of those. I'm hoping Frankie pulls one of them out to play. Reann says she doesn't care for the Beatles. She calls herself a "Stone's Girl" and admits to having a crush on Mick Jagger. I can't understand that; he has got to be one of the ugliest creatures on earth. His face reminds me of that painting by Edvard Munch, The Scream. He looks like he's wearing a pair of those red wax lips you buy at Halloween. When I asked her about his puffy lips thing, she closed her eyes in a dreamy way and said, "Oh … I could kiss those lips all day."

Big Bob's kinda quiet. He's sitting on an overturned orange crate in front of the fireplace, gazing through the window that Bev opened to allow the air to come in from the outside. The new air seems to help dilute the odors here inside, but it also adds a few other smells to the mix, like exhaust fumes and the smoke from cigarettes as people walk by on the sidewalk below. I can tell you right now, in the future when I think back on this trip, all the memories will be accompanied by the smell of cigarette smoke—it's everywhere and inescapable.

Big Bob notices me staring at him, and smiles at me. "There's never much to do around here in the evenings," he says. "This is pretty much what we do all the time. We just sit and play records. Frankie over there likes to do some pot now and then, but the rest of us mostly just drink cheap wine, get tipsy and go to sleep."

"I got a job." Frankie mutters, mostly to himself. "Booze gives me a hangover."

"And pot fries your brain," Bev answers back. I get the feeling they've had this discussion before.

I look at Frankie and ask, "Aren't you ever afraid of gettin' arrested for doing pot?"

"Are you kidding? There's too many of us smoking it for the cops to do much about it any more. If this was Podunk, Iowa, I'm sure they'd be all over us. But here in The City they just let it go."

"It's hard to hide the smell of pot. It's pretty distinct," Manny says.

"But if you're in a crowd of several thousand people, it's hard to pin an odor to one guy," Frankie says. "And we don't smoke it here in Mandy's house. We always do it on the landing out back."

"Do you smoke pot, Bev?" I ask.

"Never touch the stuff," she replies. "I tried it once but it just made me sleepy. I don't like being semi-unconscious all the time like some of the characters up here."

"It ain't like that, Bev." Frankie's speech comes out slowly and slightly slurred. "Pot just makes you feel good." He pulls a cigarette from a battered pack and lights up. Unlike pot, tobacco is smoked freely indoors—mostly by Frankie and Reann—and there is a constant haze of cigarette smoke in the living room, even with the windows open. It seems that nearly everyone living in and around Haight-Ashbury smokes something, with the exception of Bev and Big Bob, and I have no idea about Jesse. The only thing she has managed to do since Manny and I arrived is to turn over so that her face is toward the back of the couch and her back is to the room. Part of her blonde hair is spread out on the old velvet pillow and I can see now how truly dirty it is. Jesse's Levis, already low-cut, have crept down her hips to expose about three inches of her butt crack. A few shiny blonde hairs peek out of the cleft and sparkle in the light of the floor lamp—perhaps the cleanest hair on her body.

Mandy just came in through the kitchen. Wow, she's gorgeous. She's tall—I'd say close to six feet—with long, clean, brown hair and a beautiful face. If I had to pick a famous person that she looks like, it would be Natalie Wood, only much taller. And she's not wearing Levis! Her modest, knee-length skirt is pale blue with little white flowers printed on it. She is also wearing a white, short-sleeved blouse, and shiny black shoes with small heels. She looks quite … normal. There's absolutely nothing hippie about her, on the outside at least.

She looks only mildly surprised to see Manny and me sitting in her living room. "Well, Hello," she says in a tone that indicates neither acceptance nor rejection.

"Hi," I say, smiling apprehensively.

"Hi there," Manny says.

Big Bob comes to our rescue. "Hey, Mandy," he says as he stands up, grinning. "I brought some new friends home from the park. They're from Riverside, just up for the week checking out the scene."

"Oh?" Mandy's bright eyes sparkle. "Came up to see what all the fuss is about?"

"Sort of." I stand up as I gesture toward Manny, who also stands. "It was actually Manny's idea," I explain. "He's a musician and he thought if we came up he could find some music contacts." Why do I feel like a kid who's been called to the principal's office?

"Really." Mandy looks me up and down, then turns her attention to Manny. "What kind of musician are you?"

"I'm a drummer."

"Oh my," she says with mock concern. "I hope you didn't bring your drums along."

Manny grins. "They wouldn't let me take them on the plane."

"Glad to hear that," Mandy says. "And what are your names?"

"That's Manny, and I'm DH," I say, still not sure where we stand with her.

"And what do you do, DH?"

"I'm not sure yet. I haven't made up my mind. I want to take some time before I make a decision that'll affect the rest of my life."

"That's one of the most intelligent things I've heard coming from the mouth of a young man like you in a long time." Mandy looks pointedly at Frankie who is sitting at her feet, still fumbling with the records. Frankie shakes his head and mutters something under his breath.

Returning her gaze to me, she asks, "Do you have any career interests you're contemplating right now?" She might as well have asked me what I want to be when I grow up.

"I have a few. I'm currently taking some courses in astronomy. I'm fascinated by the cosmos and what goes on out there." I'm beginning to feel less like the subject of an interrogation as I get caught up in talking about my interests. "I love to read. I just finished reading a book on some new theories dealing with space travel and what they're calling bioengineering in preparation for landing on other planets. I'm also developing a strong love for painting, and writing as well. Not sure where it's all going."

I did not set out to impress her, but she's beginning to look genuinely interested in what I had to say about myself.

"I see you're writing now," she says. "Are you also interested in journalism? Is that why you're here in The City?"

"No, I just like to write. Wherever I go these days I always take my journal and make notes on my experiences. One day I might write some stories about what I've seen and heard. I think Jack London sort of did that for a living when he was getting started."

Her smile is warm and genuine now as she says, "Well, you should be able to find a ton of material up here in The City. You might even find a good half ton right here in this house." She turns her attention to Frankie. "Frankie, do you have to smoke in here all the time?" She grimaces as she waves the rising smoke away from her face.

"I don't smoke in here all the time, Mandy," he protests.

"The heck you don't," Big Bob says. "At least you could stick your head out the window and try to blow it out there."

Forgetting about Frankie and his cigarettes, Mandy turns to Big Bob. "So, what's for dinner?" she asks.

"I found some chicken in the freezer so I thought I'd make a stir fry."

She smiles at Manny and me. "You two will love Big Bob's cooking. That's really the only reason I keep him around here." Mandy smiles at Big Bob and he grins back at her.

"We've already tasted his beans down in the Park," I say.

"Ah, yes, his famous Digger Beans. Surely there has to be a cookbook in the works."

Big Bob just groans and rolls his eyes.

"Hey, that's not a bad idea," I say. "Those beans really were good, and if he cooks as good here at the house, why couldn't he write a cookbook?"

"Yeah," Manny says, "it could be illustrated with drawings of hippies, and concerts, and all the wild stuff that happens here in the District and down at the Park."

"Hmm …" Big Bob's expression has changed from scoffing to thoughtful.

"Hmm, indeed," Mandy says. "Maybe it isn't such a bad idea."

In the brief silence during which we are contemplating Big Bob's culinary and literary future, a loud growl emanates from the vicinity of Jesse's stomach over on the couch.

Mandy glances over at her and shakes her head. "It certainly sounds like it's time for dinner." We all laugh. "Get started BB. I'll go in and take a shower and get into some more comfy clothes."

The clothes she has on look pretty comfy to me—light and airy. I don't know how she could get any more comfy.

"You called him BB?" I ask, stopping her before she heads down the hallway.

"Yep, it's just easier than calling him Big Bob all the time."

"Can we call you that too, Big Bob?" I ask him.

"Sure. I never really liked 'Big Bob' anyway. Bob isn't even my real name."

"What?" Manny asks.

"It's actually, Bill. William Tyler."

"Why do they call you Bob?" I ask.

"I have no idea. When I first came onto this scene I was just about the biggest guy on the block." He raises his arm and flexes a huge bicep. "I used to work out at the gym quite a bit and I beefed up pretty good. A lot of people didn't know my name so they just started calling me Big Bob."

"Well, at least the B fits," Manny says.

"Yeah, BB's good with me," BB says.

"And it's easier for me when I write about you in my journal."

"You're kidding. You're writing about me in that thing?"

"Only when it's appropriate."

"Are you sure you aren't one of those embedded reporters out there?" Mandy's cynical side is showing again.

"I have no idea what that is, Mandy," I answer honestly.

"They're hired by newspapers and TV stations all around the world. They dress them up like hippies and plant them all over The City so they can dig up dirt for stories. Regular reporters, with cameras and all their gear, come up here all the time with their big egos and their fast talk, but they don't get much cooperation from the locals. The embedded guys pass for hippies. They try to infiltrate certain groups, even houses like this. They live with the tenants just long enough to get the dirt they want, and then POOF, they're gone. You never see them again, but a story—usually not a very flattering one—about the house they lived in or the group they hung out with for a week or so pops up in some major newspaper, or on the six o'clock news. We home owners try to recognize and unmask them when we can."

"They sound nasty to me. I promise, we're not reporters. I won't write any more if you don't want."

"I don't care," she says. "I believe you. Go ahead and write. You can even write a book about us some day if you want, but you have to wait at least twenty years before you publish it. By then I won't care." She's smiling again, and I breathe a sigh of relief.

"It's a deal," I say. "I do have a camera, but I won't take any photos. It's just one of those cheapie Kodak Instamatic things with color slide film."

"If you take photos, just leave me and my appliance business out of them, I don't really want to associate the business with the hippie thing—I might lose customers. Contrary to what you may have read, all this hippie stuff isn't that popular with some of the locals."

I smile at her. "I won't need to take any photos of you. I'll never forget how you look."

"Hmm." She cocks her head and considers me seriously for a moment. "I'm going to take that as a compliment, DH. Thank you." Then she turns once more to head for her bedroom.

"It was," I say quietly as she disappears down the hall. "And you're welcome."

Day Four

9 AM On the Bench on Haight Street

I just realized that this bench just a few doors down from the appliance store is the same one where Manny and I sat with Angie and Sissy the first day we visited Haight-Ashbury—or The Haight, as people here call it. I came out here because it's quieter on the street at this hour than it is in the apartment, making it easier for me to concentrate. I want to summarize what happened last night at Hippie Haven while everyone else was asleep, and I want to do it quickly so I don't forget anything. It was a pleasant evening full of good food and small talk and remarkable events that I will remember in detail for a very long time.

Manny has headed out to spend the day and the evening with Reann and Bev. I believe they're gonna do a tour of all the hippie venues they can get in before evening, and then hit a concert at the Fillmore. I would have gone with them, but last night, my plans changed radically—to say the least.

BB made a humongous chicken and vegetable stir-fry that we shared in the Hippie Haven living room. It was delicious and rivaled anything I've had in any oriental restaurant anywhere. He made a ton of it, too, but by the time the six of us had all had our fill, there was nothing left. That's how good it was. Of course three of the six had taken a "pot break" out on the landing just before dinner, and everybody knows what that does for the appetite. I was not one of the three doing the pot thing, so I can attest to the fact that the food was indeed out of this world.

Frankie and Reann had to have their after dinner cigarettes. The evening was muggy and still, so that even with both windows wide open the room eventually filled with smoke. As we sat in the living room drinking wine and chatting about the happenings of the day, the air became so cloudy and stinky that it was difficult for anyone to breathe, let alone an asthmatic like myself. I need to use my inhaler at least two or three times on a good day, but that kind of thick smoke is almost impossible for me to overcome.

The fumes didn't seem to bother Manny at all. I guess his occasional cigarette smoking made him immune to it—that and the fact that he conked out on one of the couches shortly after we finished eating. When Manny is asleep there is virtually nothing that can wake him up—not the loud music Frankie was playing, not the laughter, not even our voices, raised so that we could hear ourselves babble on over the music, deep in serious discussion of what ever it was we were discussing.

I sat near one of the windows and tried to wave the smoke away from my face. When Mandy saw me use my inhaler for a second time, she stood up and made her way into the kitchen where she picked up a full gallon of wine.

"Follow me, DH," she said as she headed down the hall to her bedroom.

BB looked at me and grinned. "I've been trying to get her to do that with me since day one," he said.

"I think she's just gonna give me a tour of her room."

"Sure," BB said quietly, "a tour around the world and back, you lucky guy."

The first thing I noticed about Mandy's bedroom was how incredibly neat it was—neat and beautiful. I was speechless as I turned slowly to take it all in, inhaling the aroma of old wood and furniture polish.

She smiled approvingly when she saw my reaction. "I've always been a bit of a Victorian freak," she said.

"I can see that."

She was standing next to a large wooden bed, one hand absently stroking the luminous antique wood of the upright corner post. "A lot of the old estates in England get broken up when the owners die," she said. "The heirs can't afford to keep them because of the upkeep and repairs, let alone the death taxes. They pack up the contents into big containers and ship them over here where they can get the best prices. I've got friends in the antiques business who let me know when a new shipment comes in."

The other main piece of furniture in the room was a large dresser that matched the bed. Sitting on top at one end was a beautiful art nouveau-style brass lamp in the shape of the goddess, Diana, in full flight through the woods with her bow and arrow. The satiny grain of the wood gleamed in the pool of light. An old-fashioned washbowl and pitcher painted with large flowers sat at the other end.

There was a large tapestry rug on the floor that looked like it should be hanging on a wall in a medieval castle. The scene it depicted was of a king on horseback, surrounded by his warrior men. The obligatory beautiful woman dressed in a flowing white gown was at his feet, hands clasped and looking up at the king all goggle-eyed. Several colorful posters, also classical medieval themes in the style of the Pre-Raphaelite Brotherhood, decorated the walls. In short, her room was absolutely lovely, and Mandy fit right in. All she needed was a crown.

"I thought you might want to be rescued from the smoke-filled room out there. You looked like you were having a tough time breathing," she said.

"I was, thank you," I said "I was born with asthma. Can't seem to be able to shake it."

"Jesse has asthma too," Mandy said. "That's one reason I yell at the others all the time about the smoke in the house. I think she has it worse than you, but she seems to grin and bear it."

"Doesn't she have an inhaler?"

"She used to, but I'm sure she's lost it by now. She can't remember anything. When she sets something down that's where it stays, and if her inhaler fell out of her pocket somewhere, it's history."

"I'm sorry to hear that. She's a pretty little thing."

"She's also quite bright when she's sober, but I'm afraid she's destroying her brain the way she packs that crap away in her system.

I don't even know the half of what she takes. I never see her take it, and I've looked for it several times but I can't find where she keeps it."

"I wonder if she got away from here for a little while—away from the steady stream of drugs, the ease of getting it—maybe that might give her a chance to get off that stuff."

"You mean like send her on a vacation to Alaska or something?"

"Something like that, I guess."

"I don't know. She doesn't have any money. She doesn't have any family. And right now she doesn't have any personal pride or motivation. I don't know what to do with her."

"Too bad. She looks so sweet."

"She is. She's a doll. But sometimes I feel like she's just one of my pets. A stray puppy that wandered in one day, blind and deaf, and it's my duty to try to keep her from walking into walls, and wandering out into the street." Mandy looked truly saddened by what she revealed.

I shook my head, saddened as well by the apparent hopelessness of the situation. "Such is life," I said.

After a moment of somber reflection, she brightened and changed the subject. "So, what do you think of my room?"

"It's really beautiful," I answered. "I love Victorian too, and I'm a huge fan of the PRB."

She looked at me with surprise and renewed interest. "You know the PRB?"

"The Pre-Raphaelite Brotherhood—yes, it's my favorite movement in art history, so far."

"Wow! Very few people have even heard of it."

"I know. Every time I mention it to my friends all I get back is a blank stare."

"Rossetti's my favorite," she said.

"Mine too."

"Far out!" Mandy said, and then made a face. "I hate that term."

"What term?"

"Far out."

"It kind of comes with the territory up here though, doesn't it?" I asked.

"It does, but I don't have to like it," she said. "I'm not much into all that hippie stuff out there, especially the slang. It just seems so corny."

"Then why do you have a house full of hippies?"

"It's kind of a long story. I sort of accumulated them."

"Ha, most people want to accumulate wealth, not hippies."

"I couldn't help it. Three of those guys out there used to work for my parents downstairs, but a couple of years ago things got tough and they had to be laid off. None of them had a place to sleep, and I had this big apartment up here, so in a rare fit of benevolence I told them they could stay here temporarily. Bev and Reann are actually old friends from my college days. I couldn't let them sleep in the Park."

"What about Frankie?"

"Frankie was Dad's idea. Dad was grooming him to be a manager of the store, but Frankie was much more interested in being stoned than he was in working, so Dad gently tossed him out. He came slithering back to the store two days later, begging us to help him. He'd been sleeping on a bench in the park for two nights, and it had been pretty cold. I told him he could sleep up here on the floor until he found another job, or whatever, and guess what?"

"What?"

"He found the job at the parts store, but now with the invasion of all these tourists and fake hippies from all over the country, there are no available apartments to be found anywhere in The City. I'm stuck with him."

"Can't you at least make some rules about smoking in your own home?"

"I tried that, but I gave in when they came whining to me one day and promised they'd always sit next to the open window."

"What about BB? He doesn't seem to like it either."

"BB's more of a grownup, but he's also a pussycat. He seldom complains about anything. And poor little Jesse—she doesn't smoke but she's a mess. I can't throw her out. She wouldn't last a day out there. The police would find her body floating in the bay within a week."

"Wow. It's that bad out there?"

"It didn't used to be. But now with all the strangers in town, the crime rate has really increased, and our police force doesn't seem too interested in lowering it. They just kinda go with the flow and ride with the tide." She rolled her eyes. "I think half the cops in The City are smoking pot. When they have the big festivals and the Be-Ins you can tell some of the cops are 'groovin' to the tunes' with everyone else. The cops don't even try to keep order at the events, they just stand on the outskirts ogling the girls and sneaking tokes from anybody who'll give them one. I've seen that with my own eyes more than once."

"Wow …"

"But enough of that." Mandy smiled and motioned with her hand. "Come over here and sit on the bed. I want to hear more about you."

"Actually, I think I need to hear more about you," I said as I sat on the edge of the large bed. "King size?" I asked.

"Yes, it is. Antique beds are usually smaller, but I have a friend who's a master craftsman. He was able to enlarge the frame without spoiling the design."

"Far out," I said, and we both laughed.

Mandy sat on the edge of the bed and then moved to the center where she sat cross-legged. "You don't have to sit on the edge out there, I won't bite. Come over here where it's more comfortable. It's real squishy in the middle."

I moved to the center of the bed next to Mandy. It was kind of odd being there with her. She didn't even know me, but it was obvious that she felt comfortable around me. Sitting close to her on the bed made it easy for me to get a good look at her face. She really is very pretty.

"Wait a minute," she said as she slid back to the edge of the bed. She reached down and came up with the two cups she had brought with her. She handed them to me, and then reached down again. This time she came back up with the jug of wine. She scooted back to the center of the bed and resumed her cross-legged posture, wiggling her butt to find the best position.

Remember earlier when I wrote that Mandy was gonna take a shower and get "comfy"? Well, she did take a shower, but instead of putting on different clothes, she put the same skirt and blouse back on—only without the bra and panties. Apparently that is her idea of getting comfy. I was given quite a show as she scooted off and on to the bed and settled herself cross-legged in front of me. I didn't really know where to look—I mean, I wanted to look, but then again … . She seemed to be completely unaware of the effect she was having on me. I guess it's all a part of the sexual revolution going on not just in The City, but all over. It's become normal for a person, male or female, to be half-naked and not be concerned about it. That seems especially true here in this part of San Francisco, on the streets as well as in the park. Nobody looks twice at the nudity. And even though Mandy professes not to be a hippie or to be influenced by the hippies and what they believe, right there in front of me, in full view, is a part of her that a guy isn't usually privileged to view on the first date—and I only just met this chick. I tell you, the sexual revolution is moving forward under full steam. I've had similar experiences in Riverside over the past year or so. Last summer nearly every girl I dated was willing to show me everything she had, and to do anything I wanted on the first date. Not that I necessarily followed through, but the offers were there. It didn't used to be like that.

Mandy filled both cups with wine, screwed the cap back on the jug and set it next to us there on the bed.

"So, DH, tell me how you plan to spend the rest of your stay here in San Francisco."

"I'm not really sure. We have four more days after today, and there are several places I want to visit—some things I've always wanted to see but haven't yet. I don't know if I'll ever make it back up this way again, so I'm gonna try and pack a whole bunch of stuff into those four days."

"What have you always wanted to see up here?" she asked.

"I visited UC Berkeley and Stanford last week with my friend, Bart. I really didn't get a good look at Stanford 'cause we hung around Berkeley too long. I thought Stanford was kind of pretty and I'd like to go back there."

"They're both beautiful. I am partial to Stanford of course, seeing as how I'm still a student there. Still working on that old MA. It's not easy to work it in with the business downstairs and dealing with my little hippie family out there, but I'm doing okay."

"I think BB mentioned you were studying geology. Is that right?"

"Yep, geology. Talk about a worthless degree—the study of rocks and minerals. What the heck am I gonna do with that?"

"Actually you can do a lot with that. You can even apply it to studies of space and the cosmos."

"How's that?"

"The field of astronomy covers more than just looking up at the stars and saying 'Gosh!' You can be a geologist for NASA if you want. When astronauts start bringing back moon rocks you can study those. If they bring back soil samples you can analyze those. When they start flying to other worlds you can even be in on terraforming other planets—geology is an absolute necessity for that. There are all kinds of things you can do with your degree. And if all else fails you can always teach."

"Yep. A geology teacher teaching students to be geology teachers to teach other students to be geology teachers, and on and on."

"The old never-ending argument for not becoming a teacher," I agree. "But it's the same for any field you study. What good is an art major? Unless you have a lot of connections or a lot of money you'll never make it as a famous artist. All you'll be able to do is teach. The same is true for just about every subject."

"I know. That's why I'm not in any hurry to get my degree. I think by the time I get it, I won't even be interested in geology any more." She took a long sip from her cup, stretching it out as she thought about her future. "I have a feeling I'm gonna be stuck in this appliance store for the rest of my life, maybe even taking care of those four goofballs out there to boot."

"But you love those goofballs don't you?"

"Of course I do, or else they wouldn't be there."

"Even Jesse?"

"Especially Jesse." Mandy let out a deep sigh. "She's such a helpless little flower. No, scratch that. I've known flowers that are far more productive than her. She's totally helpless."

"Maybe she'll get better," I said. "Heck, maybe they'll all get better and you can go back to living here on your own, just enjoying life."

"I can only dream."

Mandy and I sat there on the bed drinking wine like that for another hour or so, and since she had to go to work early this morning, we decided to call it a night. I got up to go back to the living room, but Mandy stopped me. "You can't sleep in there — the smoke will kill you. Why don't you sleep in here tonight?" she said as she patted her hand on the bed. And that's where I wound up, but you don't need to know the details.

I went back to the living room to get my backpack, just in case I needed something out of it during the night. I didn't want to wake anybody up, so I approached quietly and peeked around the corner. Manny was lying on the floor by the record player. Reann and Bev were lying there as well, and all three of them were asleep. Reann was using Manny's lap as a pillow. That was interesting but, given Reann's sexual persuasion, perfectly innocent. I didn't see BB or Frankie. They must have gone out for the evening.

Then I noticed Jesse. She was standing in front of the fireplace, and in the dim light from the windows I could see that her eyes were wide open. It was the first time I'd seen her awake and active. As I silently placed one foot into the room her head snapped in my direction. Her body was motionless and her face was totally without expression as her silvery blue eyes penetrated deep into my own. I was spellbound. She was Aphrodite herself rising up out of the sea-blue carpet. She could have been carved from a five foot six block of Carrara marble and then left there for passersby to marvel at throughout the ages. All she needed was a giant clamshell.

Jesse stood there as something greater than any Being I'd ever seen in all my life. Not bad for a drugged up, lay about, totally unmotivated hippie waif who had fallen on bad times. All I could do was stand there and stare at her. Her blonde hair, matted from days of neglect, somehow managed to glisten in a way that nearly blinded me. She was stunning — literally. I was totally stunned and unable to move. Then she spoke.

"Am I dead?"

She delivered the line as if she really were dead. No movement in any part of her face or her body except her lips. She had the softest, pinkest skin I'd ever seen. And the blondest hair. Even her eyebrows were blonde — nearly white. Perhaps she was dead. I couldn't tell. I couldn't even answer her question.

"I'm here … waiting," she said softly.

I finally found my voice and asked, "What are you waiting for?"

"I know you. I'm waiting for you," came her answer, her eyes unblinking, her nostrils flaring with every syllable she spoke.

"I don't believe we've met, Jesse. I just got here today while you were asleep."

"I felt you touching me with your mind," she said. "You looked at me today. I've been looked at by you."

"Yes, I did look at you when you lay on the couch."

"Perhaps I am not dead then." Every word she spoke was clear and precise. "If you touched me, then I shall go on living."

"But I didn't touch you, Jesse. I didn't come near you. I merely watched you as you slept."

"Then come touch me. Touch me now."

"I don't know … I …"

"Touch me here." She pointed up to her forehead.

I didn't know what else to do. I moved toward her slowly. I could feel the heat of her body as I came close to her. She was glowing with inner fire. And I could smell her. Her body odor was strong from having not washed in days. In any other circumstance, had it been any other person, I would have been repelled by the intensity of her odor, but I wasn't. I was captured there by everything she was. I slowly brought my hand up, extending my finger to touch her in the middle of her forehead. I both heard and felt a loud electrical "POP" as my fingertip barely touched her flesh. Static electricity? I had walked across the carpet to get to her.

At that moment, Jesse closed her eyes and began to fall. She didn't crumple to the floor like she was fainting, but she fell straight back. I went with a friend once to a tent meeting held by an evangelist who claimed he could heal people. When the people came forward, he would touch their heads and they would fall backwards. That's what happened when I touched Jesse. It only took a second or two, but it seemed as if she was falling for hours. In a way, time stood still.

I caught her before she could hit the floor, and then I guided her gently down to lay flat on the shag carpet. I placed my arm under her head for a pillow and I just sat there. I sat there staring at her face.

That's when Mandy entered.

"She just started to fall so I caught her," I said.

"It's good you did," Mandy said. "She could have split her head open on the fireplace. This isn't the first time she's fallen like this."

"Let's get her over to the couch," I said.

We lifted her up onto the couch, and I put a pillow under her head. She was so pretty.

Sensing my own thoughts, Mandy said softly, "She's rather Pre-Raphaelite, isn't she?"

"Yes, she is," I agreed. "Isn't there something we can do for her? Can't we break the drug spell somehow?"

"Well, I do have one idea," Mandy said.

"Great! What is it?"

"You told me you were gonna do some exploring tomorrow, maybe go to Stanford or Berkeley. Do you think you might put that off for a day, and do a little sight seeing closer to home? I don't mean Riverside, I mean around here. How would it be if you were to take Jesse along with you, maybe take in the downtown area, sit in the park and talk, hit a nice restaurant? Just get her away from all this. I have to work, and I heard Manny talking to Reann earlier about going to some festival events and a concert. I think it would be nice if Jesse spent some time with you. You have a very calming spirit."

"But I don't even know her. We haven't even met—I mean, not really. She might not even like me."

Mandy smiled and said, "What's there not to like?"

So, here I am on the Haight Street bench waiting for Mandy to bring Jesse out to meet me. I spent the night in Mandy's bedroom, then got up this morning, ate a bagel and some cheese, and said my formal goodbye to Mandy. I really hated that. It would be nice to spend a few days getting to know her better, but I don't know if I'll spend any more nights at Hippie Haven because of my asthma. So we said goodbye just in case I don't see her again. Mandy's a wonderful person with a big heart, and it's her big heart that convinced me to take Jesse around with me today. I have no idea what we'll do or where we'll go. Jesse was still asleep on the couch when I left, so technically, she hasn't met me yet. I can't count it as an introduction when she asked me last night if she was dead. I'm not even sure she was awake at the time. She might have been sleepwalking through that entire episode.

Where am I gonna take this little drugged-up waif? Where does one take a person who, in all probability, doesn't have much of a clue as to where they are at any given time? Will she even be able to walk? Or stay awake for that matter? Will she bring drugs with her and pop a few pills along the way? I don't want to be a part of that. She might not even wake up this morning. I might sit here for hours waiting for her and Mandy just to have them not show up.

Ah, here they come now. I'll catch up on the writing later when I get a chance.

"Here we are, DH," Mandy says brightly. "It's already been quite a morning, but things are looking up now."

"Good morning," I say, standing to greet them. It looks like I'm going to have my hands full for a while.

10:30 AM In a Little Park

I'm sitting under a tree in a secluded section of a little park. In fact, I don't see anybody else around. Of course in "hippie time" (as Big Bob would say) it's still pretty early, so most of them are still asleep.

Jesse is lying on the grass beside me. We haven't gone very far. Almost as soon as Mandy left us Jesse asked if we could sit under the trees for a while just to "ponder the sky and feel the warm breeze against our skin." She also asked me to sit close to her so I can examine her while she lies there. She actually said, "Please sit very close to me so you can examine all of me lying here."

When Mandy first brought Jesse out to meet me, she was helping her to stand and walk. When they got closer, I could see that this wasn't because Jesse was weak, but because she was limp, like a puppet or a rag doll. Her eyes were open but vacant—as if her full consciousness was anyplace but here—and she made no effort to greet me. Something flickered deep beneath the blue of her eyes as I stood there looking at her. She looked puzzled as her awareness came to rest on me. "Do I know you?" she asked in that sweet little voice of hers.

"I'm the guy that caught you when you fell." That took her by surprise. It seemed to mean much more to her than it did to me. I don't think she remembered falling into my arms last night, but who knows? I've never met anybody like this before. Ever.

I turned my attention to Mandy. "Manny was still asleep when I left this morning. Is he up and at 'em yet?"

"Oh yes. He and Bev and Reann were sitting in the kitchen eating bagels and planning out their day when I left. They're gonna be gone till the wee hours probably. They're pretty excited about it."

"So it looks like Jesse and I are gonna have the day to ourselves then." I forced a smile because I had no idea what I was getting into. Quite frankly, the whole thing made me a bit uncomfortable.

"Yep," Mandy said. "I told Jesse it would be good for her to get out of the house and into the fresh air. She's been cooped up in the house for days. Right, Jesse?" She gave Jesse's shoulder a squeeze to prompt a response.

"I guess," Jesse said softly, still looking elsewhere.

"We'll have a good time, Jesse, I promise," I told her.

She brought her focus to me again. "But I don't even know you … unless … I already know you," she said.

"Well …" I didn't really know how to answer that. I wasn't even sure what she meant.

"You met DH last night in the living room. Don't you remember?" Mandy sounded like they have had this kind of conversation before. "You passed out in front of the fireplace and DH was right there to catch you before you fell and hit your head on the fireplace stones."

"Fireplace?" Jesse asked vaguely. "What fireplace?"

"Our fireplace. In the living room at Hippie Haven where you live," Mandy said.

"I live in the sea," Jesse said. "I was in the sea last night." Once again, she looked at me. This time, her gaze seemed to penetrate beneath the surface of my eyes.

Last night I thought she looked like Aphrodite rising up out of the sea, but I never said that out loud. Surely she can't read my mind, can she?

"Well, maybe we'll walk up to the Wharf today and sit by the water."

"I am the water," Jesse said.

"Are you going to be okay?" Mandy asked her as she carefully let go of her arm. "Can you stand without me holding on to you?"

"I'll be just fine," Jesse said, still looking deep into my eyes. "DH can hold me up now. That's why he's come this far."

I pulled my attention away from Jesse to ask Mandy, "Did you tell her that I flew up here from Riverside?"

"I didn't tell her anything about you, except that you probably saved her life last night, and that you want to spend the day with her today touring The City."

"Jesse, I did fly hundreds of miles to be here with you today. I want to be with you and share my thoughts with you. I want us to have a lot of fun together and become close friends. Would you like that?"

Jesse, still looking into my eyes, paused for a moment and then said, "I'd like that. But to have true fun we must first get close. Fun follows close. Close does not follow fun. We must touch each other inside and out. It's the only way."

Mandy and I looked at each other. Mandy shrugged her shoulders and smiled. Leaning close to Mandy's ear I whispered, "How old did you say Jesse is?

"She's nineteen."

"Are you sure? Right now, out here in the sunlight, she looks like she's about twelve."

"She has a driver's license—I've seen it. She carries it in her back pocket in case somebody stops you."

Mandy obviously caught my drift. I didn't want to be stopped by the cops with an underage girl at my side.

I turn back to Jesse. "Okay, let's do this Jesse. Give me your hand and together we'll try to become close."

"It won't be bad," Mandy said brightly. "You're gonna love her. She's one of a kind."

Mandy walked away, giving us a wink and a wave as she turned to go back to her house. Jesse placed her hand in mine and smiled at least a half smile, and then we slowly headed off together.

We proceeded in silence for about half a block, then Jesse spoke softly, "We must go to the park to plan our day."

"That sounds fine to me, Jesse. We can find a nice clump of trees to sit under."

"I want to lie down while we plan," she said.

"Okay, but you won't fall asleep will you?"

"No. I'll close my eyes, but I'll be awake. I'll listen to you and you can stare at me while my eyes are closed. You can memorize my features."

"What an odd thing to say, Jesse." But I had been thinking just that thought. I wanted to place her in the sun somewhere and look at her — really look at her. I'd be content to do nothing more than stare at her all day and when darkness came, I'd light a candle and continue to stare at her into the night — to do that for days until we both starved and died. But I wondered if she even could die. There's something magical about this girl — she's many things all at once.

"I say odd things because I am odd. I'm an only child. I'm the number one." I have no idea what she meant by that.

"Well, right now you are the number one in my life," I said. "You're the most important person in my world, Jesse. Let's go find that clump of trees where you can lie down and I can sit and stare at you all I want."

I didn't want to walk all the way to Golden Gate Park, so we found a smaller one to land in not too far from The Haight, and pretty close to downtown. I don't think it's even a city park; it's more like a neighborhood park — tiny but with lots of trees and no people. We can make our plans here without being disturbed.

Jesse is lying under a lovely clump of trees, and I'm sitting next to her, examining her like she asked me to do. We still haven't started making plans for the day. Jesse told me that first I must simply sit here and fix my eyes upon her, and that I couldn't look away.

"Look at every inch of my skin. Study my face, my hair, my body. Burn holes through my flesh with your eyes."

She is odd, and that's putting it mildly. I have no idea how her mind works, but it works crazy all the time. I'm convinced that for every word she says aloud, there are a thousand more shouting out inside her lovely head. I'm also convinced that every word she says has a meaning to it beyond what a person hears.

It's good to have this time to just look at her—to examine her as she told me earlier. "Like a doctor examines a patient?" I asked her.

"No, like a spider examines a fly he's going to eat," she answered.

"You want to paint a painting of me don't you?" she asks, her eyes still closed.

"I do."

How did she know that? How did she know that I'm an artist and that I've already been pondering the possibility of painting her? How did she know about me comparing her to Aphrodite and the sea? How did she know I came all the way up here just to be with her? I didn't even know that!

She is lovely. I wish there was another word for her; lovely isn't enough. Nothing is enough. She's more than lovely. More than beautiful, much more than pretty, more than exquisite, even more than perfect. So, what does that make her? Perhaps she really is a goddess come down to Earth just to be with me. Maybe that's it. It's been a long time since the goddesses of old were worshiped or even paid any attention to. Maybe she's one of those, and she's gotten tired of being ignored so she's put on a mortal frame and come down from Olympus to walk the Earth one more time in search of those who would recognize her and give her honor. Could that be it? Am I the one she's chosen for her priest?

But at the same time she's so innocent. At first impression she has the stature of an Olympian, in reality she's only about five feet six inches — maybe even a little less. And although what comes out of her head may be the thoughts of a mature woman, or of a being far beyond a mere woman, her face is more like that of a child. It's part of her mystery. One moment her face is stern and wise, almost ancient in appearance, without time. The next moment, it is that of a twelve-year old. Which is it, really? What is she, really? Woman or child? Mortal or immortal?

Her face is perfectly shaped — not too thin or long, and not too wide or round. Her large eyes are Scandinavian in shape and in color, the most piercing of all blue, sharp as a sword and cutting both ways as they stare into a person's soul. A medium length nose that's more round at the end than it is flat or wide — a soft, warm nose. Lips that are wide on the top but even wider on the bottom creating the perfect form that lips should reflect when she smiles. I must paint her!

She is a natural blonde. Most of the girls I see today who profess to be blonde really aren't. They're fake blonds. I can tell by the black eyebrows. They dye their hair but leave the eyebrows black. Jesse has no need to dye any part of her. She's purely, softly, and wonderfully blonde. She must be Nordic. Perhaps she's not Aphrodite after all, but the goddess, Freya. Everything about her screams of the North, even her pale pink, flawless skin. Even lying there in the sun as she is now, I'd bet a thousand dollars (if I had it) that she won't get tanned or even sun burned. I bet the color she exhibits now is the way she's always been and the way she'll always be.

She told me she wouldn't go to sleep, but as I look down at her, I can see that her eyes are closed, her breathing is steady, she's quiet. A single tear has formed in the corner of her right eye. It's welled up at the edge of her eye and is getting ready to fall out and run down her cheek. Why is she crying? What am I to do if the tear is released to slide down and be lost among the grass blades and dirt particles below? Should I allow that to be the way of nature, or should I somehow prevent it from occurring? To waste a single tear from that immortal face — what could be worse than allowing that to happen?

The tear slips over the edge and begins its descent. I gently catch it on the tip of my finger. I bring the captured tear to my lips and kiss it — taste it.

"Am I food for you?" She hasn't moved and her eyes are still closed as if asleep.

"What do you mean?" I ask her.

"You've tasted my tear. You've eaten a part of me. Do I nourish you?"

"I'm sorry. I thought you were asleep."

"I'm not sorry. No one has ever tasted me before. You're the first. It had to be."

I shake my head. I'm out of my league with this girl. I'm only 19 and Jesse seems to be nineteen going on ageless. Half of what she says I just don't understand. Where's this all coming from?

"But why were you crying?" I ask.

"I was crying because your finger touched my cheek."

"But I hadn't touched you yet." I'm bewildered. "You cried before I touched you."

"I knew you would touch me."

"I'm sorry. Did I hurt you?" I didn't know what else to say.

"No. I felt your inner light. I wanted you to touch me. We must touch in order to become close."

"Yes, I remember you said that earlier."

"You need to touch me often. You may touch me anytime you wish."

It's not everyday a girl tells me that.

"Do you know anything about your family history or heritage, Jesse?" I ask her.

"Which family?"

"What do you mean, which family?" I ask.

"I have more than one family. Mandy's my family. My blood relatives are my family. My ancestors are my family. And I have another family that's not of this world."

"You mean you're an alien?" I smile.

"No. I mean I have a family that doesn't reside here where we are. They cannot be seen, only felt."

"What part of this world did your ancestors come from?" I ask.

"My grandparents came here from Norway. Do you know where that is?"

"Yes, I know where Norway is. I thought you might be Scandinavian of some sort. I just wasn't sure which country. Have you ever been there?"

"I go there often in my dreams," she said.

"Do you have vivid dreams?"

"I don't really know. Sometimes I don't know if I'm awake or if I'm dreaming. Am I dreaming now?" She asks me.

"Well, I don't think so. But then I'm not sure either. I've never had an experience like this in my life before, and I've never known anyone like you. So how can I know if I'm awake or if I'm dreaming all this?"

"And if you knew it was a dream—what then?"

"Then I wouldn't want to wake up."

"Why?"

"Because I could sit here and stare at you for all eternity and never be unhappy again."

Jesse hasn't spoken again for about ten minutes. I hope I haven't offended her. I guess I'll just sit here and continue to watch her.

"Have you made our plans yet?" She startled me. She just sat up and spoke to me, looking more alert and focused than she has been since I met her—almost normal.

"Plans?" I'd forgotten about plans. "I'm sorry. My mind's been on other things. I forgot to make plans."

"That's because you've been eating me with your eyes."

"Yes, I suppose I have been."

"And while you've been eating me, I've been making our plans."

"You have?" I straighten my back and give her my full attention.

"Yes. First we're going find a very nice restaurant. You can't live on my tears alone. Mandy gave me enough money for both lunch and dinner."

"I honestly don't eat much. I usually only have one main meal and maybe a snack later on," I tell her.

"Then we'll search for our main meal now. You can snack on more of me later."

My mind is boggled. I can take her words in many ways, but I'm sure that no matter how I decipher them, I'll misinterpret what she's said. I believe it's best if I just shut up and follow her wishes. Regardless of what happens, today is gonna go on record as the most bizarre experience of my life. Meeting and communing with Jesse is something I'll never forget. She may be right—this might be the real reason for this trip. Manny had to twist my arm to get me to come along, but here I am. And who can figure out what twists and turns my life has taken to get me here—under this tree sitting next to the most seductive and enchanting creature I could never have imagined to exist. I'm still pretty much a kid, and I haven't had many notable experiences in the nineteen years I've been alive, especially with girls, and I can count those on one hand—well maybe two—and none anything like a great passion—although there were a couple of girls last summer … Let's face it, I'm basically a novice at pretty much everything. Most of the time I have no idea what's going on with anything, let alone with girls, romance, or whatever, and this situation with Jesse isn't what I'd call any of the above. This has nothing to do with sex, romance, or love in the usual sense; it's bizarre. And it isn't me doing the leading here. It's almost entirely her. What has Mandy gotten me into?

"Come." Jesse is standing up and reaching her hand down to me. What happened to me being the one helping her? "There's a restaurant I know that Mandy and I have gone to many times, and it's a goodly walk from here. It's very expensive, but that's as it should be for the two of us. We become what we eat. You must not touch me unless I have eaten only those things that are precious and rare. I would not wish for you to be poisoned from touching me in that instant."

I take her hand as I stand up, and Jesse leads me out of the little park in the direction of the restaurant she has in mind.

We walk in silence for a few minutes; Jesse's mind is on whatever plane it occupies when she is not focused on this one, while I ponder what people have told me about her and what I have observed for myself—much of it contradictory. I need to know.

"Jesse … forgive me for mentioning this, and stop me if you don't want to talk about it …"

"You can talk to me about anything."

"Mandy and all the others back at the house told me that you are pretty much an incurable drug addict. Yesterday I watched you lying on the couch all day, drooling from your mouth and barely breathing. Your nipples were hanging out of your tank top and your butt crack was showing over the top of your jeans. Last night you seemed so stoned out of your mind that you passed out, and had I not caught you as you fell, you no doubt would have split open your head on the corner of the stone fireplace. But right now, at this moment, you're stone cold sober, very much awake and alert, with no signs of any drug abuse or withdrawals in spite of having had no drugs since at least yesterday morning. Add to that the fact—yes, I said FACT—that when we talk to each other, you're not only quite coherent—even though at times what you say completely boggles my mind—but I feel that your words make more sense than anything else I've ever heard in my life. There, that's it. I've said it."

As I spoke, a smile began to appear on her face, lighting it like a sunrise. "I love you for saying all that," she said "You are the first person to have taken notice."

"What do you mean?"

"I've never taken any drugs ever in my life."

"What?" If she's lying to me, that would be a shock, but if she's telling the truth that would be an even bigger shock. "But …"

"Just because I don't wish to be present in the moment with any given person at any given time, doesn't mean I've taken drugs. It means that I don't wish for my thoughts and my essence to intermingle with the thoughts and essences of people that aren't like me. The mixture would not be healthy."

"That's why you don't look like any of the other addicts I've known. You're way too wholesome to be a stoner. You're like that girl you resemble, Marta Kristin, very healthy."

"I do not know who she is. What I do know is that I'm an addict in the minds of those back at Mandy's house because they know only one way of viewing this world, the way that is expected, not in a way that may be different from that of a highly distorted culture and is closer to the truth of nature."

"But I saw Mandy guiding you to the bench this morning, and holding you up while you stood there."

"I allowed her to do that because that's what she thought she should be doing. I didn't wish to disappoint her. She's been a good person to me. I didn't want her to be hurt."

"Incredible." Again I was speechless. "But the drooling—I saw that with my own eyes."

"I drool when I sleep. I can't help it."

"Well now, isn't that all just something."

"I'm sorry if you felt deceived—it was not my intention. It was my intention only to exist successfully in the presence of others."

"You've got to be the strangest chick I've ever met."

Her glowing smile changed into an impish grin. "I certainly hope so."

It was nice seeing her smile; I was beginning to wonder if she even could. Now she's smiling all the time, and it's beautiful.

2:30 PM Downtown

When you're alone and life is making you lonely you can always go downtown … I guess this is the wrong town; I think Petula was singing about London. Anyway, here we are, Jesse and I, in down-town San Francisco. I never thought I'd ever be writing those words. To me, like a lot of people from Southern California, San Francisco always seemed more like a foreign country — strange and far away, and a bit mysterious. I never had a strong desire to visit, but the city does hold certain attractions for me, mainly as the West Coast center of the Beat Generation.

I've read poems and novels written by the leaders of the Beat movement and I feel an affinity for them. Even though they express themselves in unconventional ways about things that are often shocking or disturbing, their work is connected to history, both literary and cultural, and they build on it and move it forward. The hippie movement seems to have cut all ties to history and society, drifting aimlessly without connection to the past or thought for the future. There are those who say that rock music is to the hippies as jazz, poetry and novels are to the Beats, and that the hippie lifestyle is just the next step down the road from the Beats. I disagree, but the argument needs more time than I have at the moment, and more space than I have in this journal. Maybe later.

I have been fascinated by the Beats — their talent and their lives — ever since I first read *On the Road* by Jack Kerouac several years ago. Last summer I met a girl, a real Beat named Abby, and our acquaintance grew into a magical relationship. Her mother, a native of San Francisco, is actually a friend of Allen Ginsberg and several other Beat writers. I learned a lot from Abby and I hope to learn more, as our relationship never really ended. She and her mother just disappeared one day — literally vanished from the face of the earth. But that's another story.

Another thing that adds to the attraction of San Francisco is its colorful history. I've read about it in books, and it always seemed to me to be a wild and woolly place, but romantic nevertheless. I confess that a lot of my ideas about the city come from that movie about the big earthquake starring Clark Gable — great movie, but not enough to make me want to live here. I guess that's why I've always thought of San Francisco in grainy black and white images, like a newsreel or a picture in an old newspaper or encyclopedia—never in color. And before the earthquake, there was the Gold Rush. There must be hundreds of western movies that have scenes in and around the San Francisco of those days and the years that followed. As much as I enjoyed them, they still did not give me a burning desire to make the pilgrimage to San Francisco. And yet, here I am. The neon lights are indeed pretty, and there is something in the air, but with the hippie invasion, that something isn't necessarily a good thing.

My ideas about San Francisco have met the realities now that I am actually here, and the larger-than-life image I have had of the city still stands. I can see that the literature and philosophy of the Beats is perfectly suited to its romance, history and future, but the presence of the hippies dulls things for me. I don't feel the romance with them like I do with the Beats. I haven't figured it out yet, but it's different and it's not as good.

But, back to our adventures of this afternoon.

Jesse led me into a quiet residential neighborhood up on Telegraph Hill to a little restaurant called The Shadows. It was one that Bart and I had stumbled upon when we were here last week. How strange is that? It's a lovely place that serves German and Swiss food. All very tasty.

The Shadows sits just below the top of Telegraph Hill and has a beautiful view of the bay. It was a relief to be above the city where the air is crisp and clean, almost like autumn, unlike the muggy, hot, sweat-smelling stuff I've been breathing for the past three days. If I were rich I'd rent a house up on that hill and just sit there all day with all the windows open, smelling the clean Bay air. It was delightful.

We entered the restaurant through a door at the top of a flight of stairs. The hostess who greeted us gave us a long appraising look before she showed us to our table. She might have been worried that we were the first of a larger hippie mob about to invade her domain. More likely she was simply deciding whether or not to bend the dress code of the rather posh establishment.

I don't look too bad. I'm wearing Levis, a plaid shirt, and a light jacket—all clean and relatively new—and my hair is clean and neat even if it's a bit long. Jesse though, is a little rough around the edges. Her long bright blonde hair has not been washed or combed in who knows how long and is greasy and tangled. Her light blue skirt is clean, but she's still wearing the pink tank top she had on when I first saw her yesterday. The top is a bit dirty, with sweat stains under her arms. It might have been a whiff of Jesse's armpits that put the sour look on the hostess's face. To her credit, she decided to seat us anyway, probably because it was a little late for lunch and too early for dinner and the restaurant was practically empty.

The hostess settled us at a table by a window overlooking the bay and as far away from any other diners as she could get. We studied the menus she left us, and in a few minutes a waitress arrived to take our order.

"Can I be honest with you again?" I asked Jesse while we waited for our food to arrive.

"Are you ever not honest with me?" she asked.

"No."

"Then why would you ask?"

"I just don't want to hurt your feeling's by asking personal or embarrassing questions."

"You won't embarrass me," she said. "I already know what you're concerned with anyway."

"You do?"

"You were not really going to ask anything anyway, you were going to tell me that you thought it would be better if I weren't so dirty. If I were to wear cleaner clothes and wash my hair, maybe take a shower."

"Yes … that's pretty much the gist of it," I confessed.

"Does it embarrass you—me being with you with my hair looking like this?" She put her hand in her hair and mussed it even more than it already was.

"No. No, you don't. In fact, I find you quite adorable as you are. You're kind of like one of those little waifs in a Dickens novel, dirty as heck but cuter than cute. I was just concerned that you might feel a bit uncomfortable in places like this restaurant. It doesn't bother me but I thought it might bother you."

"It doesn't bother me. Dirt isn't a bad thing. Most dirt is quite sterile. It's what people do with dirt that can make it unhealthy and undesirable. This world is made up of dirt. We wouldn't be able to stand anywhere or walk anywhere if there was no dirt underneath our feet to support us."

"I never thought of that."

"Do I stink?" Jesse asked bluntly.

"Well …" How do you answer a question like that?.

"Can you smell me over there on your side of the table?"

"No, but I got a whiff of you earlier in the park."

"And was that a bad smell?"

"Well … to be honest, I thought it was kind of …"

"Erotic?" She said it, not I. "You don't have to answer," she assured me. "I know you find me attractive and you're aroused in my presence."

"I am a guy," I point out sheepishly.

"You don't have to hide it."

The waitress arrived at that moment with our lunch, and I was saved from further embarrassment. We spoke very little except to comment on the food. The mood might have been lighter if it were evening and if we had a little wine to go with our meal. As we are both only nineteen, the wine was out of the question. A walk under the stars would be nice though. Maybe later.

Just for the record, I don't care what Jesse smells like; being with her is a whole lot better than hanging around with Manny—not that I don't like hanging out with Manny, because I do—but when Manny sweats, it's gross. When Jesse sweats, it's a different story.

After lunch we started walking again. San Francisco is really different from any other city in California, or even in the world. Despite it being what I would call a "big city," it actually covers a fairly small area of land between the San Francisco Bay and the Pacific Ocean. This means that you can walk from just about anywhere to just about anywhere else. One of the main features of the city is the hills. Wherever you are, you are either going up one or down one. The houses are also unique. In some areas they look like layer cakes turned sideways — all in rows, and built close together with two or three stories. Some are painted in bright pastel colors, others are in various shades of cream and tan and grey. In some neighborhoods like China Town and The Haight there are shops and such on the street level and apartments above. The buildings in the less affluent neighborhoods are very narrow and placed right up against the sidewalk. In the wealthier sections, they are wider and have a little space in the front for some sort of garden or landscaping. These homes are truly beautiful and stand out like jewels throughout the city. Most of the streets run in straight lines, but some of the neighborhoods have been laid out in curves and circles around some of the bigger hills. One street, Lombard Street, has been nicknamed the Crookedest Street In The World. I'm not even sure that "crookedest" is a real word, but I've seen photos and it is crooked — more serpentine, really, I think.

We took our time walking, and did not really pay much attention to where we were going. It wasn't long before we found ourselves in the heart of China Town. When we finally became aware of our surroundings we noticed the way people were reacting to us. Most of them looked at us as if they wanted us to go away, but some of the men were eyeing Jesse in a way that made us both uncomfortable. At first we thought they just didn't like us because they thought we were hippies. We didn't see any hippies there — or tourists either, for that matter — so we thought maybe the Chinese people were trying to make us feel like we were not welcome there. Not that we are hippies, but I guess we might look like it to them. At any rate, it didn't feel right for us to be there so we walked as quickly as we could to get out of that neighborhood. Eventually we stumbled onto Powell Street, which, I am told, runs all the way from Fisherman's Wharf to Downtown.

We continued walking down Powell Street until we came to a small park. We were both hot and tired by then, and the little patch of grass in the shade of a tree next to a koi pond was a welcome relief. Jesse sat and looked at the brightly colored fish while I sat and looked at her.

"Those fish are really beautiful," she said. Her face was glistening with sweat, which made her look like she was covered with diamond dust. She is truly the most beautiful girl I've ever known.

"Yes, they are beautiful," I said, my eyes never leaving her face.

"You're not looking at the fish. You're staring at me again."

"I can't help it."

"It's the sweat on my face isn't it?"

"How do you know these things?"

"Because I feel everything I know. I don't just have it memorized inside my head. I feel it on the outside before it goes inward."

"You're one of a kind, Jesse."

"Yes I am. So are you. And I think it's time you put your arm around me."

I did, and immediately I could feel the heat of her body joining with my own. I pulled her close to me. Just close enough for my head to be inches from hers. I never thought body heat had an odor, but I could smell hers — not the smell of her body but of her heat — like an electrical fire; like burning wires.

She touched her cheek with her index finger. "Kiss me here," she said softly.

Her cheek was hot upon my mouth. I held it there for almost a minute before I pulled away. I could taste her salty sweat on my lips.

"You've eaten me again."

"I … I guess I have."

"What do I taste like?"

"You're very salty. But I like it."

"I'm of the sea. Salt is a part of me."

"That's twice you've told me that. Why do you believe you're of the sea?"

"As a small child I had many dreams. In nearly all those dreams I was a creature of the sea. It was a cold sea. Very cold. But I couldn't feel the cold. I could swim and frolic to my heart's content, sometimes in the day and sometimes in the night, and I never felt fear. The sea was my home. I knew nothing of humans. I knew nothing of cities. I knew only the sea."

"Those are nice dreams."

"In some of the dreams I wasn't in the water but hovering over the water, hundreds of feet in the air. At times I'd go even higher. I'd fly up beyond the atmosphere of this planet, out into the deeper space where the stars live. Then I'd play with the stars as if they were my property, my things, as if I owned them."

"I wish I could have dreams like that. That sounds wonderful."

"Kiss me again on the cheek, and linger there a while."

I held my lips pressed against her cheek for the longest time—so long that her sweat began to roll down my own face. I didn't ever want to move, to ever take my lips away. Touching her like that, smelling her smells up close, watching her eyes blink within an inch of my own—there was nothing on Earth that could compare to the feeling I received from her in those moments. I wish I could describe it. It wasn't a sexual feeling. It wasn't like anything that can be put into words. It was a closeness that's beyond any closeness known to humans. It was as if for the moment that I was joined with her I became one with her—the two of us merging into one Being. I know she could read my thoughts, and for just a moment I felt as if I could read hers. I could see what I thought were pictures in her mind. Pictures of her running through a beautiful forest, listening to the sound of her giggling along the way, as she reached out to touch leaves and limbs and tree trunks. I wasn't watching her, I was seeing through her eyes.

Jesse turned her face toward mine. Our noses were touching.

"Now breathe my breath," she said. And I did.

We sat there for several minutes, she with her eyes closed, and me gulping down every breath she breathed. Finally we lay back and down upon the grass next to the pond. We just lay there close to each other. Not speaking. Totally silent.

We soon continued walking down Powell Street, and now we are in the center of some sort of downtown business district. To be totally honest, neither of us is impressed by what we see.

I know this is supposed to be a beautiful city, and in many places it truly is, but parts of downtown San Francisco are a dirty, jumbled mess of closely packed buildings with gaudy fronts, store signs of all sizes and shapes, cars spewing out black exhaust, and people spewing out cigarette smoke. Some of the side streets in and around the downtown section are downright sleazy with burlesque theaters, seedy bars, and trashy looking apartments. We looked down one narrow street as we crossed it, and it was particularly nasty. There were bums laying on the sidewalk, some were asleep, others who were just drunk, and trash everywhere. There were rough looking characters just standing around, staring cold, angry stares, leaning up against buildings. One man was shouting at all the cars that went by. Another guy threw an empty wine bottle clear across the street at two men that were walking down the sidewalk. The bottle hit a wall and broke into a thousand pieces. The two men looked over at the man that threw the bottle, yelled some obscenities, and then walked on. Three or four little kids were running around naked and laughing in the street not twenty feet from where the bottle smashed against the wall. They never stopped or looked away from their play. They must have been used to it.

We've made it all the way up Powell to where it ends at Market. Looking back the way we came, I can see the Powell Theater and the Hotel Manx on the left side, and a hot dog joint and the

Golden State Hotel on the right. There are a lot of people in this part of town. Very few hippies and some tourists, but mostly ordinary people just going about their business. And then there are the crazies—there seems to be at least one on every block. The one on this block is a tall, thin man wearing a wig, panties, garter belt, and black stockings. If a woman went around dressed like that, she'd be arrested. Well, maybe not in San Francisco. Black Stockings Man walked right by a cop sitting on his motorcycle eating a hamburger. They just smiled at each other like they were old friends. If the man thinks he looks like a woman because he's dressed in women's clothing, that's okay with me, but surely he must know that he's the ugliest woman on the planet. I know, all big cities have their dirty spots, but I've never seen anything like that even in LA.

Several people have approached us to ask for spare change. I had to laugh and tell them I don't even have a place to spend the night, let alone a pocket full of free money to give to them. I felt sorry for one lady; she was in terrible shape. She was dressed in rags and had two little girls with her. I could smell alcohol on her breath. So maybe I don't feel too sorry for her. Jesse tells me The City is filled with people like this. At night you can find them everywhere. They sleep in the parks, in the alleys, in abandoned cars. In the daytime they all come out and do their begging bit. If you tried to give each of them a dollar, you'd run out of money real quick. At night they drink whatever cheap booze they can find until they fall asleep wherever they are. Some of the women earn money as prostitutes. I'm pretty sure that's illegal up here but I may be wrong, and anyway, no one seems to care. In fact, as I look around I can see a lot of women out here on the sidewalk that look like they might be prostitutes. They're dressed the way I would imagine prostitutes to dress—pretty tacky—and they don't seem to be going anywhere in particular.

The buildings here look old, but not too old. I'm guessing this area was destroyed in the big quake and these building were built sometime after 1906. They don't look old enough to be from the nineteenth century. The facades on the buildings would be kinda neat without all the tasteless, garish signs sticking out in front looking like open sores — the signs look like they're bleeding out from the buildings. They make things ugly.

An old man just walked by. He had long white hair, was wearing nothing but cut off Levi shorts, and every square inch of visible skin from head to toes was covered with tattoos. There was no blank space anywhere at all. He seemed to be a walking billboard for all the statements he wanted to make about his life, wearing his experiences on the outside instead of hiding them away on the inside. There's something to be said for that I suppose. I've seen some pretty elaborate tattoos — some I really liked. My father has a friend who was in the Navy and he has a tattoo of a blonde woman in a bikini. It covers his entire left arm; a beautiful thing really. The woman's legs are on his forearm, and her torso and head are on his upper arm. When he closes his arm at the elbow joint the woman folds up in the middle. Ain't that a kick? The guy that drew that tattoo could be a successful painter if he wanted to be. Maybe he is. I'm gonna check when I get back.

"Do you have any tattoos, Jesse?"

"No. I love my flesh the way it is. It's soft and without blemish."

What an odd thing to say. But I like it that she constantly surprises me with odd things. I also like it that she doesn't have any tattoos. They can look good on some girls, but on her — somehow they just wouldn't fit. She's so … smooth. And she's right, I don't see any blemishes anywhere on what she's chosen to reveal to this world. Not a freckle, not a mole. Perfect, flawless flesh.

"What do you think of this downtown area?" I ask her.

"It's very harsh." She frowns a bit as she examines our surroundings.

"Harsh?"

"Unpleasantly rough. Jarring to the senses. It's garish and harsh. I don't like it."

"I don't care for it either. But there's one place somewhere around here I want to check out before I have to go back home."

"Don't say that."

"Say what?"

"Go back home." She turns to look at me, still frowning but a different frown—sad rather than displeased. "I don't want you to go back home."

"That's very sweet, Jesse, but I have to go back home."

"Does someone need you down there where you've come from?"

"Well … I'm not sure how to answer that. I have friends there. My family loves me, I think. I have my college work. But need me?"

"I need you with me. You're not needed there. You only have things there."

"Yes, I have things there, but I have people too."

"People are things if they don't need you, and you're only a thing to them. People use other people."

"I'm pretty much out of money, Jesse. I've got three more days here in San Francisco and no place to stay, no food to eat. And I have responsibilities that I can't shirk."

"You don't need money. You can stay at Mandy's house. You can eat me and never hunger."

"I wish it was that simple, Jesse. I really do."

"We'll talk about it more later," she says. "What is it you want to see?"

"The City Lights Bookstore. Have you heard of it?"

"No, should I?"

"Not necessarily. It's not all that well known outside a certain circle of people."

"What kind of people?"

"Probably a lot of the hippies would know about it, but it's mainly something the older Beats would recognize."

"Is it one of those pot shops?"

"I don't think so. I think it just sells books, but you can find lots of intriguing books there that were written by the original Beats. Some of those guys live here in The City. Most of them are still writing."

"And you're interested in this because you're a writer?"

"I guess so. Bart and I walked by there last week. It was closed so we moved along and never got back to it. I've heard so much about it from my English professor that I really want to visit there this time. Maybe I'll buy him a book just for a lark. He'd like that."

"Do you know where it is?" she asks. "We can go there but I'm not sure I'll like it. It doesn't sound of worth or merit to me."

"I can't remember where it is from here, but I have an address. It's on Columbus Avenue, somewhere in the North Beach area. I'll bet it's easy to find."

City Lights Bookstore

We made our way to the bookstore without too many wrong turns. I feel like I have arrived at the destination of a cultural pilgrimage.

Lawrence Ferlinghetti, The Beat poet, started up City Lights Bookstore a little over ten years ago, and I understand that it's become a kind of hangout for the Beat writers and their friends. I've read some of the things they've written—Allen Ginsberg's little book, *Howl*, and *On The Road*, by Jack Kerouac, about a guy who travels around the USA trying to discover himself. The book is based loosely on Kerouac's own travels by himself and with a couple of his friends. One of them, a guy named Neal Cassady, is borderline insane in a very creative and brilliant way. My friend, Abby, once described him as "absolutely ape kookie."

Kerouac, Ferlinghetti, Ginsberg and the other original Beats are the central core of the Beat Generation. From what I have heard, this overnight hippie thing is at least partly based on and is evolving from that. I'm not sure what the Beats think about it, but that's how the media are portraying it—as an extension of the Beat philosophy and way of life. To me though, the hippie movement seems way looser and less imaginative than the Beats; not nearly as much creative output—they seem to express themselves in less artistic and constructive ways. But I guess they'll be calling this the Hippie Generation soon. Anyway, Kerouac and some of the other Beats are still kicking, and it's possible to run into a few of them around this area of The City.

Jesse examines the outside of the shop, taking in all the details — signs, posters, window displays, and such. "It doesn't look like much," she says.

"Well, it's just a bookstore."

"What kind of books does it have besides Beatnik Beat books?"

"I'm not really sure. I read an article about it and it only mentioned the Beat books. And that's just Beat, you can drop the Beatnik."

"What exactly is a 'Beat book?'"

"A book written by a Beat." I grin.

"Very funny. What does a Beat write about?"

"They mainly write about politics and contemporary cultural stuff. Lots of poetry about different ways to think about life and just stuff in general," I try to explain. I really don't know if I can put it into words. "Some of it's pretty shocking, like Ginsberg's poetry. Even Kerouac's books are a bit scandalous."

"Why?"

"Because it talks about things that are different from the way this society generally thinks is the way things are supposed to be. Things like casting your fate to the wind, hitting the road and seeing where life takes you. And some of the characters are a bit out there as far as public taste is concerned. They do and say a lotta crude and nasty stuff that most people might have a cow over."

"I understand what you're saying, but why would they want to do that? Why write about such things? It sounds like it could be depressing."

"Well, I guess that's a fair question. And I guess that 'questioning' is the answer. They seem to be questioning the way things are — trying to come up with better ways, or at least different ways of looking at things. Unlike what I'm seeing with the hippies, the Beats at least offer some solutions and avenues for a person to explore. Zen is real popular with most of them, and that's kinda different, maybe even a good thing. I need to explore Zen more."

Jesse turns to peer through the window. I can tell that she is bothered by something. "Part of the store is dark," she says. "It has a dark feeling about it."

"Dark? What do you mean?"

"There's a feeling, an energy I'm not comfortable with. I'm not sure I want to go in there."

"What do you feel?" I'm confused.

"I feel an energy of confusion and chaos. Of darkness and things that are not good. It may not be coming from the books themselves. I'm not sure where it comes from." Her face is as serious as I have ever seen it.

"Well, we don't have to go in if you don't want to."

"You should go in. You want to buy your teacher a book."

"I can buy a book from a bookstore back in Riverside."

"That won't be the same. I'll go in with you—darkness cannot harm me. We don't have to stay long."

So, do we go in or not? Jesse is clearly uneasy about going in, and I don't get it, but she has an uncanny way of sensing things, and I don't want to do anything to hurt her in any way. She pulls herself up straight and braces herself as if she is about to meet her worst enemy or confront her darkest fear.

I make the decision. "No, We won't go in. I've already made a pledge to myself that I'll come back to The City some day, and I can visit the bookstore when I do. But for now, why don't you and I just keep exploring the area. There's a lot to be seen up here and I wanna see as much as I can."

"You have three more days to see it, and you're here now," she says.

"But I may not have you with me for those days and I want to see it all with you." I smile to let her know that I mean what I say. "I don't need to go inside. And it's your turn really, what would you like to do? You've been cooped up in Mandy's house for a long time, surely there's something you'd like to see."

"I think we ought to start walking back toward the Haight. I really don't like walking around The City in the dark."

"You mean head back to Mandy's?"

"No, just back in that direction. There's another little park not far from Mandy's that I really love and we could make some memories there. It's not as crowded as Golden Gate Park or the Haight. We could have some time alone."

"I like that idea."

At that moment two men walk out the front door of the bookstore. You have got to be kidding! One of them is Lawrence Ferlinghetti—I'm sure of it; I've seen his picture. The other one is definitely Allen Ginsberg—he's pretty hard to mistake for anyone else. Ferlinghetti is carrying a well-worn card table, and Ginsberg is carrying some folding chairs. They're setting up the table in front of the store window not fifteen feet from where Jesse and I are standing. I don't know much about Beat philosophy—I've never really thought about it—but I do admire the spirit and talent that goes into the works of these two guys. To have them sitting right there so close, and to be in the same space as somebody so famous—at least within certain circles—is nothing less than awesome. Uh oh, Ferlinghetti is looking right at us. He's speaking to us!

"Well, what are you waiting for? Come over here." He motions with his arm.

I look around me to see if he's talking to somebody else. Then I look at Jesse who just looks confused as she has absolutely no idea who these guys are.

"What did we do?" she asks.

"I'm not sure. But we need to go over there."

We approached the table where Lawrence Ferlinghetti and Allen Ginsberg were sitting. AG smiled a big friendly smile and said, "sit down, young ones. You look pretty beat."

I didn't write things down as they occurred because that would have been rude, so I am recording the conversation from memory as best I can.

I couldn't believe we were being invited to sit at the same table as these two giants of the Beat movement. And Allen Ginsberg just told us that we looked pretty "Beat"—how cool is that! Or was he just playing with us. These guys probably get a lot of tourist characters horning in on their scene. I bet they get tired of the intrusion.

"Thank you," I said as we sat down. "We've been walking around for awhile."

"Where you from?" LF asked.

"I'm from Riverside, about 400 miles south of here. Jesse's from here. She lives on Haight Street."

"No," LF said, "I mean where are you really from? What's that cute little accent you've got?"

"It's an Oklahoma accent, sir. I was raised in Tulsa."

"It sounds more Irish. Do you have a name?" AG asked.

"My name's DH."

"Like DH Lawrence," LF said, smiling a big warm smile. "That's a lot to live up to."

"My name's Allen." Allen Ginsberg reached out to shake our hands. "And this is Lawrence. Ha! DH and Lawrence!" He and Ferlinghetti both chuckled.

"Nice to meet you, sirs," Jesse and I both reply in unison like a couple of nervous school kids. That gets another chuckle from AG and LF.

"What do you do, DH?" LF asked. "I noticed that little black book in your hand. Are you a writer?"

"This is my journal. I'm not much of a writer. I just like to record things I experience."

"Don't we all," AG said.

"That's what all writers do, really," LF said.

"You guys do a lot more than just record," I said.

"You mean Allen and me?" LF asked.

"The whole bunch of you," I said. "You've got a bookstore filled with not just your writing, but a lot of other Beat writers, too."

LF smiled and looked at AG. "I haven't heard that term all day," he said.

"I'm sorry," I said, shaking my head. "I sound like an idiot don't I?"

AG grinned. I think he was trying to keep from laughing. "A Beat idiot, or a regular idiot?" he asked.

"I guess when it comes to knowing anything about the Beats, I am sort of an idiot. I've read your books and I've kinda immersed myself in your culture, but I haven't got a clue to what really led you to write them. Your lives are a whole lot different than mine." Just talking to them made me feel self-conscious. I hope it didn't show.

LF turned to look at Jesse. "Do you even know what Beat means?" he asked.

"No, I'd never heard it before DH mentioned it today," she replied with complete innocence.

AG grinned again. "Who is this chick, DH?"

"She's about the smartest chick I ever met," I answered.

"What does Beat mean, Mister Ferlinghetti?" Jesse asked.

"It just means we're tired." LF smiled at her. "And please, drop the mister."

"Beat ... tired ..." AG added.

Sounding like the innocent angel she is, Jesse asked sincerely. "What are you tired of?"

"We're tired of all the commotion ... out there," AG waved his arms around.

"And that makes you a Beat?" she asked.

LF gave AG a wry smile and answered, "I guess it does. Something has to make us Beats."

I shook my head. "I wish it was all that easy."

"It's not hard to be a Beat," AG said, "but all the hippies out there are making it a lot harder than it needs to be."

"I wish they wouldn't," LF said. "Can I see that little black journal of yours, DH?" LF was asking me, personally, to see my journal!

"There's not much to see," I said shyly, quite reluctant to hand it to him.

"Any poems in there?" AG asked.

"A couple," I say, tightening my grip on the notebook.

"Come on," AG said, "gimme."

Then Allen Ginsberg, THE Allen Ginsberg reached over and took my journal out of my hand and started thumbing through it, mumbling words as he skimmed through the contents.

LF, who had been studying AG while AG studied my journal, asked, "Anything good in there, Allen?"

"Actually, this is one I really like." AG handed the book over to LF, who immediately turned his attention to my poem. I couldn't tell which one they'd chosen.

LF finally looked up at me. "Hey, this ain't too bad," he said.

"Which one is it?"

"The one about the city lights reflecting in the rain while the guy searches his soul."

"I wrote that last year during a rainy night in Riverside." Gawd! In front of the City Lights Bookstore he read MY poem about the city lights back home. I couldn't believe it was happening.

"Well, it's good." LF smiled. "Better than some of Allen's stuff." He grinned at AG.

"Ha! You're probably right." AG smiled another big smile. AG has the greatest smile ever.

LF gently closed the little book and handed it back to me. "It's a Beat poem," he said as I took it from him.

I almost drop the book. "You're kidding. I'm too young to be a Beat writer."

"No you're not!" AG said quickly. "Physical age doesn't mean a thing. It's all about the soul."

"Allen's right. You've got a Beat soul, DH," LF said, placing his hand on his chest over his heart. "You're every bit as Beat as Allen or me."

"The only thing it takes to be a Beat is a life filled with cool experiences and the ability to make personal statements about those experiences. It looks like you're on the right track with this little journal of yours." AG raised his eyebrows as I'd sometimes seen my English prof, Bill Hunter, do. It was his way of saying, "I'm right, aren't I."

I didn't know how to take these guys. Were they playing with me, or what? They seemed sincere, but for a nineteen-year-old kid to be called a Beat writer by two giants of the Beat writers — maybe even the biggest giants — I didn't know how to wrap my head around it all.

"And remember, I said *cool* experiences." AG emphasized the word cool as he said it.

Dumbfounded, I shook my head, laughed, and said, "So I have your blessing? You're actually accepting me into the Beat hall of fame?"

"I don't know if I'd go that far," LF said, "but we are accepting you."

"We here by recognize you as an official Beat Writer," AG said with a flourish of his arms. "I dub thee, Sir DH of Beatville! Rise Sir DH of Beatville!" And he patted me on my left shoulder with his open hand.

"Wow." I was totally bewildered. "I think you guys are pulling my leg a bit, but it doesn't matter 'cause I'm goin' back home tomorrow with one heck of a story to share."

"Not pulling your leg, Sir DH." LF smiled broadly. "You keep working at it and one day maybe we'll carry your books here at City Lights."

AG turned his attention to Jesse. "And what do you do, Jesse?" he asked her

"I'm just me. I do me." Jesse blue eyes looked at him unwaveringly. I can see that both men are more than a little enchanted by her, or at least by the aura of eternal naiveté that she radiates.

"What does that mean? How does one do oneself?" AG asked.

"At this time in all of time I am busy walking around The City with DH." Jesse's eyes never left his. Sometimes she reminds me of an android — no show of emotion, no outward movement.

AG and LF exchange looks — Bemused? Perplexed? Smiling at

her, LF asked, "Are you a writer too, Miss Jesse?"

"I am not, Mr. Ferlinghetti, sir."

"There you go again. Lawrence, please." He smiled at Jesse, but I could tell he didn't know quite what to do or to say in the presence of this strange little girl—I've often felt the same in the past two days.

A slightly haggard looking man joined us then. Allen greeted him saying, "Hey, Gregory, meet DH and Jesse. DH is now a famous Beat writer."

"Hey," Gregory said, raising his hand in a half-wave. In spite of his half-hearted greeting, he did not really seem to have heard what Allen had said.

Our conversation continued for about an hour, and to be honest, I think they were more impressed—or rather, intrigued—by Jesse than by anything I had to say. She showed no hesitation or nervousness while talking to these guys. In fact, she expressed herself with an unwavering certainty that both charmed and baffled the two poets. Several times Jesse revealed bits of unnatural wisdom about the poetry of nature that left them shaking their heads in perplexity. Throughout the entire fantastic discourse she remained completely calm and matter-of-fact. It was clear to both LF and to AG that they had met a bizarre, yet delightful little creature who defied their understanding. She held them spellbound in a deep state of wonder

"She's like a Faerie come to life," Allen whispered while Jesse talked about nature and the universe. I think he meant it literally. Heck, I've been thinking the same thing, like one day some crazy crystal, sparkly thing will explode out of the sky and right then and there Jesse will sprout delicate transparent wings and fly off into the heavens.

Gregory turned out to be Gregory Corso, another poet, but I couldn't get much out of him. I'm not sure if he actually lived in San Francisco or if he was just visiting, but he seemed to be great friends with LF and AG. He didn't talk much, and he seldom made eye contact. He cracked a couple of jokes, and then went into the bookstore and didn't come back out again.

LF and AG were very nice to us. Their interest in our lives—who we are and what we did—seemed genuine and not condescending. The conversation flowed around a range of literary, artistic and esoteric topics. When I mentioned my interest in being a painter, AG seemed more intrigued by that than by my interest in writing. "Painters are like poets," he said, "they both make pretty pictures. The only difference is in the medium."

LF had some words of encouragement and advice for me as well. He told me to honestly try to write important poetry, and not the corny stuff coming from the hippies in town.

They both agreed that they loved the general spirit of the hippie gathering—they were having a lot of fun with it. What they didn't like was having it associated with the Beats.

"It ain't the same," AG said. "It doesn't have focus. It needs a little Zen, maybe a little Yoga."

"DH teaches yoga," Jesse offered.

"And I've done a little yoga," AG said enthusiastically. "Come here, Sir DH." He motioned for me to come over next to him. He stood up and went into a tree pose. "Am I doing this right?"

"Looks good to me." I nodded and smiled at him. He was pretty steady in a pose that a lot of people can't retain for more than a few seconds before falling over. Finally, he wobbled a bit and had to put his foot back on the ground.

"Show me how you do it," he said.

I put myself into a tree pose, and AG studied me carefully.

He grinned at me and said, "What am I doing wrong? Your tree looks a lot better than mine."

"Your tree sucks big time Ginsberg," LF said with a chuckle.

"Come on DH, put me in that pose." AG was determined. "I gotta make this work." He grabbed my arm and pulled me over to him.

I put AG in a more difficult form of the pose with his right foot shoved way up into his crotch instead of resting on his left knee, and I held him up because it was much harder to hold his balance that way. After about twenty seconds he began to topple over, catching himself on the card table and almost collapsing it. But then he broke into laughter and patted me on the back.

"Better stick to poetry," LF said.

"I think you're right," AG said as he sat down again. Then he focused his attention on me and said seriously, "And DH, just because you teach yoga, or paint paintings, that doesn't mean you can't be a writer too. Go back home and fill that little black book with some serious poetry."

I couldn't believe that LF or AG would really be interested in poetry written by a nineteen-year-old kid from Southern California. "Sure," I said, "I'll be serious about it, but I'll never be much of a poet compared to you guys."

LF smiled and said, "You gotta start somewhere, kid."

After about an hour spent with the icons of Beat Literature, Jesse and I decided we should hit the road again. It's not a good idea to be caught walking around in San Francisco after dark. We shook hands with the poets, and they invited me to stop by and chit-chat if I was ever in The City again.

"Now that we're friends we'll take you out to dinner, show you some of the cool spots in The City when you come back," AG said.

"I'd love that." I was so excited by his invitation that I think my voice went up a few octaves.

Jesse and I took our leave and headed off in the general direction of the Haight-Ashbury neighborhood, talking as we walked

"Well, whattaya think, Jesse? Do you still feel like City Lights is a dark place? I thought they were very nice to us."

"They were very nice to us. I don't dislike them," she replied. "Mr. Ginsberg has a large and engaging smile and Mr. Ferlinghetti was quite tolerant and patient with us. Beats don't seem so bad. There's still something about the hippie movement I don't feel comfortable with, though, and I believe that was the darkness I was seeing back there. There were books of a hippie nature there in the bookstore window. I saw them."

"Care to elaborate? Allen and Lawrence didn't sound like they appreciated much of the hippie stuff either, and to be honest that kind of surprised me."

"I've been here in The City for a long time—since way before the beginning of the hippie thing—and so far I've seen nothing good come out of it. It seems to be doing the direct opposite of what those who participate in it would wish for it to do."

"What do you mean?"

"All you see in the news are pictures of happy hippies all over the place carrying flowers and dancing gleefully in the park. All you hear is the famous motto, 'Peace and Love,' but what you don't see is the chaos and lack of direction. They are accomplishing nothing but division. There are a lot of frauds up here."

"Like me?" I smiled.

"Don't be silly. You're no more of a hippie than I am, and you don't even want to be one."

"You're right about that. The one thing that stands out most for me is the lack of motivation to do anything except just demonstrate. Don't any of these people have jobs?"

"Many do not."

"I do agree that the world would be a better place if all the wars just stopped and everybody got along together," I continued, "but I can't see that happening any time soon, if ever. And, frankly, I can't see how the peace demonstrations help at all—they're just stirring people up. And it isn't just the US that has wars. Practically every country on the globe is involved in a war in some way. Even if the US was to stop participating in wars, I doubt any of the other countries would."

"I read the book titles in the window back there at City Lights," Jesse said. "The ones with the wild hippie covers were about dark things—things that cause nothing but dissension and hatred. What do those have to do with peace and love? It seems hypocritical to me. I also saw books by Mr. Ferlinghetti and Mr. Ginsberg in the window. I saw the road book you told me about. Those books were not dark to look at."

"I don't know, Jesse. Something is happening to this country—almost forcing itself upon us. It's like watching a bulldozer reshape a piece of land for a new development. The change is permanent and we may or may not regret it in the future. I'm all for peace and love, and I'm supportive of any of those who are here because they truly believe in their heart that there's a better way for us all to go. But I'd sure like to know what that way is. No one seems to be able to articulate it."

"I'm not very optimistic," Jesse said flatly.

"I hadn't noticed." I glanced at her and smiled. The frown lines on her otherwise perfect forehead were clear signs of just how disturbed she was by the recent activities here.

"There's a tension growing under the surface that's not good," she said. "Somewhere, someone is playing the hippie children like puppets on a string. I believe that strongly."

"Hard to say, but I still think there's some hope for them." In a brighter tone, I added, "I didn't really come up here for that show anyway. I came all this way just to meet you, remember?"

Her smile returned with that thought. "I'm glad you did, because I've been here waiting for you."

I glanced at Jesse to see if I could figure out what she meant by that last remark, but she was looking straight ahead, her face giving away nothing and we kept on walking.

We continued in silence for about another block when Jesse said that we were getting close to a little park where we could rest and forget that we were in the city. I told her that I would like that. The walk from City Lights had been all uphill and it would be good to get away from the city streets. Besides that, I needed some time to record our conversation with Allen Ginsberg and Lawrence Ferlinghetti while it was fresh in my mind.

6:30 PM Lafayette Park

We spotted an ice cream shop on along the way and bought ice cream cones. The sun had been bright all day, and it was pretty hot down on the streets where the buildings blocked any breeze that might cool things off.

Jesse got strawberry and I got vanilla, and we traded back and forth as we continued toward the park.

Jesse got strawberry ice cream on her lip, and we paused while I wiped it off with my finger.

"I was saving that for later," she said.

"Right, I should've left it. You did look pretty cute with an ice cream mustache." I studied her face for a moment then said, "Sometimes you look very young—much younger than nineteen."

"I know. I think you told me that already. I also heard you tell Mandy that."

"You really are nineteen aren't you? Please tell me you're nineteen."

Jesse reached into her back pocket and pulled out a beat up driver's license with her picture on it. Sure enough, she was nineteen in July.

"I'm nineteen Earth years. Why would I not be?"

"There you go again."

"Go where?" she asks, all wide-eyed innocence.

"Go getting all … bizarre and mysterious."

"Do you not like it when I get bizarre and mysterious?"

"I didn't say that. Actually, I find it nice for a change. Most people are quite predictable."

"I promise you I'll never be predictable."

"Oh, I'm sure of that."

I turned to continue walking and discovered that we were standing at the edge of an inviting tree-covered hill.

Jesse spread her arms wide as if she were inviting me into her home. "How do you like it?" she said. "It's called Lafayette Park. It isn't very big, and it's seldom crowded."

"It seems like we've been spending a lot of time in parks today."

"We have. But this one is special to me."

"And why's that?".

"Because you and I are eating ice cream cones here for the very first time."

"Aww, what a sweet thing to say."

"Come with me." She took my hand and pulled me along behind her. "I have a favorite spot here."

Jesse led me through an open playground, then up a pathway that took us to the bottom of a hilly area with trees at the top. There was no one in this park, unlike Golden Gate Park, which was, no doubt, completely packed at that time.

"The summit is just up there." She points up the path to what seems to be the highest spot. "My spot's on the other side."

It isn't a very big hill, but it is steep, and there are lots of old trees covering the mound at the top. It's really quite pretty. We finally make it to the top.

She continued to pull me along. "In here," she said.

She led me over the summit, down just a little bit, and through a dense stand of trees to a small piece of grass, where everything is blocked out except the sky over the center of the clearing.

When we reached the middle of the clearing she pushed me down to the ground. "Sit here," she commanded, and then plopped down next to me. "Now, let's lie back together."

We lay there together in the middle of the circle of old trees, gazing up at a disc of sky. The dark green leaves surrounding the deep blue sky made it seem like we were at the bottom of a deep magical well.

"What do you think?" Jesse asks.

"I love it. I can see why this is your favorite spot."

"It's beautiful at night—like looking through a telescope. You can see hundreds of stars right there in that circle. I've come here many nights and done nothing more than count stars while lying on my back right here."

"I have some more of those personal questions to ask you, Jesse. Do you care?"

"I told you before, you may ask me anything."

"You say you come here at night. This is still a pretty long walk from Mandy's house. Aren't you afraid to walk back home in the dark?"

"I don't consider Mandy's house to be my home. My home is wherever I am. This place is also my home."

"But how do you survive, Jesse?" I need to pin her down on this. "How do you buy things you need? How about food when you aren't at Mandy's house? Did you ever have a job? I really know very little about you."

"My parents left me a little money in a bank here in The City when they died. I can draw from that if I ever need to, but most of the time I don't need money. I eat at Mandy's—they always prepare much more than they need. If I'm out and around I eat at the Diggers, or occasionally I'll buy my own meal at a restaurant. And no, I've never had a job. It's not that I'm lazy, I've just never needed one."

"Wow, it must be nice not to have to work—to be able to roam around San Francisco everyday just lying under the trees, thinking wistful thoughts."

"Are you being sarcastic with me, DH?"

"No, I'm quite serious. It would be very nice to be you. I'm envious."

"Why can't you be like me? What's there to stop you?"

"Well, I suppose the first thing that pops into my head would be security. If you have some money in the bank, then you never really have to worry because you always have that to fall back on. I don't have that. And I'm not too sure if I'd stay at a place like Mandy's for long. I think it'd get pretty boring there after a while with nothing to do but listen to Frankie's records and smell cigarette smoke all evening."

"That's why I spend a lot of my time in parks." She takes a deep breath and lets it out slowly, savoring it. "The air's fresh, and it's never boring. There's always a breeze or a bird singing in the trees. Lots of color and light."

"What about when it rains. It dumps up here a lot doesn't it?"

"In the summer it doesn't matter. I just sit under the trees. I get a little wet sometimes, but it's a warm wet. I stay at Mandy's if the storms are long and drawn out. But when they're really wild I love to come to this park and sit right here and feel the strength of the storm."

"You mean you sit up on top of this hill under a tree in the middle of a storm? You gotta be kidding. What about lightning?"

"I'll never be struck by lightning." She smiles and reaches down to caress the grass.

"I don't know how you can predict that, and aren't you just a little afraid you'll be attacked by some bad guy walking through the park at night?"

"Not in this park. Not in this spot. I've never seen anyone come through here even in the day."

"So tell me more about your family—and I don't mean your other-dimensional family, I mean your blood family."

"I have no brothers or sisters. My mother was an actress in Norway. My father was a general in the US Army. They met while he was stationed in Europe. They fell in love and eventually moved to San Francisco for good."

"Your Mom was an actress? That's pretty neat."

"She was quite well known—famous really, at least in Norway. She left her fame behind when she came here with my father, but she was able to bring her savings with her. That plus my father's added up to a tidy sum. They were both killed in an accident three years ago. They left me everything. It's not millions, but if I manage it right it'll carry me through the rest of my life down here on this little world."

"I'm sorry about your parents. It's tough to lose them one at a time, but both at the same time must be terrible."

"It's not a good feeling. But it is what it is." After a moment of silent reflection she looks at me. "Are your parents alive?"

"Yes. My father's an aerospace engineer and my mother is the secretary to the boss of the Sunkist lemon factory."

She smiles and asks, "Do you get all the free lemons you want?"

"I usually don't ask for them. They're okay, but the only thing they're good for is cooking and making lemonade, and I don't do much of either. A lot of people like to suck on them or even eat them like oranges, but that's not good because the acid in them eats away the enamel on your teeth."

"What's your favorite food?" she asks.

"Pretty much everything, but I guess I'm partial to Mexican or Chinese … or maybe Italian. I love pasta just about any way it gets fixed. But I also like good old American farm food like fried chicken, mashed potatoes and gravy, bacon and eggs …"

"Maybe we should have eaten at a restaurant in China Town. There aren't any farm food places here that I know of."

"I think we were smart to get out of China Town as quick as we did. I didn't like the way everybody was looking at us."

"You mean the way they were looking at me," Jesse teases.

"That too."

"The men were looking at my tits."

"I noticed."

"My nipples are long and they poke out in front. Men like that."

"Those guys didn't look like they liked anything. They all looked tough and angry to me."

"They don't want hippies coming there because hippies don't have any money. China Town's all about the money. The meals are expensive and the waiters have been trained to get you in and out as quick as they can so that new customers can be seated."

"I like eating slow and enjoying my meal," I said.

"I do, as well."

I look up and see that the sky is rapidly turning a darker shade of blue.

"We'd better head back to Mandy's soon. Look at the sky—it'll be dark before we get back."

"Do we have to?" she asks.

"You're the one who doesn't like walking around The City in the dark."

"Why don't we just stay here for the night? It's warm and the sky's clear. It won't rain on us."

"You mean stay here on the summit all night?"

"Why not?" she says brightly. "We can watch the stars come out, and nobody will bother us. Think of how peaceful it will be. And no smoke to smell."

"I don't know. Manny's gonna be coming back with Bev and Reann. They'll all be wondering where the heck we are. They'll probably report us to the police."

"No they won't. Mandy knows you're with me so she won't be surprised at anything we do."

"Are you sure? How do you know that?"

"Positive. Everything I do surprises Mandy," she says, then smiles her mysterious, knowing smile.

"Okay, but can we send out for pizza? I'm hungry."

"You can eat some more of me. You won't be hungry long."

Day Five

It's morning and I'm sitting next to Jesse at the top of the hill in Lafayette Park. Jesse's asleep on the lawn, or at least I think she's asleep. It's hard to tell whether she's asleep or awake.

We had a wonderful evening of stargazing and more conversation about many things, but our long day of exploration was beginning to catch up to us. Just before we finally nodded off, the moon revealed itself in the circle of sky above us. Jesse stared at the moon as it emerged from the trees on one side until it was hidden by the trees on the other. My gaze shifted back and forth from the full moon to Jesse's face. The moonlight made her face glow with an aura. No, the glow came from inside her and rivaled the moonlight — soft pink, like a translucent rose petal held up in front of the sun.

Just before the moon slipped behind the surrounding treetops, I thought about the rest of the night. "It's gonna get a bit cool here tonight, I hope we can both stay warm," I said.

"Don't worry about that," she said softly. "We can curl up together and keep each other warm."

"Sounds nice. Promise not to drool on me?"

"No. Now, come closer to me and unbutton your shirt."

"What? I think that might be a bad idea. I get cold easy."

"You won't get cold, I promise." Her eyes reflected twin images of the moon as she looked at me. At that moment, lying there beside me, she appeared as the image of Titania herself. I could not have resisted anything she asked of me.

With one smooth movement Jesse sat up, and pulled her tank top over her head allowing her breasts total freedom in the night air. The sight of her naked breasts now glowing with the same light as her face was surreal. The moonlit circle at the top of the hill was suddenly transported a million miles away from anywhere to another town on another planet — to anywhere but the mundane City of San Francisco.

This experience was a first of its kind for me. Jesse sat there for a moment, smiling at me as I lay on the ground on my side looking up at her. Then she reached down, very slowly unbuttoned my shirt, and flipped it open.

"Here is what we are going to do to stay warm," she said.

She lay down on her side facing me and scooted over as close as she could get, pressing her soft breasts into my chest so that our nipples were pushing hard against each other. She was so warm. This was going to work just fine …

"Good night." She smiled, placed her lips against mine, and kissed me. Then she closed her eyes and went to sleep.

I've been awake since the first light of the new day—Day Five of my visit to San Francisco. The sky over our little hilltop circle has shifted to a brighter blue and the trees and grass have gone from shades of grey to shades of green. I can already feel the heat of a new day beginning. Jesse is still asleep on the grass beside me, and I've been enjoying the site of her lying there on her side, half curled like a child. At first she appeared as a glow against the grass, colorless in the earliest light. Now the green of the lawn is the ideal complement to the perfect shell pink skin of her legs and torso, the ivory white of her breasts, and the intense deep pink of her nipples. The sight of her is an expressionist painter's living dream. She was beautiful last night in the silver light of the moon, but the morning light reveals the soft warmth of her true colors.

Jesse opens her eyes and sits up, her breasts shifting and vibrating with every movement. She has gone from sound asleep to wide-awake with no transition at all.

"Good morning," I say. There are little bits of dried grass clinging to the side of her right breast. I reach over and gently brush them off.

She smiles at me and says, "Good morning."

"Did you sleep well?" I ask.

"Yes I did. How 'bout you?"

"Not as much as usual."

"You were too excited to go to sleep, weren't you. This was your first time sleeping with a naked girl in a park, wasn't it?"

"Yes, it was," I answered.

"Did you enjoy it?"

"Yep ... Yep, I did," I admitted honestly.

"How many naked girls have you seen before?"

"You mean besides the hippie chicks running around all over The City?"

"Besides those."

"A few," I said. "I can't really put a number on it.

"Not many, huh?"

"Okay, not many."

"I think I'd better cover my breasts before your eyeballs fall out. Can you hand me my top right there behind you?"

The strong odor of her body trailed after the shirt as I picked it up and handed it to her. Rose petals.

"Do you have to put that back on?" I asked her.

"It might be a good idea since human park people will no doubt be arriving soon—unless you don't mind me sharing these with them?" She grinned and lifted her breasts with her hands as if to offer them to me.

"You'd better put it on."

"I can always take it off later, and you can reach in and play with them any time you wish."

"That would be nice."

"We need to plan what we're going to do today," she said. "Any ideas?"

"Well ..." It took an effort to focus my thoughts as I watched her put her top back on. You know, it's not just the breasts themselves that are stimulating to a man; it's the movement of the breasts—the jiggling about when a girl moves. "I do have a couple of thoughts," I said finally.

"And ..." she prompted.

"Have you ever been to Berkeley or Stanford universities?"

"I've been to both."

"How 'bout we visit one of those?"

"It would be a pretty long walk to either one. We'd have to take a bus," she said.

"I'm game. Whattaya think?"

"Sure. Which do you prefer? I doubt we can do both in one day."

"What's your recommendation?"

"Stanford is probably the prettier of the two, but Berkeley's a little closer, I think."

"Why do you think Stanford is prettier?" I ask.

"It's smaller and it's visually more attractive than Berkeley. Berkeley's like all the other universities — big grey block buildings, and thousands of students running around looking like they have no idea where they're going.

"What do you mean by visually attractive?"

"The architecture, and the grounds. The Memorial Church has paintings and mosaics. Lots of art."

"When in doubt, opt for the art."

Jesse grinned at me. "Is that your motto in life?"

"It should be, shouldn't it? I just made it up."

"Well, I like it. You may keep it."

"Besides, I visited both universities with my friend Bart last week, and Stanford was my favorite for the very reason you mentioned — it has art. Berkeley was stale and grey. I was hoping you'd prefer Stanford, and you did."

"You are an artist. I knew you would prefer Stanford."

"You're a work of art, do you know that?" I tell her.

"I should be painted then," she says, striking a pose.

"I promise I'll paint many paintings of you when I get back ..."

"...back home?" Jesse's playful mood evaporated.

"Back to Riverside," I said gently.

"Please don't remind me you're leaving."

"Sorry."

"You should be."

"Okay … why don't we head back to Mandy's place now. I really need to check in and see how Manny's doing. I don't want him heading back to you-know-where without me."

"Would that matter?" she asks. "You could take me back with you instead."

"Don't tempt me."

"It is now my personal goal in life to tempt you."

There she goes again, saying bizarre things that confuse the heck out of me. What did she mean by that? But this time I'm not even going to ask her what she meant. I simply smile at her, reach down and take her hand and pull her up from the ground. She hugs me close and holds me there for a few moments.

"We could stay here all day," she says. "Hide behind those trees. Just cuddle the day away."

"Tempting."

"But you would grow tired of me then."

"I could never grow tired of you, Jesse."

"Yes you could."

Then she breaks the hug, grabs my hand and says, "Come on, It's time to go."

10:30 AM Back At Haight Street

We got here a few minutes ago and found Mandy's door locked. We knocked for a while and nobody answered, so we're assuming they've all gone their separate ways for the day. I do wonder how Manny made out with Bev and Reann. I don't mean that literally, as in "make out with" a girl; I mean "got along with." What if they all decided to split up and do different things? Maybe Manny didn't even spend the night here last night. If that's the case, then how in the world am I gonna find the guy? San Francisco is a big place, and with these throngs of hippies all over it'll be impossible to pick him out of a crowd.

I tore a blank page out of my journal and started writing:
Mandy, Manny, and All,

Jesse and I have been having a great time. We're now off to visit Stanford University. I hope you're all doing fine and having fun. Don't know when we'll be back, maybe late or not until tomorrow morning. We'll see you then.

DH and Jesse.

P.S. I hope Manny's still here with you Mandy, and you haven't thrown him out, or he got lost.

I fold the note in half and stick it between the door and the doorframe at eye level. I can only hope that it will be seen. "Well, that's that. I don't wanna hang around here waiting for somebody to get home, do you?"

"No," Jesse says. "I'd rather be alone with you anyway. We're having more fun than we would if we were with the others."

"I agree. I love Manny, but all that guy can talk about is music, and that gets kinda old after awhile."

"And the rest of them will come home complaining about work. I don't like to hear complaining."

"Me neither." I check to make sure the note will stay where I put it, then turn to face Jesse. "Whattaya say we go find the bus station?"

"I know exactly where it is."

"You do?"

"I do. It won't take long to get there if we can fight our way through the crowds," she says.

"They're getting thick fast. I wonder if they're having another one of those street festivals?"

"If they are, we'll never be able to get anywhere. They'll be packed in shoulder-to-shoulder here in a few minutes. We'd better hurry."

"How fast can you walk?" I ask her.

"Just try to keep up," she says with a gleam in her eye. Was that a challenge?

"Lead the way," I say.

"Why? So you can hide behind me?" She heads off at a quick pace.

"No, so I can watch your sweet little bottom bounce back and forth."

"Really," she says as I fall into step just behind her. Then both of her hands move behind her and quickly flip up the back of her skirt, flashing me a glorious full moon before letting the skirt fall back in place.

"Thanks, I needed that."

"Any time," she says without missing a step.

12:30 PM Stanford University

We made it to the bus station and, as luck would have it, the bus for Palo Alto was just getting ready to pull out. That confirmed our decision to go to Stanford. They held the bus long enough for us to buy our tickets. I say us, but actually it was Mandy's money that bought them. Thank you, Mandy.

Stanford University is nestled in a valley next to the town of Palo Alto and it has to be one of the most beautiful campuses in the entire country. The grounds are like a park; they're filled with trees that look like they grow here naturally—mostly oak, I think—and there are lots of palm trees planted along the roads and around the buildings.

We started our tour by heading for Hoover Tower. It's the tallest building on campus, so the view from the top is impressive. I'm not sure of its history, but I'm going to guess it was named after President Hoover. For all I know though, it could have been in honor of some graduate from the 30s named Fred Hoover, or maybe for the family that invented the Hoover vacuum cleaners. They must have made a bundle selling those things, maybe they gave a lot of cash to Stanford so the university named the tower after that family. Anyway, it's pretty high up here where we're standing overlooking the campus, and it makes for a lovely view, so kudos to whichever Hoover they named it after. There's probably a plaque or a sign around somewhere that explains it, but personally I like the Fred theory.

The oldest buildings and courtyards are arranged as a quadrangle — sort of like the Quad at Riverside City College, only bigger. The style is California Mission, I think, but it reminds me of those Roman houses they uncovered in Pompeii. The first thing I did when we got to the top of the tower was to scan the entire panorama, all 360°. No volcanoes, but plenty of red tiled roofs.

We'll probably spend the rest of the afternoon here just walking around enjoying the buildings and exploring the little gardens and the nooks and crannies that are tucked in everywhere. One of the students we met on the bus told us about the Memorial Church. It sounded really cool, and it's not far from the tower, so that's going to be our next stop for sure.

Inside Stanford Memorial Church

We followed a covered walkway along the outside of the buildings around the Quad. The sun was hot, but the shade of the stone building behind the columns and arches was cool. When we reached the main entrance we found that we still had a ways to go. We crossed a long courtyard lined with more columns and arches and passed under another archway before we finally came out in the Main Quad. There it was on the far side of the Quad, shining like a jewel set in a gold ring.

The front of the church is gorgeous. At the top is a big mosaic mural of Jesus hanging around with some of His disciples. He's standing up on a rise with a halo and a glow against a gold sky while all the people are below Him in various states of worship and adoration. There is more gold lower down around the arches that are the entrance to the church — angels and a pattern sort of like ivy against a gold background like a page from an illuminated manuscript. It's exquisite.

I can't help but compare this campus to some of the run down neighborhoods in The City that we saw yesterday. The Tenderloin district, so fragile and decrepit and dingy, like the people it produces, may once have been something grand — maybe not as grand as this

church, but new and proud and whole, healthy and full of hope
for the future. What happened? How did The City allow such a
district to evolve into what it is today? Why is it still like that? Why
hasn't somebody fixed it? This church was built in 1893; why isn't
it dilapidated and why aren't the disciples in the mosaic up there
tattered and holding brown bags and wine bottles? Is it money?
Is that all there is to it? Stanford U has big bucks so it can keep its
campus looking tidy and new; keep the disciples looking squeaky
clean and sober. Is it because The City ran out of money somewhere
along the line and the decay began? That's hard to believe since the
rest of The City looks pretty good. Maybe it's just the difference
between the profane and the sacred; two alternate universes trying
to exist in one spot at the same time.

The inside of the church is as impressive as the outside. The main
area is lined with arches and columns and, like the outside, looks
very Roman or Italian. The colors seem to be mainly red and gold.
The carpet on the floor is red, and the ceiling high above is exposed
wood and beams of a rich, dark-red color. The walls are decorated
with mosaics of angels and prophets all around, and the spaces in
between are filled with mosaic decoration. All of the backgrounds
of the pictures and decorations are filled in with gold. All of the
windows are stained glass and depict scenes from the life of Jesus
and other people from the Bible—big ones on the main level and
smaller ones up higher. There are also three very big ones up front
behind the altar. Some of them look familiar—probably inspired by
paintings done by artists I learned about in my art history classes.
I am sure that at least three or four of them are based on works
by some of the Pre-Raphaelite Brotherhood. There is a skylight in
the ceiling near the front of the church and the white light coming
through lands on the white marble steps of the stage-like chancel.
The whole effect seems to focus attention on the altar further back.

The cool shadows and soft light coming through the colored
glass and spilling down from the skylight are restful for tired eyes.
The church would be a nice place for people to sit in meditation

for hours Zen-ing out. I imagine there are some students who do just that on a regular basis. There might even be some Zen kids hanging in this school somewhere—it's hard to tell, since Zen people don't tend to advertise.

Earlier on campus we saw a girl wearing a brown jacket with a big OM symbol stenciled on the back. I don't think they do OM in Zen, or do they? I've noticed a lot of OM symbols on the hippies back in The Haight. I wonder if the new kids on the block are trying to take the Zen out of Beat? I wonder if they even know what it means. It's clear that the hippies are using some of the Beat stuff to build their own movement, but are they removing the Zen and replacing it with a Hindu bent? The words, "OM Kirshna Krishna" were stenciled under the OM symbol on the girl's jacket. I saw lots of similar jackets and shirts back in The City. What's the deal with that? What are they advertising?

Jesse and I have been standing for some time at the edge of the pool of light in front of the chancel soaking in the luminescence and color.

"Isn't this something, Jesse?" It seems only right to speak in a whisper.

"I've never seen anything like it," she says, "but I've not been inside many churches."

"I've visited a few of the missions. They had a sense of history and were pretty, but compared to this … it's like comparing a country church to a cathedral. It was a good idea to come here instead of Berkeley."

"That guy on the bus made Berkeley sound like a place to stay away from for a while. I'm glad we didn't go there," she says.

On the way down from San Francisco a Stanford student named Frank told us that there is a big demonstration on the Berkeley campus today and that there'd been some trouble with it already. Some of the demonstrators started throwing things at innocent people who were just walking by and the cops had to be called out to break it up. Some folks had been seriously injured and the cops wound up using tear gas and who knows what else. Not good. Why can't these people just speak their peace, march a little, and go home? I don't get all the drama; it seems so childish. What good does it do to hurt people and destroy property? All that does is damage the cause they're trying to build up. And it ticks me off because I really wanted to go to Berkeley either today or tomorrow. I may never get another chance, but if it's going to be like that kid said, then I don't want to get in the middle of it. We'll just have to see.

Jesse is standing a few feet in front of me. Her hair catches a shaft of colored light from one of stained glass windows and turns it into a halo. And why not? I'm still not sure who or what Jesse really is. Maybe she's a real angel come down here to visit with me for a while and then at a moment when I least expect it, she'll just vanish into the air. Maybe it'll even happen in this chancel while I am standing here staring at the back of her golden hair. And you know something else? Two days ago her hair was so dirty and greasy that it stuck to the pillow she was laying on. Now, I'll swear, it's as clean as if she'd just washed it today. I'm not kidding. Her hair looks like she just stepped out of a fashion magazine, like one of those Breck girls, and she hasn't been anywhere near a shower in at least three days, probably more like a week or two.

I walk up behind her, place my arms around her, pull her toward me, and bury my face in her hair. The top of her head comes just about even with my mouth.

"You smell good," I tell her.

"You mean you like my stinky hair?"

"It doesn't stink. It just smells like you smell on a hot day."

"It should stink. I haven't washed it in two weeks." She pulls some of her hair around to smell it. "Hmm. It doesn't stink." She holds some up to look at. "It looks clean."

"Told ya."

"Too bad. I was gonna have you wash it for me when we get back to Mandy's." She smiles.

"I can still do that."

"We'll have to find a way to get it dirty again first."

"Mud wrestling?"

"Why don't we go outside and walk around a bit. I'm sure to sweat buckets and then you can throw dirt in my hair."

I took Jesse's hand and led her outside. I don't plan on throwing dirt in her hair, but I do think it's time to head back to The City. We've seen what I came here to see and we're gonna get hungry pretty soon.

We walk out of the dark church into the bright sunlight and are blinded for a moment. It's a beautiful day here on the Stanford campus. It might be nice to go to school here. It's too bad that all I can afford is a city college back in Riverside. If I could, I'd probably attend a place like this, even though I'm not so sure an expensive college gives you any better education than a cheap one. I think the people who go here are mainly paying for the ambience of the place, not necessarily for the subjects they take. I find it interesting that all the unruly "peace" marches happen at these big, expensive schools and not at the little community colleges. I have a theory about that. I think most of the students that go to places like this have been spoiled rotten all their lives. They've always gotten their way and never had to work for it, and these schools are designed to cater to that kind of mentality. I think the courses offered in places like these may actually be less difficult to pass than the ones in the regular city colleges because the hoity-toity schools don't really care about education; they care about keeping the rich kids and rich parents happy. I think they really do teach stuff at RCC. Up here I think they just drink coffee and talk about stuff. I think kids are more inclined to demonstrate and start riots in expensive schools because they're bored from sitting around talking all day. That, and they also know that they won't get into trouble for doing those things here. Money talks. The Stanford student on the bus told us that if he could, he'd participate in the Berkeley demonstration.

"So, what they were actually demonstrating against?" I asked.

"Capitalism and Big Money," he said.

Ok, the same old excuse. What I wanted to ask him was, "How much money do your parents make? What does it cost to send you to Stanford? Ain't that the pot calling the kettle black?" but I didn't say a word. A lot of this stuff goin' on up here just doesn't make sense. It's all kind of romantic in a way—a bit exciting and even fun—but it defies logic.

"Have you ever thought about goin' to one of these schools, Jesse?" I ask her on the way to the bus stop.

"Of course not. I'd never do that."

"Why not?"

"Because these schools have no life in them. I can't be in any of them for very long without dying."

"What do you mean by that?"

"Universities make you into what they want you to be, not what you were born to be," she replies calmly.

"Okay …"

"You attend their classes and they fill your mind with information you don't know. How do you know the information they instill within you is accurate and true? You don't. The reason you attend the university in the first place is because of a void of information within your brain. Instead of discovering on your own what truth really is, you pay someone else to fill that void for you. But if their information is incorrect or biased in any way, then you're no longer yourself, you're a clone of the university. What you've really done is murdered your soul, because your soul may have had other ideas for your future, and you've destroyed any chance of making those ideas reality. Universities are roadblocks on the path of individuality. They are assassins of truth."

"You really are something, Jesse," I tell her. "I don't know where you get all the ideas you come up with, but I find it difficult to argue with any of them."

"I get the ideas from my own Spirit. I don't get them from university professors."

And though she has, once again, boggled my mind, just for a moment the thought flashes through my own center of existence that I could sit at her feet for days and listen to her teachings and never grow bored. Given the choice of a full scholarship to Stanford University, all expenses paid, or the opportunity to sit at the feet of Jesse and soak up her thoughts, I'd take Jesse any day.

5 PM Another Chinese Restaurant

When Jesse and I got back from Palo Alto, we figured we'd walk around a bit before heading back to Mandy's place — should we decide that's where we want to spend the night — since we were already downtown. Guess who we ran into on Market Street? Manny, Bev and Reann!

Jesse had said that she knew of a good Chinese restaurant where she and Mandy had eaten several times, and she thought I might like to try it out. While we were walking down Market Street back toward Haight, we noticed three slow moving, hippie-looking characters in front of us. Even though we could only see their backs, I knew that the one in the middle had to be Manny. So we picked up our pace. It became obvious who they were when we caught up with them.

"Got any spare change?" I said, disguising my voice a little as we came up behind them.

"No spare change. Just a little change," Manny replied without looking back, as if he had become used to hearing the question.

"Come on, jerk," I said. "You got more money than I have!"

"Who the hell you calling a jerk?" Manny said as he whipped around to confront what he thought was a rude hippie begging for money. Then his scowl turned to a grin. "DH! You idiot. I coulda slugged you."

"You've never slugged anybody in your life, Manfred." Manfred is what I call Manny when I'm teasing him.

"Where've you two been?".

"Here, there, everywhere." I smiled.

"Jesse? You okay?" Bev is clearly puzzled that Jesse is alert, quite sober, and walking around.

"Why shouldn't I be?" Jesse asked, smiling.

"Well … because …"

"Because you look kinda normal," Reann, also puzzled, bluntly completed Bev's statement.

"What's goin' on, Jesse?" Bev asked.

"I'm not sure what you mean?"

"The last time we saw you back at the house you were nearly comatose." Bev said.

"Not really," Jesse said. "I've never been comatose in my life."

Before anyone could say anything else, I said "We all need to go somewhere to sit down and talk. I think there are some misconceptions about Jesse that need to be cleared up."

"Ok …" Reann said, still looking at Jesse with some suspicion.

"Where were you guys heading?" Manny asked.

"To the Chinese restaurant down around the corner," Jesse said.

"The one Mandy goes to all the time?" Bev asked.

"Yes, that's the one."

Bev gave Jesse another long look up and down. "Jesse, I'll swear, you look really good," she said.

"Thanks, Bev."

"Yeah, I don't know what the heck you're doing, but keep doing it," Reann said. She, too, was beginning to believe her eyes.

"I'm doing this." Jesse said calmly.

"We can talk about it at the restaurant," I said. "You're all gonna need to be sitting down."

"I don't have any money for the restaurant," Manny said. "I blew my wad last night and this morning. But I got a really cool tie-dye shirt to take back to Riverside with me."

"That's okay Manny," Jesse said. "This'll be my treat. I'll pay for everyone."

Bev and Reann, stupefied, looked at each other. The last time either of them saw Jesse she was asleep on the couch, drooling all over the pillow. Everyone thought she was a complete dope head, and now she's buying them lunch.

I was right about them needing to sit down to hear what we were about to tell them. I waited until after we were served our food and had begun to eat before I started to fill them in on all that had transpired between Jesse and me. Not just the places we went together, but some of the background about who Jesse really is. Needless to say, Bev and Reann were floored.

"Mandy's gonna be shocked," Reann says. "It's hard to believe. You're telling us that you've never taken drugs in your entire life? That basically you've just been putting us on all this time."

"I wasn't putting you on intentionally, Reann. I was merely acting the way I believed you all wished to see me act. I was trying to make you all happy," Jesse says.

"Well, it's a bit odd. An odd way to make us happy," Bev says. "But I guess I can believe you. I don't know how you could make a story up like that and not have it be real."

"Big Bob's gonna fill his pants when he hears all this," Reann says.

Bev closes her eyes and shakes her head. "That's a mind image I didn't need."

"No kidding," Reann says. "But he was the one who seemed to talk about Jesse the most. He's the one who kept yakking on about her being high day in and day out."

"He shouldn't have said those things without discussing it with me first," Jesse says. "That wasn't very nice of him."

"No it wasn't," Bev agrees. "But in his defense, you didn't help matters by looking like a zombie all the time."

"I suppose I didn't. But in all sincerity I meant only to be nice to you all. It would hurt me deeply if I hurt any of you."

"Why did you decide all of a sudden to become normal again?" Bev asks sarcastically.

"That was my fault. Mandy gave her to me for safe keeping yesterday, and actually," I look at Jesse and smile, "she ended up being the one to lead me around."

"I found in DH someone I could trust with everything that I am." Jesse met my gaze, her piercing blue eyes drilling right through my own.

"Well, DH," Bev says, "it looks like you're a bit of a miracle worker. You know, even if Jesse has been leading us all on about the drug stuff, it doesn't change the fact that she was disturbed enough emotionally to hide everything from us. Emotions can be just as bad as drugs sometimes." She directs a smile at Jesse. "I can't find fault in you for acting the way you did, Jesse."

"I love you Bev," Jesse says. She returns Bev's smile, then expands it to include Reann. "I love you all, even Big Bob. I just want you all to be happy."

Manny leans over and says to me quietly, "I feel like I'm eavesdropping on a private counseling session."

"It's okay Manny. The counseling was all done last night under the stars."

"Really?" Manny leans back and gives me a wicked grin.

It's good to see Jesse finally able to express her true nature with her friends, and to see her friends beginning to accept her for who she is. "I have a feeling that Hippie Haven's gonna be a lot more fun now that Jesse's being who she's supposed to be," I say.

Always one who has his priorities in order, Manny asks, "Does anybody want that last eggroll?"

"We can order more, Manny," Jesse assures him.

"And you're not broke?" Although Bev seems to be fine with Jesse's explanation, Reann is still not satisfied. "All this time I thought you were a homeless, poverty stricken bum off the street, and that you were just kind of using us a little. Weren't you?"

"If you'll remember, Reann, I never asked you or anybody for a penny. I slept on the couch, and I ate very little at the house. And Mandy, whose house it is, never ever spoke badly to me about anything." Jesse's tone and demeanor is kind and almost apologetic as she correctes Reann.

"I'm sure that when Mandy learns all this she'll be very happy for Jesse and welcome her with open arms," I tell Reann. "Jesse didn't mean any harm. She was just trying to help things make sense in her mind." I smile and add, "And believe me, her mind is quite an amazing thing."

"I like you, Jesse," Manny says, smiling at her. "Anybody who can put up with DH all night is a hero in my book."

"Thanks, Manny, my semi-best friend," I say.

"You're welcome. So what the heck have you guys been doing for the last two days, especially last night—if you know what I mean?" He finishes his question with that Groucho Marx waggle of his eyebrows.

"That's a long story," I begin. "But to summarize, we did a heck of a lot of walking, ate at The Shadows …"

"Wow, nice place," Bev interjects.

"… stopped at City Lights Bookstore and chatted with Ferling-hetti, Ginsberg and Corso for about an hour …"

"What!" Manny realizes that his sudden exclamation has drawn the attention of everyone else in the restaurant. He continues in a more subdued tone, "What? I mean, what? You did what? You gotta be kidding!"

"Nope." I confess that my reply was delivered with a degree of smugness as I was enjoying Manny's reaction.

"Why would he be kidding? We did just as DH said we did," Jesse says to Manny, then she continues to the whole group. "I'm not sure I really liked that bookstore, but it was an interesting hour. I think Allen was probably the nicest. At least he was the funniest."

"Allen?" Manny can hardly believe what he's hearing. "You called him Allen? You gotta be kidding. You called Allen Ginsberg by his first name?"

"We did," I tell him. "And I think you're right, Jesse, he was the funniest of the three. Gregory didn't say much and he never actually sat down to talk. He stood there for a while and then went inside the store. We were starting to go somewhere else when Lawrence and Allen brought out the chairs and a table. It looked like something they did all the time. It was Lawrence who noticed us and invited us to join them. He was very nice and asked us a lot of questions about who we are and what we do in life. He seemed genuinely interested."

"And you called him Lawrence? He didn't tell you to call him Larry?" Manny is having a hard time believing this.

"I didn't think it was appropriate to shorten his name to Larry, given his stature in the community and the fact that it was the first time we'd ever met him. I suppose the next time we see him we'll be able to call him Larry."

"Get out of here." Manny shakes his head. "Now you're playing with me."

"A little," I confess. "I doubt we'll ever see any of them again, but we did have a good time talking with them."

"They're giants in the Beat Movement! And no small potatoes in contemporary literary circles, either. Just wait till Bill Hunter hears that you actually got to talk with them — he'll have a frigging cow."

"He probably will. But enough about us. What have you guys been doing?"

I really do want to hear about their adventures, but Manny is not ready to switch topics. "Wait a minute. What did you talk about with them?"

"A little of this, a little of that. They wanted to read my journal." I casually wave the ever-present little book for all to see.

"You're kidding!" Manny almost falls out of his chair. "Did you let them read it?"

"Actually, Allen grabbed it from me. He wouldn't take no for an answer."

"I don't believe you," Manny says flatly.

"It's true, Manny," Jesse confirms. "Allen took his journal and read through parts of it, then Mr. Ferlinghetti took it from Allen, and he read some of it. They loved DH's poems.".

Again, Manny expresses his astonishment. "OH MY GAWD!" And once again we have the attention of the entire restaurant. The waitress gives us a look that says we'd better not do that again.

"Lawrence said that I should keep writing and one day I might have my own book in City Lights Bookstore."

"And Allen made DH into a real Beat," Jesse announces proudly even though I don't think she really knows what that means.

"Huh?" Manny looks at me for clarification.

"It's no big deal," I explain. "We were talking about the Beat movement and the writings of the Beats, and they told me I was a Beat writer because my poetry was 'so deep and introspective' or something like that."

Jesse picks up the story again. "So then DH told them he wasn't worthy of being called a Beat writer because he didn't think his stuff came anywhere near to being as good as the stuff Allen and Mr. Ferlinghetti wrote. But they insisted that it's all a matter of the heart and mind."

I continue the narrative as my audience reacts with increasing astonishment. "Lawrence told me it's all about the soul, then Allen told me that all it takes is a life filled with cool experiences and personal statements, with the emphasis on cool."

Manny is shaking his head in disbelief and envy. "This is all a dream," he says. "Why didn't I go with you instead of doing the hippie thing? I think I'm gonna be sick."

Then Jesse delivers the coup de grace. "And then Allen made DH a knight."

"A what?" Bev asks. "How can a Beatnik make somebody a knight?"

"Lawrence told me I had a 'Beat soul' and that I was every bit the Beat as Allen or he was. I said he must be kidding, and he said, 'No, I'm not.' He was quite serious."

Reann, ever the skeptic, leans back in her chair and rolls her eyes. "I'm not sure I'm believing this, but it's a hell of a story."

"It's all true," Jesse says.

"If Jesse says it's true then I believe it is," Bev says. "There's something about Jesse that tells me she never lies."

"Get back to the story," Manny says, impatient with the interruption. "What's this knight business?"

"Nobody made me a knight." I tell them smiling. "After they went on about my poetry I said, 'So I have your blessing? You're actually accepting me into the Beat hall of fame?' I was just kidding—kinda sarcastic really—but then Allen said, 'We hereby recognize you as an official Beat writer.' He raised his right hand, brought it down on my left shoulder, and said, 'I dub thee, Sir DH of Beatville! Rise Sir DH of Beatville!' Then he grinned at me and shook my hand. That was that."

"That was that," Manny repeats softly, shaking his head again. Then his excitement gets the better of him. "That was all there was to it? Do you realize that even if you're a lousy writer you just got the blessing of the two biggest Beat guys around? It's like the Pope giving an imprimatur to a book by some no-account Catholic writer. You can tell people about this and you'll be able to be somebody!"

"I don't know …" I say.

"What an honor," Reann says. "I can hardly believe it, but I do."

"So that was the end of the conversation?" Bev asks.

"We talked for a little while longer. Mainly about the differences between the Beats and the hippies," I say, grateful for the opportunity to share some of the more thought provoking aspects of the conversation. "I got the impression that Lawrence and Allen have a lot of fun with the hippie thing, but they aren't too impressed by the hippies themselves. They didn't seem too happy with the way everyone compares the hippie movement to the Beats when they are really quite different.

Our little corner of the restaurant went quiet for a few minutes, each of us absorbed in our own thoughts on the subject, and then Bev breaks the silence. "Well, what a day you two have had," she says. "I'm with Manny. I'm really envious. I don't know what to say."

It's time to shift gears. "That's enough about Jesse and me," I say "What have you guys been doing?"

"We've been having a great time," Bev says brightly. "We spent all day yesterday doing the same sort of things you were doing—just walking around, checking out the hippie scene."

"Can't get enough of that," Reann says dryly.

"It was sort of fun," Manny says. "We saw some pretty interesting things."

"Sure did," Reann says. "And we smelled some pretty interesting things too."

"What are you talking about?"

Bev puts her hand on Reann's shoulder and says, "Let me tell it." Reann just shruggs her shoulders.

"Apparently yesterday was one of the designated Street Fests, so everywhere we went it was wall to wall people. Some were residents and others were tourists, but it was so hot and humid, that by the end of the day they all smelled just as bad. And there was pot everywhere. Right out in the open. We couldn't walk ten feet without sucking in somebody else's stale smoke."

"We were high most of the day and into the evening just from inhaling the pot in the air," Manny adds. "I didn't mind it, but the ladies here weren't too happy."

"I wasn't happy," Bev says. "I know they were all trying to make some sort of point, although I'm still not sure what that point is, but they shouldn't have the right to ruin the atmosphere for everyone else." Reanne and Manny nod vigorously in agreement.

"The problem was that you couldn't get away from it," Manny says. "It wouldn't have been so bad had it been localized in pockets around the city, but everywhere we went, there it was. There were cops all around, but they didn't do anything about anything."

"With that many people it was probably impossible to do anything," I say. "I mean, who do you arrest? If a hundred thousand people are all participating in a crime, who do you collar? You can't handcuff them all and take them in. Where they gonna put them?"

"That's their problem," Bev says. "That's what we pay them for. And if it was me, I wouldn't have allowed this mass invasion in the first place."

"San Francisco seems to be gaining a reputation for catering to the renegades and free spirits of society," I say. "That's not necessarily a bad thing. Change has to come from somewhere I guess, and someplace or somebody has to allow it."

Reann scowls. "Yes, but at the expense of the people who live and work here and pay their taxes?" She has a point.

To lighten things up, I ask, "Did you meet anybody you liked?"

"Oh yeah," Manny says. "There were a lot of nice people. I think the really nice ones were the people who actually live here. The tourist hippies were pretty silly, though. I didn't care for them.

"They stood out like sore thumbs," Reann says. "They were all clean."

Bev snickers and explains, "Their clothes were neat and tidy, like they ironed their pants and shirts before they went out on the streets."

"Their Levis were brand new," Manny adds. "You could hear them make that new denim rustle sound when they walked."

Bevs laughter fades as she considers a more serious thought. "There were some locals who had some interesting things to say though. I actually agreed with some of it."

"If you could get them to talk about something besides Hendrix, Janis Joplin, and pot," Reann adds.

"That even got old for me," Manny said. "There was that girl we met over by the Japanese statue — her name was Freedom. She had some interesting things to say."

Bev rolls her eyes and said, "You just liked her because she was topless and had huge tits."

"What?" I ask.

"Manny here got the hots for this chick who was doing nude yoga on the lawn in front of the Buddha statue in Golden Gate Park."

"Well maybe … but she had some good stuff to say. She could

actually carry on a conversation using words over five letters long," Manny says defensively.

Reann laughed. "And every time she bent over to touch her toes her tits drug on the ground. I'll bet she got nipple rash from that."

"So, Manny, what did this Freedom girl have to say that was so interesting?" I ask. "Did she tell you why she was involved with the hippies?"

"She's a local yoga teacher. Her classes have doubled in size since all the people started swarming up here. She's making big bucks off it," he says.

"I did hear that hippies are really into yoga," I say. "That's kinda neat."

"But it's a myth apparently," Manny says. "Freedom said that the real hippies never come to her class—just the out-of-towners in their brand new yoga outfits. The tourist hippies have been told that the real hippies do yoga, so they figure they have to take a yoga class just to be able to tell their friends back home they did. But most hippies don't do yoga. They're too busy trying to think of ways to not do anything at all, so they don't have time to do yoga."

"Really? That's strange," I say.

"Everything in The City is strange right now," Bev says. "I just want all these people to go home so we can get back to normal."

"I'm sure that one of these days everybody's gonna look back on this crazy little invasion and think it was all just one big love fest," Reann says. "Thousands of young people smoking pot, running around naked, and having a happy time. The City's gonna be looked upon as the new Garden of Eden, or something like that, and that's all well and good. All right, you all had a nice vacation but what came out of it? There's more to it than dope and music. Something's shady. Something doesn't make sense."

"I agree," says Bev. "It's much more complex than what it first seems to be."

We grow silent again as we ponder that last exchange. After a few moments I say, "Jesse was telling me that she has felt a darkness in the air. It's not really my place to comment because, quite frankly, I'm one of those tourists you were talking about. But for what it's worth, I agree with Reann. I can't help but think that there's something behind all of this. This whole hippie thing seems to be a façade disguising a less obvious motive. I kind of sense that darkness thing, too. I think Jesse might be right."

"Well, I think there are some nasty characters hiding in the woodwork," Reann says. "These massing hoards and all the unrest are intentional. Stuff like that doesn't just come together over night. This had to be planned out by somebody with a brain for the bad."

"For what reason though?" Bev asks.

"I don't know. Just to stir things up and cause anxiety I guess."

Manny turns to Jesse and just looks at her for a moment. His expression suggests that he is sizing her up, or is seeing her in a new light. "So, Jesse," he says, "what about the darkness thing?"

Jesse is looking at the paper napkin in her lap. She has been fidgeting with it and now it's in shreds. With an effort she stills her hands by clasping them together, and raises her eyes to the rest of us at the table. "I'm not sure," she says. "It's just something I feel."

"Jesse has these 'feelings,'" I explain.

"You mean like ESP?" Bev asks.

I can see that the mention of ESP has made Jesse uncomfortable, so I try to answer for her. "We've talked about that. She certainly does have an uncanny sense of intuition."

"Interesting," Manny says. "That seems to be a popular subject for conversation up here in The City. Freedom told me she was a psychic."

"I talked about such things with another girl when Manny and I first got here," I add.

Bev brought an eggroll to her mouth where it hovered while she said, "Here in San Francisco everybody thinks they're a psychic." She takes a big bite of eggroll. "It seems to be part of the hippie thing. They all want to be connected to something bigger than they are," she adds, waving the eggroll for emphasis.

"It's one big identity crisis," Reann says. "A bunch of lonely, insecure people with no real goals in life coming together from all over the country, wearing costumes and distorting their own self-centered desires into a national movement so that it makes them look normal."

"Wow," says Manny. "That's quite a mouthful."

But Reann is just getting started. "Well it's true," she says. "If you don't have a job or don't want one, don't wanta go to college, don't have any money or maybe have more than you know what to do with, if you come from a bad family or just one where your parents 'don't understand', if your friends are all losers—then whattaya do?"

Manny rubs his chin in mock thoughtfulness. "Let me guess—you start a movement."

Reann ignores Manny and continues. "The Beats have been writing books and poetry for nearly twenty years, and they're still at it. What do these hippies do? How many hippie writers and poets can you think of? Yeah, the stuff the Beats put out seems rough sometimes and challenges the way people think, but it's based on intellect and experience. The hippies like it because they think it gives them permission to behave any way they want to just because they can. It's all reaction and show for them. That's why your buddies, Allen and Lawrence, are so suspicious of the hippie thing. They worked hard to get where they are. So far, none of the hippies have had the discipline and drive to produce anything of substance. Maybe that will come with time."

"When Big Bob first brought Manny and me to Hippie Haven we thought we were gonna be meeting a family of hippies living out their dreams. Boy were we wrong."

"None of us are hippies," Reann says. "And that's kinda my point. I'm not sure any of the people out there on the streets really are either. I think most of 'em are just here for the circus. When they go back home all the beads and tie-dye will come back off, and they'll have to make some real life decisions. Go to college? Get a job? Raise a family?"

"I think a lot of them will end up staying here, living off The City," Bev says.

Jesse has withdrawn again and has resumed fidgeting with what remains of her napkin. In an effort to draw her out I ask, "What do you think, Jesse?"

"I think this conversation is dark."

"What do you mean?"

"I don't want to be negative at such a lovely dinner gathering, but for weeks now I've only been able to see people in black and white. They have no color. Only nature—animals, the parks, the trees—has color now."

Bev shifts in her seat to look directly at Jesse. "I'm not sure I understand what you just said, Jesse dear. You mean that literally?"

"I meant exactly what I said. All of the people out there on the streets are black and white. The tie-dyed shirts, the colored bell-bottoms, the banners they carry—there's no color. I see it all in black and white, like a newsreel on TV. It's only when I find a place to sit quietly in a park that I see color. But even in a park, when a person walks by, that person is in black and white."

"Oh my," Reann says. "That's really weird. Maybe you ought to go see an eye doctor."

Jesse pins Reann with the full force of her gaze. "I don't think so," she says. "I don't think so at all."

"How do you explain it?" Manny asks.

"It's all a part of the darkness. When DH and I were at the bookstore, those men were almost in color—like the color was trying to come through, but there was darkness all around them. It was as if their souls were imprisoned by the darkness and trying to escape. They didn't look healthy, and parts of the bookstore were black and white."

"What about us? Are we in black and white?"

"Yes, Manny. DH is the only one in color."

"Why's that? Why is he so special?" Reann seems almost offended by Jesse's statement.

Jesse turns her gaze on her and says calmly, "Because he ate me."

Manny is startled by her answer. "I beg your pardon?" he says, exchanging looks first with Bev and then Reann.

Seeing their obvious discomfort at Jesse's statement I quickly explain. "She means that I ate one of her tears. Yesterday I saw a tear running down her cheek. I touched it with my finger then put my finger to my mouth to kiss it."

Reann relaxes back into her chair and laughs. "For a minute there I thought she was giving us a little too much information."

Bev raises her hands as if to surrender. "Jesse dear, I'm sorry but I don't get any of this. I don't understand where the heck you're coming from, but it does make for a fun conversation."

"Let's change the subject," I say.

"To what?" Manny asks.

"I don't know. How about what we're gonna do after we leave this place?"

"I don't know about the rest of you, but I'm pretty tuckered. I think I'll just head back home and take a nap," Bev says.

"I'm not too tired. I might try to catch a movie or something," Reann says.

"I could get into that," Manny says. "You want company?"

"Sure, if you promise not to talk about rock bands during the movie."

"I promise."

"What are you and Jesse gonna do, DH?" Bev asks.

"We haven't talked about it. I'm sure we'll think of something."

"Should we tell Mandy you'll be back tonight?"

"Probably. I'm up for a quiet evening. I can't recall any time in my life when I walked so much. I know it's gotta be good exercise, but I could use a break."

"We're all gonna need showers tonight." Manny puts his nose in his armpit. "I smell pretty ripe."

"Jeez, Manny …" Bev says.

"I think we'd better finish up here and start heading back home,"

Reann says. "This little party's getting weird."

Civic Center Bench 7:30 PM

We parted company on the sidewalk in front of the restaurant; Bev headed back to Hippy Haven, Manny and Reann off to find a movie, and Jesse and I to nowhere in particular. We found a bench on Van Ness near the Civic Center where we can rest our feet while we decide what to do next. Neither one of us wants to go back to Hippie Haven just yet.

"If we go back to the house, it'll be like saying goodbye," Jesse says softly.

"What do you mean?"

"You and I will no longer be alone. We'll no longer be able to touch each other or to see the stars together. We'll be forced to follow the ways of those who exist in that house."

"It is a kind of depressing thought after what we've experienced together. Listening to that boring music …"

"Smelling cigarette smoke …"

"We don't have to go back just yet. What would you like to do?"

Jesse looks at me and smiles. "It doesn't matter, as long as I can be where I can touch you."

During the course of our conversation there has been a small but steady stream of people on the sidewalk passing us by — singles, couples, and small groups — all intent on their own business and paying us no heed. Now however, a couple that has just walked by has stopped. It looks like they are having a discussion of some sort. They have turned around and are walking back toward us. One of them is an attractive Japanese woman, about twenty-five years old. She is wearing a nice green dress and is carrying a small black handbag in one hand and a little black book in the other. The other person is a tall white guy with wavy grey hair, maybe in his forties, wearing dark grey slacks and a grey sport coat. Mormons? Jehovah Witness? Are we going to be proselytized right here on the streets of San Francisco?

The woman speaks first. "My name is Cheryl Nakayama. Bill and I saw you two sitting over here and we thought you'd be fun to talk to." She turns and motions to her friend. "This is Bill Davison. How are you folks this evening?"

Why do I feel like they're getting ready to sell us a set of encyclopedias?

"We're just fine?" I thought I knew what was coming, so what I just said was really more of a question than a statement.

Bill reaches out his hand to shake mine. "What's your name?" Reluctantly but out of habit, I shake his hand and return the introduction.

"I'm DH, and this is my girlfriend, Jesse." Jesse turns to look at me, a hint of a smile on her pretty pink lips. I think she liked it that I called her my girlfriend.

"So," Cheryl asks, "where are you two from?"

"Jesse's from here in The City, and I just came up a couple of days ago from Riverside."

"Where's Riverside? Is that in California?" Bill asks.

"It's down around LA — about 65 miles east of there. Pretty little town surrounded by orange groves."

"Nice!" Cheryl says, smiling broadly. In fact, she doesn't seem to be able to stop smiling. It's like her face is glued in that position. "Are you here visiting family?"

"No, just up for the sights."

"The City's pretty busy these days," Bill says, then his expression changes. "Lot's of lonely people up here right now." He reminds me of a funeral director.

Cheryl looks at Bill, puts on a similar mask and adds, "Yes, so many who seem to be lacking something in their lives."

Oh boy, here it comes.

"Jobs?" I smile sarcastically.

"Oh, that was clever." Cheryl goes back to the smile that sells encyclopedias.

"Who are you two?" Jesse asks bluntly. "Do you live here?" She's not going to play the game of smiles.

"Yes we do," Bill says. Now he's smiling the same smile as Cheryl. "We have an apartment not too far from here."

"So, you two are married," I say.

"Oh, no." Cheryl is quick to reply, and now her smile is saying "How absurd!" Out loud she says, "No, we've chosen not to marry."

So, they're not Mormons.

"We've chosen to live our lives not for ourselves but for spiritual endeavors," Bill explains.

Okay, now I'm getting it. I'll bet these guys are some of those Krishna people that hand out flowers and candy to people in airports.

"And why do you do that?" Jesse asks. Her question seems to put Bill and Cheryl into a slight state of confusion. It's not in their script?

"Well ... it's what we believe," Bill stammers. Smile is gone.

"It's a part of our faith," Cheryl adds with a little more composure than Bill.

Here we go. Here comes the punch line.

"And what faith is that?" I ask. Drum roll please ...

Cheryl looks quite happy to answer, "We are Nichiren Shoshu Buddhists. We follow the teachings of the great priest, Nichiren Daishonin, whose primary purpose was to teach the Three Great Secret Laws. We have a group that meets here in The City at our apartment every week."

OK ... that's not what I was expecting. I glance over at Jesse. She also looks puzzled, but not uncomfortable. She even has a slight smile on her face—although one thing I've learned about Jesse is that her smiles are often precursors to a very bizarre line of conversation.

True to form, she asks, "It's a spiritual group, but its laws are secret?"

"Some laws are so sacred and so powerful that they should not be shared with everyone. Only with those who are worthy to share," Cheryl replies solemnly.

"And how does one become worthy to share these laws?" I ask.

"If you attend only one of our meetings we'll tell you what the laws are. After that, you are welcome to join with us and learn the details of each law and how it applies in your own life. When you become proficient, then you can share them with others." Bill sounds like he's been doing this a long time.

I nod my head and look interested. Actually I am interested, but probably not for the reasons Bill might think. "Very interesting," I say.

Jesse looks at me like I had just gone crazy. She leans over and whispers, "It doesn't sound interesting to me."

"Would you two like to attend one of our meetings?" Cheryl asks. "We're having one tonight …" she pauses to check her watch. "… in about half an hour."

"It would take me an hour just to find your meeting place on the map. We don't have any idea where anything is here in this berg. We're just roaming around having fun together." I smile thinking that'll be the end of that.

But Bill is not at all put off. "No problem!" he says. "We can take you there. We have a car."

"You have a car in San Francisco?" I ask. "Well that makes two I've met so far."

"Yes we do — a brand new Mercedes," he declares proudly.

"Well, that's real nice of you, Bill," I tell him, "but Jesse and I are kinda tired. We're probably just gonna head home, grab a quick bite to eat and hit the hay. But thanks anyway." I smile, and I mean it — these two seem nice enough.

"Have you ever eaten real Japanese food?" Cheryl asks.

"No, I haven't."

"I haven't either," Jesse says. "Do you have it flown in daily?"

"You have a quick wit, young lady," says Bill, back in salesman mode. "No, but we make it fresh daily at our apartment. And as far as your being tired is concerned, our meetings are quite restful. We sit on the floor, eat and talk. That's all it is. If you get tired you can even stay the night. You'd have to sleep on the floor, but there are those who do that. They say the carpet is quite comfortable."

"Can you wait just a minute? I'd like to talk this over with Jesse and we'll get back to you." I get up, take Jesse's hand and lead her far enough away from the bench so that Cheryl and Bill can't hear us.

"What do you think, Jesse?"

"I think these guys are loony," she says.

"I'm not ready to rush to judgment yet, and how often do you get to ride in a brand new Mercedes, eat real Japanese food for free, and sleep on a plush carpet instead of Mandy's old ash-covered shag back at the house?"

"You have a point," she says. "But whatever they're selling, I ain't buying. If you think this is a legit Zen thing, it isn't. This is nothing more than a cult like all the other cults here in The City. There are hundreds of them. You have to watch out or they'll take your money and run."

"I say we go along with it. It might be fun." I smile encouragingly.

"If we can sit somewhere off to the side and I can hold you while the meeting's going on, I'll go. But I don't think I want to sleep there. I want to sleep somewhere alone with you."

"Then that's exactly the way it's going to be."

9 PM Nichiren Shoshu Buddhist Meeting

We told Cheryl and Bill that we'd go with them to their little Buddhist meeting, but we wouldn't make any promises about joining up or even hanging around for long. They laughed and Cheryl told us, "We're used to rejection. We don't mind. At least we'll have given you a nutritious meal, and maybe even planted a seed of goodness in your hearts."

How can you not like people like that? They're both sweet as sap running down a tree trunk, but as we were walking the couple of blocks to where their car was, Jesse whispered to me, "This could be a trap you know. These people could be kidnapping us." That's what Angie said that morning when she and I had breakfast in the deserted Chinese place. What's with these San Francisco girls and their fear of being kidnapped by Orientals?

We finally came around a corner, and there next to the curb was a brand new, shiny black Mercedes. What a sweet looking ride. "Look at that!" I whispered to Jesse. "If they kidnap us, it'll have been worth it for a ride in that baby." She gave me a look that left no question as to what she thought of that statement.

Regardless of what these guys' spiritual beliefs have to offer, I don't think Jesse needs any of it. She could write a book and start her own cult; these people would just get in her way. In fact, I'll bet she'd wind up converting them.

It didn't take us long to get to where we were going. The car pulled up to the curb in front of a swanky looking apartment building. I took a minute to look around as we stepped out.

"Wow! A new Mercedes and a place like this? Your little group must have a bit of cash saved up. This looks pretty posh to me."

"Cheryl owns this apartment complex," Bill said. "She lets our group have one of the larger apartments rent free. The Mercedes is hers, too. I just do the driving."

I turn to Cheryl. "Must be nice," I say.

She smiles like a satisfied cat. "It is. It's very nice, and it's all the result of my participation in the Nichiren Shoshu faith."

Jesse is still not buying it. "I don't get it," she says. "How can a belief in God, or a religion have anything to do with your prosperity?"

"We don't teach belief in God. You don't have to have belief in a God to follow the teachings of Buddhism. We have no rules. We merely adhere to certain principles."

"So you're atheists?"

"Some are, some aren't. It's not a requirement to believe in God."

"Well, that might be a problem 'cause I believe in God." Jesse is not giving up. "I don't believe in religion—that hasn't done much good for anything—but I do believe that there's a Creator God up there somewhere who made all this stuff down here and keeps an eye on it."

"You can believe that if you wish, Jesse," Bill says. "We never attempt to remove beliefs from people, just to add clarifications to them."

"Actually, our rules and principles might just reinforce your personal beliefs." Cheryl says.

"We'll see." Jesse looks skeptical.

I, too, am skeptical. I also believe in God in pretty much the way Jesse just described her belief. But we've come this far and I'm up for some Japanese food. Right now, it's all about the food for me.

We enter through the big glass doors into a lobby that makes the building seem more like a hotel than an apartment complex. The lobby is huge. Three crystal chandeliers the size of Volkswagens hang from the ceiling and there are potted plants the size of trees scattered around. One of those chandeliers—let alone, all three—must have cost more than everything my family owns. This building must be worth a fortune. In the wall opposite the entrance are a couple of elevators. Two attendants—a cute little redheaded girl and a guy who looks like he ought to be giving lessons at the local Gold's Gym—man a reception desk next to them. The desk and all the other woodwork in the lobby look like mahogany.

The attendants immediately recognize Cheryl, the owner of the building and their boss, and come to attention and Cheryl acknowledges them with a smile. The redheaded girl goes to the elevator, pushes a button to open the door, and salutes us as we enter. She follows us into the elevator and takes us up to the fifth floor. We exit the elevator and walk down the hall, leaving the attendant behind.

The opulence of the lobby is carried through to the corridor. It's so plush that I'd be happy to sleep out in the hall any night of the week; I can't imagine what the apartments are like. The distance between the doors to the units suggests that the apartments must be huge—maybe thousands of square feet. They are made from the same wood—a glowing, deep sienna-red mahogany—as the desk and other furnishings in the lobby. Each one is a seven-foot tall work of art, uniquely and elaborately carved with a stylized oriental figure in the center.

When we reach the last door, Cheryl opens it and invites us in. I don't think we have any reason to fear being kidnapped by these people. The place is magnificent, as I had expected based on the lobby and the hallway. It is also filled with—you guessed it—Buddhists: male and female, young and old. They are all seated on the floor and are chanting something that I can't quite make out.

"It's our principle mantra," Bill explains when I ask him what it is. "The words, Nam Myoho Renge Kyo, are the Japanese pronunciation of a blend of Sanskrit and Chinese words that mean, 'Devotion to the Mystic Law of the Lotus Sutra. The chanting has many purposes that you'll discover as you move along in your exploration of our faith."

"We have very few doctrines or dogmas," Cheryl clarifies. "The one thing we all do share in common is the practice of chanting these words."

"So, they're like a magic spell?" Jesse asks.

"No, not magic. They're just words that are tuned to certain frequencies in this universe, so that when you repeat them as a chant you become more attuned to the universe."

Jesse is still not sold on this Buddhist stuff. "I wasn't aware that I was out of tune with anything."

Bill smiles as he gears up for the hard sell. "You're not out of tune with anything, Jesse. But sometimes everyone has a bad day, or an emotional problem, or something that sets them off. This chanting we do merely helps to ease tensions and bring a little relief."

Well said, Bill. His explanation takes a little off the edge of Jesse's skepticism, but neither Jesse nor I are swallowing the whole thing. I've had some experience with other religions. I've actually studied quite a few, and I find them all to be pretty much the same. Each one has a core belief that makes everybody feel good when they join up, but just when you get comfortable with the rituals and whatnot, somebody brings out the BOOK—that five-inch-thick book of rules and regulations you must follow in order to be a part of the club. Every religion on this planet has its own rules and regulations, its own rituals and costumes, and they fight with each other because one BOOK cover is a little bit different from the other BOOK cover, even though the rules and regulations are pretty much the same on the inside. That's the biggest difference — the cover. That, and the silly costumes they come up with — black shirts with a little white square in the center at the top; red robes with a funny little red cap; white and gold robes with a cone-shaped hat; orange robes and a bald head. For crying out loud, why do you have to wear a costume to get into heaven? It ain't a costume party up there.

The chanting is over now and the people are rising up from where they were seated on the thick plush carpet. When we came in, we had left our shoes in the tiled entry along with a dozen or so other pairs. The carpet throughout the rest of the apartment is so thick that my toes are almost buried.

Cheryl catches the eye of a young woman across the room and motions to her to join us. Wow! What a knockout. She's about five feet ten inches tall, full figured, and has long reddish hair flowing down her back. She is wearing a red and white striped mini dress cut low in the front and showing mucho cleavage. Not exactly what I'd expect to find at a Buddhist meeting, and not exactly the outfit to be worn while kneeling or sitting cross-legged on the floor.

"Jesse and DH, I want you to meet Marian." The lovely Marian reaches out to shake hands with us and Cheryl continues the introduction. "We met them down on Van Ness and invited them to our meeting tonight. They were gracious enough to agree to come."

How could I have been so suspicious of these people? They're genuinely nice; everyone even looks nice. There isn't a hippie in the crowd, and the smell is of Marian's lovely perfume rather than of body odor — or worse. And there isn't even the hint of smoke, cigarette or otherwise. What a big difference there is between this place and Hippie Haven. If it wasn't for the fact that I am not the slightest bit interested in what they have to offer, I just might get used to this place. Don't get me wrong, I've studied Buddhism and some of it, especially Zen, makes some sense. What they are doing here seems to be kinda like Zen, but it's not—it's a whole 'nother ball game. It will take more than a group of happy chanters to convince me.

"I'm so pleased to meet you two." Marian's smile could knock a man out at fifty feet. I swear I saw one of those little cartoon sparkles wink off her perfect white teeth. "I suppose Cheryl and Bill have told you all about us," she continues.

"Marian is our group leader," Bill informs us.

"Yes, I believe they covered it pretty well." I smile back at Marian.

"What did you think of our chanting, Jesse?"

"I found it … interesting. It had a pleasant tone to it." Jesse's response is wary but polite.

"That's the frequency tuning I told you about," Bill says.

"Maybe you'll join us later for our midnight chant? It only lasts about ten minutes and it's quite lovely," Marian says.

"I'm not sure we'll be here that long." Jeez … Midnight. I'm already worn out from two days of walking all over the city.

"As luck would have it, you're just in time for our evening meal," Cheryl says. "It always follows the evening meditation and chant."

"That must be what I've been smelling since I walked in. It does smell good," I said.

"Tonight we're having miso soup, sushi, a lovely vegetable salad, and some boiled rice," Bill says. "It's very tasty and there's plenty of it. We serve it buffet style in the dining room. Follow me." And we do.

This place just keeps getting better. The dining room is next to the kitchen. A large double door stands open giving a clear view from one room into the next. The kitchen is huge—big enough for an entire hotel, not just one apartment—and there is a full uniformed staff preparing the evening meal.

"The staff you see in the kitchen isn't employed by the apartment complex." Cheryl must have been reading my mind. "They are members of this group doing a sacrificial work detail. It's all part of our service program."

"What's the service program?"

"We teach classes and hold week-long workshops here. We charge a fee for those and people who can't afford to pay can work it off by doing service—the cooking, housecleaning, et cetera," she explains.

"That's pretty neat. So this isn't like some of the other cults that are just in it for the money."

Bill is quick to respond. "Oh no. First of all, we don't see ourselves as a cult; we're a part of the Buddhist faith which is a recognized religion. Second, we don't need the money. I'm the only salaried person here and we don't pay rent—Cheryl owns the building and donates the space—so our needs are few. Cheryl has all the money in the world, so she doesn't require anything. In fact, no one here tonight is paying anything. This is our weekly gathering for group meditation and chanting, discussion, and socializing—those are always free and open, even the food, most of which is donated by Cheryl as well. There is a fee for our workshops and special classes, but they are minimal, only just enough to cover material costs.

"You keep saying Buddhist faith, but if you don't believe in God, then who or what do you have faith in?" Jesse asks.

"That's a great question, Jesse," Bill says. "We use the word faith more in a generic sense. To us, it just means believing what we teach."

"But we do have faith in many things," Marian says. "We have faith in the future, in science, in ourselves … even in you two, DH and Jesse."

"You have faith in us?" I ask. "What for? What about?"

Marian smiles at us again and says, "Well, personally, I have faith that you'll enjoy yourself here tonight, and that regardless of whether you join our group or not, you're going to go back home with a brand new understanding of so-called cults like this one."

She might be right.

People are starting to line up to fill their plates at the buffet tables along the side of the dining room, so we join them. There is a dazzling assortment of Japanese food, deserts, and drinks. Who knows what I'll discover when I get over there to fill up my plate. I'm glad I didn't eat a lot at the Chinese restaurant earlier.

Four long, low, shiny black tables are arranged in a square in the middle of the room. There are pillows on the floor to sit on around the outside of the square so that everyone can see everyone else while we eat. The center of the square contains four statues of Buddha sitting shoulder to shoulder, each one facing a table. There is a little fountain trickling gently in front of each statue. It's really quite nice.

10:30 PM Buddhist Apartment Living Room

Dinner was over at about ten o'clock, and the next chanting session doesn't start until midnight. Cheryl said that the time in between is free time. Some people take a nap in one of the bedrooms, and some go out into the city for a drink or just to explore. Most sit around in the living room and talk about stuff.

"We try to steer clear of politics," Bill said. "That always leads to arguments and we try to avoid conflict of every nature here." I'm all for that.

I had the pleasure of sitting between Jesse and Marian during dinner. Marian started out kneeling in the traditional Japanese fashion, but it wasn't long before she shifted to Indian style—quite a challenge for her in that mini dress, and quite a challenge to me as I could not help but look. She kept giving me sideways glances throughout the meal, and wriggling her butt, which made her dress ride up even higher on her thighs. Pretty soon a full view of her white panties pushed up into her crotch was revealed. I was feeling increasingly uneasy—seriously. At one point she picked up one of her sushi roll things. She looked at me and slowly took a bite off the end, making a point of licking the piece that remained in her hand. She held the piece out toward my mouth, saying that I should try it as it was quite delicious and different from the sushi in restaurants. I thought it odd that she was sharing hers with me, since I had one just like it on my own plate, but I took a bite anyway, not wanting to cause a problem. After I took my bite she brought it back to her own mouth and ate the remaining part. Under any other circumstances I would swear it was a come on. We just shared spit on that sushi thing with her crotch in full view, and she was the one that started it. Then she smiled and said, "You can have some more if you want." Only there wasn't any more sushi on her plate.

I told her I was getting pretty full, and I turned to see if Jesse had seen all that sushi sharing, but she was in a deep conversation with Cheryl, who was seated on her other side. I was glad, 'cause I didn't want Jesse to think that I was flirting with Marian, 'cause I wasn't.

We finished eating, and people began to leave the table. Marian seemed to make a special effort to rise from her seat slowly, first unfolding her legs and carefully positioning her feet, then moving her derriére close to my face as she got up. She stood over me as I started to rise, smiled down at me seductively, and walked slowly into the living room. I had not imagined it—she was coming on to me.

I helped Jesse up and we, too, headed for the living room. We made our way over to a corner on the far side where we made ourselves comfortable on the plush carpet, the solid wall of the room behind us, and a glass wall on our right. The glass wall extends the entire length of the apartment and is made of sliding glass panels with nearly invisible seams so that you can't tell that it's a door. Outside is a deck that also extends the length of the apartment overlooking the city.

After a few minutes of trying to catch up in my journal, I find my gaze pulled toward the scene outside the window. "What a view," I said.

"Yes," Jesse responded. "If we were alone out there on the deck it would be quite romantic."

"Can't we be romantic in here?"

"With all these bead counters belching their sushi breath everywhere?"

All the Buddhists have a little round ring of beads that they carry in their pocket or wear on their wrists. I'm not sure what it means, but they seem to fiddle with them constantly, regardless of whatever else they're doing.

"It is a bit different here, I'll give you that."

"It's too sterile," she said "Not that I love the way Hippie Haven looks or smells, but I'm afraid to touch anything in here."

I have to agree with her. The place is filled with what could pass for museum pieces, all of them oriental. There are Japanese statues of a religious sort that I am not familiar with, and a bunch of Buddhas, including one in the corner across the room that must be eight feet tall. Even the furniture looks like art. The two black couches are decorated all over with Japanese drawings done in white — they look like originals done by hand. Arranged around the room are three perfectly polished glass coffee tables with nothing on them, not even a fingerprint. Jesse is right; the place is so perfect and everything is so nice that it is a bit uncomfortable. Sterile is a good word for it.

"I feel like I'm in the lobby of a hotel," she said.

"Do you want to go?" I asked.

"Do we need to stay? I mean, would it be impolite if we leave?"

"We never promised them we'd stay."

"Where would we go? It's getting close to eleven o'clock."

"Back to Mandy's?"

"I don't want to go back to Mandy's. I want to be alone with you."

"Just tell me where you want to go and we'll go there."

"I do have one idea," she said.

"Okay."

"There's another park here in The City, and it's not far from here. In fact, it's near Mandy's place so if we decide to, we can always head there from the park and be there in just minutes."

"Is this another park that is special to you?"

"It will be after tonight." She smiled for the first time since we got here.

"Oh?" I smiled with anticipation.

"Lafayette Park was a special park because I always went there alone to get away from people. It was my island of refuge. But this one can be Our Park. I've only been there a couple of times. It's small and sits up on a hill. Actually, the whole park is a hill, I think. It's very secluded and covered in trees. Since it's late and already dark, I doubt anyone will see us up there."

"There's a big moon tonight," I said.

"That'll be good for us. It's very dark there and the trees are really thick, but I'll bet we can find a spot where we can see the moon."

"Let's do it."

We stand up, but before we can start toward the door, Marian walked over.

She smiled at me and said, "You really have to come out on the landing and take a look at the view. It's glorious!"

"Well, we were just getting ready to leave," I told her. I stepped closer to Jesse to make it clear that we are together.

"It'll only take a few minutes," Marian said. "You won't regret it." She directed her last statement at me along with another big smile.

I looked at Jesse and she gave a slight nod to let me know it's okay, but I can tell by the look on her face we'd better not tarry out on the landing. She's ready to make tracks for the park.

Suddenly, the glass panel in the wall beside us started to slide open. Jesse and I jumped a little, startled, but Marian is laughing and pointing across the room. Bill is standing over there laughing, his finger on one of the many buttons on a control panel. Clever.

Marian, Jesse, and I went through the opening and across the balcony to the railing at the outer edge where we held on tight, as it was a long drop to the street below. The real sight, though, was beyond the drop. Marian wasn't kidding — it was glorious. Beyond the railing, The City was laid out in all its nighttime splendor, and beyond that, the harbor lights, and the lights of boats and ships sparkled on the dark waters of the bay. It was a sight no artist could paint. It was more than a scene; it was a feeling. An artist would have to be able to feel it all and then paint that feeling. There's nothing like a San Francisco night—nothing. This has to be the most beautiful city in the world. I could have stood out there all night until the sun came up.

"It's beautiful isn't it?" Marian said.

"It certainly is," I agree.

"I never get tired of it," she continued, "and it never changes. I've been coming out here for years and it doesn't make any difference what day it is or what year it is, it always takes my breath away."

"It's something alright."

Marian turned to look straight at me. "It's one of the most romantic spots in The City," she said softly.

"San Francisco is a romantic town," Jesse said as she took hold of my right hand. There was a definite edge to her voice.

"I've actually slept out on this landing several times," Marian said while securing my left hand.

I can't believe it. Both of the girls have latched onto me at the same time. It's like a scene from a movie. This is not good. There has to be something about this crazy town, something in the air that causes people to go bonkers with the romance stuff. I'm just a kid, for crying out loud, and girls are coming onto me like I look like I know what I'm doing!

"Can you feel the energy in the night air?" Marian asked softly.

What I can feel is Marian pushing herself closer to me—real close—and kind of squirming around a little. Then shes placed my left hand, which is still firmly in the grip of her right, on her bottom—her naked bottom. All that wriggling must have been to get her miniskirt up around her waist.

"Can you feel it?" she repeated herself, this time whispering in my ear.

"Um … yeah … I can feel it."

Just then a voice from the living room came sailing out through the night air like a rescuing angel on golden wings. "Hello? Hello out there. Is that you, DH and Jesse?"

It's Bill. Good old Bill. Thank heaven for Bill.

Bill's presence made it much easier to leave than I thought it was going be. We stopped in the entry to get our shoes. When I looked up, Marian was there, too, looking ready to leave. The midnight chant is about to start, and the group leader is leaving? Not a good advertisement for the cult.

Jesse and I thank Marian for all the food and the interesting evening, and we tell her that we'd think about coming back again to try out a chant or two. Marian smiled at that, reached into her pocket, and pulled out a business card. "I do hope you decide to come back," she says. Then she handed it to me, but not before kissing the back of it, leaving a lipstick lip print. "Call me any time and I'll make sure you get a royal treatment."

"That Marian vamp was coming on to you," Jesse said when we were in the hall. She seemed more than a little irritated.

"Nonsense, I'm just a kid. A woman like that wouldn't come on to a poor little boy like me. I think she was just being nice." I didn't mention what Marian had done during dinner or out on the landing.

"I don't think so," Jesse said. She paused for a few moments before adding, "Would you like to make love with an older woman like that?"

"What?"

"She looks like a movie star, she's got money …"

"Jesse …" I grasped her shoulders and turned her around to face me. I look her right in her eyes and say, "Close your eyes."

"Why?"

"Just do it."

She closed her eyes. I took her left hand and lifted it up over her head. "Hold that there," I said. Then I took her head gently in my hands, turned it to the left and then directed it down a bit.

"What are you doing?" she asked with her eyes still closed.

"What do you smell? Take a deep long sniff."

"All I can smell is my stinky old armpit."

"Right."

"So?

"THAT is the reason I would never leave you for Marian. No matter what she did, no matter how hard she tried, Marian could never produce that smell." I grinned.

"I ought to slap you," Jesse said as she quickly lowered her arm.

So here we are, sitting under a streetlamp at the edge of Buena Vista Park. We stopped here where the light is good so that I could catch up my journal while everything is still fresh in my mind. I'm all caught up now, and we are rested and ready for the climb up the steep path to the top of the hill.

At the Top of the Hill in Buena Vista Park

We were both winded when we got up here because we were full from eating all that Japanese food, but the walk in the moonlight was lovely. Our seat on the log of a tree that died and fell to the ground many years ago gives us a complete view of one of the nicer neighborhoods in San Francisco. The air has cooled a bit and the mugginess has disappeared.

Although the full moon makes it bright enough to write in my journal, the shadows in the surrounding trees are too dark to make out details. The park must be gorgeous in the daytime. The atmosphere seems almost primeval, and some places are distinctly eerie, giving me a feeling kind of like the feeling you might get in a haunted house.

"Do you feel that, Jesse?"

"You mean the feeling that someone's watching us?"

"Exactly." I'm whispering just in case it's true.

"The park is completely deserted," she says. "The police patrol this area because a lot of rich people live down there in that neighborhood. They try to keep vagrants out of here after dark. We got lucky. We got in without being noticed."

"It's weird. I sure feel something."

"You may be feeling the ghosts that roam the park."

"What?"

"They say it really is haunted. There are supposed to be some Gold Rush pioneers buried up here somewhere, and it's said that they walk the place at night, scaring anyone who dares come up the hill."

"You're kidding me."

"No, I'm not. Someone once told me that there are some old tombstones up here somewhere, but I've never found them."

"So you brought me to a haunted park? Great."

"Are you afraid?" She grins at me. I can see the moonlight reflecting off her wet teeth.

"No, I'm not afraid. Not as long as I have you here to protect me."

"Silly thing. I'll protect you." She giggles. Man, she sounds cute when she giggles.

"I'm not sure I'm too happy about the old dead pioneers watching us all night though."

"Aww, come on. Let's give the old guys something to look at."

Jesse stands up and quickly pulls her tank top down to free her breasts. She spreads her arms wide and starts shaking her breasts back and forth saying, "Come on you old geezers! Look all you want!"

I just sit on the log and watch. I've never seen a more seductive sight.

It's getting too dark to write now, so I'm gonna close this off and bring it up to date tomorrow morning. Besides, there are a couple of things I need to attend to right away.

Day Six

Last Night in Buena Vista Park

We stayed awake for quite some time chatting about things in general, and doing all the other things a guy and girl would do when the girl is sitting topless next to him, but it was after we had lain down and tried to go to sleep that stuff really started to happen.

All I can figure is that our voices must have been carried on the still, clear night air to the neighborhood surrounding the hilltop park. At any rate, it wasn't long before we heard other voices coming toward us. Apparently someone had called the police. We didn't really know what to do. If there was a fine for trespassing on city property after a certain hour, neither one of us could pay it. We doubted that they would arrest us for such a simple thing, but we didn't really know what to expect, so we hid in the bushes and hoped we wouldn't be discovered.

As the policemen came closer, we could make out their words quite clearly. It sounded like there were at least a half dozen of them making their way up here from several directions. Fantastic! These guys won't arrest all the people for breaking serious laws during these hippie fests up here—vandalizing cars, smoking pot, public nudity, theft, fist fights, drug overdoses—but they'll send half the force out to capture a couple of silly teenagers kissing in the woods. How professional is that?

We had brought nothing with us and we hadn't lit a fire; even the spot where we were going to sleep was just soft grass, so there was no evidence that anyone had been camping up here. The only thing that could happen is that the police would accidentally stumble over us as we crouched in a patch of scratchy bushes.

I was wearing Levis, so I was not too uncomfortable, but Jesse was still wearing the same short skirt she'd been wearing for the past couple of days.

"I think a spider crawled into my butt," she whispered.

"You're kidding," I whispered back.

"No, I can feel it crawling around down there."

"Shush." The police were getting closer. "I'll see if I can get it out."

Reaching under her dress, my hand went looking for the spider. My search was methodical and quite thorough, but I didn't find the spider.

"He must have jumped off," I said.

Jesse giggled. "I was just kidding. There wasn't any spider."

"Hush." I had to stifle my own chortle. "We're gonna get caught."

The policemen were closer and we could now hear their conversation clearly as they wandered around looking for us. They seemed to be sticking to the paths and not venturing much into the brush, so we weren't too worried about getting caught. The closest they came to us was about twenty feet.

"You know this place is haunted," said one cop to his partner.

"I've heard that, but you don't believe in ghosts do you?" replied the partner.

"I don't know," Cop One said. "There might be something to it."

"Well, I don't believe in them," said Cop Two. "And if we do see any, don't worry, I'll protect your sorry ass."

"Ha Ha … big man," said Cop One.

I decided to try a little experiment to get the cops away from us. I picked up a couple of small rocks, and I threw one into the bushes on the other side of the little clearing where we had spent the evening.

"What the hell was that?" Cop One asked.

"I don't know," Cop Two replied.

Then I threw the other rock behind the cops and into another patch of brush.

"That came from over there," Cop One pointed.

"I heard it," Cop Two said. "It's probably just nuts fallin' off the trees."

"These trees don't have nuts," Cop One replied.

"Neither do you, Bailey!" Cop two laughed.

"Yeah, real funny. You wouldn't laugh if some glowing specter jumped outta the bushes on top of you."

"That all depends upon whether or not the specter was male or female," Cop Two said.

Just then two more cops came into the clearing.

"Anything up here?" Cop Three asked.

"Just a bunch of ghosts, but Bailey's got 'em covered," Cop Two said with a laugh.

"Is that right, Bailey?" Cop Three asked. "You got the ghosts covered?" All the cops but Bailey laughed.

I threw three more pebbles behind the four cops. It made a pretty good rustle.

"What was that?" Cops Two and Three said at the same time.

"Maybe it's the ghost," Cop One said sarcastically. "I told you there's somethin' up here."

"Well, either there really is a ghost, or it's just some freak of nature." Cop Four said. "It don't matter. Let's get outta here. I'm thinkin' the lady who called us probably had a little too much to drink tonight. Come on, we got better things to do."

Jesse and I stayed in the bushes and listened while the cops headed down the hill. We finally came out of hiding when we heard their cruisers pull away. The whole episode had taken about an hour and a half, so it was close to 3 AM when we lay back down on the grass again. We were careful to speak only in whispers after that just in case any little old ladies still had their ears tuned in our direction.

"Well, that was fun," I said.

"Yes it was, and we learned a new game that might come in handy some day."

"You mean tossing pebbles to confuse the cops?"

She grinned at me. "I mean Playing Spider."

The Next Morning

We've been awake for a while discussing our plans for the day—sort of. I have to leave tomorrow and fly back to Riverside. Jesse's not too happy about that, and I don't want to talk about it either, so we've both been pretty quiet.

I'm sitting on the ground with my back against a tree and my knees up. Jesse is sitting on the ground next to me, hugging my legs and resting her chin on my left knee. I've sorta been catching up on my writing, but mostly just staring out into space—looking out at the cityscape below the hill. It really is beautiful. I'm gonna miss that part of The City, the beauty part, but I don't think I'll miss the derelict part.

"I have to pee," Jesse says. She stands up, walks a few feet away, raises her skirt, and squats down. She's barefoot and her pee splatters all over her feet. She doesn't seem to care.

"You should put your shoes back on," I tell her. "We should probably head on out."

"Out to where?"

"I'd kinda like to walk around town a bit more today, maybe pick up some souvenirs to take back with me."

"Are you sure you want to go back?" she asks, still squatting, her head down.

"It's not a matter of wanting. It's a matter of necessity. There's a big difference. If I had my way, I'd rather just lay back down with you right here, stare into your eyes, go to sleep and never wake up again."

Jesse looks up at me. She cocks her head first to the right and then to the left. She tries to speak, but the words don't come out.

"Jesse … you know if I could I'd stay here with you I would. Or I'd take you with me if I thought I could hide you away in my room where no one would find you."

"What would they do if they found me?"

"I don't know, but I don't think they'd like it."

"Do you love me?"

"Of course I do." I walk over to her, squat down in front of her, and kiss her on her forehead.

"But are you in love with me?"

"Jesse, how long have we known each other?"

"I don't know. Maybe for eternity."

"I mean in the here and now. We've known each other for three days. How can you be in love with anyone after having known them for only three days?"

"I'm in love with you." She touches my cheek.

"But you hardly know me. You know virtually nothing about me. I may be a fun guy to spend time with, but you might not like me at all if you really got to know me."

"All I have to do is look into you and I know you. I love what I see. I see you in color," she says softly.

"I know you do … and I can't deny that means something … but …"

"But I still can't go with you tomorrow."

I stand up, take her hand, and pull her up. "Let's not ruin what time we have left. Come on, let's go do a little shopping and see what this day brings."

So off we go—down the hill to the neighborhood below, over a block, and we're back on Haight Street. It's pretty quiet this morning, like the first day we got here. Nothing much seems to be going on. I'm not sure where to go to find something really good to take back with me. There are a ton of head shops in this neighborhood, but I don't want anything associated with the drug culture—that's not what I want to remember about this trip. I just want something that'll reflect this time and place in history, and that will also be useful to me somehow.

"I know a little store back on Market Street. I think they'll have what you want," Jesse says. "We'll have to go around the park and head back south to get there though."

"Sounds good to me."

The Hippie Store on Market Street

We walked down Haight until we hit Castro, turned right, and in no time we were on Market Street. Market Street's probably one of the most well-known streets in The City. They had a big anti-war parade here back in April that pretty well closed it down. It's a wide street, so there must have been quite a crowd. The march was a big deal, albeit a bit unruly. They had tons of cops out on motorcycles and even on horses. I wonder about horses in crowds like that. They must be pretty well trained not to buck and bolt with all the noise going on. I wasn't there, but I imagine it was probably a lot like any other day here now, especially in the Haight. The crowds are massive and sometimes out of control; that's what the cops are for I guess, although I have yet to see anyone get arrested. Anti-war posters are a common sight on the streets and in the parks, and the other day on Haight Street Jesse and I saw a semi-naked guy who'd crucified himself on a couple of boards put together like a cross. His arms were outstretched on the cross piece, but instead of being nailed to it, his wrists were tied in place. He just walked around the Haight like that. He'd tacked a big poster to the back of his cross that said, "BAN WAR! LOCK UP LBJ!" He was pretty ineffective though, because his knots kept coming undone from his hands (which were also tied to the sign) and the cross bounced around on his back which made his little poster flop around so much that you couldn't read it unless it stopped flopping and it was turned the right way out. He looked silly trying to keep the sign right side up. He'd fix it, then he'd walk a few feet and it would flop over again, then he'd fix it again and walk another few feet and there it went again, flopping over. He finally got mad, tore the sign off, threw it on the ground, leaned the cross up next to a building and walked away.

There were no marches, no posters, and no nitwits out today; Just the obligatory cops sitting on motorcycles here and there. They all seem friendly enough.

"Can you read their name badges, Jesse? I wonder if Bailey from last night is out here."

"If we find him we ought to ask him if he's afraid of ghosts," she says.

"That might not be a good idea. It sounded like his buddies were picking on him and he might not be in a very good mood."

Cops aren't bad people; I like cops. I know some cops back home and count about a half dozen among my personal friends. They're all good guys and they have a tough job that nobody else is willing to do. The ones in Riverside do seem to be more "with it" than the cops up here—more like a part of the community rather than just referees. Some of these guys here don't act like they're too concerned with enforcing the laws. They let a lot of stuff slide and then they laugh about it. It's almost as if they've become calloused to the constant abuse of the law that seems to be happening here in San Francisco with the recent invasion. I sense a feeling of indifference among them, almost resentment, although I don't know what it is they might be resenting. They get paid to do the job, and they should be doing it, even though it might be a bit overwhelming at times. Dealing with hundreds of thousands of people, and most of them antagonistic to any type of authority, law enforcement included, has to be tough. In a way I feel kinda sorry for the cops. I doubt they asked for all this when they signed up for the job. I don't think anybody saw it coming.

Jesse tugs at my sleeve and points. "Up here on the left," she says.

I can see the sign—THE CITY TIDE in large red letters. It's not a very big place, but it looks like it might be packed to the gills with all kinds of cool hippie stuff.

Jesse and I walk in and notice that although the store is narrow, it goes back quite a ways, and it really is packed full of stuff. It would take days to search through everything. I can see three or four people who look like they might work here. One, a skinny middle aged man with long, stringy black hair and really bad teeth, is sitting at a cash register to the right as we walk through the front door. A blonde girl wearing what appears to be a man's white dress shirt and a pair of cutoff jeans, is sorting stock in one of the big bins on the left. Her shirt is completely unbuttoned in front allowing her breasts to flop around freely as she scoops up little rubber animals, separates them by species, and replaces them in the bins. Another girl with short brunette hair is sweeping the floor near the middle of the store. There is a Doors song being piped in from somewhere and she's dancing and singing along while she sweeps.

I look around. So much stuff.

"If you can't find it here, you won't find it anywhere," Jesse says. "But most of the good stuff is in the back. The stuff up front is for the tourists."

She leads me down the center aisle about two-thirds the length of the store, until will find ourselves in an area that does indeed look promising. There are racks of clothes, belts, jackets, ties … Hmmm, ties. There's an idea.

"Need some help?" Another girl with brunette hair—shoulder length this time—appears from out of nowhere.

I return her smile. "I'm just looking. I'm from out of town and I thought I'd find something nice to take back home with me, just so I could remember the trip."

"Well, all of the clothes you see back here are handmade in San Francisco by local people. The stuff up front I can't guarantee. Are you thinking about a shirt? A hat?"

Jesse smiles and points to a display. "I saw him ogling those ties over there."

"Those are my favorites," the brunette says. "Take a look."

Jesse and I walk over and start going through the dozens of ties of every color, pattern, and shape. I'm not too turned on by tie-dye, of which there are plenty, but I kinda like the paisley prints—nothing says "hippie" like paisley—and these ties are actually quite well made. I thought they'd have been manufactured en masse by machines, or kids in India, just so there'd be enough to go around with all the hoards of people flooding into San Francisco, but that's not the case.

Two ties catch my eye; one is dark blue with pink and purple paisley designs all over it, and the other is bright red with green and blue designs. I'm not sure which one I like best.

Jesse hands me a tie she found. "Check this one out," she says.

The tie she picked out is a pale yellow or cream color, and the paisley design is done in brighter yellow, blue, and rust-red. It's really very different and looks rather classy. It's not as gaudy as the others, nor as bright, and the material is good quality—I'm guessing cotton—not that shiny, in-your-face material most ties are made of.

"I love this!" I say as I take it from her. I turn to the brunette and ask, "Where did this one come from? It doesn't have label on the back."

She smiled and said proudly, "I made it, and I guarantee the quality. I don't make very many, but when I do, I put everything into it."

"That's why it looks so nice. It's very well made, and quite pretty," I tell her. "Good eye, Jesse."

"Would you like to buy it?" the girl asks.

"Yes, I would. So it's a real product of this hippie scene up here, not a cheap deal from India or Japan?" I asked, just wanting to make sure I don't go home with something from Sears Roebuck.

"It's as real as it gets," she says. "I've lived here for many years, over on Haight. I make clothes for a living. If you knew what to look for, you would find my shirts and ties on a lot of people out there in the street. George Harrison was in not too long ago and bought several things I made."

"Go on! George Harrison? Really?"

"Yep. And one of the shirts he bought is made out of the same fabric this tie was cut from."

"You're kidding! I mean, you don't have to lie to me. You've already got a sale."

"That's why you know I'm not lying." She grinned. "He really did. He bought a shirt and he took what was left of the bolt of fabric with him so that nobody else could copy the shirt. If I hadn't already cut this tie out before he came in, you wouldn't be buying it now."

I turn to Jesse. "How cool is that?" I say.

"Pretty cool," she replies, not looking too impressed, but then things are not her thing.

"Well, I honestly wasn't expecting this. Jesse, you're magic." I smile at her.

She returns my smile and says, "Yes I am. Are you sure you don't want to take me back with you tomorrow?" My smile fades a bit.

"Where are you from?" the brunette asks.

"Riverside," I tell her, glad to have an excuse to look somewhere else. "Down south, about sixty-five miles east of LA."

"I've never been to LA," she says. "Always wanted to go there, though."

"It's different from here, that's for sure."

"How so?"

"It's a lot bigger. You could set this city down in the middle of LA and it wouldn't make a dint."

"Wow!" I can almost see her mind wrestling with that image. "So, are you guys having these big crowds down there like we're having up here?"

"Not really. There are plenty of hippie wannabes down there, but they haven't blown it out of proportion like you guys have up here. I think there's a lot more stuff down south to keep their minds occupied—the beach, Disneyland, Knott's Berry Farm. It's also a lot more spread out, and there's no really central place for people to gather like Golden Gate Park up here."

She slowly shakes her head and says, "Yeah, it's crazy here man. Part of it's good, but part of it's bad. You know? My business is booming here now, but shoplifting has become a big problem since these homeless kids all moved in. It never used to be, but now I get lifted about the same amount of stuff as I sell."

"You're kidding."

Then Jesse quietly says, "It's all a part of the darkness."

"The what?" The brunette looks puzzled.

"Jesse has a theory about this hippie phenomenon," I explain. "Actually, it's more of an intuitive prophecy. She says that underlying all the peace and love stuff, there's a certain element of darkness controlling everything from the shadows."

"You mean like good and evil? You mean the devil's behind it?"

"I never mentioned the devil," Jesse says. "Just the darkness."

The girl is almost frowning now in an effort to comprehend what Jesse is saying. "Are you saying the hippies are all evil?" she asks. Then her face brightens and she is smiling again. "By the way, my name is Katya." She reaches out to shake hands, Jesse's first, then mine.

"Pretty name, Katya. I'm DH, and this is Jesse. Jesse lives here, over on Haight."

"Thanks, it's a Russian name. It's the short form of Yekaterina, but Katya to you guys." She grins. "And Jesse's a local huh? We locals are getting more rare with every passing day. Hey, if you guys have a little time, why don't we catch a bite to eat together? Jerry up there can watch the store."

"Sounds good to me," I say. I look at Jesse and she nods her head in the affirmative. I think she's glad that the subject was gracefully changed.

"Great!" Katya says. "I'm famished."

"So you own this place?" I ask.

"I do. I have for several years. My parents owned it before they passed away, and they left it to me. They used to operate a fabric store in here. When they died I decided to jazz it up a bit, so I started adding some different stuff to the inventory. Nothing fancy, mostly just tchotchke, but I like to think it's a cut above what you find in most of the tourist shops. I make more on some of the junk up front than I ever did on bolts of cloth. I try to keep this back part for classier things—like that tie you just bought." She grinned.

"That's quite a history. And you're a real native-born hippie?" I say. "We've had a hard time finding those lately."

"I sure am, first generation. My parents emigrated from Russia in 1919. Katya points to a door in the back. "I've got a little apartment back there. Why don't you come back and sit for a minute while I change clothes and then I'll take you two out to eat—my treat, DH. I wouldn't want you to go back home without having a real, true hippie experience up here." She laughs.

"Jesse and I have had some experiences alright. But quite honestly, I'm not very impressed by the whole hippie thing. I kind of agree with Jesse about there being a darkness involved. I just can't quite put my finger on it."

"Being a real hippie, I should probably be offended by that, but I'm not. I'm not so convinced about all the peace, love, and good wishes stuff either. It just came outta nowhere. Usually when something good happens up here, it's the result of lots of thought and planning within the community. These happenings and be-ins popped up overnight like they'd been thoroughly planned somewhere else, and then brought here and manufactured into a sensation almost immediately. Last January is when it really started, and it's been growing every day. But it doesn't really seem to be accomplishing anything. It just looks like a bunch of immature kids marching in the streets, giggling, smoking pot, and breaking things. I get the feeling that there might be some not-so-nice grownups in the wings who are using the kids to stir things up."

"Katya, you don't look old enough to have owned this store for so long, but you sound pretty gown up for a hippie."

Katya grins at me and says, "I'll be forty-five tomorrow."

"You look like you're only about twenty! I honestly thought you were our age when I first saw you over here." I truly am amazed.

"Happy birthday, Katya. You do look young for your age."

"Thank you, Jesse. Clean living I guess, and no drugs. Now, come on back with me and have a seat. I'll get dressed quickly. There's a Russian restaurant down the street that has incredible food. My mother brought all the old recipes with her in her head when they left Russia, and she was a wonderful cook, so I know good Russian food when I taste it." She smiles and leads the way to her apartment.

"There's a little bit of Russian in my background, too," I say as we head for the back of the store. "Not much, but enough for me to be interested in the culture."

"Then you'll love my little place. My parents were only able to bring a few of their most treasured family heirlooms with them when they came to this country, but once they got established—they both had a good head for business—they kept an eye out for Russian art and artifacts. They also had a good eye for a bargain. The apartment is packed with the treasures and trinkets I grew up with."

Katya opens the door to her apartment and invites us in.

"Holy cow," I say as I step through. Jesse steps in to stand beside me. Her eyes grow wide and her hand comes up to cover her mouth as if she is experiencing a minor shock.

It's like stepping into a wonderland. Every nook and cranny and every spot on the walls is filled with some kind of decorative object, and the main theme seems to be Christmas. There must be a dozen Christmas trees in the living room, complete with lights, ornaments, the works. And reindeer! Dozens of reindeer standing on tabletops, perched on ledges, and tucked into spaces in the bookshelves. The walls are covered with paintings. What appear to be real Russian icons are hung in prominent areas, giving them the respect they deserve. Other paintings of the Russian countryside—mainly in winter—fill the spaces in between. These, too, look like originals. Everywhere I look there are antique glass ornaments and little statues. Ornate lamps hang from the ceiling and stand on the tables and the floor. An elaborately decorated urn—a samovar, I think—stands on a large sideboard, surrounded by a collection of teacups of every possible description. I could spend several days here just studying Katya's family treasures.

"It's like walking into Santa's house," Jesse says.

"My Mother collected the Christmas stuff. She loved Christmas. In fact, most of what she was able to bring with her is related to Christmas. My parents were devout Christians—members of the Russian Orthodox Church. Life after the revolution became difficult for anyone with religious convictions. The leaders were atheists and I think they did not like the idea of anything but themselves having authority in the lives of anyone. All of the holidays had to be celebrated quietly so as not to draw attention, harassment, or worse. Christmas trees were still openly displayed after the Revolution, although any religious significance had to be downplayed. That wasn't hard to do as the decorated evergreens were also associated with pagan celebrations of midwinter going back long before Christianity. I think that these days the Christmas trees are officially recognized as New Year trees glorifying the State and having nothing to do with religion.

"At any rate, Mother loved Christmas trees. She brought what she could with her and continued to collect trees and ornaments all her life. The attic upstairs is full of them."

As she told her story, I tried to imagine what life must have been like for her parents, and what it cost them to leave so much behind and come to this country. Some of these ornaments truly are priceless. "I hope you have a good security system in here," I said.

"Oh I do!" Katya said emphatically. "Every door and window is wired and the police substation is a just a few doors down."

"Are those real Russian Icons?" I ask.

"Yes, they are. Very real and very old."

"They must be worth a fortune," Jesse says. "They're quite beautiful."

"So, Jesse, do you see darkness in this room?" Katya asks.

Jesse turns around slowly taking in the room and everything in it. When she is facing Katya she stops, looks directly at her, and smiles. "No," she says, "I see color here. Color and light."

"Is Katya in black and white or is she in color?" I ask. Katya gives me a puzzled look, not understanding what I was asking.

"She's in color."

"I'm glad to hear that," I say. Jesse's proclamation is indeed a relief.

Katya looks from Jesse to me. "Huh?" These last comments have gone entirely over her head.

"It's a long story. We'll tell you over Russian food," I assure her.

"You'd better." She looks again at Jesse, then she smiles and says, "Now hang on a minute. I've got to get out of these rags and into something a little cooler. I'll just be a minute."

Katya disappears into what I presume to be her bedroom. I turn to Jesse, who is now staring deeply into the face of the Virgin Mary in the big icon over the fireplace.

"It's lovely, isn't it," I say.

"Yes, she is. This room is so much more alive than even the chancel at the Stanford church. That pales to grey when compared to this."

"Maybe that's because the mosaic art in the Chancel isn't as old. I find that newer art often lacks the feeling or spirit of older art."

"I think it's more that the artist who painted this icon was so emotionally involved with his subject that his soul entered into the work and stayed there. The Stanford church was manufactured by many professionals who were just doing a job—a very good job, but still—and not created by a single, dedicated artist."

She never ceases to amaze me. "Wow, that's what I've always said. Some artists merely paint, but others like Van Gogh and Botticelli become what they paint, and their paintings become a part of them."

Jesse turns and looks at me—almost sadly. "You'll never paint me if you go back tomorrow. You'll never become me."

"I'll paint you, Jesse. The first painting I do will be you."

"But I'll never see it."

"Never say never. You never know." I smile at my own wit, but she doesn't notice and turns back to the icon.

"I always know."

I sit on the couch, content now to watch Jesse. I don't even see the paintings and other ornaments in the room any more. Jesse is a work of art far greater than any icon ever created. I'll be leaving her tomorrow. I want to study her carefully and remember everything about her. I will paint her, and I no doubt will cry sad tears of longing with every stroke of the brush on the canvas—just as I touched her tear that first day with her. Just as I ate her. I'll carry her with me forever, and I'll never be able to forget her. I don't want to forget her.

Katya emerges from the bedroom a few minutes later, ready to go. She is really gorgeous, for a woman in her forties—or any age, for that matter. Manny would call her hot if he could see her. There's something about her age and maturity that makes that lovely exterior even more attractive.

She gives us a big smile and says, "Okay kids, let's go pig out."

11 AM at the Russian Restaurant

Katya was well known at the restaurant, so they gave us a good table in the corner by the window where we could talk and watch the people go by on the sidewalk outside. Katya ordered the house sampler plate for all of us. It included about a dozen samples of different traditional Russian dishes on one large plate and was one of the most expensive things on the menu, but Katya wouldn't argue—it was her treat.

When the food was set before us, Jesse's eyes grew almost as large as the massive plate in front of her. "I'll never be able to eat all this," she said.

I echoed the sentiment. "Whoa—that's a lot of food."

The food was delicious and, contrary to our first impression, I don't think any of us will have difficulty eating all of it.

We ate in silence for a few minutes, intent on tasting a little bit of everything on our plates. Katya seemed to enjoy watching us enjoy ourselves.

I pause for a moment when I complete the first tour of my plate. "This is incredibly good," I say. "Thanks, Katya."

"Yes, Katya, this is delicious. Thank you," Jesse says.

"I'm just happy to have someone to share a meal with." Katya smiles at us. "I don't get to do this very often."

"Well, this little experience is gonna be one of the highlights of my visit to The City. You know, I came up here with virtually nothing, and I've somehow managed to be carried along all week without starving, or having to go without any of the comforts of life for that matter. I've met some very nice people up here." I look at Jesse. She smiles but does not meet my eye.

"What do you guys do? Do you work?" Katya asks.

Jesse answers first. "I'm not working right now. I'm in between experiences."

"But you manage to support yourself? You're not sleeping in the park are you?" Katya asks.

Jesse and I smile at each other, and I reply, "Actually, we've slept in a couple of parks, but not because we had to. Jesse lives with some folks over on Haight. I stayed there with them one night, but I think we both prefer the parks."

Katya smiles and shakes her head. "Sleeping in the park by choice. That's a new one on me."

"It's another long story," I say.

"You two seem to have a lot of interesting experiences packed into just one short week in San Francisco."

"That we do," I agree.

Jesse is blushing a bit. It seems as if she has been withdrawing—going inward—since this morning. I know she's upset that I have to go back to Riverside, but there isn't much I can do about that. My family, my friends, my college, everything I am is there. I know Jesse doesn't have deep roots here in San Francisco, at least none that she recognizes, but there's no way I could bring her back with me.

"So, what is it that you two have done that makes it all so interesting? Care to elaborate?" Katya asks, lightening the mood somewhat.

I run down the list of the places we've been, the parks, the people, the Buddhists, the police—she laughed at that one—and I told her about meeting Ginsburg and Ferlinghetti, and visiting Stanford. But mainly she was curious about the interactions we had with the so-called hippie movement. I gave her the best synopsis I could of all the people we'd met. I talked mainly about the folks at the

Hippie Haven: Big Bob, Frankie, Bev, Reann, and Mandy. I told her about Digger Auntie. I didn't mention anything about Angie or Sissy, or even Manny, because that experience was before I met Jesse and I didn't want her to be excluded from the conversation. Jesse actually did very little talking at the table. I did most of it, but somehow the conversation kept coming back around to Jesse, or something she'd said to me, or a funny little thing I'd done with her. It made me realize that the past week had been centered entirely around her and on what she had somehow magically awakened within me. When I go back to Riverside tomorrow, whether I like it or not, I'll be going back a changed man, bringing a big part of Jesse back with me in both my heart and my mind. Or perhaps I'll be going back less full — less full of myself. Maybe there'll be a big hole in my soul where Jesse has been residing these past few days. Maybe I won't be bringing anything back with me. Maybe I'll just be empty. Very empty.

I'm going to be just as sad as Jesse when we say our goodbyes in the morning.

"Sounds like you've had quite a time here, both of you," Katya says. "What do you have planned for the rest of the day? I don't know how you're going to top what you've already experienced, but surely you need to do something special for the last day."

"I have no idea," I tell her. "I've already done far more than I expected to do, and I'm taking back enough information to fill a book, should I ever decide to write one." I smile. "I'm gonna let Jesse decide."

"And I take it that's what you do, DH. You're a writer?"

"I really haven't made up my mind what I am yet. I'm still goin' to college, but nothing is certain even there. I still haven't declared a major. But yes, I do some writing. I keep a journal. I hope one day, in the distant future, the words I write in this little book will mean something. I also paint."

"Pictures or houses?"

"Pictures," I say. "Art is really my first choice as far as possible majors are concerned, but it's probably a bad choice. After all, what can a person do with a degree in art except maybe teach art, and I'm not sure I want to be a teacher."

"Do you want to be a famous painter?"

"I don't think about that much. I'd like to make a living at it, but that's a tough road to go down. I've made a new friend, Frank Reed, who's trying to do that. He works pretty hard at it. It's a full time job just selling your personality to the galleries, never mind your paintings. I keep hoping some of Frank will rub off onto me so that I can immerse myself more into the art business—even though that doesn't really trip my trigger either. I just want to paint."

Jesse, who has been silent for a while, looks at me and says, "You'll never be a famous artist."

"I won't?"

"It takes a violent, aggressive person to climb to the top in the art world. If you were to do that you'd no longer be in color. You'd be in black and white just like all the others. You won't let that happen."

I know she's right. Jesse's always right, and that's what scares me about her. She seems to get her information from somewhere else, not of this world. She sizes things up in an instant, and then spits out the wisdom of the ages as if she were born to it. I have no idea where that wisdom comes from, or how it gets into her—I just know it is.

I can see that Katya, too, is beguiled by Jesse. Addressing her directly, Katya says, "Young lady, you really are something. You don't say much, but when you do I don't believe I've ever heard anything like it."

"I think I once told her the same thing," I say.

"You're the one who ought to be writing the book, Jesse," Katya continues. "I'm pretty sure you have much to say that you haven't said yet."

"I'm just me being me," Jesse says.

Katya just shook her head. Then she brightly directed our attention to our most immediate concern. "So, let's decide what you two will do to finish off this beautiful day."

"I suppose we could just go back to Mandy's place and visit with them. Then I'll get up and head back to Riverside tomorrow morning," I say without enthusiasm.

Jesse remains silent. She appears withdrawn, as if there were a veil between her and the world around her. Then the veil lifts and she looks at Katya and me. She is resolute when she speaks. "But I don't want to go back there. I'd rather not. I can no longer be a part of them."

"Why not?" I ask.

"I'm not like them."

"I know that, but you get along with them and they like you. It works well for you. Where would you go, what would you do without them?"

"I'd find a way. I've always found a way," she says. "Besides, I've already decided. I'll buy them each a gift. I'll take them their gifts, thank them for all they've done for me, and then I'll find my way."

I know that there is more to Jesse than meets the eye, but I am concerned about her going off on her own. "Jesse, I know you have a little money saved up so you could afford to live on your own, but a move like that just seems a bit drastic."

"No, it's not. They're heavy and I'm light. They're cloudy and I'm pure. If I stay there any longer I'll become stained and spotted. It's time for me to move on."

"I'm not sure I understand what you just said," Katya says, "but you certainly seem to have thought it all out very thoroughly."

"It's what she does," I say.

"And you have some extra cash, Jesse?" Katya asks.

"Yes, I do. I have a bank account with enough to make me quite comfortable." Jesse has undergone a subtle change since she first began to speak of her plans. What was once a waifish, faerie-like girl has been transformed into a young woman who knows who she is and what she can do.

Katya studies her for a moment, reassessing her evaluation of

Jesse. Finally she smiles and says, "Well, you're a big girl. You can make your own decisions."

I can see that Katya is right, but I am still troubled. "But are you sure? You aren't just doing this to make me feel bad about not taking you to Riverside with me?"

"No I would never do that." She looks at me and gives me the sweet smile that I have come to love over the past few days. "We're both young and we have many years ahead in which to live our lives. It would be wrong to make such a permanent choice as that in this early stage of our development. I can see that. Besides, I kind of like it up here. I'd miss my parks."

I smile back at her and say, "I'm gonna miss those parks too."

She reaches over and touches my hand. "Maybe one day I'll come visit you in Riverside and you can show me your parks."

"I hope so," I say.

"You know, Jesse," Katya says, "you can always bunk with me for a while if you want. Just to get your head focused on where you really want to go. I can even put you to work out front. I could use the help."

"Thank you, Katya, that's very kind of you, but I want to find a little place of my own. I'm thinking about looking for an apartment over by Buena Vista Park."

"Some of those are pretty expensive," Katya says.

"If I ever get in a bind, I'll come here and put in an application."

"I'll hire you in a heartbeat."

We sat in there for quite some time just chatting and savoring all the wonderful food. We all left the restaurant and walked down to the corner together. We thanked Katya for the meal and promised to keep in touch. Jesse told her that she would let her know when she got settled on her own. Then Katya went back to her shop and we went back toward the Haight.

We walked slowly, both to stretch out the time we had together and to finalize our plans. Jesse decided that it would be best if we headed back to Hippie Haven so she could talk to the group about her leaving. She'll stay with them as long as it takes to find an apartment and then she'll move out. I also needed to locate Manny and make plans with him for our departure tomorrow.

"Is there anything special you'd like to do this evening, Jesse?" I asked.

"No. I think I should spend the evening with Mandy and the crew at the Haven. They've done so much for me and I think I owe them a little time before I leave them for good. That will also give them a chance to get to know the real me a little better."

"That's a good idea. I think at least a couple of them had a hard time dealing with the difference between what you appeared to be and who you really are."

Even though we had been walking slowly and taking the longest way back, we arrived back at Hippie Haven all too soon. We found the place filled with loud music and smoke—cigarette with a hint of something else."Ah, the real world. Manny and the others were happy to see us both and were curious to know what we'd been doing. We gave them a brief run down and then Jesse told them her plans. They were surprised and sad to hear that she would be leaving. Mandy tried to talk her out of it, but Jesse's mind was made up. She did agree to spend a few more nights with them while she went house hunting, and they agreed to do everything they could to help her find a nice place to live.

I spent much of that last hour or so at Hippie Haven just listening to the conversation, watching the interactions of the residents of the house, and reflecting on my experiences here in San Francisco. I came to realize just how good people can be to each other. I also thought that Jesse was making a big mistake by leaving that group because, for better worse, they'd become a family—a bit dysfunctional, yes, but family nevertheless.

I was able get a few minutes in the kitchen alone with Jesse before

Manny and I left for the last time. Neither of us said much—we were pretty talked out by then—but we hugged each other for a long time, and then I held her face gently between my hands and tenderly kissed her lips. I gave her my mailing address and she promised to keep in touch with me. Whether she will or not, I have no idea.

2 PM Golden Gate Park

So here we are, sitting on a bench in Golden Gate Park. I have just finished bringing my journal up to date while Manny has been observing the daily parade of characters.

"So, DH, what do we do now?"

Manny has just asked the eternal question, and this time I have a real answer. I dig my wallet out of my back pocket and extract a piece of paper from behind my photo of the Rossetti painting.

"What the heck is that?" Manny asks as I hold up the magic scrap triumphantly.

"This should solve our problem for the evening," I explain. "It's the phone number Angie gave me. She told me to call her before we leave."

"Cool!" Manny's face lights up. "Maybe we can spend some time with her and Sissy before we head out mañana."

"We do need to say goodbye to them. They were really nice to us."

"They were," Manny says. "And I kinda like them. To be honest, I've just about had it up to here with the hippies. I'm ready for normal."

"You're kidding? I thought you felt some sort of tribal camaraderie with this whole scene."

"I thought I would when we first arrived, but not so much now. I'm kinda hippied out."

"How come?"

"Well, while you were having a great time running around with that sweet little Jesse chick, I've been flopping around from place to place trying to find whatever it is to be found up here. Quite frankly, I can't seem to find it."

"So you got a good taste of the scene?"

"That I did. I attended one of those be-ins, but I was so far back in the crowd that all I got out of it was a sunburn. I met dozens of local hippies, visited a couple of hippie pads in the Haight. It was the same thing everywhere I went."

"Whatta you mean?" I ask.

"It was boring! Geez, I never thought I'd see the day when I'd get tired of music."

"You're kidding."

"I'm not kidding. If I hear that Hendrix album one more time, I'll blow my brains out. All these people do is lay around stoned out of their heads, listen to loud music, and eat crap food all day. If you try to start a meaningful conversation with them it always comes back to Hendrix, or the Dead, or one of the other bands. It's all they talk about. And none of them have any get-up-and-go at all. They're like slugs, except when they're at a festival. At festivals everybody's stoned or drunk and dancing around looking like the undead, or they're throwing Frisbees back and forth endlessly."

"It does sound a bit boring."

"Boring isn't strong enough. I was ready to go home yesterday, but now that you mention seeing the girls again, I think that would be cool. They're real people. They know all the big words, and they eat real food. The official hippie meal seems to be refried beans with crumbled up hamburger mixed in. I don't know how many plates of that crap I've had. Everywhere I went, that's what they were serving."

"But you had a little cash. Why didn't you get some restaurant food?" I ask.

"I wanted to save the cash to buy something to take back to my sister—the sick one, remember? I thought she'd like a real hippie something or other just to cheer her up."

"I'm sorry all that stress has to be on your shoulders while you're here trying to enjoy things."

"It is what it is."

Manny's younger sister, Shanie, is such a nice kid. I've known her as long as I've known Manny and his Mother. She's always been a very active girl—loves to have fun, real friendly and a kick to hang around. It's really too bad she's not doing well, and it's too bad that Manny has to worry about her all the time. But I understand, family's family. I'd feel the same if she was my sister, if I had a sister.

"Well, I've got some extra cash that I haven't spent yet. If you're short, I can help some. With only one night left here we aren't likely to spend much."

"Unless we take the girls out to a nice place."

"You got something in mind, Manfred?"

"No. But don't you dare suggest anything that has to do with loud music, hippies, or beans."

"You'll still drink some wine if Sissy can get us some, won't you?"

"Oh yeah. I need to drink my troubles away." His face brightens with anticipation of the evening yet to come.

"Okay, now all we have to do is find a pay phone. I think I've got a dime in my pocket."

We found a pay phone at the edge of the park. I inserted my dime and dialed the number. Angie answered on the first ring.

"'Bout time," she said. I could hear a smile in her voice.

"Good to hear you too, Ang."

"Have you missed me?" she asked.

"I really have," I said. And I meant it. Even while I was running around with Jesse, Angie's face would pop into my mind now and then, and I'd wonder what she was doing and if I'd get a chance to see her before Manny and I had to skip back to Riverside.

"Are you sure?" she asked.

"I'm positive."

"What have you two been doing out there in the wild? Sissy and I thought we'd hear from you before now."

"There's way too much to tell you here on the phone. Are you guys able to meet us somewhere so we can get together again? We have to head back home tomorrow."

"Where you at?"

"We're at a phone booth on the east side of Golden Gate Park."

"Stay right there. I'll call Sissy and we'll be there in a few."

Back Together with Angie and Sissy

I'm back on the bench in the park. Angie is sitting beside me, and having her there just feels right. Sissy and Manny are lounging on the grass in front of us, laughing and talking about Manny's experiences with the hippies. I told them all to give me just a few minutes to catch up on my notes.

Sissy's car pulled into a parking space not far from our bench. The car had barely stopped when both doors were flung open and the sisters came running toward us with their arms wide open, barely taking time to slam the doors shut. It was like a family reunion. Angie's freckled face lit up with a big grin made me feel like a million bucks.

The big surprise was that Angie was wearing her baseball uniform. Apparently she has a ballgame scheduled for today, and when I called she'd just gotten dressed. She looks really cute in that outfit—a typical baseball uniform, grey and pink with red pinstripes and the team name, the Scrappers, in red across the front—and I'll bet Angie is just that, a scrapper, out on the field. She's a tough Tessie.

She leans against me and says, "Are you finished yet?"

"I guess."

"Did you write something nice about me?"

"I wrote about that cute freckled face of yours."

"Did you mention the way my nose crinkles up when I smile?" She smiles.

"You're a cutie, there's no denying that."

"You like my uniform?"

"I love it."

She stands up and strikes a pose with her left hand on her hip and her right hand behind her head. "You think it make me looks sexy?"

"I think you're just kidding, but it actually does make you look kinda sexy." I smile. "But then, you'd look sexy wearing a potato sack."

"Really? Potato sacks are short. My butt would hang out in the back."

"Well …" I smile at the image that comes to my mind. "I'd call that sexy."

"Are you just trying to butter me up or do you really mean it?"

"I really mean it," I tell her seriously—then I grin. "Of course, I always have liked Doris Day. You really do look like her, and you kinda act like her, too. She's a tomboy just like you. You could be her younger sister."

"You're not the first person to tell me that. I guess it isn't too bad."

"It's good. Doris Day's a babe."

"Really?" She sounds surprised that I said that. "Do guys really think she's attractive? I mean, I think she's kinda cute, but I never thought of her as a babe."

"That's because you're just a tomboy and not a real boy."

"Okay, I'll take your word for it."

Manny and Sissy are getting restless. Manny keeps looking at his wrist for the watch he left at home in Riverside.

"You catching a bus, Manny?" I ask.

"No, but we don't have another week to spend up here, and I'd kinda like to do some stuff with the girls before we go home. We're gonna run out of time if you two don't quit flirting."

"We could always go watch Angie play ball," Sissy says.

Angie throws up her hands in protest. "Nope. No way. I'm gonna call and tell them I can't make it today. We need to do some important stuff with the guys here before they head back."

"Wait a minute." Now it's my turn to protest. "I think it would be a kick to watch you play ball. What do you think Manny?"

"Actually, that might be fun. It sounds like a perfectly normal thing to do, and I'm up for normal. I've had enough of those hippie festivals."

"You're kidding," Angie says. "You guys really want to come to a ball game?"

"Will there be any food there?" Manny asks.

"They've got a food stand," Sissy says. "All you can get is pizza, popcorn and cokes, but it's real good pizza."

"Let's do it. I Loooooove pizza!" Manny is up and halfway to the car before the rest of us can catch up.

"I just hope you don't get bored and leave half way through the game," Angie says as she starts the car. "Once it starts, I'll have to play through to the end. I won't be able to quit."

"I doubt we'll get bored. I love baseball," I say. "We won't leave till the last out."

"Okay, let's do it," Angie says as she pulls out into the flow of traffic. "We've got about 20 minutes to get there. The game starts at four."

At the Ball Game

This was a really good idea. It's been an exciting game so far and we're having a great time. I haven't been to a baseball game in a long time, and to have a friend playing in the game makes it even better. These so-called amateurs are much more fun to watch than the professionals any day. They play the game strictly for the love of it, and they play it well. They're in a time out for now, and I think the spectators need a break from the action as much as the players.

Angie's been a fireball running around the bases. She's had three opportunities so far in the game — two home runs and a strong hit to left field that got her all the way to third base, which is where she is right now. It'll be up to one of her teammates to send her home after the time out. The two teams are pretty evenly matched, and the score is tied right now at three to three. The Scrappers will be up one over the Beamers if Angie touches home plate.

I think Manny's getting hoarse from yelling. He's been like a little kid—standing up, waving his arms, screaming his head off. He once told me he didn't really care for baseball, but he's pretty happy right now. Of course, we've also been stuffing ourselves with pizza since we got here, so that adds to his current state of euphoria.

I can tell that Sissy's been to a lot of these games. She knows all the players by name, including some of the players on the opposing team. She has the rules down pat, knows whenever anybody screws up, and cusses at the umpire when she thinks he made a bad call. It's as much fun watching her as it is watching the game.

Angie is the star of the afternoon, though. What a player! She knocked both of her homers over the centerfield fence. Remind me not to arm wrestle with her any time soon.

"Whattaya think?" Sissy asks between bites of pizza.

"I think Angie's gonna come on home, and if I was that catcher I'd get the heck out of her way," I say.

"Me too. Little Sis is like a bulldog on the field. She's only been injured a couple of times, but she's accidentally sent some opposing players out of the game several times, even in practice. She's stocky and hard as a rock. If she runs you down, you go flying a bit before you hit the ground."

"I didn't know baseball got that violent," Manny says.

"You know you're loving it," I tell him.

"I didn't say I didn't like it. But I don't think I'd like to play it."

"It can get pretty rough at times," Sissy says, "but I wouldn't call it violent—not like football or basketball."

"I'm not a basketball fan myself," I say. "It just looks like a bunch of tall guys running back and forth trying to keep the ball away from each other. A bit of a kid's game to me."

"Me neither," Sissy says. "You're right, DH, there's no real thinking involved. I don't care how many play diagrams they draw up, it's still just a bunch of tall guys running back and forth."

"It seems like it's mainly luck if the ball goes through the hoop," Manny says. "Especially the long shots."

"In baseball every player has to be constantly thinking about what could happen next," I say. "Planning out all the plays in your head and trying to read the other team's mind in between plays, and when the ball is in play, things happen fast and there's a lot to keep track of—not just where that tiny ball is going, but where your teammates are, and where the runners are, where everybody is going, and when they will get there. There's a lot of strategy happening as opposed to just brute strength."

"And Angie's got a brain in that little head of hers," Sissy says proudly.

"That *pretty* little head of hers," I add.

She looks at me and asks, "You like her a lot don't you?"

"I do," I tell her, but I'm not sure I want to talk about it.

Sissy smiles at me and winks. "Well, she likes you a lot, too."

"A match made in heaven." Manny sends Sissy a knowing grin, then turns to me. "I think she's the best prospect you've had in life so far, DH."

"Has he had some losers, Manny?"

"Not many. To be honest, he hasn't dated much."

"That ain't a bad thing," Sissy says. "That just means he isn't out to lay every chick that comes along."

"I'm sitting right here," I say quietly.

"Oops," Sissy says with fake contrition, "I forgot. We'd better clam up, Manny. Angie will beat us up if we scare off her new boyfriend."

"For crying out loud," I say, rolling my eyes.

I am saved from further humiliation when the umpire blows his whistle to restart the game. Angie is standing at third base looking like a real pro. She is leaning forward with her weight on the balls of her feet, every muscle tensed, and ready to spring into action when the ball is hit. The girl who is up at bat looks like she could hit the ball with some force if she puts her weight into it. She's about twice Angie's size, but unlike Angie, she seems to be more fat than muscle. We'll soon see. She's got two strikes and two balls right now and …

CRACK! The ball goes right over the head of the player at

second base and out into center field. The ball bounces once, and the center field player scoops it up and throws it to the catcher. Meanwhile, Angie launches herself toward home plate just as the batter takes her swing. The catcher is watching the ball, and Angie is almost there and going full speed. The ball is in the air, the catcher is reaching for it, and suddenly Angie's feet have left the ground and she is literally flying toward home base. It's over in an instant. Angie creams the catcher as she slides in over the plate, knocking her aside as the ball goes sailing past. She's safe and the Scrappers are ahead of the Beamers by one.

Angie went down hard when she hit the catcher, but she's getting up now and dusting herself off. She appears to be OK, but it looks like she got a cut to her forehead; I can see some blood over her left eye.

"Is she okay?" I ask Sissy.

"Oh yeah. Happens all the time. If she's walking and smiling at the same time she's just fine."

She is walking and smiling as she wipes the blood off her forehead with her sleeve. She looks up, finds us in the stands and, grinning from ear to ear, waves at us with both hands. Then she blows us a kiss. What a sweetie.

Sissy nudges me in the ribs and says, "That kiss was for you, Dumb-Dumb boy."

"It was for all of us," I protest.

"Yeah, right," Manny says.

"I'm sure it was," I mumble, just a little embarrassed.

"Look at her struttin' her stuff all the way to the dugout," Sissy says. Angie is indeed strutting—dancing, almost. "She knows she's got this game locked up."

"You gotta give the whole team some credit, Sissy. It takes more than one player to win a game," Manny says.

"Are you kidding? If Angie wasn't on this team they wouldn't win a single game. She's a tiger."

"I believe that, Sissy," I agree.

Angie was too excited to sit down when she reached the dugout and continued to pace back and forth, a big smile on her face. As I watched her I felt a big wave of something warm like liquid honey flowing through my veins. Tenderness? Is it tenderness? No, it's something stronger than that. I didn't feel this around Jesse. Jesse was wonderful, but she was such a mystery, and as hard as I tried I could never feel truly close to her. If anything, I felt a distance between us. That's why when she told me she loved me and asked if I was "in love" with her I had a hard time answering directly. I love Jesse in some way, but not in this way—not like I'm feeling for Angie right now. I want to be down there in the dugout with her, hugging her, laughing with her—sharing everything. I love the way she laughs. She's happy all the time.

"You okay, DH?" Sissy's voice breaks through my thoughts and I realize that I haven't sat down again yet. I must have been staring out into space.

"Yeah ... I'm fine."

Sissy gives me a knowing look then says, "You got it bad, don't you?" Can she read my mind? Gawd, I'm embarrassed. I can't hide anything from anybody. I sit down, not taking my eyes off Angie.

"I guess I do, Sissy. I guess I really do."

Manny, too, has not missed a thing. "Man oh man, this is better than any hippie love fest I've been to this week. We've got a real love story goin' on here," he says gleefully.

Sissy pokes him in the arm with her finger. "Pay attention, Manny. You might learn something." Was that a hint of ice in her voice?

Manny changes the subject, thank heaven. "I can't believe I'm gonna say this, but I sure wish I had some wine. I think it'd be nice to be just a little bit loopy for the last couple of innings."

"I've got some." I think Sissy must have been a Girl Scout; she's always prepared—at least when it comes to wine.

"Is it legal to drink wine here?" Manny asks.

"Oh come on, Manny. Look around!"

She's right. There are quite a few people openly enjoying

adult beverages.

"This is San Francisco," she says. "What difference does it make if it's legal or not. Nobody cares."

"Where've you been hiding it?" Manny asks.

She pulls the large bag that she uses as a purse out from under the seat. "Right here. Three bottles of Chablis with screw caps. And …" She pulls out a stack of plastic cups, and holds them up, smiling triumphantly.

"Why didn't you tell us sooner?" I ask.

"I was saving it for the fifth inning. I didn't want to run out early."

"Perfect timing," I said. "We're in the fifth now."

"I plead the fifth—hand me a cup," Manny says.

Sissy discretely fills three cups with wine, handing one each to Manny and me and keeping the last for herself, and then packs the bottle back into her purse. I'm not much of a Coke drinker, and that's about all you can get here except for the little water fountain back by the snack stand, so the wine tasted pretty good.

"These three bottles should last us through the next four innings," Sissy said.

"What if it goes into extra innings?" I ask.

"Then I'll have to go out to the car and get some more. I've got a case of this stuff in the trunk." She smiles. "I used to be a Girl Scout—you know, be prepared, and all that crap." I knew it!

Now that we have the wine business out of the way I notice that the players on the field are just standing around looking relaxed. "So, why aren't they playing out there?"

"Another time out," Sissy replies.

"If they didn't have so many time outs the games wouldn't be so long," Manny says.

"The longer they are, the more fun they are, Manny," I say. "If they didn't have time outs they'd have to add another five innings just to give the spectators their money's worth."

"It's all free, and it's a family thing," Sissy says. "Some of the people even bring picnic lunches. A great way to spend an afternoon."

The umpire blows the whistle and the game gets going again.

7:30 PM *The End of the Game*

The game was a long one, and it was close all the way to the end. The score was tied at five to five in the bottom of the ninth inning, with two out and two runners on base. I held my breath as Angie stepped up to the plate. The pitcher wound up and launched the ball, and WHAM — Angie knocked another homer over centerfield. The two runners rounded the bases and headed for home, followed by Angie. The scrappers beat the Beamers eight to five.

"Wow!" Sissy exclaimed. "What a squeaker. That was about the tightest game Angie's played this year."

Angie broke away from her celebrating teammates and ran in from the field with a big grin on her face. We made our way down the bleachers to greet the conquering hero.

"Whoooie!" whooped Angie as she reaches us.

"Ang!" Sissy yelled as Angie grabbed her and gave her a big hug.

"Eight and five!" Angie shouted "The unbeatable Scrappers!"

"The unbeatable Angie!" I said. "You hit all the homers!"

"Awww …" Angie released Sissy and hugged me hard and long. Then she looked up into my face with that heart-stopping grin and said, "Did you like the game? Did you really like it?"

"Of course I did," I said truthfully. "I haven't had this much fun in years."

Angie smiled even bigger, and then she kissed me. A long kiss.

"I loved having you up here watching me," she said.

"I loved being up here watching you. I could do this every day."

"You could?"

"I could … if I could."

"I know …" The smile left her face. "You're leaving tomorrow."

"I wish I didn't have to." And that was the truth. I was beginning to not exactly like the idea of going back to Riverside. Yeah, my family's there and I love my family, but what else is there? College? RCC is a great school, and I'm making a few friends there that I like, but … I mean … what would happen if I never went back, never attended RCC, never met new friends down there? What would it hurt? How would it change the outcome of my life? Of my future? They say if you live in the future and you go back to your past in a time machine you have to be careful what you do so you don't mess up the future timeline. If that happens you might stop existing or something. Well, I feel like that now. I feel like I'm in the future right now and going back to Riverside is like going back to my past. If I go back and attend RCC and meet new friends, that's gonna change the future for me—at least that's the way I see it. If I stay here, I'd have a future with Angie, get married and have kids, maybe become a Beat writer, who knows. So what timeline do I choose? Which one am I supposed to choose. Sometimes I think all of this past-present-future stuff really isn't in our hands anyway, it's in the hands of someone "up there" who's planning every thing out for us and no matter what we do, it ain't gonna make any difference.

"I wish you didn't have to either." Her smile hadn't completely left her face but the hint of a frown was right there on the edge.

"Come on you two," Sissy said. "Let's not get all maudlin. The night's still young and we need to think of something to do that'll keep our minds off the big departure tomorrow."

"Our minds, Sissy? You don't want them to go either, do you?" Angie said.

"Well, I have gotten kind of used to them. But don't forget, I'm gonna be heading out of here in a few days too. Gotta go back to school … get that degree … get that job."

"Yadda, yadda, yadda," Manny added.

Sissy perked up. "UCLA isn't very far from Riverside—I can come visit you guys. Or you can come visit me."

"And I'll be the only one sitting up here all alone in this crazy city," There was still a little smile on Angie's face, but I think I saw a tear in the corner of her eye?

"Don't you ever go down to visit Sissy?" I asked her.

"I haven't much. It's a long drive. But it looks like I might be doing it more in the near future."

"When you come to visit Sissy, Manny and I can drive into LA and we can have some time together."

"When? Once every six months?"

"As often as possible," I told her. "It's all we can do."

"Okay, we got that all fixed." Sissy slapped her hands together like a teacher calling her class to attention. "Now cut it out. Let's think about tonight. What are you guys up for?"

Manny whispered something in Sissy's ear, then he stepped back, grinned at her and waggled his eyebrows like Groucho Marx.

"Manny! I oughta slap you." Sissy said, repressing her own grin. "Hmm ... maybe ..."

"Maybe what?" Angie asked.

"None of your business, Ang," Sissy said quickly, still looking at Manny.

Angie looked at Manny, then back at her sister. "I can guess."

"So can I," I said, looking at Manny.

"Seriously. What are we going to do?" Sissy asked after clearing her throat.

"Well, I do have one idea." I hope the girls go for it.

"Let's hear it," Sissy urges.

I looked at Angie and blurted it out in one quick breath. "Manny and I've never been to your house, Angie."

"Oh ... oh, no ... It's a mess. We need to go somewhere else."

"Come on!" Manny said. "We should at least get to see it once before we go."

"Yeah, just once, and then you'll never have to see us again."

Angie looked stricken. "Don't say that!"

"We can go see your place, and then we can do whatever you want for the rest of the evening."

"Oh ... all right."

"You're gonna love it." Sissy seemed to like the idea. "And I know she has plenty of wine 'cause I filled her up yesterday."

"That's all I need to hear," Manny said.

Angie's House

Sissy was right—I do love Angie's house. And I gotta stress that it isn't an apartment, it's a real house in a nice neighborhood near Buena Vista Park.

There is no front yard at all, but a long flight of steps starts at the sidewalk and rises to a small porch and the front door. Angie lead the way, unlocked the door, and motioned for us to enter. As we emerged from the entry hall into the living room, I could see that Angie was right—the place is a mess, and most of it seems to be baseball related. In one corner is a stack of dirty and scuffed rubber bases. I could see five different baseball shoes scattered around on the floor; I'm guessing that they all have mates that are hiding out somewhere else. A brief inventory of the coffee table includes: two hardballs, a softball, five magazines; a glass half full of what appears to be orange juice; a handful of bobby pins, a pair of toenail scissors and a little pile of what I assume to be clipped toenails; a small plate covered with the remains of a sausage, egg, and toast breakfast; one shoe and a pair—make that two pairs—of dirty white socks. Through the archway separating the living room from the dining room I can see that the table is strewn haphazardly with magazines, some open and some closed, and all having something to do with baseball.

The main piece of furniture in the living room is a tan couch of good quality, based on what I can see peeking out from under the various piles that occupy most of its surface. Apart from a baseball jacket draped over the back and a pair of shoes tied together by the laces and dangling over one arm, the piles on the couch seem to be somewhat organized—t-shirts of various colors in one pile, dirty white socks in another, several pairs of pants and shorts, and another pile of panties. I think Angie must have been gathering up clothing for the laundry.

There is a pizza box on the floor in front of the couch next to a pile of newspapers, since there is no room on the coffee table, and a coffee cup sits precariously on the arm of the couch that's not occupied by the shoes. The wall opposite the couch is entirely filled with built-in cabinets and shelves. The shelves support an eclectic assortment of books and knick-knacks, and in the center presiding over the whole scene is a large TV, turned on but with the sound off.

I went to an art show in LA a while back. The guy had filled room-sized spaces with found objects—junk, abandoned cars, appliances, furniture, you name it—to create total environment sculptures. I think he must have used Angie's living room for practice.

"Oh no," Angie said as she followed us in. "I told you the place was a mess, I just didn't remember how bad it really was." She covered her face with her hands and emitted a pathetic moan.

"Well," I began cautiously, "it looks like it might be very nice … underneath the mess."

Angie turned to me, her hands still covering her mouth, her eyes like those of a puppy caught eating a shoe. Then she dropped her hands, smiled, and shrugged her shoulders. "What can I say? It's me!"

I laughed. "It's exactly how I pictured it in my mind before we ever got here," I told her.

"Holy cow." Manny said. "Somebody fought a war in here and you lost."

Sissy, of course, went over to the stairway and sat on a step and just started laughing.

I picked a dirty sock off the coffee table and held it up. "The latest baseball fashion?"

"Oh, geez." Angie grabbed it out of my hand. "It stinks!" She stuck it in her pocket and I laughed again.

"You should've given me a few minutes to pick it all up first," Angie said as she hustled around tidying what she could.

"But how would you have gotten the dump truck through the front door?" Manny grinned.

"Very funny," she said. She looked at the armload of stuff she had just picked up, shook her head, then let it all fall back to the floor. "Oh pooft. I am what I am."

I stepped up behind her, gave her a hug, and kissed the top of her head. Her hair was still sweaty from the ball game.

"I love the messy you," I said. "I wouldn't have you any other way."

Angie turned her head to look up at me, "You're just saying that."

"No, I'm not. I'm not exactly a neat freak myself."

"Yeah," Manny said. "You should see his room back home. They don't call it 'The Hole' for nothing."

"The Hole?" Sissy said.

"It's a long story," I told her.

"We gotta hear that some day," Sissy said.

Her cheeky grin made me feel that I have to defend myself. "It's not a bad story. I shared a bedroom with my brother and I wanted a room all to myself, so my grandfather measured off a corner in my parents' big garage, and built a little room for me. It has two windows in it, and my brother came up with the idea of painting a replica of a French poster on one of the windows. The poster was labeled 'Le Trou,' The Hole. I have no idea why it was labeled that, it just was. So we started calling my room The Hole. It just stuck."

"It's a true story," Manny sighed. This is not the first time he's heard this story. "Only thank heaven you just got the short version."

"Interesting," Sissy said.

"I told you it wasn't a bad story. Kinda silly really."

"I think it's sweet," Angie said. "Maybe I ought to name my little house."

"How about 'La Décharge?'" Sissy suggested.

"What does that mean?" Angie asked.

"The Dump." Sissy tried not to laugh.

"Very funny."

"I think it's kinda catchy," Manny said, grinning.

We really need a change of subject. "Okay you guys, I want a tour." And Angie gladly led the way.

The house is not all that big, but it has lots of class—aside from the mess. I'm not sure what the actual artistic and architectural style is called, but it has a lot of art deco touches. It also reminds me of some of the homes I've seen in Palm Springs—I think they call it "modern" down there. If I had to guess, I'd say it was built sometime between 1935 and 1955.

A large archway separates the living room from the dining area and kitchen. The kitchen is all pink and white—pink and white tile countertops, pink stove and refrigerator, pink and white curtains. The handles on all the cabinets and drawers are bright chrome, as are a few small items such as the toaster and coffee pot. It looks really sharp. There is also a lot of glass—a glass-topped table in the dining room that matches the end tables and coffee table in the living room.

Since the house is built on a hillside, every section is on a different level. The living room is down a couple of steps from the entry, and the kitchen and dining area are up a couple from there. There are two bedrooms; one is downstairs from the living room and the other is upstairs from the kitchen. The two bathrooms are beautifully tiled and chromed like the kitchen. The larger one upstairs is all yellow, and the smaller one halfway down to the other bedroom is pink like the kitchen.

There is a large glass door in the dining area that opens onto a patio in the small backyard. The yard is beautifully landscaped, and in the middle is a small swimming pool—not too common in San Francisco. There is also a deck off the upstairs bedroom with a stairway leading down to the patio. It really is a spiffy little house. One of the neatest things about it is that it sits up near the crest of the hill, so the view from both the deck upstairs, and the patio is incredible, day or night—as good as the view from the Buddhist apartment; maybe even better.

The only other thing of note, is that Angie's bedroom wasn't nearly as messy as the living room, except for a few piles of clothing ready for the laundry. The pile of underwear included bras as well as panties, which speaks to the fact that Angie is NOT a hippie, nor is she one of the countless girls that run around San Francisco braless.

When we returned to the living room, Angie raked all the stuff from the couch onto the floor and into a corner so we could sit down. Angie is sitting next to me on the couch, and Sissy and Manny are on the floor on the other side of the coffee table.

"Hey, guys," Angie said, "want to go swimming?"

"That might be fun. It's certainly a good night for it," Manny said.

That does sound like a good idea. "It's still pretty warm out there, especially for San Francisco," I said.

"What do we do for swim suits?" Manny asked.

Sissy got "that look" again, then said, "We girls have suits. You guys will just have to swim naked."

"And scare all the wildlife away?" I asked.

"You can't be all that bad," Angie said.

"How about if we all get naked!" Sissy said. "We'll go outside. Angie and I will turn our backs while you guys get undressed and slip into the water, then you can turn your backs while we get undressed and slip in."

"I guess …" Angie said, not sounding too convinced of the idea.

"Sounds good to me," Manny said.

"Wait a minute…" I said. "I think we ought to talk about this for a minute.

"Why do you always have to analyze things?" Manny frowned.

"I'm not analyzing anything. I'm just not sure it's a good idea to all get naked in a pool."

"It'll be okay." Sissy smiled in an attempt to reassure me. "You'll be under water and Angie and I won't peek."

"Not much." Angie grinned not so reassuringly.

"Good," Manny said. "It's settled."

"Great! I'll grab the wine," Angie said.

Day Seven

Catching Up on Last Night

We went outside around 8:30. At first we just walked around enjoying the warm summer night and admiring the view. It was beautiful beyond words, although I'm sure I'll come up with some. The lights of the city were like sparkling stars—a reflection of the cosmos above. I could almost imagine it being a giant, clear lake mirroring the Milky Way. Having read the Egyptian Book of the Dead recently, I couldn't help but think of how the ancient Egyptians built an entire system of gods and goddesses around the stars. They believed that some of the stars were reflections of their underworld realm they called the Duat—especially the constellation Orion. The Duat is where the old gods and goddesses roam around in the after life. I always thought that gods and goddesses were supposed to be eternal, never die, until I started reading books about Egyptian history and religion, but apparently they were alive once, then they died to become the gods and goddesses. Some archaeologists even believe the pyramids were laid out on Earth to reflect the stars in the Orion constellation up yonder, and those stars were believed to be home to the gods. I saw a picture once that kind of backs that up. The relative positions of the three largest Pyramids seem to match the stars of Orion's belt almost exactly. I doubt that the other ancient houses and buildings match anything in the heavens, but it's fun to ponder stuff like that.

Sissy brought a jug of wine out and set it and some cups on the patio at the shallow end of the pool along side of the stack of towels she had brought out earlier. "Okay guys, we're turning around now. Let us know when you're in the water," she said.

When Manny and I were safely in the water, he said, "Your turn, ladies."

We kept our backs turned until we heard two splashes and Angie said, "We're in."

"Wanta play tag?" Manny asked.

"Good try, Manny," Angie said. "But if you tag me you'll lose your front teeth."

"Don't worry, I'm not gonna mess with you. I saw how you slammed those homers into centerfield."

"She can drive nails with her fist," Sissy said.

The night was clear and bright—unusual for San Francisco at this time of year. There was a lot of light coming from the city down the hill, but up hill in the other direction it was dark enough to see the stars coming out.

"Look up," I said.

"It's so lovely," Angie said softly.

"That it is," I said, but my gaze kept moving back and forth from the stars to Angie. The beauty of the night sky was competing with her beauty, and the sky was losing. Angie was aware that I was staring at her. I caught her more than once turning her head to meet my gaze with hers. There was always that brilliant smile on her face when she did.

The four of us talked about many things last night. The air was warm and so was the water, and the wine flowed freely. Since the wine jug was sitting at the shallow end of the pool, it was impossible to get a refill without giving at least a flash of naked body parts to the other three people in the pool. After a couple of hours of that, and probably because of the effect of the wine, we all just gave up trying to hide anything. Angie eventually ended up on one side of the pool with me, and Manny ended up on the other side with Sissy. It wasn't like an orgy or anything—that never happened. None of us wanted to spoil the innocent fun of the moment or the relationships we were forming. But Angie did spoon up in front of me, and I held her like that while we talked and wondered about what lay out there in the farthest parts of the galaxy.

At some point in the conversation Angie said to me, "You told us earlier you were taking some astronomy classes in college?"

"Yes, I did," I said while kissing the back of her head.

"We talked about all that stuff when we first met you. Aliens and outer space …" Sissy said.

"But the topic never gets old, Sissy," Angie said. "I love talking about astronomy and what strange things might be 'out there.'"

"Oh yeah," Sissy said, rolling her eyes.

"You know a lot about those stars, don't you?" Angie said. "I figured that out from our first conversation."

"I guess … a bit more than the average guy on the street maybe."

"There are trillions of stars in deep space aren't there?"

"Yes, there are," I said.

"And most of those stars have planets?"

"Yep."

"Then the chances are really pretty good that there are at least billions of planets out there with people on them." She smiled.

"The chances are very good. In fact, I'd say it's true."

"So what I said when we talked about this before just might be true. There just might be another young alien couple, millions of light years out in outer space, who are sitting in their own swimming pool staring right at us."

"You're worried about being seen naked by aliens millions of miles away?" Manny asked.

"No. I think it's kind of romantic." Under the water she moved my hands off her stomach upward onto her breasts.

"Yes …" I said. "Yes, it is romantic."

"I wouldn't care if they could see me," Sissy proclaimed. "They probably think we look weird anyway. Everybody knows that aliens look like lizards, and since we don't look like lizards, the aliens are probably repulsed by us."

"I doubt that," I said.

"Oh no, here we go," Manny sighed. "You just gave him an opening for a long lecture on aliens."

"If it's not too long, I'd like to hear what he has to say," Angie said.

"Just think about it," I said. "If everything in the universe is made up of the same elements, and if life forms all begin basically in the same way, then why should the life forms on other planets be any different than those on this planet? The trees on another planet would be the same as the trees here, and the people would be too. In order for an alien to look like a lizard, then that alien would need to be a lizard. In that case, he wouldn't be sitting in a swimming pool looking out toward us, he'd be on a warm rock somewhere looking out toward us. If there are people out there, and I believe there are, then except for some minor differences, they'd look very much like us. Their language would probably be different, but that's another story."

"And you can hold that story for another time, please," Manny said.

"I never thought of it that way," Angie said. "It makes a lot of sense though."

"Yes it does," I said. "The building blocks of life are exactly the same all over the universe. Why would life look any different somewhere else? It's science."

"It's all Hollywood's fault," Sissy said. "Humans get all their information about outer space from the movies, not from the science."

Angie smiles at her sister. "Why, Sissy, that was rather profound,"

"And it's true," I said. "Every idea you have about what an alien might look like comes from TV or the movies. And, guess what? About 80% of them look like big lizards."

"Even comic books," Manny said.

"But when you look at the science, there's just no justification for aliens looking any different from us. For all we know, super advanced aliens could be here on Earth right now walking among us and we wouldn't even know it," I said.

"I never thought of that," Sissy said. "Hey, you two guys appeared out of nowhere. How do we know you aren't aliens?"

"You mean us and the hundreds of thousands of other people coming up here from out of nowhere?" Manny said sarcastically.

"Well, there's that," Sissy said.

"Baloney," Angie said. "None of us are aliens. We're having too much fun to be aliens." She turned her head, smiled, and pushed her backside even tighter against me.

"You're probably right," Manny said. "Aliens are always grumpy. They carry ray guns and growl all the time. Look at Godzilla."

"He isn't an alien, silly," Sissy said. "He's an Earth monster."

"But he looks like a lizard."

"Okay, this is getting silly," Angie said. "Can't we talk about something else?"

"You're the one who wanted to talk about astronomy," Sissy said.

"Lizards aren't astronomy."

"Maybe we should call it a night," Sissy said. "I don't know about you, but I'm getting a bit tired and we've got a big day tomorrow."

"Oh, I don't want to!" Angie said. "The sooner tomorrow comes, the sooner DH and Manny leave."

"Well, we can't stay out here in the pool all night," Sissy said.

"Why not?" Angie protested.

"Because we'll look like prunes in the morning."

"What about us guys? We don't have any place to stay tonight unless we sleep in a park somewhere," Manny said.

"Don't be silly," Angie said. "You're going to sleep here. When do you have to be at the airport?"

"Two o'clock," I said.

"Okay, here's the plan," Angie said. "We go to bed, we get up early and make some breakfast …"

"I still need to buy a couple of things before we head back," I remind her.

"After breakfast we go buy whatever it is you need, we get a little lunch and then head for the airport," Angie said. "I don't like that last part, but I guess it has to be."

"I don't like it either," I said, "but it's the only way it can be for now. And don't forget, you and Sissy promised to visit when you're down our way."

"You can count on it," Angie said.

"Okay, who wants to go first?" Sissy asks.

"We will," Angie said. She grabbed my hand and we moved to the shallow end, and up the steps. We headed for the sliding glass door leading into the living room, each of us wrapped in a towel so that we wouldn't make puddles on the floor.

As Angie and I stepped out of the pool, I heard Manny say, "Yep, you two are sisters alright. Even your butts look the same."

That was closely followed by the sound of a light slap and Sissy saying, "You aren't supposed to be looking at her."

I followed Angie up to her bedroom where we sat cross-legged on her bed facing each other. Angie took both of my hands in hers and held them. We sat there like that for the longest time, just staring into each other's eyes.

Angie spoke first. "I have to memorize your face. I want to be able to bring your face into my mind any time I want."

"Even when you're hitting home runs?"

"Even then. But most of all I want to be able to see it at night when I've gone to bed and I'm laying here all alone. I want to see your face smiling down at me."

"I don't think it's possible for me to forget your face," I said.

"Am I that memorable?"

"Are you kidding?" I grin at her. "All I have to do is think of Doris Day."

"Oh that's nice. Just what I want to hear — that you'll be thinking about another girl instead of me."

"No, I won't," I assure her. "I was kidding. I'll be thinking about you." I pause for a moment to admire her perfect, athletic body, sitting there in front of me in all its glory. "All of you."

"Is that all you'll remember me for — my naked, freckly body?"

"No. I'll also remember the very first night we met, when you walked in with the stuff to fix up Manny's heel. I'll remember watching you sleep in the hotel bed. I'll remember the fun we had at the little Chinese restaurant where the girl couldn't speak English, and most of all I'll remember the baseball game today. The way you strutted around like a banty rooster, yelling out instructions and cheering on your teammates. The way you slammed those balls over the fence and then ran like a bat out of hell, kicking up clouds of dirt behind you. And the way you grabbed me and hugged me after the game. The way your hot body smelled after all that aggressive exercise. And the way that million dollar smile of yours flashed up at me … the sparkle in your eyes …"

"Is that all?" She smiled coyly.

"One more thing."

"What's that?" she asked.

"I'm gonna remember how it felt lying next to you in this bed tonight. I'm gonna remember everything we did … do."

"Well then, the night's going by pretty fast. I think it's time we started making those memories." She moved toward me …

In the Morning

It's now nine o'clock in the morning. Angie and Sissy are making breakfast in the kitchen and Manny is out in the pool. He wanted one more swim before we headed home.

"I wish I could afford a pool. I could get used to this," he says.

"I could get used to a lot of things up here, Manfred."

"Maybe you ought to just stay up here, DH," Manny says. "Angie's head over heels for you, and she's absolutely gorgeous. I'd stay if I could. I really like Sissy, but I have to get home. My sister's sick, my mother's alone, and the band counts on me."

"Your mom can take care of herself." I look at him knowingly. "But I understand about your sister — that's a no-brainer."

"She's scared us a couple of times now. Her heart's just failing and the doctor said there isn't much he can do for her."

"You do need to get back. Plus, your band wouldn't be a band without you."

I like Manny a lot; he's a good guy. I don't know the other guys in his band well enough to think one way or the other about them, but I don't think they like me much. When I sit in on their practice sessions in Manny's garage I get the impression they'd rather not have anybody listen to them. Their music is fairly good, as rock music goes, but they don't seem to have any motivation. They seem perfectly content to sit around for hours on end, day after day, playing their stuff, dreaming about fame, but seldom leaving the garage — never having the desire to do so. Except for Pet, the singer. One time Pet came over to The Hole to visit. I was surprised because I'd never actually been around her when she was alone; she always had at least one of the band guys with her. Anyway, she came into The Hole and sat down on my bed.

"You're a painter, right?" she asked after a few moments of awkward — to me, anyway — silence while her eyes took in all the details of the small room.

"Yes, I try to be." Where is this going?

"Well, this is going to sound a bit odd, but I was wondering if you'd paint a painting for me to give to my boyfriend?"

"It all depends. What would you like me to paint?"

"Me. Only without all these clothes." She looked at me and smiled hopefully.

I didn't know what to say. Part of me was dancing a jig. While Pet has some pretty spectacular scenery to offer — from an artistic point of view — her current boyfriend is a guitar player in Manny's band. What's he going to think about her posing naked for me?

Long story short, I told her I'd think about it, but so far it hasn't happened. Pet's a bit of a pothead, and like most potheads she doesn't always finish what she starts, or make good on promises or plans. She just forgot about it, and I wasn't about to remind her. I have had some other interesting times with Pet though, when no one else has been around. She's always liked me, and on a few occasions she's gone out of her way to show me just how much she likes me, if you know what I mean.

Oh well, that has nothing to do with our plans for the day, which are to have breakfast, go out for a last walk in The City, pick up a few trinkets to take back to Riverside, sit down for one last chat in a park somewhere, and then be driven by Angie and Sissy to the airport where they will see us off.

I am so not looking forward to that send off. The memories of the experiences I have had and the people I have met here in San Francisco will stay with me for the rest of my life. Those memories will blur in time into a colorful impression of the reality of the experience. The vision of Angie, however, will remain in my head with crystal clarity, probably forever.

The sounds coming from the kitchen have changed, and now Sissy is making an announcement. "Breakfast is ready! Clear a spot on the table and we can bring the food out. Everybody can serve themselves."

I stand up and head inside, yelling to Manny along the way, "Come on man, soup's on!"

"Soup? For breakfast? You gotta be kidding!"

The dining table looks pretty much the way it did when we arrived last night, only there might even be a few more things on it, but that's hard to tell. How do you clear a space for a full meal for four people? Using my arm as a bulldozer, I start at one end and push everything to the other end where it all falls off onto the floor in one big neat pile of total disorder.

Angie comes around to the dining area with a big pan full of scrambled eggs in one hand and a platter piled with enough sausage patties to feed an army. She sets them down in the center of the table, then steps back and looks around.

"Where'd you put all my stuff?" she asks.

I point to the floor at the end of the table.

Her eyes grow big with horror. "Oh no! How am I ever gonna find anything in that mess? I had it all organized. I knew where everything was!" She really is chewing me out.

Then she starts to laugh. "Just kidding." She comes over and plants a big sloppy kiss on my cheek. "Had you goin', didn't I?"

Sissy comes around with more food—a plate full of toast and

another large skillet filled with fried potatoes. "Where's Manny?" she asks

"He's coming," I said. "He thinks we're having soup for breakfast."

"How'd he get that idea? Sometimes I wonder about that goofball." Sissy shakes her head.

Manny comes in with a towel wrapped around his waist. Even though he's the last to come to the table, he's the first to worm his way in to get a plate and start scooping up food.

"First one served has to do the dishes." Angie may be smiling, but I think she is at least half serious.

Manny rolls his eyes. "Great. Always picking on the short guy."

The rest of us fill our plates and then we all head into the living room. Angie and I sit on the couch while Manny and Sissy sit on the floor on the other side of the coffee table. It's pretty quiet for a few minutes while everybody shovels food into hungry mouths. It really is good.

My plate is half empty before I pause to take a breath. "Just like my mother makes," I tell the girls.

"He's telling the truth," Manny says around a mouthful of sausage. "I've had his mom's cooking."

Angie grins, pleased with herself and pleased by the compliments. "Well, thanks. Sissy and I both love to cook. If you were staying longer we could prove that to you."

"I wish," I said.

"So, let's not go there again," Sissy says. "Where are we headed after breakfast?"

"I still need to buy a couple of things. I promised Bill Hunter I'd pick him up some local magazines that have stuff about the hippie convention. He'll never make it to San Francisco himself, so the magazines would help him talk about it in class."

"I know just the place to get what you want, but you'll have to take a deep breath before you go in. It reeks of incense," Angie says.

"You mean that head shop around the corner—Sweet Willie's, or something like that?" Sissy says.

"That's the one."

"Gawd, what a dump. But he does have magazines."

"Sounds like just the place," I say. "I hate incense. I wouldn't be surprised if they found out that smoke from incense is just as bad as smoke from cigarettes."

"That would explain why all those hippies cough all the time," Angie says.

"Yeah … those deep phlegmy coughs …" Sissy adds.

Manny puts down his fork and makes a face. "Please, not while I'm eating scrambled eggs."

After a brief pause I ask, "Any suggestions about the magazine I should buy?"

"There's one that's fairly popular — Ramparts," Sissy says. "I've looked at the covers, but I've never actually read it. It looks kinda radical and I'm pretty sure its main audience is the hard-core hippies, dopers and misfits of the world. I'll bet your English Prof would get a kick out of it."

"That's the very one I had in mind. I heard about from a friend down south. We'll look for one of those."

"What else do you want to buy?" Angie asks.

"I've been thinking about that. In all honesty, I don't think I'm as keen on buying something as I was when I first got here. I thought it'd be neat to bring home some genuine memorabilia of the hippie movement, but now that I've been here for a week and gotten to see it up close and personal, nothing really appeals to me any more. I already bought a paisley tie, so that may be the extent of it."

"That's okay," Manny says. "I don't feel like doing much walking anyway. When I get back to Riverside I'm never going to walk anywhere ever again. If can't take a car I ain't goin'."

"How are your heels, Manny?" Angie asks.

"They kind of scabbed over. Not bad, I guess."

"That's good," Angie says smiling.

"We won't be doing much walking today. We'll just pick up the magazine and hit one of the parks and relax for a while," I assured him.

"We should be at the airport by 1:30."

"It's about twelve miles from here, and it takes about fifteen to twenty minutes to get there if there isn't a problem along the way," Sissy says.

"So wherever we are at the time, we need to leave around one PM," I say.

Angie's smile has faded. "Do we have to talk about it?" she says.

"I don't like it either, but it's good to make a plan."

"It's a little after ten now, so we ought to get a move on," Manny says. "We can talk more at the park."

Buena Vista Park 10:30 AM

Buena Vista is a lovely little park and it's near Angie's house, which will give us more time to visit before we head to the airport. I had mixed feelings about coming here since this is where Jesse and I spent our last night together. I'm still a little confused about that entire relationship — I'm gonna have to think about it for a while. I made sure we didn't climb all the way to the top of the hill. I wanted to keep the memories that Jesse and I made together that night separate from the memories that Angie and I are making. We found a beautiful spot under some trees about halfway up and overlooking the bottom part of the park.

The park is really quiet this morning — no kids running around yelling and screaming, just a few girls in bikinis laying on towels sunbathing, and a handful of zombie-like hippies roaming around in the distance. There are a couple of long-haired guys, shirtless, barefoot and wearing Levis throwing a Frisbee back and forth with a girl who is wearing a very short tie-die skirt and what looks like a man's white t-shirt that's been cut way low on the top, and way short on the bottom, while two other girls on the ground nearby are smoking cigarettes and watching. At least I think those are cigarettes.

I don't really know what to talk about in these last couple of hours here in The City. I'd like for the conversation to be meaningful, but what the heck does that mean? Manny and I came up here to see what this hippie movement is all about and I think we got a fairly good picture, but I'm sure the picture I got is gonna be different from the pictures other people get. I know for a fact that many, if not most of the kids up here smoking pot, playing rock music, and doing not much of anything else, are gonna have great memories of their time here. They're gonna think back and get a big smile on their faces and say, "That was the most fun I've ever had in my life," or something like that. Or they'll proudly state, "I was there when it all came down! I was there for the whole hippie deal and it was just wonderful! It was so meaningful! A highlight in the history of America." And I know I'm gonna make some people mad when I say this, but I still have to say it. It has been fun, but I'm not so sure it's been very productive, or even meaningful. What has this big gathering really accomplished? I'm just being honest here. And when it finally comes to an end, and it surely must, what mark for good will it leave, if any?

The other night at Hippie Haven, Mandy told me that she thought all the hoopla about the war and capitalism and the like was little more than a convenient cover for a bunch of young people goofing off and having fun — that the hippies were using the war as an excuse for their own non-productivity within society; that being a so-called hippie was nothing more than putting on a costume to disguise a lazy person on the inside. In all honesty I have to ask, could Mandy be right? Because I just don't see what all this chaos is going to accomplish. I'm sure it's gonna make the history books, no doubt about that, but what will the books say about it? Just what good is it gonna do for the world?

I've met a lot of really nice people this week, but the nicest ones haven't been the hippies. They've been the Mandys and the Angies and the Big Bobs and the Katyas — none of whom truly identify with the hippie movement. Not even Jesse. She often put on the facade of a hippie, but in reality she didn't even come close.

And those folks down there in the park below us — who are they and what's really inside their heads? What do they plan to do with their lives? Do they have any goals for the future, or are they up here just so they can have a part in making a statement about the world? And what exactly is that statement? What ever it is seems to be buried in chaotic and immature activity.

I know it's probably really cool, hip, in, and groovy to be here in The City protesting and marching and be-bopping to the loud music in the park, but where will all these people be in thirty years? What will they be thinking then? I guess time will tell, although just what I haven't a clue. I'm sure some of these folks may turn out to be rocket scientists, but some may be axe murderers. In the end, people are just people. It's almost a flip of a coin as to how any one of them will turn out. Long hair and even dope smoking on one day could turn into herb teas and a crew cut the next. People change. Some get off to a bad start and wind up good, and others start off good and become bad.

I can only worry about myself I suppose. I doubt that I'll ever do drugs of any type, but I have thought of letting my hair grow a bit. Not because I want to be a hippie, but because I just want to see what it's like. Maybe that's the answer to why all these people are really here. Maybe it has nothing to do with politics and peace and love, and nothing to do with the war. Maybe all these folks just want to see what it's like to be something they are not back home. This City is the laboratory where an identity crisis can be worked out without the pain of your friends and relatives giving you a hard time about it.

Oh well, in a few hours I'll be home and all this will be a vague dream. Angie is sitting next to me right now, and she's very real. Manny and Sissy are leaning up against a tree nearby.

"What are you thinking?" Angie asks.

"Just running things around in my head. It's been a short week but I've sure packed a lot into it."

"You've packed more of The City into this week than I have in years," she says. "Have you had a good time?"

"I have. It's different than I thought it would be—The City, the people, the hippie thing, everything."

"In a good way or a bad way?"

"A little of both." I smile. "San Francisco is beautiful. I could live here. I love the fresh ocean air hitting my face all the time when it isn't ninety-five degrees and I'm standing in a crowd of sweaty, smelly strangers."

"I'm betting that's the bad part."

"Part of it. The congestion up here isn't like anything I've ever seen. I live near LA, one of the most populated cities in the world, and I've never seen crowds there like I've seen here."

"It wasn't always like this," Angie says. "The invasion brought all that on. I used to walk down Haight Street in the morning and I could count on one hand the people I'd run into. It was peaceful, quiet, and everybody smiled and said hello. I guess that's gone now."

"That's too bad," I say, wishing I could have experienced that Haight-Ashbury.

"I think that's probably the worst thing about the invasion. San Francisco will never be the same again. There used to be a kind of wild innocence about The City—if that makes sense."

"I think I know what you mean," I say.

"The romance of The City has sort of been tarnished," she continues. "A few years ago when a person thought of San Francisco, they thought of cable cars, hills, beautiful old mansions, pretty houses all painted up, the restaurants and night life, the wharf—romantic things. They thought of the music, the cool jazz, late night jazz, and the art, and the culture. But nobody sees that any more. They just see the throngs of unkempt people wandering around, filling up the parks, and messing up the routine of those who actually live here. I ran into a resident friend of mine in Golden Gate Park the other day. She told me she won't even bring her family out to a park any more. She has small kids, and some of the people hanging around in the parks are a bit unsavory. She's scared to let her kids play there."

"The way you just described it is pretty much the way I've always thought of San Francisco until I came up here, but probably the main impression I'll take with me back to Riverside will be the hippie thing," I tell her. "That scene has tainted all my earlier images."

"It's like something dark has fallen on us up here," Angie says seriously, bringing Jesse's words to my mind.

"Somebody else told me the same thing a couple of days ago," I say.

"Oh well, not much we can do about it, I guess." She sighs. "The city fathers apparently don't mind because they aren't doing much about it either."

"It's probably hard to do anything about such an overwhelming situation," I say. "Can you imagine the crowd control at one of the be-ins?"

"I guess so." Angie lets out another deep sigh and is silent for a few moments. "But I sure miss my town," she continues. "It's not right. It's not their's. They don't live here. When they leave, they'll go back to their own towns and leave mine a mess."

"Look at the bright side," I say. "Not all the people are bad. I've met some great folks up here."

She turns to look at me and smiles. "I hope I'm one of those."

I smile back at her. "You're number one on the list. I'm gonna miss you Angie."

"You just don't know how much I'll miss you." Her eyes glisten wetly and she looks away from me, but I pull her to me and we kiss. That's when I get hit in the head by a small acorn, or pebble or something.

"None of that in public!" I look up to see Manny and Sissy grinning at us.

"Oh hush, Manfred. It's the last chance we're gonna get."

Angie waves them over. "Come on and join us, you two."

They walk over and sit down in front of us. Sissy says, "Manny and I were just talking about all the things he did over the week."

"It's a small world," I say. "We were doing the same thing."

"You boys split up for a couple of days didn't you?" she asks.

"Yes, we did. Manny got hooked up with a couple of girls who wanted to do the concert thing. I wasn't really into that, so I went my own way."

"Anything exciting happen on your half of the trip, DH?" Sissy asks.

"Not much really." I look at Manny, and he shrugs his shoulders and looks away. I really don't want to mention Jesse if I don't have to, and I can tell that Manny's gonna respect that. "I did get to visit City Lights Bookstore. I met a couple of writers there."

"I think I've heard of that place but I've never been there," Sissy says.

"It's kind of an old Beat hangout. It specializes in books by ..."

"Old Beatniks?" Angie smiles.

"You got it." I grin.

"You got to meet some writers?" Sissy asks. "What does that mean?"

Manny butts in, "It means he got to meet Allen Ginsberg and Lawrence Ferlinghetti, and I didn't. They're famous!"

"I've heard of Ginsberg, but I haven't heard of the other guy," Sissy says.

"The other guy owns the bookstore," Manny says.

"They're both poets from the original Beat scene," I explain, "and Lawrence, especially, is a helluva good one. Anyone who professes to identify with the Beats owes him a debt of gratitude. He and his bookstore became the heartbeat of the movement. There might have been a Beat Movement without the City Lights Booksellers and Publishers, but it probably wouldn't have lasted very long, and it certainly wouldn't have had the cultural and social influence — for better or worse — that it has. His efforts provide the active vehicle for its continuation.

"Well, I guess that's something then," Sissy says. "Not my cup of tea, but I suppose it's neat that you got to meet some famous writers, since you're a writer too."

"It was pretty neat. Other than that, my time away from Manfred was pretty uneventful. I bussed down to Stanford and saw a few things there. I hit a couple of restaurants. Walked through China Town and got a weird feeling. Spent one night in a park and almost got arrested."

"What?" exclaimed the three of them.

"It's a long story, but I got away," I say, dismissing it with a wave of my hands.

"Are you a fugitive now?" Manny asks. "Do we even want to be seen with you?"

"Could be. I guess I'd better go into hiding."

"You can hide at my house," Angie says. "I'll keep you safe."

"Tempting. Very tempting," I tell her, wishing I could. "Oh, I almost forgot, I got hijacked by some people in a Buddhist cult. They took me to an apartment, fed me some exotic food, then they allowed me to escape."

"Right," Manny says sardonically.

"I'm not kidding" I protest, then I confess, "But I wasn't really kidnapped, I went willingly. I was wandering around the Civic Center area, when an attractive couple, a Japanese girl named Cheryl and some Caucasian guy named Bill, approached me. They talked to me for a while, and then asked me if I wanted to attend one of their meetings. I said, 'What the heck?'"

"That's a good way to disappear in this town," Angie says."

"Angie's right," Sissy agreed. "People get stolen here all the time."

"I wasn't too worried. These folks looked more like Mormon missionaries than people-stealers."

"Still, I hope you don't do that again," Angie says looking seriously concerned.

"I won't. They drove me to a really ritzy apartment complex and took me up to their meeting. It was one of the most boring things I've ever experienced. A bunch of people were sitting around meditating and chanting something in Japanese. Cheryl was the only Japanese person there—everybody else was Caucasian—and a couple of them looked to be pretty flush with cash."

"I don't think I could ever be Buddhist," Angie says.

Sissy agrees. "Not if you have to meditate and chant all day. That would bore me to tears. A lot of these hippies are Buddhist wannabes—I've heard that from more than one. I wonder if they really understand what Buddhism's all about?"

"Kerouac wrote a book called Dharma Bums," Manny says. "I read it in Bill Hunters class last semester. I kinda liked it. There's a lot of Zen Buddhist stuff in it. I imagine quite a few hippies have read it."

"Aren't Buddhists atheists?" Sissy asks.

"I'm not sure," Angie says.

"Heck if I know," Manny says.

"I think they're sort of atheists but not quite." I explain. "I think it depends on what kind of Buddhist a person wants to be. I don't think any of them believe in a Creator God like Christians do, and Buddha wasn't God, he was just a guy, a philosopher."

"I can't imagine not believing in God," Angie says. "Nobody can prove God really exists, but somehow it's kinda comforting to think He does exist—that He's up there somewhere watching out over everything."

"You mean like an alien?" Manny says, grinning mischievously.

Sissy buries her face in her hands and cries, "No, no, no! Not the alien thing again."

"I don't think God is an alien," Angie protests. "I don't know what He is, but I believe in Him and that's enough for me. If others want to disbelieve, then that's their thing."

"Kinda like ghosts," Sissy says. "Nobody's ever really seen one."

"Lots of people claim they have," Manny says.

"But they don't have any real proof," Angie says. "There's a few photos floating around out there, but they could be anything—bad film, stray light, ground fog. I think it's a bunch of bunk."

"Like Bigfoot," Manny says. "There's that one picture of Bigfoot that everybody shows around and it looks so stupid, like a man in a gorilla suit. How do they believe in that stuff?"

"I don't think any of it really matters one way or the other in the scope of all things," I say.

Manny leans back against the trunk of the tree we are sitting under, spreads his arms wide, and looks up to the sky to ask the universe, "Does anything matter?"

In response, Angie sits up straight and answers the question, the tone of her voice expressing her frustration and sadness. "Yes, something matters. What matters is that in just a little while we're gonna be driving you two to the airport, and all we're talking about are Buddhists, ghosts, and Bigfoot!"

"Somehow that seems appropriate," Manny says. "Just like ghosts, in a couple of hours we'll vanish—POOF—like we were never here."

"Well, I don't like it," Angie pouts.

"I'm not too happy with it either," Sissy says quietly.

"You live in LA now, Sissy. At least you'll be able to visit them on a regular basis," Angie says.

Sissy looks at Manny and smiles. "Yeah, that's a plus."

"We've had this conversation already," Manny says.

I hug Angie tightly. "You'll see us again."

"I don't care about Manny," she says. "I don't want to lose you."

Manny puts on a show of being hurt. "Thanks a lot,"

"I didn't mean it that way," Angie says, giving him a friendly punch in the arm.

I give her another squeeze. "You aren't gonna lose me. You know exactly where I'll be. When you come down to LA to visit Sissy I'll drive in to visit you."

"But that's not the same as being with you all the time."

"I know, but it's the best we can do."

"Enough already!" Manny says.

"Yes," Sissy says.

Angie sits up straight and turns to me. "Oh hey, DH, you forgot to get your magazine."

"I did, didn't I. I sort of forgot it on purpose. I didn't want to waste time looking for it."

"I'll bet they have Ramparts at the airport," Sissy says. "They've got a big magazine kiosk down there — it's got magazines from all over the world."

"If they don't have it there you guys can get me one and mail it to me. I gave my address to Angie."

Our conversation starts to slow down. There isn't much left to be said, and we are beginning to repeat ourselves. Pretty soon we are sitting in silence, just staring down the hill at the people below, each of us lost in our own thoughts. The girls both look sad, especially Angie. For the first time since I've been with her, there is not a trace of a smile on her face. Her eyes are distant and sad, with tears barely hanging on to her lashes, not quite ready to fall but seriously thinking about it.

Sissy seems to be better than Angie at hiding her emotions, but I can tell that she's going to miss Manny, and that's great for him. I don't think he's ever had a real girlfriend before. He's dated a few of the girls that like to hang around his band, but they're mostly just young groupies that only care about being seen with someone from the band and not about any type of relationship with him. Sissy's the first girl with a real brain that I've ever known Manny to spend any time with.

I can't tell what Manny's thinking. He may just be thinking about getting back home and beating on his drums — getting back to the band. They practice together several hours a day, every day, so a week is a long time for him to be away. He's really the one who holds the group together. Guitarists are a dime a dozen but a good drummer is hard to find, and Manny is a good drummer. I never thought the drummer did more than just sit on a stool and beat the heck out of the drumheads, but he takes it very seriously. He writes down all the notations and comments about all the songs they play during practice so that their performances are top notch and professional.

Without warning, a Frisbee sails through the air and lands in front of us, just grazing the top of Sissy's head and breaking our reverie.

The Frisbee is followed by a girl running to catch it. "I'm so sorry, guys!" she yells out. "I never was very good at this Frisbee stuff, and now—well, I'm just about hopeless." It becomes clear what she means as she gets closer—she is quite pregnant. "Did I hit anybody?" she asks.

"You just parted my hair a bit," Sissy says good-naturedly.

"I'm so sorry," the girl says, and smiles. Her smile is very engaging.

The Frisbee has fallen right in front of me. When she reaches down for it, her enlarged breasts spill over the top of her shirt, proving that gravity still works here on Earth. Manny watches in fascination.

While picking up the Frisbee in her left hand, she extends her right hand to me and introduces herself. "I'm Nanny," she says. The complicated motion causes her boobs to do a wavy little dance in front of me. She's definitely pregnant—there are wet spots around her nipples and her navel pokes through her thin shirt. Manny grins at Sissy who is sitting next to him, and Sissy slaps him on the back of his head.

"Nice to meet you, Nanny. I'm DH, this is Angie, and that's Manny and Sissy there behind you."

She's a pretty little thing. I say "little" because the only things about her that are big are her breasts and her belly. She is quite small and fragile looking otherwise. In fact, her arms and legs are downright skinny and her face is thin and gaunt as well. Her long, thin, naturally red hair falls down past her shoulders, and besides looking like it could stand a wash, it doesn't have the shine that healthy hair should have.

"Nice to meet you guys," She smiles broadly, showing a dimple in spite of the thinness of her face. "Hey, this is far out. You all from The City or just passing through?"

"Manny and I are from Riverside, and Angie and Sissy live here."

"Cool! Locals." Nanny says, reaching over to shake Angie's hand, then Manny's and Sissy's. "I love meeting new people."

"Nanny is an unusual name," I remark.

"It's just what everybody calls me. My real name is Barbie."

"Why do they call you Nanny?" Angie asks.

"Because I live in a communal house and I take care of all the kids while the others are at work."

"I get it," Sissy says. "Like a nanny."

"Yeah, that." She laughs and caresses her swollen belly. "And I also seem to be pregnant all the time." Two out of eight of the kids are mine, and I have one in the oven."

"I take it you're a local," I say.

"I was born here twenty-seven years ago today." she says proudly.

"Happy birthday!" the four of us chorus.

"You're a local for twenty-seven years and you're living in a communal house?" Sissy asks.

"I can't afford my own place. All the cheaper places have gone to all the non-locals who are pouring in. I also lost my job."

"How'd you lose it?" Sissy asks.

"You care if I sit down?" She makes a face as she points to her belly.

"Of course not. Join us." Angie says, scooting over a bit to make room for her in our circle.

Nanny eases herself down and sits cross-legged, Indian fashion between Angie and Sissy directly in front of Manny and me. Making no effort to pull her skirt down around her knees, she leaves Manny and me a wide open, sunlit view of all her pantyless lower charms. Like most of the other girls I've met here in The City, she didn't seem to think anything of it.

"I was working at a department store here in The City when I got pregnant with my second baby. I worked for the same store when I had my first one, and I had to take some time off. I guess they didn't want to give me time off for the second baby, so they let me go. I haven't been able to find work since then, so I hooked up with a house over in the Tenderloin."

"Oh my," Sissy says, genuinely concerned. "That's not a very good neighborhood for anybody, let alone a pregnant woman."

"It's not too bad," Nanny says. "There's a lot of hippie houses over there now. I live on Ellis Street and there's at least three communal houses on my block."

"So you must be a real hippie," Manny says.

"Huh?" Nanny gives him a puzzled look.

"You're not one of the phony tourist hippies like we've been meeting lately," Manny explained.

Her face brightened with understanding. "I'm part of the movement, if that's what you mean. I guess I have been since the beginning."

Now we're getting somewhere. So far all we've had to go on is observation and conjecture. Maybe we can get some real info from this girl instead of relying on our own vague impressions. I'm not prepared to write off the entire hippie cause just because of some bad smells and dirty clothes. If Nanny can answer a few questions, then I might change my limited and semi-negative opinion of it all.

I'm noticing now that Nanny has a couple of tattoos — dead giveaways she really is a true hippie. One is a small multi-colored peace symbol very high up on the inside of her left thigh, and the other on her right arm is a blue and green rendition of the well-known hand with the two-fingered peace salute above the word, "love." Most of the wannabe tourists don't have permanent tattoos advertising the cause. They wear buttons, 'cause those are easy to take off. I suppose they don't want to take the chance that they won't be able to get behind a movement they know little about, and they don't want to get saddled with a peace sign tattoo for the rest of their life. If they plan on being a biology teacher, or something else in the system back home, hippie tattoos might not be a good thing.

"Well, this is good timing then," I tell her. "Manny and I have only been here a week and we're having a hard time figuring out what it's all about. Angie and Sissy have lived here all their lives and they're not too sure, either. Can you tell us exactly what a hippie is, and what all these people are really doing up here?"

She took some time to gather her thoughts before she began to speak. "I don't know if I can define it all for you. There are different kinds of hippies, but I think the main thing we all have in common is that we're unhappy with the state of the country and we want it to change."

"What are you unhappy with?" Angie asks.

"That's where things get muddy," Nanny says. "Different people or groups are unhappy about different things, depending on how they think things should be or what they think is important. I've heard a pretty long list of grievances since I've been in the movement."

"Like what, for instance?" I ask.

"Well, like war—not just waging war, but the brutality of war. Some hippies think that war for a just cause is cool, but a war like Viet Nam is stupid. We're not doing anything over there except killing people and getting killed. Nobody's gonna win that one.

"Because of the war, almost everyone's against the draft. None of my guy friends want to be forced to go over there and get killed for nothing. Tommy, the guy down there with the guitar, told me he wouldn't mind getting killed in a war if somebody was attacking California. But Viet Nam? Nah.

"A lot of hippie girls want to legalize abortion. They got themselves in trouble and they can't support their babies, so they want to get rid of them. I don't buy into that one. I love my babies. I can't imagine killing one of them.

"Some of us are against materialism. It seems like everybody's buying more and more stuff, and we think there should be a limit to the stuff a person can hoard. Like, some people have five cars. What's that all about? That's why a lot of hippies drive VWs—they're small and cheap and unpretentious. A lot of kids just hitchhike. They think that the less they use machines the better the world will be. But I think it's kind of hypocritical to give up your car and then make other people drive you all around. You're making them do what you said you wouldn't do, and you're doing it because you're too lazy to walk. That's not right. Some of the locals do walk. If you've lived here in The City all your life, you know where everything is. Nothing's really too far away around here—you can walk just about anywhere in an hour or so.

"I think a lot of the younger hippies are against going to school and holding down a job, so a lot of them drop out of school and live up here in the communal houses. If they get enough people together in a group and they land a few jobs, they can even pool their money and pay rent on an apartment. But some just don't wanta work. They just wanta lay around all day getting stoned and listening to records. I like getting stoned, but I'd kill for a job right now. I'm thinking about my kids. I don't want them to grow up in a hippie house. I want them to make something of themselves.

"I think the bottom line is that we're all just looking for our own personal Eden. I'm not sure it really exists, and I have big doubts that anything we do up here in The City will bring it about, but it's all about trying. You know, if you feel something's wrong you should try to change it. If you feel something's right you should try to become a part of it." Nanny smiles, looks at each one of us in turn, then shrugs her shoulders. "That's about it," she says.

"What about the free sex thing?" That question comes from Manny, of course.

Nanny looks at him and grins. "Yeah, everyone wants to know about that. Most hippies want more sexual freedom. They don't like all the laws, mainly the one about having to be twenty-one to get hitched. If you fall in love you should be able to live with the person you fall in love with, even if you're only fifteen. Love really is what it's all about. I know a lot of girls who are pregnant and under eighteen. I know two that are only thirteen. I'm not sure about having babies at thirteen, but I am for the free love thing, obviously. I'm on my third kid and I'll have a hundred if I can. And, hey, I really like sex! What's wrong with liking sex?" Nanny looks right at me with a big grin on her face. "When you get right down to it, if everybody had sex all the time they wouldn't want to fight wars. Sex just feels good. What's there not to like?"

"Wow," I say, "that's a lot of info."

"There's a lot more than that," Nanny says. "Every hippie up here is a little different from every other hippie. They all wanta make their own rules, and some of those rules don't agree with each other."

"That's kinda what I've been thinking," I say. "You guys all seem to have the right kind of heart, but the actual goals are a bit fuzzy, let alone how to reach them."

"I guess so," Nanny says thoughtfully. "But I've thought about it a lot, and that's a pretty good rundown of what you'll get from talkin' to most people."

I nod my head in agreement. "Its right on par with the discussions the four of us have had this week."

"Cool," Nanny says. "Brothers and sisters in the storm."

"What storm?" Sissy asks.

"The storm of life," Nanny answers.

"You think life's a storm all the time?" Angie asks.

"Not all the time, but most of it, I think. It's been pretty hard on me these past few years." Suddenly Nanny looks very tired and worn.

"What do you see in your future, Nanny?" Angie asks.

"I can't see much right now," she answers. "No silver linings. I'll soon have three kids to feed and I don't have a penny in my pocket. Food's no problem—the Diggers give us beans or stew every day. The stew's kinda watery, but the beans are always good. I'm worried about my kids. They're real skinny and their color is bad. I don't think they're real healthy right now. If we go on like this much longer, I'm not even sure they'll make it. My oldest, Tad, looks the worst and now he's got a bad cough. I don't know what that's about."

"Don't you have anybody besides the other hippies you can go to?" Sissy asks. "Any family? Where are your parents?"

"My mom died when I was just a kid, and my dad's a drunk. I don't even know where he's at. I don't have any brothers or sisters. These hippies are all I've got—they're family now."

"Can you go to a doctor?" I ask. "You can always take Tad to the emergency room at the hospital. I think you can do that for free."

"I did that once, a few weeks ago. They gave him some pills and told me that was about all they could do. They said he had a bad cold and he was malnourished. They told me to feed him more. I took him home and made him eat more beans, but that hasn't helped. He's pretty weak. My daughter looks like a walking skeleton."

"And now you're having another kid?" Manny asks. "You think it's a good idea to bring a third kid into the world when you're having trouble taking care of the other two?" A good question, but not too tactful.

"I know … I'm stupid. I blew it when I got pregnant. I wasn't very careful, but nobody is around here. It's kind of a badge of honor for a girl to be poking out in front. All the guys think it's sexy, and all the girls think it makes them a grown woman. I don't care about no badges, I just love kids. But I may not have to worry. I'm not so healthy myself. I'm liable to lose this one." She caresses her belly tenderly.

I glance at Angie and Sissy and notice that they both have tears welling up in their eyes. Manny is looking at the ground and playing with the grass—anything to avoid looking at Nanny. He's been known to get a little misty eyed on occasion.

"Hey Nan!" We look down the hill to see the guy Nanny called Tommy waving to get her attention. "We gotta jam. We're gonna be late, Dude."

"He calls you Dude?" I ask.

She smiles. "Everybody calls everybody Dude here."

"Is Tommy the father of your kids?"

"I'm not sure," she says. "Every guy in the house has had me."

"Wow … okay …" I look at her and I really don't have anything to say.

"So, it's real nice meeting you all." She shakes my hand. "I hope you and Manny have a nice trip back to Riverside. I knew another guy from there once."

I wondered how she had "known" him, but I didn't ask. Instead I said, "It's been really nice talking to you, Nanny. You've cleared up a lot of questions that we've been puzzling over all week."

"I'm glad." She smiled. "I like helping people. It makes me feel good to do that."

Angie reaches out and takes Nanny's hand in both of hers. "It was nice meeting you, Nanny. I hope your future gets brighter. Maybe something magical will happen to you soon. Never lose faith."

"I'm afraid I lost that years ago," Nanny says. "But I wish you a good future too, Angie. And you too, Sissy."

Sissy reaches over and takes her hand, "Take care of those kids, Nanny." Unfallen tears rimmed Sissy's eyes.

"You okay honey?" Nanny asks. "You cryin'?"

"Just allergies," Sissy says.

"Oh yeah … I get those too," Nanny says. "Well, I'll see you all. Take care. Gotta hurry. We're headed over to Haight. There's a big march this afternoon." Without looking back, she heads down the hill to join her friends.

This just ain't right. I call down to her, "Wait a minute, Nanny!"

I jog down to Nanny and pull out my wallet. I really hadn't spent much money since the first day we got here, so I still have almost a hundred dollars left. What do I need that for? I reach into my wallet and pull it out. I grab her hand, place the money in it, and squeeze her hand into a fist.

"Happy birthday. See if you can use this to help your little family."

She looks down into her hand and sees all the cash. It must look like a million dollars to her. She breaks into tears, grabs me, and hugs me as tight as her swollen belly will allow. She releases me and steps back. Looking up into my eyes, tears pouring down her face, she asks, "Are you an angel?"

Angels of one kind or another have been front and center three times during my visit here in San Francisco, and now I seem to be playing the part of one. What a bizarre turn of events this is. I squeeze her fingers around the bills in her hand and tell her, "Just take this money. Hide it in your pocket if you have one and don't tell anybody you have it. Not even Tommy. Do you hear me? Use it for you and the kids and nobody else."

"I won't tell anybody, I promise." Nanny wipes the tears from her face with the back of her hand and reaches up to plant a kiss on my cheek. "You are an angel. I know you are." Then she turns and runs down the hill toward her hippie friends who await her at the bottom. They all look up toward me, smile, wave, and head out of the park. When they reach the edge of the park, Nanny turns back and blows a kiss to me.

I return to Angie, Sissy and Manny who are all standing around looking like three wet puppies that just came in out of the rain.

"Did you give her some money?" Manny asks. "I saw you pull your wallet out."

"I couldn't help it. I had to."

"How much did you give her." Sissy asks.

"Everything I had."

Angie hugged me to her, trying to hide her tears. "That's the sweetest thing I've ever seen anyone do."

"Maybe it'll help her."

"Please don't go. I don't want you out of my life," Angie pleads, hugging me tighter.

"That is pretty cool, DH," Manny says. You gave her all of it?"

"I don't need it any more. I'll be home in a few hours. I'll be greeted by a family that loves me, I'll eat a good home cooked meal, and sleep in a nice cozy bed. Nanny doesn't have anything."

1:30 PM at the San Francisco International Airport

All good things must come to an end, and so, too, our stay in The City is coming to its conclusion. Angie, Sissy, Manny, and I are here at the airport waiting for the announcement that will tell us it's time to board the plane. Angie is sitting next to me, her head on my shoulder, her tears wetting my shirt. Manny is sitting on the other side of me, staring out the window at the runway. Sissy is pacing the floor over by the check-in desk, her arms crossed tightly against her chest and her eyes downcast. No one seems to be in the mood to do any talking. What more could we say?

It's been a wild week, and I hate for it to end like this. I don't want my last image of Angie to be a tearful one, but the old saying, "parting is such sweet sorrow," seems to be the order of the day. I turn to Angie and gently lift her chin with my finger. I look into her eyes and I tell her, "I really am taking you with me inside my heart."

"That doesn't help," she says. "I know I'm being selfish wanting you to stay here with me, but I can't help it. I'm just an old fashioned girl and …"

I don't let her finish her sentence. Our kiss is interrupted by the announcement that our flight is now boarding.

And that's that. Manny and I pick up our backpacks and head for the gate while the girls stand and watch us go.

Before I get very far, Angie comes up behind me. I turn and hold her to me, kissing her one last time. She releases her hold on me and takes a step back, handing me a shoebox-sized package wrapped in bright red paper and tied with string. She had taken the box out of the trunk of Sissy's car when we arrived at the airport earlier, saying that it was for me and that I couldn't open it until I was on the plane. I had forgotten all about it.

"I hope this will help you remember me," she says as she places the box in my hands.

I give her a quick kiss on the forehead, then turn to catch up with Manny on the boarding ramp. We look back. Angie and Sissy are still standing there. They are both crying now as they wave at us. Manny and I wave back, and then turn to get on the plane.

We find our seats and get buckled in for takeoff. The suspense is too much for me; I have to open the package and see what Angie has gifted me — probably a collection of Ramparts magazines. I break the string, rip off the bright red paper, and take off the lid. Whatever is inside is buried in tissue paper. Any other package I would have dived right into, but this time I slowly and carefully fold back the layers to reveal the treasure. I reach in, and slowly pull out the most precious, most valuable, thing Angie could have given me — her baseball glove.

Epilogue

After all I've seen and heard during my seven days here in The City, the one question that has not been answered by any of the hippies, the Beats, or even the locals is, "Why?" Why all of this noise and nonsense? Where is the substance? Where is the truth?

It seems to me that the drugs, loud music, crazy costumes, and even the protests are all products of a shallow human culture having little or nothing to do with finding peace, love, awakening, or anything like that. They are decoys manufactured for the purpose of calling attention to superficial issues and problems while diverting awareness and energy from the real cause of the discontent and injustices of this world. While these activities may make the participants feel good for the moment, I believe that true peace and even what the hippies are calling enlightenment can only be achieved through regular and deep personal reflection and the cultivation of the awareness of the greater universal and creative forces.

I think the show of protests and marches and the gaudy circus-like atmosphere are a false face that conceals a deeper yearning of the soul; perhaps even a search for God. And therein lies all of the frustration I see manifested in the rebellious attitudes and actions of many of those taking part in this "invasion." Therein lies the reason behind the sudden surge in popularity of the Buddhist and Hindu philosophies and religions. While considered by many to be more "spiritual" than the more familiar and often scorned western religions, they are still only worldly constructs arising from the limited minds of men. The frustration comes from the fact that God cannot be found in any of those things, not even religion. If anything, I believe that God can only be found when a person wakes up one day, dumps the drugs, the music, the costumes, the ego, the religion, and says, "Here I am—just ME—without the superficial cultural garbage that I've been gathering all my life.

Just me, a brand new naked baby again. Talk to me God."

These people are looking for what they truly desire in all the wrong places—the easy paths that lead nowhere except into realms of egotistical and physical gratification and meaningless fun. They need to close out the noise and go off somewhere into nature, into the desert, deep into the mountains, or just a quiet corner of their own home or garden. Alone in silence and in solitude, ready to listen.

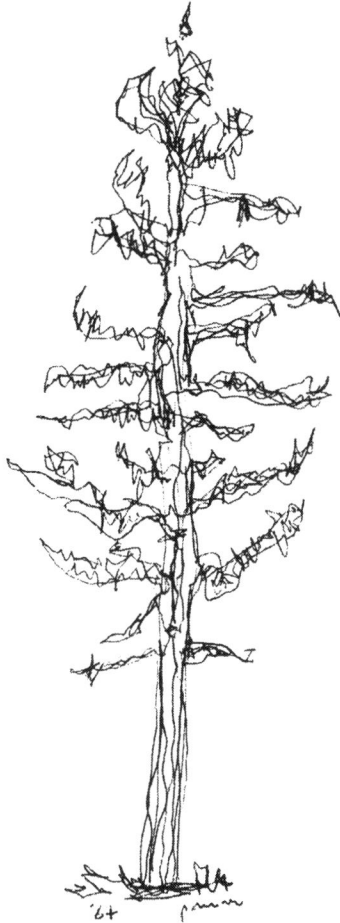

About the Author

Born in Kansas and raised in Southern California, the life of DH Parsons has been varied and interesting. His education has resulted in degrees and awards in Art, Public Education, and Comparative Religion. He has served as a teacher of art, journalism, English, and history in both public and private schools, and as a Dean of students and assistant principal in public secondary schools. It is his life-long love for creative expression however, that has given shape and meaning to his life.

Highly imaginative as a child, he first put brush to canvas while still in high school. Painting prodigiously throughout his life, his works have been exhibited in a number of venues.

DH's writing skills developed as an alternate outlet for his creative urges. As with painting, he began keeping a personal journal while still in high school. Over the years the journal has become a valuable reference and source of inspiration for further creative work of either paint on canvas, or pen on paper.

Prompted by his creativity and intellectual curiosity, DH's independent inquiries have moved him toward the study of things of a more transcendent nature. With this in mind, he founded the Bliss-Parsons Institute (www.bliss-parsons.com), dedicated to the exploration and expression of Truth through the examination of history, culture, and the arts.

DH Parsons maintains an active career as a writer, a painter, and an inspirational speaker throughout the Mid-Western United States.

76781048R00161

Made in the USA
Columbia, SC
26 September 2019